NOV 1 9 2007

D0201473

somewhere
in the city

ST. HELENA PUBLIC LIBRARY
1492 LIBRARY LANE
SAINT HELENA, CA 94574-1143
(707)963-5244

ST. HELENA LIBRARY

MAY 1 6 2012

somewhere

ST. HELENA PUBLIC LIBRARY
1492 LIBRARY LANE
SAINT HELENA, CA 94574-1143
(707)963-5244

somewhere
in the city

Marcia Muller

PEGASUS BOOKS
NEW YORK

Pegasus Books LLC
45 Wall Street, Suite 1021
New York, NY 10005

Collection copyright © 2007 by Marcia Muller

Introduction copyright © 2007 by Marcia Muller

First Pegasus Books edition 2007

Dust to Dust (1982) first published in *Specter!*
Cattails (1982) first published in *The Web She Weaves*
Cave of Ice (1986, with Bill Pronzini) first published in *Boy's Life*
Deceptions (1987) first published in *A Matter of Crime*
The Time of the Wolves (1988) first published in *Westeryear*
The Place that Time Forgot (1990) first published in *Sisters in Crime II*
Final Resting Place (1990) first published in *Justice for Hire*
Somewhere in the City (1990) first published in *The Armchair Detective*
Silent Night (1990) first published in *Mistletoe Mysteries*
Benny's Space (1992) first published in *A Woman's Eye*
The Wall (1993) first published in *Criminal Intent I*
Forbidden Things (1994) first published in *The Mysterious West*
The Cracks in the Sidewalk (1996) first published in *Women on the Case*
The Lost Coast (1995) first published in *Deadly Allies II*
The Holes in the System (1996) first published in *Ellery Queen's Mystery Magazine*
Up at the Riverside (1999) first published in *Irreconcilable Differences*
The Indian Witch (2001) first published in *No Place for a Lady*
The Season of Sharing (2001, with Bill Pronzini) first published in *Crippen & Landru*
The Cyaniders (2003) first published in *Time of the Wolves*

All rights reserved.

Library of Congress Cataloging-in-Publication Data is available.

ISBN: 978-1-933648-34-7

10 9 8 7 8 6 5 4 3 2 1

Interior design by Maria Fernandez

Printed in the United States of America
Distributed by Consortium

For Mary DeYoe, Carolyn Treakle, and Mary Zimmerman
Three of the Fabulous Four

Contents

Introduction

Short stories are a particularly difficult form of writing for me. They must be well thought out, carefully constructed, and every word must count. Since I'm a seat-of-the-pants plotter and—I have to admit it—flagrantly verbose in my first drafts, my initial efforts at short fiction were rambling, full of irrelevant detail, and way, way too long. When I tried to rein myself in, the result was stilted, lacking in depth of character and description, and—quite frankly—boring. Such words as "contrived," "lifeless," and "pointless" were also mentioned by the few editors who were unfortunate enough to read them.

I'd about given up on short stories and decided I was primarily a novelist when a friend—now my husband, Bill Pronzini—gave me a valuable piece of advice: "Write a story as if you're writing a novel. It won't end up being as long, because short-story ideas seldom can sustain a novel's length. Then go back and edit the hell out of it. None of what you put down on paper is graven in stone."

So I began writing in my usual manner and produced manuscripts that were not long enough to be novels but nevertheless were ungainly until I went back and slashed with the old blue pencil. Over time I was turning out some fairly decent work that regularly sold. Of course, now that I use a computer the process is a lot easier, as the delete key is just a fingertip away!

The stories in this collection represent a journey of nearly thirty years, during which I've learned a great deal and have also honed my writing skills. The early stories took me a month or more to write; the later ones went off to the publishers within a week or two. But, other difficulties aside, I've never had any lack of inspiration for the plots, characters, and situations offered up here.

For instance, the first story in the collection, "Dust to Dust," was inspired by the workmen on a Victorian house I was having restored finding a tiny nook under the stairs that had been covered over many years before with wallboard. The nook contained coat hooks and a bench in which people stored wet overshoes. My bench was empty, but in the story . . .

Many of my stories have been suggested by places. "Deceptions" is set at Fort Point at the southern base of the Golden Gate Bridge; it took me nearly five years to concoct a plot that would support that setting. Similarly, the idea for "The Place That Time Forgot" came to me after several visits to on old store and former lending library full of merchandise that had to have been there since the fifties. "Final Resting Place" came about because I'd always been interested in the Columbarium, a multistoried classical building that is the only place of burial—inurnment, actually—left in San Francisco. And "Up at the Riverside" stemmed from a visit to a very bizarre garage sale at an old, falling-down hotel in the Russian River area north of the city.

Short fiction has given me an opportunity to experiment with other genres than the mystery, although these tales always have some criminous element. "Cattails" is a horror story but also concerns a murder. "The Time of the Wolves," which was nominated for a Spur award by the Western Writers of America, is the best western story I've written—even though it was made into the middle segment of an egregiously bad TV movie, "Into the Badlands," starring Bruce Dern in an over-the-top performance. The film was supposed to be a pilot for a new "supernatural western" series on the USA network—and you can imagine what happened to that idea.

Many writers will expand a published short story into a novel—a process Raymond Chandler called "cannabalizing." It's perfectly legitimate; after all, you can't plagiarize yourself, and what emerges as the novel is usually quite different from the story. "The Cyaniders" is not a pure example of this, but it did form the basis for the history of the contemporary town depicted in my 2003 novel *Cyanide Wells*. In fact, I wrote the story so I could become familiar with the past of the area I intended to depict in my fictional Soledad County, California.

Of course, there's nothing like personal experiences—especially bad ones—to encourage a writer to work out his or her feelings about the events in fictional form. On October 17, 1989, Bill and I had spent the day in San Francisco and were planning to have dinner with friends. Authorities on the subject tell you there's no such thing as "earthquake weather," but many of us who've gone through quakes can feel it—a mugginess, murky clouds, a stillness in the air as if waiting for something to happen. We didn't recognize the weather for what it was that day, but it made me feel unwell, so we cancelled our dinner plans and drove home to Sonoma County. Fifteen minutes after we arrived, the quake hit, and even at seventy-five miles from its epicenter, we were badly shaken. TV coverage and phone service was restored the next day; as calls began coming in from friends who lived in the city and on the San Francisco peninsula, I became increasingly depressed by the death, destruction, and disruption the quake had caused. The title story of this collection, "Somewhere in the City," was my therapy—an attempt to show people at their absolute best when the disaster struck.

I hope you'll enjoy this decades-long journey in storytelling.

—MARCIA MULLER
May 8, 2007

The Wall
1993

I

I'd been on the Conway case for close to twenty-four hours before I started paying serious attention to Adrian's bedroom wall. A big oversight, considering it was dark purple and covered with a collage of clippings and photographs and junk that looked like it had been dug out of a garbage can. But then I've never been too quick on the uptake on Monday mornings, which was the only other time I'd seen it.

The wall, the missing girl's mother had explained, was a form of therapy, and even though its creation had more or less trashed the room, she—the mother, Donna Conway—considered it well worth the cost. After all, a sixteen-year-old whose father had run off a year and a half ago with a woman of twenty whom she—the daughter, Adrian Conway—insisted on calling "Dad's bimbo" needed *something*, didn't she? And it was cheaper than paying for a shrink.

Or for any more self-help books, I thought, *if* there are any left that you don't already have.

The Conway house made me damn twitchy, and not just because there wasn't a book in it that didn't have the words "relationship" or "self" in its title. It was in San Francisco's Diamond Heights district—a place that looks like some alien hand has picked up an entire suburb and plunked it down on one of our southeastern hills. The streets are cutesily named— Jade, Topaz, Turquoise—and the Conways', Goldmine Drive, was no exception. The house, tucked behind its own garage and further hidden from the street by a high wall, was pretty much like all the other houses and condos and apartments around there: white walls and light carpeting and standard modern kitchen; skylights and picture windows and a balcony with a barbecue that could hardly ever be used because the wind would put icicles on your briquettes up there. The view was nice enough, but it couldn't make up for the worn spots on the carpet and the cracks that showed where the builder had cut corners. When Donna Conway told me—for God knows what reason—that the house was the sum total of her divorce settlement, I started feeling depressed for her. I didn't get much myself when I got divorced, but a VCR and half the good silverware were at least hockable, and from the rust on the FOR SALE sign out front, I gathered that this house was not.

Anyway, Adrian Conway had been missing for two weeks by the time her mother turned for help to the firm where I work, All Souls Legal Cooperative. We're kind of a poor man's McKenzie, Brackman—a motley collection of crusaders and mainstream liberals and people like me who don't function too well in a structured environment, and one of the biggest legal-services plans in Northern California. Donna Conway was a medical technician with a hospital that offered membership in the plan as part of their benefits package, so she went to her lawyer when she decided the police weren't doing all they could to find her daughter. Her lawyer handed the case to our chief investigator, Sharon McCone, who passed it on to me, Rae Kelleher.

So on a Monday morning in early November I was sitting in Donna Conway's drafty living room (God, didn't she know about weather stripping?), sipping weak instant coffee and wishing I didn't have to look at her sad, sad eyes. If it weren't for her sadness and the deep lines of discontentment that made parentheses around the corners of her mouth, she would have been a pretty woman—soft shoulder-length dark hair and a heart-shaped face, and a willowy body that about made me green with envy. Her daughter didn't look anything like her, at least not from the picture she gave me. Adrian had curly red-gold hair and a quirky little smile, and her eyes gleamed with mischief that I took to be evidence of an offbeat sense of humor.

Adrian, Donna Conway told me, had never come home two weeks ago Friday from her after-school job as a salesclerk at Left Coast Casuals at the huge Ocean Park Shopping Plaza out near the beach. Turned out she hadn't even shown up for work, and although several of her classmates at nearby McAteer High School had seen her waiting for the bus that would take her to the shopping center, nobody remembered her actually boarding it. Adrian hadn't taken anything with her except the backpack she usually took to school. She hadn't contacted her father; he and his new wife were living in Switzerland now, and the police there had checked them out carefully. She wasn't with friends, her boyfriend, or her favorite relative, Aunt June. And now the police had back-burnered her file, labeled it just another of the teenage disappearances that happen thousands and thousands of times a year in big cities and suburbs and small towns. But Donna Conway wasn't about to let her daughter become just another statistic—no way! She would pay to have Adrian found, even if it took every cent of the equity she'd built up in the house.

I'd noticed two things about Donna while she was telling me all that: She seemed to harbor the usual amount of malice toward her ex's new wife, and an even larger amount toward Adrian's Aunt June.

On Monday I went by the book: talked with the officer in Missing Persons assigned to Adrian's case; talked with the classmates who had seen her leaving McAteer that Friday; talked with her supervisor at Left Coast Casuals and the head of security at Ocean Park Plaza. Then I checked out the boyfriend, a few girlfriends, and a couple of teachers at the high school, ran through the usual questions. Did Adrian use drugs or alcohol? Had she been having romantic problems? Could she be pregnant? Had she talked about trouble at home, other than the obvious? No to everything. Adrian Conway was apparently your all-American average, which worked out to a big zero as far as leads were concerned. By nightfall I'd decided that it was the old story: gone on purpose, for some reason all her own; a relative innocent who probably hadn't gotten far before becoming somebody's easy victim.

Sad old story, as sad as Donna Conway's eyes.

It was the memory of those eyes that made me go back to take a second look at Adrian's room on Tuesday afternoon—that, and the thought that nobody could be as average as she sounded. I had to find out just who Adrian Conway really was. Maybe then I could locate her.

I started with the collage wall. Dark purple paint that had stained the edges of the white ceiling and splotched on the cream carpet. Over that, pictures cut from glossy magazines—the usual trite stuff that thrills you when you're in your teens. Sunsets and sailboats. Men with chiseled profiles and windblown hair; women in gauzy dresses lazing in flower-strewn meadows. Generic romance with about as much relationship to reality as Mother Goose.

But over all that were the words. They leaped out in bold type: black, white, red, and other primary colors. GO FOR IT! HOT. GONE FOREVER. STOLEN MOMENTS. FEAR. YES, NO, MAYBE. LOST. THE RIGHT STUFF. WHAT'S IN/WHAT'S OUT. FLASH, COLOR, CURVES, SPLASH, JUST DO IT! And many more . . .

Words as typical as the pictures, but interesting because they seemed important to a young woman who lived in a house where there wasn't a single book, unless you counted her school texts and her mother's stacks of mostly unread paperbacks on self-improvement.

Now, I'm no intellectual giant. I scraped through Berkeley by the skin of my teeth, and for years afterward all I could make myself read were shop-and-fucks. I still don't read what passes for literature these days, but I do get mighty uncomfortable in a place where there aren't any old dust-catchers—as my grandmother used to call them—lying around. Apparently Adrian was fond of the written word, too.

Tacked, nailed, and glued to the words—but never completely covering them—was the junk. A false eyelash, like the hairy leg of a sci-fi spider. A lacy red bra, D-cup, with the nipples cut out. A plastic tag like the stores attach to clothing to prevent shoplifting. A lid from a McDonald's carry-out cup, Coke-stained straw still stuck through the opening.

Broken gold neck chain, pair of fake plastic handcuffs, card with ink smudges on it that looked like fingerprints. Egret feather, dismembered doll's arm, syringe (unused). Lottery ticket with 7s rubbed off all in a row, $2.00 value unclaimed. And much, much more . . .

Not your standard teenage memory wall. A therapy wall, as Adrian's mom had put it? Maybe. I didn't know anything about therapy walls. The grandmother who raised me would have treated me to two years of stony silence if I'd trashed my room that way.

Donna Conway was standing in the door behind me. She must have felt my disapproval, because she said, "That wall was Adrian's only outlet for her pain. She adored her father. After he left us, she needed a way to begin healing."

So why didn't she hire out to a demolition company? I thought. Then I scowled, annoyed with myself. Next thing you knew, I'd sound just like my boss, Sharon McCone. The generation gap wasn't something I needed to leap yet.

Donna was watching my face, looking confused. I wiped the scowl off and said, "Just thinking. If you don't mind, I'd like to spend some time alone with the wall." Then I started to blush, hearing how truly stupid that sounded.

She didn't seem to notice. Maybe because her daughter had put a private part of herself into the wall, it had become a sort of being to her. Maybe people who were "rediscovering and healing" themselves, as she'd said she was, were either too sensitive or too vulnerable to make fun of other people who expressed sudden desires to commune alone with inanimate objects. Whatever, she just nodded and left, closing the door so the wall and I could have complete privacy.

I sat down on Adrian's brass daybed, kicked off my shoes, and drew my legs up on the ruffly spread. Then I took a good look at the mess on the wall. It had been a long-term project. Adrian started it, Donna had told me, the day the divorce papers were served. "We made an occasion of it," she said. "I had champagne and caviar, Adrian had Coke and a pizza. We painted. I guess it was the champagne that made me paint the edges of the rug and ceiling."

Now I replayed that. She hadn't painted the rug and ceiling because she was drinking champagne; the champagne had made her do it. So perfectly in tune with the philosophies of some of the books I'd glimpsed in passing. This was a household where little responsibility was ever assigned or acknowledged. Not healthy for an adult, and definitely bad for a teenager.

Back to the wall, Rae. You should be able to decipher it—after all, you were a psych major.

First the purple paint. Then the layer of pictures. Idealized, because she was trying to look beyond the bleak now to a better future. Next the layer of words. She was trying to talk about it, but she didn't really know how. So she used single words and phrases because maybe she wasn't ready for whole sentences. Hadn't worked through her feelings enough for whole thoughts.

Finally the layer of junk. Pretty ordinary stuff, very different from the pictures. Her feelings were more concrete, and she was trying to communicate them in concrete form. Unconsciously, of course, because doing it deliberately would be too sophisticated for a kid who'd never been in therapy. Too sophisticated for you, Rae—and you *have* been in therapy. Too bad they didn't encourage you to make a wall like this. Now, that would've given them something to eyeball at All Souls . . .

Back to *this* wall. She's gone through a process of sorts. Has piled concrete things and real words on top of idealized pictures and vague words. And then one day she's through. She walks out of this room and goes . . . where? To do what? Maybe if I knew what the very last thing she added to the wall was . . .

I left the room and found Donna in the kitchen, warming her hands around a cup of tea. "What were the last things Adrian put up on her wall, do you know?" I asked.

For a moment she looked blank. Then she shook her head. "I never looked at the wall before she left. It was her own private thing."

"You never talked about it?"

"No."

"What *did* you talk about?"

"Oh . . ." She stared down into the teacup. "I don't know. About the healing process. About everyone's potential to be."

I waited for her to go on. Then I realized that was it. Great conversational diet for a kid to sink her teeth into: healing process, potential to be.

What happened when Adrian was worried about an exam? When she hurt because her favorite guy didn't ask her to the dance? When she was scared of any one of all the truly scary things kids had to face in this city, in this world? Where did she retreat to lick her wounds?

I was getting mad, and I knew why. Like Adrian, I'd grown up in a home where everything was talked about in abstractions. In my case, shoulds and shouldn'ts, what-will-people-thinks and nice-girls-don'ts. I knew where Adrian Conway retreated: not to a nest of family affection and reassurance, but into a lonely lair within herself, where she could never be sure she was really safe.

I wasn't mad at Donna Conway for her arm's-length treatment of her daughter, though. I was mad at my dead grandmother, who raised me after my parents were killed in a car wreck. Donna Conway, even though she wasn't able to deal with emotion, had said she was willing to spend her last dollar to get Adrian back. Grandma wouldn't have given two cents for me.

I wanted to go back to All Souls and talk the case over with Sharon, but when I got to Bernal Heights, where the co-op has its offices, I made a sidetrip to our annex across the triangular park from our main building. Lillian Chu, one of the paralegals who worked our 800 line, lived in Diamond Heights, and I thought she had a kid at McAteer. Maybe there was something going on with Adrian Conway that the classmates the police and I had questioned couldn't or wouldn't tell.

Lillian was just going off shift. Yes, she said, her son Tom was in Adrian's class, and he was due to pick her up in about five minutes. "We're going shopping for new running shoes," she added. "The way he goes through them, I should have bought stock in Reebok."

"Could I talk with Tom for a few minutes?"

"Sure. I've got to run over to the main building and check about my payroll deductions. If you want, you can wait here and I'll send Tom in."

I sat in Lillian's cubicle, listening to phones ringing and voices murmuring on the 24-hour legal hot line. After a while a shaggy-haired young guy with a friendly face came into the cubicle. "You Rae? Mom says you want to talk to me."

"Yes, I want to ask you about Adrian Conway. Her mom's hired me to find her."

Tom Chu perched on the corner of the desk. His expression was still friendly, but a little guarded now. "What do you want to know?"

"Anything you can tell me."

"You mean like dirt."

"I mean anything that might help me locate her."

Tom looked uncertain.

"This isn't a game," I told him. "Or a case of a mother trying to find out more than her daughter wants her to know. Adrian's been missing for over two weeks now. She could be in serious trouble. She could even be dead."

"Yeah." He sighed heavily. "Okay, I don't really know anything. Not facts, you know? But . . . You talk with her boyfriend, Kirby Dalson?"

"Yes."

"What'd you think of him?"

"What do *you* think of him?"

"Bad news."

"Why?"

Tom drew one of his legs up on the desk and fiddled with the lace of his sneaker; from the looks of the shoe, Lillian *should* have invested in Reebok. "Okay," he said, "Kirby's . . . always into something. Always scamming. You know what I'm saying?"

"Drugs?"

"Maybe, but I don't think they're his main thing."

"What is?"

He shrugged. "Just . . . scams. Like a few times he got his hands on some test questions beforehand and sold them—for big bucks, too. And for a while he was selling term papers. Scalping sports and concert tickets that you knew had to be stolen. He's always got a lot of cash, drives a sports car that everybody knows his folks didn't buy for him. He tells his parents he's got this part-time job in some garage, but all the time he's just scamming. The only job he ever had was cleaning up the food concession area at Ocean Park Plaza, but that didn't last long. Beneath him, I guess."

"What about Adrian—you think she was in on his scams?"

"She might've been. I mean, this past year she's changed."

"How?"

"Just . . . changed. She's not as friendly anymore. Seems down a lot of the time. And she's always with Kirby."

"Did this start around the time her father left?"

He shook his head. "After that. I mean, her old man left. Too bad, but it happens." His eyes moved to a photograph on Lillian's desk: the two of them and a younger girl, no father. "No," he added, "it was after that. Maybe six months ago."

"Do you remember anything that happened to Adrian around that time that might have caused this change?"

He thought. "No—sorry, I know Adrian okay, but she's not really a good friend or anything like that."

I thanked him and asked him to call me if he thought of anything else. Then I walked across the park to the freshly painted Victorian where our main offices—and the attic nest where I live—are.

The setup at All Souls is kind of strange for a law firm, but then even the location is strange. Bernal Heights, our hillside neighborhood in the southeastern part of the city, is ethnically mixed, architecturally confused, and unsure whether it wants to be urban or semirural. At All Souls we're also ethnically mixed; our main building is a combination of offices, communal living space, and employees' separate quarters; and most of us don't know if we're nineties progressives or throwbacks to the sixties. All in all, it adds up to an interesting place to work.

And Sharon McCone's an interesting person to work for. That afternoon I found her behind her desk in the window bay at the front of the second floor—slumped spinelessly in her swivel chair, staring outside with that little frown that says she's giving some problem a workover. She's one of those slim women who seem taller than they are—the bane of my pudgy five-foot-three existence—and manages to look stylish even when she's wearing jeans and a sweater like she had on that day. When I first came to work for her, her dark good looks gave me attacks of inferiority because of my carrot top and freckles and thrift-shop clothes. Then one day I caught her having her own attack—mortified because she'd testified in court wearing a skirt whose hem was still pinned up waiting to be stitched. I told her she'd probably started a new fad and soon all the financial district power dressers would be wearing straight pins around their hemlines. We had a good laugh over that, and I think that's when we started to be friends.

Anyway, I'd just about decided to stop back later when she turned, frowned some more, and snapped, "What?"

The McCone bark is generally worse than the bite, so I went in and sat in my usual place on her salmon-pink chaise longue and told her about the Conway case. "I don't know what I should do next," I finished. "I've already talked with this Kirby kid, and if I come back at him so soon—"

"Aunt June."

"What?" I'd only mentioned Adrian's favorite aunt and Donna's apparent dislike of her in passing, and Sharon hadn't even looked like she was listening very hard. She'd been filing her nails the whole time—snick, snick, snick. Someday I'm going to tell her that the sound drives me crazy.

"Go see Aunt June," she said. "She's Adrian's closest relative. Mom disapproves of her. Go see her."

If it didn't save me so much trouble, I'd hate the way she puts things together. I stood up and headed for the door. "Thanks, Shar!"

She waggled the nailfile at me and swiveled back toward the window.

II

Adrian's aunt's full name was June Simoom—no kidding—and she lived on Tomales Bay in western Marin County. The name alone should have tipped me off that Aunt June was going to be weird.

Tomales Bay is a thin finger of water that extends inland from the Pacific forty-some miles northwest of San Francisco. It's rimmed by small cottages, oyster farms, and salt marsh, and the largest town on its shores—Inverness—has a population of only a few hundred. The bay also has the dubious distinction of being right smack on top of the San Andreas Fault. Most of the time the weather out there is pretty cold and gloomy—broody, I call it—and it's a hefty drive from the city—across the Golden Gate Bridge, then through the close-in suburbs and rolling farm-land to the coast.

It was after seven when I found the mailbox that June Simoom had described to me over the phone—black with a silver bird in flight and the word WINGSPREAD stenciled on it, another tipoff—and bounced down an unpaved driveway through a eucalyptus grove to a small cottage and a couple of outbuildings slouching at the water's edge.

My car is a 1964 Rambler American. A couple of years ago, when I met my current—well, on-again, off-again—boyfriend, Willie Whelan, he cracked up at his first sight of it. "You mean you actually *drive* that thing?" he asked. "On the *street*?" No matter. The Ramblin' Wreck and I have gone many miles together, and at the rate I'm saving money, we're going to have to go many more. Barring experiences like Aunt June's driveway, that is.

The cottage was as bad off as my car, but I know something about real-estate values (money is my biggest fascination, because I have too little of it), and this shoreline property, bad weather and all, would have brought opening offers of at least a quarter mil. They'd have to demolish the house and outbuildings, of course, but nature and neglect seemed already to be doing a fine job of that. Everything sagged, including the porch steps, which were propped up by a couple of cement blocks.

The porch light was pee-yellow and plastered with dead bugs. I groped my way to the door and knocked, setting it rattling in its frame. It took June Simoom a while to answer, and when she did . . . Well, Aunt June was something *else*.

Big hair and big boobs and a big voice. My, she was *big*! Dressed in flowing blue velvet robes that were thrift-shop fancy, not thrift-shop cheap (like my clothes used to be before I learned about credit and joined the mil-lions of Americans who are in debt up to their nose hair). Makeup? The-atrical. Perfume? Gallons. If Marin ever passed the antiscent ordinance they kept talking about, Aunt June would have to move away.

She swept—no, *tornado'd*—me into the cottage. It was one long room with a kitchen at the near end and a stone fireplace at the far end, all glass overlooking a half-collapsed deck. A fire was going, the only light. Outside I could see moonshine silvering the bay. June seated me—no, forced me down—onto a pile of silk cushions. Rammed a glass of wine into my hand. Flopped grunting on a second cushion pile nearer the hearth.

"You have news of Adrian?" she demanded.

I was struggling to remain upright in the soft nest without spilling the wine. "Umpfh," I said. "Mmmm-r!"

Aunt June regarded me curiously.

I got myself better situated and clung to the wine glass for ballast. "No news yet. Her mother has hired me to find her. I'm hoping you can—"

"Little Donna." She made a sound that might have been a laugh—*hinc, hinc, hinc.*

"You're Donna's sister?" I asked disbelievingly.

"In law. Sister-in-law. Once removed by divorce. Thank God Jeffrey saw the light and grabbed himself the bimbo. No more of those interminable holiday dinners—'Have some more veggies and dip, June.' 'Don't mind if I do, Donna, and by the way, where's the gin?' " Now she really did laugh—a booming sound that threatened to tear the (probably) rotten roof off.

I liked Donna Conway because she was sensitive and gentle and sad, but I couldn't help liking June, too. I laughed a little and sipped some wine.

"You remained close to Adrian after the divorce, though?" I asked.

"Of course." June nodded self-importantly. "My own flesh and blood. A responsibility I take seriously. I tried to take her under my wing, advise her, help her to deal with . . . everything." She flapped her arms, velvet robe billowing, and I thought of the name of the cottage and the bird on her mailbox.

"When was the last time you saw her?"

Now June's expression grew uncertain. She bit her lip and reached for a half-full wine glass that sat on the raised hearth. "Well. It was. . . . of course! At the autumnal equinox firing."

"Huh?"

"I am a potter, my dear. Well, more of a sculptor in clay. I teach classes in my studio." She motioned in the direction of the outbuildings I'd seen. "My students and I have ceremonial firings on the beach at the equinox and the solstice. Adrian came to the autumnal firing late in September."

"Did she come alone, or did Donna come, too?"

June shook her head, big hair bobbing. "Donna hasn't spoken to me since Jeffrey left. Blames me for taking his side—the side of joy and loving, the side of the bimbo. And she resents my closeness to Adrian. No, my niece brought her boyfriend, that Kirby." Her nose wrinkled.

"And?"

"And what? They attended the firing, ate, and left."

"Do you know Kirby well?"

"I only met him the one time."

"What did you think of him?"

June leaned toward the fireplace, reaching for the poker. When she stirred the logs, there was a small explosion, and sparks and bits of cinder flew out onto the raised stone. June stirred on, unconcerned.

"Like my name," she murmured.

"What?"

"My name—Simoom. Do you know what that is?"

"No."

"A fierce wind of Africa. Dry. Intensely hot. Relentless. It peppers its victims with grit that burns and pits the skin. That's why I took it—it fits my temperament."

"It's not your real name?"

She scowled impatiently. "One's real name is whatever one feels is right. June Conway was *not*. Simoom is fitting for a woman of the earth, who shelters those who are not as strong as she. You saw the name on my mailbox—Wingspread?"

"Yes."

"Then you understand. What's your last name again?"

"Kelleher."

"Well, what does that mean?"

"I don't know. It's just an Irish name."

"You see my point? You're alienated from who you are."

"I don't feel alienated. I mean, I don't think you have to proclaim who you are with a label. And Kelleher's a perfectly good name, even though I'm not crazy about the Irish."

June scowled again. "You sound just like Adrian used to. For God's sake, what's *wrong* with you young women?"

"What do you mean—about Adrian, that is?"

"Well, there she was, given a wonderful name at birth. A strong name. Adrian, of the Adriatic Sea. The only thing Donna did right by her. But did she appreciate it? No. She wanted to be called Melissa or Kelley or Amanda—just like everyone else of her generation. Honestly, sometimes I despaired."

"You speak of her in the past tense, as if she's dead."

She swung around, face crumpling in dismay. "Oh, no! I speak of her that way because that was before . . . before she began to delight in her differences."

"When was that?"

"Well . . . when she started to get past this terrible thing. As we gain strength, we accept who and what we are. In time we glory in it."

In her way, June was as much into psychobabble as her sister-in-law. I said, "To get back to when you last saw Adrian, tell me about this autumnal equinox firing."

"We dig pits on the beach, as kilns. By the time of the firing, they've been heating for days. Each student brings an offering, a special pot. The gathering is solemn but joyful—a celebration of all we've learned in the preceding season."

"It sounds almost religious."

June smiled wryly. "There's also a great deal of good food and drink. And, of course, when the pots emerge from the earth, we're able to sell them to tourists for very good money."

Now that I could relate to. "What about Adrian? Did she enjoy it?"

"Adrian's been coming to my firings for years. She knows a number of my long-term students well, and she always has a good time."

"And this time was no different?"

"Of course not."

"She didn't mention anything being wrong at home or at school?"

"We spoke privately while preparing the food. I'm sure if there had been problems, she would have mentioned them."

"And what about Kirby? Did he enjoy the firing?"

Wariness touched her face again. "I suppose."

"What did you think of him?"

"He's an adolescent boy. What's to think?"

"I didn't care for him," I said.

"You know him?"

"I've spoken with him. I also spoke with a classmate of his and Adrian's. He said Kirby is always into one scam or another, and that Adrian might have been involved, too."

"That's preposterous!" But June's denial was a shade weak and unconvincing.

"Are you sure Adrian didn't hint at problems when you spoke privately with her at the firing?"

"She's a teenager. Things are never right with teenagers. Adrian took her father's defection very badly, even though he and I tried to explain about one's need for personal growth." June gave her funny laugh again— *hinc, hinc, hinc.* "Even if the growth involves a bimbo," she added.

"June," I said, "since you were so close to Adrian, what do you think happened to her?"

She sobered and her fingers tightened on the shaft of the poker. "I can't tell you. I honestly can't hazard a guess."

Her eyes slipped away from mine, but not before I saw something furtive in them. Suddenly she started stirring the fire, even though it was already roaring like crazy.

I said, "But you have suspicions."

She stirred harder. Aunt June wasn't telling it like it was, and she felt guilty.

"You've heard from her since she disappeared, haven't you?" Sharon taught me that little trick: no matter how wild your hunch is, play it. Chances are fifty-fifty you're right, and then their reactions will tell you plenty.

June stiffened. "Of course not! I would have persuaded her to go home. At the very least, I would have called Donna immediately."

"So you think Adrian's disappearance is voluntary?"

"I . . . I didn't say that."

"Assuming it is, and she called you, would you really have let Donna know? You don't seem to like her at all."

"Still, I have a heart. A mother's anguish—"

"Come off it, June."

June Simoom heaved herself to her feet and faced me, the poker clutched in her hand, her velvet-draped bigness making me feel small and helpless. "I think," she said, "you'd better leave now."

When I got back to All Souls, it was well after midnight, but I saw a faint light in Sharon's office and went in there. She was curled up on her chaise longue, boots and socks lying muddy on the floor beside it. Her jeans, legs wet to the knees, were draped over a filing cabinet drawer. She'd wrapped herself in the blanket she keeps on the chaise, but it had ridden up, exposing her bare feet and calves, and I could see goosebumps on them. She was sound asleep.

Now what had she gotten herself into? More trouble, for sure. Was she resting between stake-outs? Waiting for a call from one of her many informants? Or just too tired to go home?

I went down the hall to the room of an attorney who was out of town and borrowed one of his blankets, then carried it back and tucked it around Sharon's legs and feet. She moaned a little and threw up one hand like you do to ward off a blow. I watched her until she settled down again, then turned off the Tiffany lamp—a gift long ago from a client, she'd once told me—and went upstairs to the attic nest that I call home.

Sometimes I'm afraid I'll turn out like Sharon: illusions peeled away, emotional scars turning white and hard, ideals pared to the bone.

Sometimes I'm afraid I won't turn out like her.

We're already alike in some ways. Deep down we know who we are, warts and all, and if we don't always like ourselves, at least we understand what we are and why we do certain things. We often try to fool ourselves, though, making ourselves out to be smarter or nobler or braver than we are, but in the end the truth always trips us up. And the truth . . .

We both have this crazy—no, crazy-*making*—need to get at the truth, no matter how bad it may be. I guess that's how we're most alike of all. The withheld fact, the out-and-out lie, the thing that we just plain can't understand—none of them stands a chance with us. For me, I think the need began when my grandmother wouldn't tell me the truth about the car wreck my parents were killed in (they were both drunk). With Sharon, I don't know how the need got started—she's never said.

I didn't used to feel so driven. At first this job was a lark, and I was just playing at being a detective. But things happen and you change—Sharon's living proof of that—and now I'm to the point where I'm afraid that someday I'll be the one who spends a lot of nights sleeping alone in her office because I'm between stake-outs or waiting for a phone call or just too tired to go home.

I'm terribly afraid of that happening. Or not happening. Hell, maybe I'm just afraid—period.

III

The next morning it was raining—big drops whacking off my skylights and waking me up. Hank Zahn, who pretty much holds the budgetary reins at All Souls, had let me install the skylights the spring before, after listening to some well-orchestrated whining on my part. At the time they seemed like a good idea; there was only one small window in the part of the attic where my nest is, and I needed more light. But since then I'd realized that on a bad day all I could see was gray and wet and accumulated crud—nothing to lift my spirits. Besides, my brass bed had gotten crushed during the installation, and although the co-op's insurance covered its cost, I'd spent the money on a trip to Tahoe and was still sleeping on a mattress on the floor.

That morning I actually welcomed the bad weather because my rainwear being the disguise it is, it actually furthered my current plan of action. For once the bathroom (one flight down and usually in high demand) was free when I needed it, and in half an hour I was wrapped in my old red slicker with the hood that hides nearly my whole head, my travel cup filled with coffee and ready to go. As I moved one of the tags on the mailboxes that tell Ted Smalley, our office manager, whether we're in or out, I glanced at Sharon's. Her tag was missing—she's always setting it down someplace it doesn't belong or wandering off and completely losing it—and Ted would have quite a few things to say to her about that. Ted is the most efficient person I know, and it puzzles him that Sharon can't get the hang of a simple procedure like keeping track of her tag.

The Ramblin' Wreck didn't want to start, and I had to coax it some. Then I headed for Teresita Boulevard, up on the hill above McAteer High School, where Kirby Dalson lived. I'd already phoned Tom Chu before he left for school and gotten a good description of Kirby's car—a red RX-7 with vanity plates saying KS KAR—and after school started I'd called the attendance office and was told that Kirby hadn't come in that morning. The car sat in the driveway of his parents' beige stucco house, so I U-turned and parked at the curb.

The rain kept whacking down and the windows of the Wreck kept steaming up. I wiped them with a rag I found under the seat and then fiddled with the radio. Static was all I got; the radio's as temperamental as the engine. Kirby's car stayed in the driveway. Maybe he had the flu and was bundled up in bed, where I wished I was. Maybe he just couldn't face the prospect of coming out in this storm.

Stake-outs. God. Nobody ever warned me how boring they are. I used to picture myself slouched in my car, wearing an exotic disguise, alert and primed for some great adventure. Sure. Stake-outs are so boring that I've fallen asleep on a couple and missed absolutely nothing. I finished my coffee, wished I'd brought along one of the stale-looking doughnuts that somebody had left on the chopping block in All Souls's kitchen. Then I started to think fondly of the McDonald's over on Ocean Avenue. I just love junk food.

About eleven o'clock the door of the Dalson house opened. Kirby came out wearing jeans and a down jacket and made for his car. After he'd backed down the driveway and headed toward Portola, the main street up there, I started the Wreck and followed.

Kirby went out Portola and west on Sloat Boulevard, toward the beach. By the time we'd passed the end of Stern Grove, I realized he was headed for Ocean Park Plaza. It's a big multistory center, over a hundred stores, ranging from small specialty shops to big department stores, with a movie theater, health club, supermarket, and dozens of food concessions. It was built right before the recession hit by a consortium of developers who saw the success that the new Stonestown Galleria and the Serramonte Center in Daly City were enjoying. Trouble is, the area out there isn't big enough or affluent enough to support three such shopping malls, and from what the head of security at Ocean Park, Ben Waterson, had told me when I'd questioned him about Adrian the other day, the plaza was in serious trouble.

Kirby whipped the RX-7 into the eastern end of the parking lot and left it near the rear entrance to the Lucky Store. He ran through the rain while I parked the Wreck a few slots down and hurried after, pulling up the hood on my slicker. By the time I got inside, Kirby was cutting through the produce section. He went out into the mall, skirted the escalators, and halfway to the main entrance veered right toward Left Coast Casuals, where Adrian had worked before she disappeared.

I speeded up, then slowed to the inconspicuous, zombielike pace of a window shopper, stopping in front of the cookware shop next door. Kirby hadn't gone all the way inside, was standing in the entrance talking with a man I recognized as Ben Waterson. They kept it up for a couple of minutes, and it didn't look like a pleasant conversation. The security man scowled and shook his head, while Kirby went red in the face and gestured angrily at the store. Finally he turned and rushed back my way, nearly bowling over a toddler whose mom wasn't watching her. I did an about-face and started walking toward Lucky.

Kirby brushed past me, his pace fast and jerky. People in the mall and the grocery store gave him a wide berth. By the time I got back to the Wreck, he was already burning rubber. The Wreck picked that minute to go temperamental on me, and I knew I'd lost him.

Well, hell. I decided to run by his house again. No RX-7. I checked the parking lot and streets around McAteer. Nothing. Then the only sensible thing to do was drive over to the McDonald's on Ocean and treat myself to a Quarter Pounder with cheese, large fries, and a Diet Coke. The Diet Coke gave me the illusion I was limiting calories.

I spent most of the afternoon parked on Teresita. I'd brought along one of those little hot apple pies they sell at McDonald's. By the time I finished it, I'd had enough excess for one day.

I'd had enough of stake-outs, too, but I stayed in place until Kirby's car finally pulled up at around quarter to five. I waited until he was inside the house, then went up and rang the bell.

While I was sitting there, I'd tried to figure out what was so off-putting about Kirby Dalson. When he answered the door, I hit on it. He was a good-looking kid—well built and tall, with nice dark hair, even when it was wind-blown and full of bits and pieces of eucalyptus leaves like now, but his facial features were a touch too pointy, his eyes a touch too small and close-set. In short, he looked rodenty—just the kind of shifty-eyed kid you'd expect to be into all kinds of scams. His mother wouldn't notice it, and young girls would adore him, but guys would catch on right away, and you could bet quite a few adults, including most of his teachers, had figured it out.

The shiftiness really shone through when he saw me. Something to hide there, all right, maybe something big. "What do you want?" he asked sullenly.

"Just to check a few things." I stepped through the door even though he hadn't invited me in. You can get away with that with kids, even the most self-assured. Kirby just stood there. Then he shut the door, folded his arms across his chest, and waited.

I said, "Let's sit down," and went into the living room. It was pretty standard—beige and brown with green accents—and had about as much character as a newborn's face. I don't understand how people can live like that, with nothing in their surroundings that says who or what they are. My nest may be cluttered and have no particular decor, but at least it's *me*.

I sat on a chair in a little grouping by the front window. Kirby perched across from me. He'd tracked in wet, sandy grit onto his mother's well-vacuumed carpet—another strike against him, even for a lousy house-keeper like me—and his fingers drummed on his denim-covered thighs.

"Kirby," I began, "why'd you go to see Ben Waterson today?"

"Who?"

"The security head at Ocean Park Plaza."

"Who says I did?"

"I saw you."

His little eyes widened a fraction. "You were following me? Why?"

I ignored the question. "Why'd you go see him?"

For a moment he glanced about the room, as if looking for a way out. "Okay," he finally said. "Money."

"Money? For what?"

"Adrian, you know, disappeared on payday. I thought maybe I could collect some of what she owed me from Left Coast."

"Owed you for what?"

He shook his head.

"For *what*, Kirby?"

"Just for stuff. She borrowed when she was short."

I watched him silently for a minute. He squirmed a little. I said, "You know, I've been hearing that you're into some things that aren't strictly legal."

"I don't get you."

"Scams, Kirby."

His puzzled look proved he'd never make an actor.

"Do I have to spell it out for you?" I asked. "The term-paper racket. Selling test questions when you can get your hands on them."

His fingers stopped their staccato drumming. Damned if the kid didn't seem relieved by what I'd just said.

"What else are you into, Kirby?"

"Where're you getting this stuff, anyway?"

"Answer the question."

Silence.

"What about Adrian? Did you bring her in on any of your scams?"

A car door slammed outside. Kirby wet his lips and glanced at the mantel clock. "Look," he said, "I don't want you talking about this in front of my mother."

"Then talk fast."

"All right, I sold some test questions and term papers. So what? I'm not the first ever who did that."

"What else? That wouldn't have brought in the kind of cash that bought you your fancy car."

"I've got a job—"

"Nobody believes that but your parents."

Footsteps on the front walk. Kirby said, "All right, so I sell a little dope here and there."

"Grass?"

"Uh-huh."

"Coke? Crack?"

"When I can get them."

"Adrian use drugs?"

"A little grass now and then."

"She sell drugs?"

"Never."

A key turned in the front-door lock. Kirby looked that way, panicky. I asked, "What else are you into?"

"Nothing. I swear."

The door opened.

"What did you get Adrian involved in?"

"I didn't—" A woman in a raincoat stepped into the foyer, furling an umbrella. Kirby raised a hand to her in greeting, then said in a low voice, "I can't talk about it now."

"When?"

He raised his voice. "I have to work tonight, I'll be at the garage by seven."

"I'll bring my car in then. What's the address?"

He got a pad from a nearby telephone table and scribbled on it. I took the slip of paper he held out and glanced at it. The address was on Naples Street in the Outer Mission—mostly residential neighborhood, middle-class. Wherever Kirby wanted to meet, it wasn't a garage.

—⚬⚬—

By seven the rain was really whacking down, looking like it would keep it up all night. It was so dark that I had trouble picking out the right address on Naples Street. Finally I pinpointed it—a shabby brown cottage, wedged between two bigger Victorians. No light in the windows, no cars in the driveway. Had Kirby been putting me on? If he had, by God, I'd stomp right into his house and lay the whole thing out for his parents. That's one advantage to dealing with kids—you've got all kinds of leverage.

I got out of the Wreck and went up the cottage's front walk. Its steps were as bad off as the ones at June Simoom's place. I tripped on a loose board and grabbed the railing; its spindles shook. Where the bell should have been were a couple of exposed wires. I banged on the door, but nobody came. The newspapers and ad sheets that were piled in a sodden mass against the threshold told me that the door hadn't been used for quite a while.

After a minute I went back down the steps and followed the driveway alongside the house. There were a couple of aluminum storage sheds back there, both padlocked. Otherwise the yard was dark and choked with pepper trees. Ruts that looked like they'd been made by tires led under them, and way back in the shadows I saw a low-slung shape. A car. Kirby's, I thought.

I started over there, walking alongside the ruts, mud sucking at my sneakers. It was quiet here, much too quiet. Just the patter of rain in the trees overhead. And then a pinging noise from the car's engine.

It was Kirby's RX-7, all right. The driver's side door was open, but the dome light wasn't on. Now why would he leave the door open in a storm like this?

I moved slower, checking it out, afraid this was some kind of a setup. Then I saw Kirby sitting in the driver's seat. At least I saw someone's feet on the ground next to the car. And hands hanging loose next to them . . .

I moved even slower now, calling out Kirby's name. No answer. I called again. The figure didn't move. The skin on my shoulders went prickly, and the feeling spread up the back of my neck and head. My other senses kicked into overdrive—hearing sharper, sight keener, smell . . . There was a sweet but metallic odor that some primitive instinct told me was blood.

This was Kirby, all right. As I came closer I identified his jeans and down jacket, caught a glimpse of his profile. He was leaning forward, looking down at his lap. And then I saw the back of his head. God. It was ruined, caved in, and the blood—

I heard somebody moan in protest. Me.

I made myself creep forward, hand out, and touched Kirby's slumped shoulders. Felt something wet that was thicker than rainwater. I pulled my hand back as he slumped all the way over, head touching his knees now. Then I spun around and ran, stumbling through the ruts and the mud. I got as far as the first storage shed and leaned against it, panting.

I'd never seen a dead person before, unless you counted my grandmother, dressed up and in her coffin. I'd never touched one before.

After I got my wind back, I looked at the car again. Maybe he wasn't dead. No, I knew he was. But I went back there anyway and made myself touch his neck. Flesh still warm, but nothing pulsing. Then I turned, wiping my hand on my jeans, and ran all the way down the driveway and straight across the street to a house with a bright porch light. I pounded on the door and shouted for them to call 911, somebody had been murdered.

Afterward the uniformed cops who responded would ask me how I knew it was a murder and not natural causes or an overdose. But that was before they saw Kirby's head.

IV

I sat at the oak table in All Souls's kitchen, my hands wrapped around a mug of Hank Zahn's superstrength navy grog. I needed it more for the warmth than anything else. Hank sat next to me, and then there was Ted Smalley, and then Sharon. The men were acting like I was a delicate piece of china. Hank kept refilling my grog mug and trying to smooth down his unsmoothable wiry gray hair. Every now and then he'd take off his horn-rimmed glasses and gnaw on the earpiece—something he does when he's upset. Ted, who likes to fuss, had wrapped me in an afghan that he fetched from his own room upstairs. Every few minutes he'd tuck the ends tighter around me, and in between he pulled on his little goatee. Men think women fiddle with our hair a lot, but really, they do more of it than we do.

Sharon wasn't saying much. She watched and listened, her fingers toying with the stem of her wineglass. The men kept glancing reproachfully at her. I guess they thought she was being unsympathetic. I knew differently. She was worried, damned worried, about me. And eventually she'd have something to say.

Finally she sighed and shifted in her chair. Hank and Ted looked expectant, but all she did was ask, "Adah Joslyn was the inspector who came out from Homicide?"

I nodded. "Her and her partner . . . what's his name? Wallace." Joslyn was a friend of Sharon's—a half-black, half-Jewish woman whose appointment to the top-notch squad had put the department in good with any number of civil-rights groups.

"Then you were in good hands."

I waited. So did Ted and Hank, but all Sharon did was sip some wine and look pensive.

I started talking—telling it once more. "He hadn't been dead very long when I got there. For all I know, whoever killed him was still on the scene. Nobody knows whose house it is—neighbors say people come and go but don't seem to live there. What I'm afraid of is that Adrian Conway had something to do with Kirby's murder. If she did, it'll about kill her mother. I guess I can keep looking for her, can't I? I mean, unless they tell me not to?"

Sharon only nodded.

"Then maybe I will. Maybe I ought to take a look at that bedroom wall of hers again. Maybe . . ." I realized I was babbling, so I shut up.

Sharon finished her wine, took the empty glass to the sink, and started for the door. Hank asked, "Where're you going?"

"Upstairs to collect my stuff, and then home. It's been a long day."

Both men frowned and exchanged looks that said they thought she was being callous. I watched her leave. Then I finished my grog and stood up, too.

"Going to bed?" Ted asked.

"Yes."

"If you need anything, just holler."

"I'm upset, not feeble," I snapped.

Ted nodded understandingly. Sometimes he's so goddamn serene I could hit him.

Sharon was still in her office, not collecting anything, just sitting behind her desk, where I knew she'd be. I went in there and sat on the end of the chaise longue. After a few seconds, I got up again, and began to pace, following the pattern of the Oriental rug.

She said, "I can't tell you anything that'll help."

"I know."

"I'd hoped you'd never have to face this," she added. "Unrealistic of me, I suppose."

"Maybe."

"But maybe not. Most investigators don't, you know. Some of them never leave their computer terminals long enough to get out into the field."

"So what are we—unlucky?"

"I guess." She stood and started putting things into her briefcase. "You're going to keep looking for Adrian?"

"Yes."

"Good."

I stopped by the fireplace and picked up the gorilla mask she keeps on the mantel. It had a patch of hair missing right in the middle of its chin; I'd accidentally pulled it out one day during a fit over something that I couldn't even remember now. "Shar," I said, "it never gets any easier, does it?"

"No."

"But somehow you deal with it?"

"And go on." She put on her jacket, hefted the briefcase.

"Until the next time," I said bitterly.

"If there is one."

"Yeah." I suspected there would be. Look at what Sharon's life has been like. And yet, seeing her standing there—healthy and reasonably sane and looking forward to a good night's sleep—made me feel hopeful.

She came over to me and gave me a one-armed hug. Then she pointed at the gorilla mask and said, "You want to take him to bed with you tonight?"

"No. If I want to sleep with a gorilla, I'll just call Willie."

She grinned and went out, leaving me all alone.

After a while I put the gorilla back on the mantel and lay down on the chaise longue. I dragged the blanket over me and curled up on my side, cradling my head on my arm. The light from the Tiffany lamp was mellow and comforting. It became toasty under the blanket. In a few minutes, I actually felt sleepy.

I'd stay there tonight, I decided. In some weird way, it felt safer than my nest upstairs.

Donna Conway called me at eight-ten the next morning. I'd already gone down to my office—a closet under the stairs that some joker had passed off as a den when All Souls moved into the house years before—and was clutching a cup of the battery acid that Ted calls coffee and trying to get my life back together. When my intercom buzzed, I jerked and grabbed the phone receiver without first asking who it was.

Donna said dully, "The backpack I told you Adrian always took to school with her? They found it where poor Kirby was murdered."

I went to put my cup down, tipped it, and watched coffee soak into my copy of the morning paper. Bad day already. "They—you mean the police?"

"Yes. They just brought it over for me to identify."

"Where was it? In the yard?"

"Inside the house. It'd been there a long time because the yogurt—she always took a cup of yogurt to work to eat on her break—was spoiled."

Not good at all.

"Rae, you don't think it means *she* did that to Kirby, do you?"

"I doubt it." What I thought it meant was that Adrian was dead, maybe had been dead since shortly after she disappeared—but I wasn't going to raise *that* issue yet. "What else was in the pack besides the yogurt?"

A pause. "The usual stuff, I guess. I didn't ask. I was too upset."

I'd get Sharon to check that out with her friend Adah Joslyn.

Donna added, "The police said that Kirby was the one who rented the house, and that there was a girl with him when he first looked at it who matched Adrian's description."

"When?"

"Late last July. I guess . . . well, with teenagers today, you just assume they're sexually active. Adrian and I had a talk about safe sex two years ago. But I don't understand why they thought they needed to rent a place to be together. I'm not home all that much, and neither are Kirby's parents. Besides, they couldn't have spent much time at that house; Adrian worked six days a week, after school and on Saturdays, and she was usually home by her curfew."

I thought about Kirby's "job" at the nonexistent garage. Maybe Adrian's had been a front, too. But, no, that didn't wash—the store's manager, Sue Hanford, and the plaza security man, Ben Waterson, had confirmed her employment both to me and the police.

"Rae?" Donna said. "Will you keep on looking for her?"

"Of course."

"Will you call me if you find out anything? I'll be here all day today. I can't face going to work."

I said I would, but I was afraid that what I'd have to tell her wouldn't be anything she'd want to hear.

"Yeah, the little weasel wanted to pick up her pay, in cash." Ben Waterson plopped back in the metal chair behind the front desk in the Ocean Park Plaza security office. Its legs groaned threateningly under his massive weight. On the walls around us were mounted about two dozen TV screens that monitored what was going on in various stores in the center, switching from one to another for spot checking. Waterson glanced at one, looked closer, then shook his head. "In cash, no less, the little weasel said, since he couldn't cash her check. Said she owed him money. Can you imagine?"

I leaned against the counter. There wasn't another chair in the room, and Waterson hadn't offered to find me one. "Why'd he ask you for it, rather than Ms. Hanford? Adrian was paid by Left Coast Casuals, not the plaza, wasn't she?"

"Sue was out and had left me in charge of the store." Waterson scratched at the beer belly that bulged over the waist of his khaki uniform pants. "Can you imagine?" he said again. "Kids today." He snorted.

Waterson was your basic low-level security guy, although he'd risen higher than most of them ever go. I know, because I worked among them until my then boss took pity on me and recommended me to Sharon for the job at All Souls. It's a familiar type: not real bright, not too great to look at, and lacking in most of the social graces. About all you need to get in on the ground floor of the business is never to have been arrested or caught molesting the neighbors' dog on the front lawn at high noon. Ben Waterson—well, I doubted he'd been arrested because he didn't look like he had the ambition to commit a crime, but I wasn't too sure about his conduct toward the neighborhood pets.

"So you told Kirby to get lost?" I asked.

"I told him to fuck off, pardon my French. And he got pissed off, pardon it again, and left."

"He say why Adrian owned him money?"

"Nah. Who knows? Probably for a drug buy. Kids today."

"Did Adrian do drugs?"

"They all do."

"But did you ever know *her* to do them?"

"Didn't have to. They all do." He looked accusingly at me. From his fifty-something perspective, I probably was young enough to be classified as one of today's youthful degenerates.

I shifted to a more comfortable position, propping my hip against the counter. Waterson scanned the monitors again, then looked back at me.

"Let me ask you this," I said. "How well did you know Kirby Dalson?"

His eyes narrowed. "What the hell's that supposed to mean?"

I hadn't thought it was a particularly tricky question. "How well did you know him?" I repeated. "What kind of kid was he?"

"Oh. Just a kid. A weasel-faced punk. I had a daughter, I wouldn't let him near her."

"You mentioned drugs. Was Kirby dealing?"

"Probably."

"Why do you say that?"

He rolled his eyes. "I told you—kids today." Then, unself-consciously, he started picking his nose.

I didn't need any more of this, so I headed downstairs to Sue Hanford's office at Left Coast Casuals.

Hanford was a sleek blonde around my age, in her late twenties. One of those women who is moving up in the business world in spite of a limited education, relying on her toughness and brains. On Monday she'd told me she started in an after-school job like Adrian's at the Redwood City branch of the clothing chain and had managed two of their other stores before being selected for the plum position at the then new plaza. When she saw me standing in her office door, Hanford motioned for me to come in and sit down. She continued working at her computer for a minute. Then she swiveled toward me, face arranged in formally solemn lines.

"I read in the paper about the Conway girl's boyfriend," she said. "So awful. So young."

I told her about Adrian's backpack being found in the house, and she made perfunctorily horrified noises.

"This doesn't mean Adrian *killed* Kirby, does it?" she asked.

"Doubtful. It looked as if the pack's been there since right after she disappeared."

For a moment her features went very still. "Then Kirby might have killed . . ."

"Yes."

"But where is the . . . ?"

"Body? Well, not at the house, I'm sure the cops would have found it by now."

"Or else she . . ."

"She what?"

"I don't know. Maybe she ran away. Maybe he frightened her somehow."

Interesting assumption. "Are you saying Adrian was afraid of Kirby?"

Quickly she shook her head. "No. Well, maybe. It was more like . . . he dominated her. One look from him was all she needed, and she'd do whatever he wanted her to."

"Give me an example."

"Well, one time I saw them at a table near the food concessions in the middle of the mall. He had a burger, she was spooning up her yogurt. All of a sudden, Kirby pointed at his burger, then jerked his chin at the condiment counter. Adrian got up and scurried over there and brought him back some katsup."

"So he pretty much controlled her?"

"I'd say so."

"What else?"

She shrugged. "That's about the best example I can give you. I didn't really see that much of them together. We try to discourage our girls from having their friends come into the store during working hours."

"When I spoke with you earlier this week, you said you doubted Adrian was a drug user. Are you sure of that?"

"Reasonably sure. I observe our girls very carefully. I can't have anything like that going on, especially not on store premises. It would reflect badly on my abilities as a manager." Her eyes lost focus suddenly. "God, what if something has happened to Adrian? I mean, something like what happened to Kirby? That would reflect badly, too. The damage control I'd need to do . . ."

I said wryly, "I don't think that as store manager you can be held responsible for what happens to your employees during off-hours."

"You don't understand. It would reflect badly on my abilities to size up a prospective employee." Her eyes refocused on my face. "I can see you think I'm uncaring. Maybe to some degree I am. But I'm running a business here. I'm building a career, and I have to be strong. I have a small daughter to raise, and I'm fiercely protective of her chances to have a good life. I'm sorry Kirby Dalson's dead. If Adrian's also been killed, then I'm sorry about that, too. But, really, neither of them has anything to do with me, with my life."

That's the trouble, I thought. The poet, whoever he was, said no man is an island, but nowadays *every* man and woman is one. A whole goddamn continent, the way some of them act. It's a wonder that they all don't sink to the bottom of the ocean, just like the lost continent of Atlantis is supposed to have done.

V

I wanted to drive by the house on Naples Street, just to see what it looked like in the daylight. The rain had stopped, but it was still a soppy, gray morning. The house looked shabby and sodden. There was a yellow plastic police line strip across the driveway, and a man in a tan raincoat stood on the front steps, hands in his pockets, staring at nothing in particular.

He didn't look like a cop. He was middle-aged, middle height, a little gray, a little bald. His glasses and the cut of his coat were the kind you used to associate with the movers and shakers of the 1980s financial world, but the coat was rumpled and had a grease stain near its hem, and as I got out of the Wreck and went closer, I saw that one hinge of the glasses frame was wired together. His face pulled down in disappointed lines that looked permanent. Welcome to the nineties, I thought.

The man's eyes focused dully on me. "If you're a reporter," he said, "you'd better speak with the officers in charge of the case." He spoke with a kind of diluted authority, his words turning up in a question, as if he wasn't quite sure who or what he was any longer.

"I'm not a reporter." I took out my ID and explained my connection to the case.

The man looked at the ID, nodded, and shrugged. Then he sighed. "Hell of a thing, isn't it? I wish I'd never rented to them."

"This is your house?"

"My mother's. She's in a nursing home. I can't sell it—she still thinks she's coming back someday. That's all that's keeping her alive. I can't fix it up, either." He motioned at the peeling facade. "My business has been in a flat-out slump for a couple of years now, and the nursing home's expensive. I rented to the first couple who answered my ad. Bad judgment on my part. They were too young, and into God-knows-what." He laughed mirthlessly, then added, "Sorry, I didn't introduce myself. Ron Owens."

I'd inched up the steps toward the open front door until I was standing next to him. I shook his outstretched hand and repeated my name for him.

Owens sighed again and stared glumly at the wet street. "It's a hell of a world," he said. "A hell of a thing when a kid dies like that. Kids are supposed to grow up, have a life. At least outlive their parents." Then he looked at me. "You said the girl's mother hired you?"

"Yes. I haven't come up with any leads, and she's getting frantic. I thought maybe if I could see the house . . ." I motioned at the door.

For a moment Owens hesitated. "What the hell—they said they were done there. Come on in, if you want."

I followed him into a narrow hallway that ran the length of the cottage. "Were you here when they found the girl's backpack?"

"Did that belong to her? Yeah. I came over and let them in as soon as they contacted me. First time I'd been here since the kids rented it. Place is a mess. I'm glad I stored most of my mother's things in the sheds and only left the basic furnishings. They didn't exactly trash it, but they didn't keep it, either."

Mess was the word for it. Dust—both natural and from fingerprint powder—saturated all the surfaces, and empty glasses and plates stood among empty bottles and cans and full ashtrays in the front room. Owens lead me back past a bathroom draped in crumpled and mildewy-smelling towels and a bedroom where the sheets and blankets were mostly on the floor, to a kitchen. It contained more dirty crockery and glassware. Wrappings from frozen entrees and fast food overflowed the trashcan. A half-full fifth of Jim Beam stood uncapped on the counter. The entire place reeked.

"The cops went through everything?" I asked.

"Yeah. They didn't think anybody had been here for a while. At least not last night. There weren't any muddy footprints inside, and the door was blocked by a few days' worth of newspapers."

"Where did they find the backpack?"

"Front room. I'll show you."

The table where the backpack had been was just inside the living room door. What was left there was junk mail and ad sheets—the sort of stuff you drag inside with you and dump someplace until you get around to throwing it out. "So," I said, "this was where she'd leave the pack when she arrived. But why not pick it up again when she left?"

Ron Owens made a funny choking sound, and I realized he'd jumped to the obvious conclusion. "No," I said quickly, "the cops would have found evidence if she was killed here. Did you see what was in the pack?"

He shook his head. "One of them said something about there being no money or ID"

Adrian had been smart, carrying her cash and ID someplace else where it wouldn't be snatched if somebody grabbed the pack on the street or on the bus. Smart, too, because if she'd had to run out of this house suddenly —if Kirby had frightened or threatened her, as Sue Hanford had suggested —she'd at least have had the essentials on her.

I'd seen enough here, so I thanked Owens and gave him one of my cards in case he thought of anything else. I was halfway down the front walk when I remembered to ask him if I could see the sheds where he'd stored his mother's things.

For a moment he looked puzzled at the request, then he shrugged and fished a key ring from his pocket. "Actually, it wouldn't hurt to check them."

We ducked under the police line and went up the driveway. The trees dripped on the muddy ground where Kirby's car had been parked. There were deep gouges and tracks where the tow truck had hauled it out. Other than that, you would never have known that anything unusual had happened there. It was just an ordinary backyard that the weeds and blackberry vines were trying to reclaim.

Ron Owens fitted a key into the padlock on the first shed. Unfastened it and then the hasp. The door grated as he opened it.

There was nothing inside. Nothing at all except for a little heap of wood scraps.

Owens's face went slack with surprise. Then bright red splotches blossomed on his cheeks. "They cleaned me out," he said. "Check the other shed."

We hurried back there. Owens opened it. Nothing except for some trash drifted in the corners.

"But how did they . . . ?" He held up his key ring. "I had the only . . . There were no other keys."

I looked closely at the padlock. Cheap brand, more pickable than most. My boyfriend Willie would have had that off of there in five minutes, max—and he's out of practice. Willie's a respectable businessman now, but there are things in his past that are best not discussed.

"You better call the police," I told Owens.

He nodded, shoulders slumping. "I'm glad my mother will never have to find out about this," he said. "Her good china, Grandma's silver, the family pictures—all gone. For the first time I'm glad she's never coming home. There's no home left here anymore."

I watched Owens hurry down the drive to a car with a mobile phone antenna on its trunk. I knew how he felt. For me, the word "home" has a magical aura. Sometimes I can actually *see* it—velvety green like the plants in my nest at All Souls, gold and wine-red like the flames in a good fire. Silly, but that's the way it is for me. Probably for all of us people who've never had a real home of our own.

I turned away and looked back into the empty shed. Adrian had had a real home, but she'd left it. For this shabby little house? I doubted that. But she'd been here shortly after her schoolmates had last seen her, and then she'd probably fled in fear. For where? *Where?*

I decided to consult the therapy wall once more.

VI

The Conway house was warm for a change, and Donna had closed the drapes to hide the murky city view. Adrian's room, though, was frigid. Donna saving on the heating bill now that Adrian was gone? Or maybe the registers were closed because Adrian was one of those human reptiles who never need much warmth. My ex-husband, Doug, is like that: when other people are bundled in two layers of sweaters, he's apt to be running around in his shirtsleeves.

Before she left me alone, Donna said, "My sister-in-law called and said you'd gone to see her."

"Yes, Tuesday night."

"What'd you think of her?"

"Well, she's unconventional, but I kind of liked her. She seems to have a heart, and she certainly cares about Adrian."

Donna pushed a lock of hair back from her forehead and sighed. She looked depressed and jumpy, dark smudges under her eyes. "I see she's fooled you, too." Then she seemed to relent a little. "Oh, I suppose June's got a good heart, as you say. But she also has an unfortunate tendency to take over a situation and tell everyone what to do. She's the original earth mother and thinks we're all her children. The straw that broke it for me was when she actually advised Jeffrey to leave me. But . . . I don't know. She seems to want to patch it up now, and I suppose for Adrian's sake I should."

The words "for Adrian's sake" hung hollowly in the cold room. Donna shivered and added, "I'll leave you alone with the wall now."

Honestly, the way she acted, you'd have thought the wall was my psychiatrist. In a sense that was what it *had* been to her daughter.

I sat on Adrian's bed like the time before and let the images on the wall speak to me. One, then the other, cried out for attention. Bright primary colors, bold black and white. Words, pictures, then more words. And things—incongrous things. All adding up to . . . what?

After a while I sat up straighter, seeing objects I hadn't noticed before, seeing others in a new light. What they communicated was a sense of entrapment, but not necessarily by the family situation. Material relating to her absent father—GONE FOREVER, THE YEAR OF THE BIMBO, a postcard from Switzerland where Jeffrey Conway now lived—was buried deep under more recent additions. So were the references to Adrian's and her mother's new life—JUST THE TWO OF US, A WOMAN ALONE, NEW DIRECTIONS. But on top of that . . .

Fake plastic handcuffs. Picture of a barred window. NO EXIT sign. SOLD INTO WHITE SLAVERY. Photo of San Quentin. Images of a young woman caught up in something she saw no easy way out of.

I got up and went over to the wall and took a good look at a plastic security tag I'd noticed before. There were similar ones on the higher-priced garments at Left Coast Casuals. Next to it, the word "guilt" was emblazoned in big letters; smaller repetitions of it tailed down like the funnel of a cyclone. My eyes followed them, then were caught hypnotically in the whorls of a thumb-print on a plain white index card.

On top of all these were Adrian's final offerings. Now that I'd discovered a pattern, I could tell which things had been added last. FREEDOM! Broken gold chain. A WAY OUT. Egret feather and silhouette of a soaring bird. She was about to break loose, fly away. I wasn't

sure from what, not exactly. But guilt was a major component, and I
thought I knew why.

I started searching the room. Nothing under the lingerie or sweaters or
socks in the bureau drawers. Nothing pushed to the back of the closet or
hidden in the suitcases. Nothing under the mattress or the bed. Nothing
but school supplies in the desk.

Damn! I was sure I'd figured out that part of it. I had shameful personal experience to guide me.

The room was so cold that the joints of my fingers ached. I tucked my
hands into my armpits to warm them. The heat register was one of those
metal jobs set into the floor under a window, and its louvers were closed.
I squatted next to it and tried to push the opener. Jammed.

The register lifted easily out of its hole. I peered through the opening
in the floor and saw that the sheet metal furnace duct was twisted and
pushed aside. A nail had been hammered into the floor joist, and something hung down from it into the crawl space. I reached in and unhooked
it—a big cloth laundry bag with a drawstring. I pulled the bag up through
the hole and dumped its contents on the carpet.

Costume jewelry—rings, bracelets, earrings, necklaces—with the price
tags still attached. Silk scarves. Pantyhose. Gloves, bikini underpants,
leather belts, hair ornaments. They were all from Left Coast Casuals.

Although the items were tagged, the tags were not the plastic kind that
trip the sensors at the door. Left Coast Casuals reserved the plastic tags
for big-ticket items. All of the merchandise was brand-new, had never
been worn. No individual item was expensive, but taken together, they
added up to a hell of a lot of money.

This told me a lot about Adrian, but it didn't explain her disappearance.
Or her boyfriend's murder. I replaced the things in the bag, and the bag
beneath the flooring. Then I got out of there and went to bounce this one
off Sharon.

Sharon was all dressed up today, probably either for a meeting with
one of our tonier clients or a court appearance. The teal blue suit and
silk blouse looked terrific on her, but I could tell she wasn't all that

comfortable in them. Sharon's more at home in her jeans and sweaters and sneakers. The only time she really likes getting gussied up is for a fancy party, and then she goes at it with the excitement of a kid putting on her Halloween costume.

She said she had some time on her hands, so I suggested we stop down at the Remedy Lounge, our favorite bar and grill on Mission Street, for burgers. She hesitated. They serve a great burger at the Remedy, but for some reason Sharon—who's usually not fastidious when it comes to food—is convinced they're made of all sorts of disgusting animal parts. Finally she gave in, and we wandered down the hill.

The Remedy is a creaky local tavern, owned by the O'Flanagan family for longer than anybody can remember. Brian, the middle son and night-time bartender, wasn't on yet, so we had to fetch our own food and drinks. Brian's my buddy, and when he's working, I get table service—something that drives everybody else from All Souls crazy because they can't figure out how I manage that. I just let them keep guessing. Truth is, I remind Brian of his favorite sister, who died back in '76. Would you refuse table service to a family member?

While we waited for the burgers, I laid out the Adrian Conway situation for Sharon. When I was done, she went and got our food, then looked critically at her burger, taking off the top half of the bun and poking suspiciously at the meat patty. Finally she shrugged, bit into it, and looked relieved at finding it tasted like burger instead of entrail of monkey—or whatever she thinks they make them from. She swallowed and asked, "All the stuff was lifted from Left Coast Casuals?"

"Uh-huh."

"Employee pilferage." She shook her head. "Do you know that over forty-three percent of shrinkage is due to insiders?"

I didn't, but Sharon's a former department-store security guard and she keeps up on statistics. I just nodded.

"A lot of it's the employers' fault," she added. "They don't treat their people well, so they don't have a real commitment to the company. The clerks see it as a way of getting even for low wages and skimpy benefits."

"Well, whatever Adrian's reasons were," I said, "she dealt with the loot in the usual way. Once she got it home, it wasn't any good to her. Her mother would notice if she wore a lot of new things and ask where she got the money to buy them. Plus she felt guilty. So she hid the loot away were Donna wouldn't find it and—more important—where she couldn't see it and be reminded of what she'd done. Out of sight, out of mind. Only it doesn't work that way. She was probably aware of that bag of stuff hanging between the floor joists every minute she was in that room. She probably even dreamed about it."

My voice had risen as I spoke, and I couldn't keep an emotional quaver out of it. When I finished, Sharon didn't say anything, just watched me with her little analytical frown. I ate some of my burger. It tasted like cardboard. I drank some Coke. My hand shook when I set the glass down.

"Anyway," I said, "Adrian being a shoplifter doesn't explain the important things. Did you ask Adah Joslyn what was in the backpack, like I asked you to?"

"I've got a call in to her."

She was still watching me. After a moment I gave it up. "All right," I said, "I used to shoplift."

"I suspected as much."

"Thanks a lot!"

"Well, you did get pretty worked up for a moment there. You want to tell me about it?"

"No! Well, maybe." I took a deep breath, wishing I'd ordered a beer instead of a Coke. "Okay, it started one day when I was trying to buy some nail polish. The clerk was off yapping with one of the other clerks and wouldn't stop long enough to notice me. So I got pissed, stuck the bottle in my purse, and walked out. Nobody even looked at me. I couldn't believe I'd gotten away with it. It was like . . . a high. The best high I'd ever felt. And I told myself the clerk had goaded me into it, that it was a one-shot thing and would never happen again."

"But of course it did."

"The second time it was a scarf, an expensive scarf. I had a job interview and I wanted to look nice, but I couldn't afford to because I didn't have a job—the old vicious circle. I felt deprived, really angry. So I took the scarf. But what I didn't count on was the guilt. By the day of the interview, I knew I couldn't wear the scarf—then or ever. I just tucked it away where I wouldn't have to see it and be reminded of what I'd done. And where my husband wouldn't find it."

"But you kept stealing."

"Yeah. I never deliberately set out to do it, never left the apartment thinking, today I'm going to rip some store off. But . . . the high. It was something else." Even now, years after the fact, I could feel aftershocks from it—my blood coursing faster, my heart pounding a little. "I was careful, I only took little things, always went to different stores. And then, just when I thought I was untouchable, I got caught."

Sharon nodded. She'd heard it all before, working in retail security.

I looked down at my half-eaten burger. Shame washed over me, negating the memory of the high. My cheeks went hot, just thinking about that day. "God, it was awful! The security guy nabbed me on the sidewalk, made me go back inside to the store office. What I'd taken was another scarf. I'd stuffed it into a bag with some underpants I'd bought at Kmart. He dragged it out of there. It was still tagged, and of course I didn't have any receipt."

"So he threatened you."

"Scared the hell out of me. I felt like . . . you know those old crime movies where they're sweating a confession out of some guy in a back room? Well, it wasn't like that at all, he was very careful not to do or say anything that might provoke a lawsuit. But I still felt like some sleazy criminal. Or maybe that was what I thought I deserved to feel like. Anyway, he threatened to call my employer." I laughed—a hollow sound. "That would really have torn it. My employer was another security firm!"

"So what'd you do—sign a confession?"

"Yes, and promised never to set foot in their store again. And I've never stolen so much as a stick of gum since. Hell, I can't even bring myself to take the free matchbooks from restaurants!"

Sharon grinned. "I bet one of the most embarrassing things about that whole period in your life is that you were such a textbook case."

I nodded. "Woman's crime. Nonsensical theft. Doesn't stem from a real need, but from anger or the idea you're somehow entitled to things you can't afford. You get addicted to the high, but you're also overcome by the guilt, so you can't get any benefit from what you've stolen. Pretty stupid, huh?"

"We're all pretty stupid at times—shoplifters haven't cornered the market on that."

"Yeah. You know what scared me the most, though? Even more than the security guy calling my employer? That Doug would find out. For a perpetual student who leaned on me for everything from financial support to typing his papers, he could be miserably self-righteous and superior. He'd never even have tried to understand that I was stealing to make up for everything that was missing in our marriage. And he'd *never* have let me forget what I did."

"Well, both the stealing and Doug are history now." Sharon patted my hand. "Don't look so hangdog."

"Can't help it. I feel like such a . . . I bet you've never done anything like that in your life."

Sharon's eyes clouded and her mouth pulled down. All she said was, "Don't count on it." Then she scrubbed her fingers briskly on her napkin and pushed her empty plate away. "Finish your lunch," she ordered. "And let's get back to your case. What you're telling me is that Adrian was shoplifting and saw a way to break free of it?"

"A way to break free of something, but I'm not convinced it was the shoplifting. It may have been related, but then again, it may not." My head was starting to ache. There was too damn big a gap between the bag of loot under the floor of Adrian's room in Diamond Heights and the abandoned backpack in the living room of the house on Naples Street. I'd hoped Sharon would provide a connection, but all she'd done was listen to me confess to the absolutely worst sin of my life.

She looked at her watch. "Well, I'll try to find out what you need to know from Adah later this afternoon, but right now I've got to go. I'm giving a deposition at an upscale Montgomery Street law firm at three." Her nose wrinkled when she said "upscale."

I waved away the money she held out and told her I'd pick up the tab. It was the least I could do. Even though she hadn't helped me with the case, she'd helped me with my life. Again.

I've always felt like something of a fraud—pretending to be this nice little person when inside I'm seething with all sorts of resentments and peculiarities and secrets. But since I've been with All Souls, where people are mostly open and nonjudgmental, I've realized I'm not that unusual. Lately the two me's—the outside nice one and the inside nasty one—are coming closer together. Today's conversation with Sharon was just one more step in the right direction.

VII

I'd come up with a plan, an experiment I wanted to try out, and while it probably wouldn't work, I had a lot of time on my hands and nothing to lose. So after I finished my burger, I went back up the hill to our annex and got Lillian Chu to call her son Tom at McAteer and command his presence at my office as soon as school let out. When Tom arrived, he'd traded his friendly smile for a pout. To make up for my high-handedness, I took him to the kitchen and treated him to a Coke.

Tom perched on one of the counter tops and stared around at the ancient sink and wheezy appliances. "Man," he said, "this is really retro. I mean, how can you people *live* like this?"

"We're products of a more primitive era. You're probably wondering why I—"

"Pulled this authority shit. Yeah. You didn't have to get my mom to order me to come here."

"I wasn't sure you would, otherwise. Besides, the people at McAteer wouldn't have called you to the phone for me. I'm sorry, but I really need your help. You heard about Kirby, of course."

The anger in his eyes melted. He shook his head, bit his lip. "Oh, man. What an awful . . . You know, I didn't like the dude, but for him to be *murdered . . ."*

"Did you hear that Adrian's backpack was found m the house whose backyard he was killed in?"

"No." For a few seconds it didn't seem to compute. Then he said, "Wait, you don't think *Adrian* . . . ?"

"Of course not, but I'm afraid for her. If she's alive, it's possible Kirby's killer is after her, too. I need to find her before anyone else does."

Tom sat up straighter. "I get you. Okay, what can I do to help?"

"You have a group of friends you hang out with, right? People you can trust, who aren't into anything—"

"Like Kirby was."

"Right."

"Well, sure I do."

"Can you get some of them together this afternoon? Bring them here?"

He frowned, thinking. "Today's Thursday, right?"

"Uh-huh."

"Okay, football practice'll be over in about an hour, so I can get hold of Harry. Cat and Jenny don't work today, so they should be around. Del— he's just hanging out these days. The others . . . probably. But it'll be getting close to suppertime before I can round them all up."

"I'll spring for some pizzas."

Tom grinned. "That'll help. At least it'll get Del and Harry here."

I realized why when I met Del and Harry—they each weighed around two hundred pounds. Harry's were all football player's muscle, but Del's were pure flab. Both waded into Mama Mia's Special like they hadn't eaten in a week. Even the girls—Anna, Cat, Jenny, and Lee—had appetites that would put a linebacker to shame.

They perched around the kitchen on top of the counters and table and chopping block, making me wonder why teenagers always feel more at home on surfaces where they have no right to plant their fannies. Each had some comment on the vintage of the appliances, ranging from "really raunchy" to "awesome." The staff couldn't resist poking their noses through the door to check out my young guests, but when Tom Chu, who knew full well who Hank Zahn was, pointed to him and called, "Hey, Rae, who's the geezer?" I put a stop to that and got the meeting under way. After shutting the swinging door and shouting for them to get serious, I perched on the counter next to Tom. Seven tomato sauce–smudged faces turned toward me.

I asked, "Do all of you know what brainstorming is?"

Seven heads nodded.

"What we're going to do," I went on, "is to share information about Kirby and Adrian. I'll ask questions, throw out some ideas, you say whatever comes into your heads. Anything, no matter how trivial it may seem to you, because you never know what might be important in an investigation."

The kids exchanged excited glances. I supposed they thought this was just like *Pros and Cons*.

"Okay," I began, "here's one idea—shoplifting."

Total silence. A couple of furtive looks.

"No takers? Come on, I'm not talking about any of you. I could care less. But think of Adrian and Kirby."

The angelic-looking blonde—Cat—said, "Well, Adrian took stuff from the place where she worked sometimes. We all suspected that."

"I didn't," Harry protested.

"Well, she *did*. At first she thought it was a giggle, but then . . ." Cat shrugged. "She just stopped talking about it. She'd get real snotty if you mentioned it."

"When was this?" I asked.

"Sometime last spring. Right about the time things started getting very heavy between her and Kirby."

"When she started sleeping with him," Del added.

"Okay," I said, "tell me about Kirby's scams."

Beside me, Tom muttered, "Dope."

"Test questions." Anna, a pretty Filipina, nodded knowingly.

Cat said, "He sold stuff."

"Like L.L. Bean without the catalog." The one sitting cross legged on the shopping block was Jenny.

I waited, letting them go with it.

Harry said, "Kirby'd get you stuff wholesale. He sold me the new Guns N' Roses CD for half price."

"You wanted something," Anna added, "you'd give him an order. Kirby filled it."

"A real en-tree-preneur," Del said, and the others laughed. All of them, that is, except Lee, a tiny girl who looked Eurasian. She sat on the far side of the oak table and had said nothing. When I looked at her, she avoided my eyes.

Jenny said, "It's not funny, Del. Kirby was so into money. It was like if he got enough of it, he'd really be somebody. Only he wouldn't've been because there was no one there. You know what I mean? He had nothing inside of him—"

"Except money hunger," Tom finished.

"Yeah, but don't forget about his power trip," Cat said. She looked at me and added, "Kirb had a real thing about power. He liked pushing people round, and I think he figured having money would mean he could push all he wanted. He really was a control freak, and the person he controlled best was Adrian."

"Jump, Adrian," Harry said. "How high, Kirby?"

Anna shook her head. "She was getting out from under that, though. Around week before she disappeared, we were talking and she said she'd about had it with Kirby, she was going to blow the whistle and the game would be over. And I said something like, 'Sure you are, Adrian,' and she goes, 'No, I've worked it all out and I've got somebody to take my side.' And I go, 'You mean you got another guy on the line who's going to stand up to Kirb?' And she goes, 'Yes, I've got somebody to protect me, somebody strong and fierce, who isn't going to take any shit off of anybody.' "

"Did you tell the cops about that when they came around?" Del asked. Anna tossed her long hair. "Why should I? If Adrian took off with some guy, it's her business."

I caught a movement to one side, and turned in time to see Lee, the silent one, slip off the table and through the swinging door to the hall. "Lee?" I called.

There was no answer but her footsteps running toward the front of the house. I was off the countertop and out the door in seconds. "Help yourself to more Cokes," I called over my shoulder.

By the time I spotted her, Lee was on the sidewalk heading downhill toward Mission. As I ran after her I realized what truly lousy shape I'd let myself get into these past few months, what with the caseload I'd been carrying and spending too much time with Willie. There's only one kind of exercise that Willie likes, and while it's totally diverting, it doesn't do the same thing for you as aerobics.

Lee heard my feet slapping on the pavement, looked back, and then cut to the left and started running back uphill through the little wedge-shaped park that divides the street in front of All Souls. I groaned and reversed, panting.

At the tip of the park two streets came together, and two cars were also about to come together in a great blast of horns and a shout from one of the drivers that laid a blue streak on the air. Lee had to stop, I put on some speed, and next thing I knew I had hold of her arm. Thank God she didn't struggle—I had absolutely no wind left.

Lee's short black hair was damp with sweat, plastered close to her finely fashioned skull, and her almond-shaped eyes had gone flat and shiny with fear. She looked around desperately, then hung her head and whispered, "Please leave me alone."

I got my breathing under control—sort of. "Can't. You know something, and we have to talk. Come on back to the house."

"I don't want to face the rest of them. I don't want any of them to know what I've done."

"Then we'll talk out here." There was a makeshift bench a few yards away—a resting place one of the retired neighborhood handymen had thrown together for the old ladies who had to tote parcels uphill from the stores on Mission. Hell, I thought as I led Lee over there, he'd probably watched me trying to jog around the park before I totally lost it in the fitness department, and built the thing figuring I'd need it one of these days. Eventually I'd keel over during one of my workouts and then they'd put a plaque on the seat: *Rae Kelleher Memorial Bench—Let This Be a Warning to All Other Sloths.*

I gave Lee a moment to compose herself—and me a moment to catch my breath—and looked around at the commuters trudging up from the bus stop. The day had stayed gray and misty until about three, then cleared some, but new storm clouds threatened out by the coast. Lee fumbled through her pockets and came up with a crumpled Kleenex, blew her nose and sighed.

I said, "It can't be all that bad."

"You don't know. It's the worst thing I've ever done. When my father finds out, he'll *kill* me."

I tried not to smile, thinking of all the kids down through the ages who had been positively convinced that they would be killed on the spot if they were ever caught doing something wrong. I myself was in college before it occurred to me that parents—normal, sane parents, that is—don't kill their offspring because kids are too damned expensive and troublesome to acquire and raise. Why waste all that money and effort, plus deprive yourself of the pleasure of becoming a burden to them in your old age?

"Maybe," I said to Lee, "he won't have to find out."

She shook her head. "No way, not this."

"Tell me about it, and then we'll see."

Another tremulous sigh. "I guess I better tell somebody, now that Kirby's been murdered and Adrian . . . but I'm afraid I'll go to jail."

Big stuff, then. "In that case, it's better to come forward, rather than be found out later."

Lee bit her lip. "Okay," she said after a moment. "Okay. I didn't know Kirby very well, just to say hi when I'd see him around, you know? But then one day last August he came to my house with these pictures while my parents were at work."

"What pictures?"

"Of me taking stuff from where I work. You know that stationery and gift shop at Ocean Park Plaza—Paper Fantasy? Well, I worked there full time last summer and now I go in three days a week after school. I kind of got into taking things—pen-and-pencil sets, jewelry, other gift items. I didn't even want them very much. I mean, the stuff they sell is expensive but pretty tacky. But it made me not feel so bad about having this crummy job . . . Anyway, that's what Kirby's pictures showed, me taking jewelry from the case and stuffing it under my sweater." Lee's words were spilling out fast now; I was probably the only person she'd ever told about this.

"There was no way you could mistake what I was doing," she went on. "The pictures showed it clear as could be. Kirby said he was going to go to my boss unless I did what he wanted. At first I thought he meant, you know, sex, and I could have died, but it turned out what he wanted was for me to steal stuff and give it to him. I said I would. I would have done anything to keep from being found out. And that's what I've been doing."

"So Kirby got the merchandise he was selling by blackmailing people into shoplifting for him. I wonder if that's the hold he had over Adrian?"

"It might have been. When they were first going together, they were, you know, like a normal couple. But then she changed, dropped all her friends and other activities, and started spending every minute with Kirby. I guess he used her shoplifting to get control of her."

"What about the other kids? Do you know anybody else who was stealing for Kirby?"

"Nobody who'll talk about it. But there's a rumor about a couple of the guys, that they take orders and just go out and rip off stuff. And a lot of the things he has for sale come from stores where I know other kids from school work."

Kirby had had quite a scam going—a full-blown racket, actually. And Lee was right: There was no way this could be kept from her father. She might even go to juvenile hall.

"The pictures," I said, "did Kirby say how he took them?"

"No, but he had to've been inside the store. They were kind of fuzzy, like he might've used a telephoto."

"From where?"

"Well, they were face on, a little bit above and to the left of the jewelry counter."

"Did you ever see Kirby in the store with a camera?"

"No, but I wouldn't've noticed him if we were busy."

"Would you have taken something while the store was busy?"

"Sure. That's the best time." Lee seemed to hear her own words, because she hung her head, cheeks coloring. "God, those pictures! I looked like a *criminal*!"

Which, of course, she was. I thought about Kirby and his corps of teenaged thieves. What if he'd tried to hit on the wrong person? Homicides committed by teenagers, like all other categories, were on the upswing . . .

"Lee," I said, "you're going to have to tell the cops investigating Kirby's murder about this."

She nodded numbly, hands clenching.

The phrase "shit hitting the fan" isn't a favorite of mine, but that was exactly what was about to happen, and a lot of perfectly nice parents were going to be splattered, to say nothing of their foolish but otherwise nice children. Parents like Donna Conway. Children like Adrian.

I pictured the pretty redhead in the photo Donna had given me—her quirky smile and the gleam in her eyes that told of a zest for living and an offbeat sense of humor. I pictured her quiet, concerned, sad mother— a lonely woman clinging to her stacks of self-help books for cold comfort. Maybe I could still find Adrian, reunite the two so they could lean on each other in the tough times ahead. If Adrian was still alive, there had to be a way.

And if she was dead? I didn't want to think about that.

VIII

Lee and I went back to All Souls, where the rest of the kids were standing around the foyer wondering what to do next, and while she escaped to my office to call her father, I thanked them and showed them out. Tom Chu hung back, looking worried and throwing glances at my office door. Since he was the one who had put this together for me, I filled him in on some of what Lee had told me, after first swearing him to secrecy.

Tom didn't look too surprised. "I kind of suspected Lee was in trouble," he said. "And you know what? I think Del might've been mixed up with Kirby, too. He got real quiet when Lee ran out on us, and he left in a hurry right afterward."

"Those're pretty shaky grounds to accuse him on."

"Maybe, but Del . . . I told you he's basically just hanging out this fall? Well, where he's hanging out is Ocean Park Plaza."

Ocean Park Plaza—the focus of the whole case. I thanked Tom and gently chased him out the door so Lee wouldn't have to deal with him when she finished calling her dad.

Her father arrived some fifteen minutes later, all upset but full of comforting words, and agreed to take Lee down to the Hall of Justice to talk to Adah Joslyn. I called Joslyn to let her know a witness was on her way. "Adah," I added, "did Sharon ask you what was in Adrian Conway's backpack?"

"Yeah. I've got the property list right here." There was a rustling noise. "Some raunchy-smelling yogurt, makeup, a Golden Gate Transit schedule, couple of paperbacks—romance variety—and an envelope with the phone number of the Ocean Park Plaza's security office scribbled on it."

"Security office? You check with them?"

"Talked to a man named Waterson. He said she'd lost her ID badge the week before she disappeared and called in about getting it replaced. What is this—you trying to work my homicide, Kelleher?"

"Just trying to find a missing girl. I'll turn over anything relevant."

When I got off the phone, Lee and her father were sitting on the lumpy old couch in the front room, his arm protectively around her narrow shoulders. He didn't look like much of a teenaged killer to me; in fact, his main concern was that she hadn't come to him and admitted about the shoplifting as soon as "that little bastard"—meaning Kirby—had started hassling her. "I'd've put his ass in a sling," he kept saying. I offered to go down to the Hall with them, but he said he thought it would be better if they went alone. As soon as they left, I decided to head over to Ocean Park Plaza, check out a couple of things, then talk with Ben Waterson again.

The mall wasn't very crowded that night, but it was only Thursday, and the merchants were still gearing up for a big weekend sales push designed to lure in all those consumers who weren't suffering too much from the recession—getting started early on the Christmas season by urging everybody to spend,

spend, spend in order to stimulate the economy. The sale banners were red, white, and blue, and really, they were making it sound like it was our patriotic duty to blow every last dime on frivolous things that—by God!—had better be American-made if Americans made them at all. Even I, much as I love to max out my credit cards, am getting totally sick of the misguided economists' notion that excess is not only good for the individual but for the nation. Anyway, the appeals from the politicians and the business community probably wouldn't meet with any more success with patrons of the Ocean Park Plaza this coming weekend than they had with downtown shoppers the previous one, and tonight they were having no effect at all.

When I got to Paper Fantasy I found I was the only browser—a decided disadvantage for checking out the possible angles from which Kirby might have taken the photographs of Lee. I checked anyway, under the suspicious eyes of the lone clerk. Over there was the counter where Lee had been standing when she'd five-fingered the jewelry, and from the way she'd described the pictures, Kirby would have had to be standing not only in front of it, but some three feet in the air. Impossible, unless . . .

Aha! There it was—a surveillance camera mounted on the wall above and to the left of the counter. One look at that and I recalled the banks of screens in the security office upstairs, closed-circuit TV that allowed you to videotape and photograph.

I hurried out of Paper Fantasy—possibly provoking a call to security by the clerk—and headed for Left Coast Casuals.

Only two salesclerks manned the store, and there were no customers. I wandered up and down the aisles, scanning for the cameras. There were four, with a range that covered the entire sales floor. While stealing jewelry, Adrian would have had to stand around here, in plain sight of that one. For lingerie, camera number two would have done the observing. Stupid. How could the kids *be* so stupid?

Of course I knew the answer to that—anybody who's ever shoplifted does. The cameras are there, sure, but you just assume they're not recording your particular store at the time, or being monitored. And you're certain that you're being oh-so-subtle when actually you're about as discreet as a moose picking its way through a bed of pansies. And then there's that urge that just washes over you—ooh, that irresistible impulse, that heady pulse-quickening temptation to commit the act that will bring on that delicious soaring high.

Yeah, the kids were stupid. Like I'd been stupid. Like a drug addict, an alcoholic, a binge-eater is stupid.

"Ms. Kelleher?" The voice was Sue Hanford's. "Can I help you?"

I swung around. She'd come out of the stock room and stood a few feet away from me, near the fake angora sweaters. "I was just looking the store over once more, before going up to see Ben Waterson."

Her face became pinched, two white spots appearing at the corners of her mouth. "You won't find him in the office. I know, because I just called up there. I'll tell you, I've about had it with him not being available when I need him."

"This happens a lot?"

"Well, yesterday morning around eleven-thirty. He said he'd come and talk about the problem I've been having with a gang of girls who are creating disturbances outside and intimidating my customers, but then he never showed up. I called and called, but he'd taken off without saying why. He didn't come back until six." But yesterday morning at around eleven-thirty I'd seen him just outside the store, arguing with Kirby Dalson. Waterson had claimed Sue Hanford was the one who was away, leaving him in charge. "Were you in the store all day yesterday?" I asked.

She nodded. "I worked a fourteen-hour shift."

"And today?" I asked. "Waterson wasn't available again?"

"Yes. He took off about half an hour ago, when he's supposed to be on shift till nine-thirty."

"I see."

"Ms. Kelleher? If you do go up there and find Ben has come back, will you ask him to come down here?"

"Sure," I said distractedly. Then I left the store.

A taco, I thought. There was a taco stand down in the food concession area. Maybe a taco and a Coke would help me think this one through.

Okay, I thought, reaching for Gordito's Beef Supreme taco—piled high with extra salsa, guacamole, and sour cream—somebody in the security office here has been getting the goods on the kids who are shoplifting and turning the evidence over to Kirby so he could blackmail them into working for him. If I wasn't trained not to jump to conclusions I'd say Ben Waterson, because his behavior has been anything but on the up-and-up lately. Okay, I'll say it anyway—Ben Waterson. Kirby was a good contact man for Waterson—he knew the kids, knew their weak spots, and after they ripped off the stuff he would wholesale some of it at school, keeping Waterson out of the transaction. Kind of a penny-ante scheme, though, if you think about it. Would hardly have brought in enough to keep Kirby, much less Waterson, in ready cash. And there had to be something in it for Waterson. But then there were the other kids—like Del—who didn't work here but ripped things off for Kirby, maybe big-ticket items, here and at other malls as well. And there was the rented house on Naples Street.

Those storage sheds in the backyard—sheds full of Ron Owens's mother's things, that Owens claims were worth quite a bit—I'll bet all of that got fenced, and then they filled up the sheds with new merchandise while they tried to find a buyer for it. Not hard to find one, too, not in this town. Neighbors said a lot of people came and went at Naples Street, so it could have been a pretty substantial fencing operation.

I know a fair amount about fencing, courtesy of Willie Whelan, who in recent years, thank God, has "gone legit," as he puts it. So far the scenario made sense to me.

The taco was all gone. Funny—I'd barely tasted it. I looked longingly at Gordito's, then balled up the wrappings and turned my attention back to the case.

Where does Adrian fit into all this? Last spring she starts to change, according to her school friends. She's been taking her five-finger employee discount for a while, oblivious to what Kirby and Waterson are up to. Then Kirby comes to her with pictures, and suddenly he's got the upper hand in the relationship. Adrian's still pretty demoralized—the father leaving, the mother who's always spouting phrases like "potential to be"—so she lets Kirby control her. Did she steal for him? Help him with the fencing? Had to have, given that she was familiar enough with the Naples Street house to walk in and plunk her backpack down in the living room. I'm pretty sure she slept with him—even the other kids know that.

Okay, suppose Adrian does all of that. Maybe she even glamorizes the situation as young women will do in order to face themselves in the morning. But fetching the condiments for the hamburgers of a young man who can damned well get them himself grows old real fast, and after a while she starts to chafe at what her therapy wall calls "white slavery." So, as she tells her friend Anna, she's decided to "blow the whistle and the game would be over." How? By going to the cops? Or by going to the head of mall security, Ben Waterson?

I got up, tossed my cup and the taco wrappings in a trash bin, and headed for the security office.

Waterson wasn't there. Had left around six after a phone call, destination unknown, the woman on the desk told me. I persuaded her to check their log to see if Adrian Conway had reported losing her ID badge about a week before she disappeared, as Waterson had told Adah Joslyn. No record of it, and there would have been had it really happened.

Caught you in another lie, Ben!

Back down to the concession area. This time I settled for coffee and a Mrs. Fields cookie.

So Adrian probably went to Waterson, since she had the phone number of the security office scribbled on an envelope in her backpack. And he . . . what? Lured her away from the mall and killed her? Hid her body? Then why was her backpack at Naples Street? Waterson would have left it with the body or gotten rid of it. And would Waterson have gone to such lengths, anyway?

Well, Kirby was murdered, wasn't he?

But would Kirby have kept quiet if he thought Waterson had murdered his girlfriend? The kid was a cold one, but . . . Maybe I just didn't want to believe that anybody that young could be that cold. And that was poor reasoning—if you don't believe me, just check out the morning paper most days.

Another thing—who was this person Adrian had talked about, who would take her side and not take any shit off of anybody? Maybe Waterson had played it subtle with her, pretended to be her protector, then spirited her off somewhere and—

The prospects for her survival weren't any better with that scenario.

I was so distracted that I bit clear through the cookie into my tongue. Swore loud enough to earn glares from two old ladies at the next table.

Back to Ben Waterson. Kirby came to the mall the other day and argued with him—not about getting hold of Adrian's back pay, as they both claimed, because Waterson lied about Sue Hanford leaving him in charge at Left Coast Casuals. And right after the argument, Kirby stormed out of the mall and drove off burning rubber. Waterson took off around that time, too. And tonight Waterson left again, after a phone call around six—about the time the kids, Del preceding them, left All Souls. Did Del or another of them warn him that everything was about to unravel? Is Waterson running, or did he leave for purposes of what Sue Hanford calls damage control?

Damage control. I suppose you could call Kirby's murder damage control . . .

I got up, threw my trash in the bin, and began walking the mall—burning off excess energy, trying to work it out. If only I knew what Kirby and Waterson had argued about. And where they'd each gone Wednesday afternoon. And why Kirby had asked me to meet him at the Naples Street house. Had Waterson found out about the meeting, gotten there early? Killed Kirby before he could talk with me? And what about Adrian? If she was dead, where was her body? And if she was alive—

And then I saw something. It wasn't related to my case at all, was just one of those little nudges you get when you have all the information you need and are primed for something to come along and help you put it all together. I'm sure I'd have figured it out eventually, even if it hadn't been for the poster of the African veldt in the window of a travel agency—a poster that made the land look so parched and windswept and basically unpleasant that you wondered why they thought it would sell tours. But as it was, it happened then, and I was damned glad of it.

IX

The Wreck and I sped through the night, under a black sky that quickly started leaking rain, then just plain let go in a deluge. The windshield wipers scraped and screeched, smearing the glass instead of clearing it.

Dammit, I thought, why can't I get it together to buy a new car—or at least some new wiper blades? No, a whole car's in order, because this defroster isn't worth the powder to blow it to hell, and I'm so sick of being at the mercy of third-rate transportation.

Then I started wondering about the tread on the Wreck's tires. When was the last time I'd checked it? It had looked bad, whenever, and I'd promised myself new tires in a few hundred more miles, but that had to be several thousand ago. What if I got a flat, was stranded, and didn't reach Adrian in time? She was probably safe; I didn't know for sure that Waterson had figured it out. Hell, *I'd* barely done that. Could anybody manage, without knowing Adrian the way I did from her therapy wall?

The rain whacked down harder and the wind blew the Wreck all over the road. My shoulders got tense, and my hands actually hurt from clinging to the wheel. Lights ahead now—the little town of Olema where this road met the shoreline highway. Right turn, slow a little, then put the accelerator to the floor on the home stretch to Aunt June's.

She lied to me—that much was obvious at the time—but I hadn't suspected it was such a big lie. How could I guess that Adrian was with her—right there on the premises, probably in June's studio—and had been with her since shortly after her disappearance? Maybe I should have picked up on the fact that June didn't seem all that worried about her niece, but otherwise I'd had no clues. Not then.

Now I did, though. The Golden Gate Transit schedule in Adrian's backpack, for one. Golden Gate was the one bus line that ran from the city to Marin County, and she would only have needed it if she planned a trip north. There had been no one with a Marin address other than June Simoom on the list of people who were close to Adrian that the police had checked out. And then there was the graphic evidence on the therapy wall—the soaring bird so like the symbol of June's place, Wingspread, next to one broken gold chain and the word FREEDOM. But most of all it was Adrian's own words that had finally tipped me: "somebody to protect me, somebody strong and fierce." That was June's way of describing herself, and Adrian had probably heard it enough to believe it. After all, her aunt had taken the name of a fierce, relentless African wind; she had called her home Wingspread, a place of refuge.

But there was another side to June—the possessive, controlling side that Donna Conway had described. Frying pan to fire, that's where Adrian had gone. From one controlling person to another—and in this case, a control freak who probably delighted in keeping the niece from the hated sister-in-law. June hadn't called Donna after my visit to make peace; she'd probably been fishing to find out if I'd relayed any suspicions to her.

I slowed to a crawl, peering through the smears on the windshield and the rain-soaked blackness for the mailbox with the soaring bird. That stand of eucalyptus looked about right, and the deeper shadows beyond it must hide Tomales Bay. Hadn't the road curved like this just before the turnoff to the rutted driveway? Wasn't it right about here . . . ?

Yes! I wrenched the wheel to the left, and the Wreck skidded onto the gravel shoulder.

What I could see of the driveway looked impassable. Deep tire gouges cut into the ground, but they were filling with muck and water. Better not chance it. I turned off the engine—it coughed and heaved several times, not a good sign, Willie had recently told me—and then I got out and started for the cottage on foot.

The wind blew even stronger now, whipping the branches of the trees and sending big curls of brittle bark spiraling through the air. The rain pelted me, stinging as it hit my face, and the hood of my slicker blew off my head. I grabbed at it, but I couldn't make it stay up, and soon my hair was a sodden mess plastered to my skull.

Adrian, I thought, you'd better be worth all this.

I couldn't see any lights in the cottage, although there was a truck pulled in under the trees. That didn't mean anything—the other night June had relied on the fire for both heat and light, and there was no reason she would have turned on the porch lamp unless she was expecting company. But what kind of a life was this for Adrian, spending her entire evenings in darkness in that crumbling shack? And what about her days— how could she fill the long hours when she should have been in school or working or doing things with her friends? If her mother hadn't hired me and I hadn't figured out where she was, how long would she have hidden here until reality set in and she began to want to have a life again?

My slicker was an ancient one, left over from my college days, and its waterproofing must have given out, because I was soaked to my skin now. Freezing, too. Please have a fire going, June, because I'm already very annoyed with you, and the lack of a fire will make me truly pissed off—

Movement up ahead, the door of the cottage opening. A dark figure coming out, big and barrel-shaped, bigger than June and certainly bigger than Adrian . . . Ben Waterson.

He came down the steps, hesitated, then angled off toward the left, through the trees. Going where? To the studio or the other outbuilding?

I began creeping closer to the cottage, testing the ground ahead of me before I took each step. Foot-grabber of a hole there, ankle-turner of a tree root here. At least the wind is shrieking like a scalded cat so he can't possibly hear me.

The cottage loomed ahead. I tripped on the bottom step, went up the rest of them on my hands and knees, and pushed the door open. Keeping low, I slithered inside on a splintery plank floor. There was some light at the far end of the room, but not much; the fire was burning low, just embers mainly.

What's that smell?

A gun had been fired in there, and not too long ago. I opened my mouth, tried to call to June, but a croak came out instead. The room was quiet, the wind howling outside. I crept toward the glowing embers . . .

There June was, reclining on her pile of pillows, glass of wine beside her on the raised hearth. So like the other night, but something was wrong here, something to do with the way she was lying, as if she'd been thrown there, and why was the fireplace poker in her hand— Oh God June no!

I reeled around, smashing my fist into the wall beside me. My eyes were shut but I could still see her crumpled there on the gaudy silk pillows, velvet robes disarrayed, hand clutching the poker. Why was she still holding it? Something to do with going into spasm at the moment of death.

Disconnected sounds roared in my ears, blocking the wind. Then I heard my voice saying bitterly to Sharon, "Until the next time," meaning until the next death. And Sharon saying to me, "If there is one."

Well, Shar, this is the next time, and I wish you were here to tell me what to do because what I'm about to do is go to pieces and there's a killer somewhere outside and a helpless young woman who I promised to bring back to her mother—

Go to the phone, Rae, and call the sheriff.

It wasn't Sharon's voice, of course, but my own—a cool, professional voice that I'd never known I had. It interrupted the hysterical thoughts that were whirling and tumbling in my brain, calmed me and restored my balance. I dredged up memories of the other night, pictured an old-fashioned rotary-dial phone sitting on the kitchen counter. I felt my way until I touched it, and picked up the receiver. No dial tone.

Maybe the storm, maybe something Waterson had done. Whatever, there wasn't going to be any car full of Marin County Sheriff's deputies riding to my rescue.

You'll just have to save yourself—and Adrian.

With what? He's armed. I don't even have a flashlight.

Kitchen drawer. I felt along the edge of the warped linoleum counter, then down to a knob. Pulled on it. Nothing in there but cloth, dishtowels, maybe. Another knob, another drawer. Knives. I took one out, tested its sharpness. Another drawer, and there was a flashlight, plus some long, pointed barbecue skewers. I stuck them and the knife in the slash pocket of my slicker.

And then I went outside to face a man with a gun.

The wind was really whipping around now, and it tore the cottage's door from my grip and slammed it back against the wall. I yanked it closed, went down the slick, rickety steps, and made for the eucalyptus trees. As I ran I felt the flashlight fall from my slash pocket, but I didn't stop to find it. Silly to have taken it, anyway—if I turned it on, I'd be a target for Waterson.

Under the trees I stopped and leaned against a ragged trunk, panting and feeling in my pocket for the knife and the skewers. They were still there— not that they were much of a match against a gun. But there was no point in stewing over the odds now. I had to pinpoint those outbuildings. If I remembered correctly, they were closer to the shore and to the left of this grove.

I slipped through the trees, peering into the surrounding blackness. Now I could make out the shoreline, the water wind-tossed and frothy, and then I picked out the shapes of the buildings—two of them, the larger one probably the studio. Roofs as swaybacked as the cottage's, no lights in either. Windows? I couldn't tell. They sat across a clearing from me, a bad way to approach if there were windows and if Waterson was inside and looking out. A bad way if he was outside and looking in this direction.

How else to get over to them, then? Along the shore? Maybe. June had said something about a beach . . .

I went back through the trees, their branches swaying overhead, ran for the cottage again, then slipped along its side and ducked under the half-collapsed deck. The ground took a sudden slope, and I went down on my butt and slid toward the water. Waves sloshed over my tennis shoes—icy waves.

Dammit! I thought. What the hell am I doing out here risking pneumonia—to say nothing of my life—for a thieving teenager I've never even set eyes on?

I pulled myself up on one of the rotten deck supports—nearly pulling it down on my head—and started moving again. Then I stopped, realizing there was no beach here now, just jumbled and jagged rocks before the spot where the sand should begin. The beach was completely submerged by the high storm-tide.

Stupid, Rae. Very stupid. You should have realized it would be this way and not wasted precious time. You should have gotten back into the Wreck as soon as you found June's body and driven to the nearest phone, called the sheriff's department and let them handle it.

No time for recriminations now. Besides, the nearest phone was miles away, and even if I had driven there immediately, the deputies wouldn't have gotten here fast enough to save Adrian. I wasn't sure *I'd* gotten here fast enough to save her.

I crawled back up the incline and looked around, trying to measure the distance I'd have to run exposed to get to the shelter of the outbuildings. From here it was twenty, maybe twenty-five yards. Not that far—I'd go for it.

I hunched over, made myself as small as I could, and started running—

not much of a run, but still the longest, scariest of my life. I kept expecting the whine of a bullet—that's what you hear, Sharon's told me, before you hear the actual report, and she ought to know. You hear the whine, that is, if the bullet doesn't kill you first.

But all I heard was the howl of the wind and the banging of a door someplace and the roaring of my own blood in my ears. Then I was at the first outbuilding, crouching against its rough wood wall and panting hard.

The banging was louder here. When my breathing had calmed, I crept around the building's corner and looked. Door, half off its hinges, and no sound or light coming from inside. I crept a little closer. Empty shed, falling down, certainly not June's studio.

I moved along until I could see the larger building. The space between the two was narrow, dark. I ran again, to a windowless wall and flattened against it, putting my ear to the boards and trying to hear if anyone was inside.

A banging noise, then a crash—something breaking. Then an angry voice—male, Waterson's. "Where the hell is it?"

Sobbing now, and a young woman saying, "I *told* you I don't know what you're talking about. Where's Aunt June? I want—"

"Shut up!" It sounded like he hit her. She screamed, and my hand went into my pocket, grasping the knife.

More sobbing. Waterson said, "I want those pictures and the negatives, Adrian."

"*What* pictures? What negatives? I don't know anything about them!"

"Don't give me that. Kirby said you were holding them for him. Just tell me where they are and I'll let you go."

Sure he would. He'd shoot her just like he had June, and hope that this would go down as a couple of those random killings that happen a lot in remote rural areas where weirdos break into what look like empty houses for stuff to steal and sell for drug money.

"I wouldn't hold *anything* for Kirby!" Adrian said through her sobs. "I'm scared of him!"

"Then why did he come out here yesterday after he tried to hit me up for money? Coming to get his evidence to prove to me that I'd better pay up, that's why. And don't lie to me about it—I followed him."

"No! I didn't even see him! He figured out where I was and wanted to talk me into going back to the city. I hid from him, and Aunt June ran him off."

So this was where Kirby had gone when I'd lost him. I remembered the eucalyptus leaves in his hair, the sand on his shoes when I'd talked with him at his parents' house—probably picked up while he was skulking around outside here, looking for Adrian after June had told him he couldn't see her. Waterson had not only followed Kirby here, but later to the Naples Street house, where he'd killed him.

There was a silence inside the studio, then Adrian screamed and cried some more. He'd hit her again, I guessed. Then he said, "I'm not going to ask you again, Adrian. Where're the pictures?"

"There *aren't* any! Look, Kirby's always bullshitting. He had me fooled. I was going to go to you about what he was doing at the plaza, until I saw you at the house with him, making a deal with that fence."

That was what had made her run out of the Naples Street place so fast she'd left her backpack—made her run straight to Aunt June, the only person she'd told about the trouble she was in, the person who'd offered to take her side and shelter her. Well, June had tried. Now it was up to me.

I started moving around the building, duck-walking like my high-school phys ed teacher had made us do when we goofed off in gym. Inside, I heard Waterson say, "You never knew about a hidden camera at that place in the Outer Mission?"

"No."

"Kirby never asked you to take pictures of me doing deals with the fences?"

"Neither of us took any pictures. This story is just more of Kirby's bullshit."

Waterson laughed—an ugly sound. "Well," he said, "it was Kirby's last shovelful of bullshit. He's dead."

"What . . . ?" Adrian's question rose up into a shriek.

I stopped listening, concentrated on getting to the corner of the building. Then I peeked around it. On this side—the one facing the water—there was a window and a door. I duck-walked on, thanking God that I still had some muscles left in my thighs. At the window I poked my head up a little, but all I saw were shadows—a big barrel-shaped one that had to be Waterson, and some warped, twisted ones that were downright weird. The light shivered and flickered—probably from a candle or oil lamp.

The door was closed, but the wind was rattling it in its frame. It made me think of how the wind had torn the cottage door from my grasp. I stopped, pressed against the wall, and studied this door. From the placement of its hinges, I could tell it opened out. I scuttled around to the hinged side, paused, and listened. Adrian was screaming and sobbing again. Christ, what was he *doing* to her?

Well, the sound would hide what I was about to do.

I stood, pressed flat as could be against the wall, then reached across the door to its knob and gave it a quick twist. The door opened, then slammed shut again.

"What the hell?" Waterson said.

Heavy footsteps came toward the door. I tensed, knife out and ready.

Don't think about how it'll be when you use it, Rae. Just do it—two lives are at stake here, and one's your own.

The door opened. All I could see was a wide path of wavery light. Waterson said, "Fuckin' wind," and shut the door again. Well, hell.

I waited a few seconds until his footsteps went away, reached for the knob again, and really yanked on it this time. The wind caught the door, slammed it back, and it smashed into me, smacking my nose. I bit my lip to keep from yelling, felt tears spring to my eyes. I wiped them away with my left hand, gripped the knife till my right hand hurt.

The footsteps came back again, quicker now, and I grasped the knife with both hands—ready, not thinking about it, just ready to do it because I had to. When he stepped outside, I shoved the door as hard as I could with my whole body, slamming him against the frame. He shouted, staggered, reeled back inside.

I went after him, saw him stumbling among a bunch of weird, twisted shapes that were some sort of pottery sculptures—the things that had made the strange shadows I'd glimpsed through the window. Some were as tall as he was, others were shorter or stood on pedestals. He grabbed at one and brought it down as he tried to keep his balance and raise his gun.

The gun went off. The roar was deafening, but I hadn't heard any whine, so his shot must have gone wide of me. Waterson stumbled back into a pedestal, flailing. I lunged at him, knife out in front of me. We both went down together. I heard the gun drop on the floor as I slashed out with the knife.

Waterson had hold of my arm now, slammed it against the floor. Pain shot up to my shoulder, my fingers went all prickly, and I dropped the knife. He pushed me away and started scrambling for the gun. I got up on my knees, grabbed at the base of the nearest sculpture, pushed. It hit his back and knocked him flat.

Waterson howled. I saw the gun about a foot from his hand and kicked out, sending it sliding across the floor. Then I stood all the way up, grabbed a strange many-spouted vase from a pedestal. And slammed it down on his head.

Waterson grunted and lay still.

I slumped against the pedestal, but only for a moment before I went to pick up the gun. The room was very quiet all of a sudden, except for sobbing coming from one corner. Adrian was trussed up there, dangling like a marionette from one of the support beams, her feet barely touching the plank floor.

She had the beginnings of a black eye and tears sheened her face, and she was jerking at her ropes like she was having some kind of attack. I located the knife, made what I hoped were reassuring noises as I went over there, and cut her down. She stumbled toward a mattress that lay under the window and curled up fetuslike, pulling the heavy blanket around her. I went over to Waterson and used the longer pieces of the rope to truss *him* up.

Then I went back to Adrian. She was shivering violently, eyes unfocused, fingers gripping the edge of the blanket. I sat down on the mattress beside her, gently loosened her fingers, and cradled her like a baby.

"Sssh," I said. "It's over now, all over."

X

I was lolling around All Souls's living room on Friday night, waiting for Willie and planning how I'd relate my triumph in solving the Conway-Dalson case to him, when the call came from Inspector Adah Joslyn.

"I just got back from Marin County," she told me. "Waterson's finally confessed to the Simoom murder, but he denies killing Kirby Dalson."

"Well, of course he would. Dalson was obviously premeditated, while the poker in Simoom's hand could be taken to mean self-defense."

"He'll have to hire one hell of a lawyer to mount a defense like that, given what he did to the niece. But that's not my problem. What is is that he's got a verifiable alibi for the time of Dalson's death."

"What?"

"Uh-huh. Dalson didn't leave his parents' house until six-twenty that night. Six to seven, Waterson was in a meeting with several of the Ocean Park Plaza merchants, including Adrian Conway's former boss."

I remembered Sue Hanford saying Waterson had taken off the morning before Kirby was killed and hadn't come back until six. I hadn't thought to ask her how she knew that or if he'd stayed around afterward. Damn! Maybe I wasn't the hotshot I thought I was.

Adah asked, "You got any ideas on this?"

Unwilling to admit I didn't, I said, "Maybe. Let me get back to you." I hung up the phone on Ted's desk, then took the stairs two at a time and went to Sharon's office.

She wasn't there. Most of the time the woman practically lived in her office, but now when I needed her, she was gone. I went back downstairs and looked for her mailbox tag. Missing. There was one resting on the corner of the desk, like she might have been talking with Ted and absent-mindedly set it down there. I hurried along the hall to the kitchen, where five people hadn't yet given up on the Friday happy hour, but Sharon wasn't one of them. Our resident health freak, who was mixing up a batch of cranberry-juice-and-cider cocktails, said she'd gone home an hour ago.

I said, "If Willie shows up before I get back, will you ask him to wait for me?" and trotted out the door.

Sharon doesn't live far from All Souls—in Glen Park, a district that's been undergoing what they call gentrification. I suppose you could say her brown-shingled cottage—one of a few thousand built as temporary housing after the '06 quake, which have survived far better than most of the grand mansions of that era—has been gentrified, since she's remodeled it and added a room and a deck, but to me it's just nice and homey, not fancy at all. Besides, things are always going wrong with it—tonight it was the porch light, shorting out from rain that had dripped into it because the gutters were overflowing. I rang the bell, hoping it wouldn't also short out and electrocute me.

Sharon answered, wearing her long white terry robe and fur-lined slippers and looking like she was coming down with a cold—probably from the soaking she'd gotten Tuesday night, which meant I would be the next one in line to get sick, from the soaking I'd gotten last night. She looked concerned when she saw me on the steps.

Last night, after I'd dealt with the Marin authorities and driven home feeling rocky and ready to fly apart at the slightest sound or movement, she'd come over to the co-op—Ted had called her at home, I guess—and we'd sat quietly in my nest for a while. Neither of us had said much—there was nothing to say, and we didn't need to, anyway. This second horror in a week of unpleasantness had changed me somehow, maybe forced me to grow up. I wasn't looking to Sharon for wisdom or even comfort, just for understanding and fellowship. And fellows we were—members of a select group to which election was neither an honor nor a pleasure.

Tonight I could tell that she was afraid I was suffering delayed repercussions from the violent events of the week, so I said quickly, "I need to run some facts by you. Got a few minutes?"

She nodded, looking relieved, and waved me inside. We went to the sitting room off her kitchen, where she had a fire going, and she offered me some mulled wine. While she was getting it, her yellow cat, Ralph, jumped into my lap. Ralph is okay as cats go, but really, I'm more of a dog person. He knows that, too—it's why he always makes a beeline for me when I come over. The little sadist looked at me with knowing eyes, then curled into a ball on my lap. His calico sister, Alice, who was grooming herself in the middle of the floor, looked up, and damned if she didn't wink!

Sharon came back with the wine, wrapped herself in her afghan on the couch, and said, "So run it by me."

I did, concluding, "Adrian couldn't have killed Kirby. Her hysterics when Waterson told her he was dead were genuine."

"Mmmm." Sharon seemed to be evaluating that. Then she said, "Maybe one of the other kids Kirby was blackmailing?"

"I thought of that, too, but it doesn't wash. Adrian talked a little while we were driving to Point Reyes to call the sheriff. She said none of the kids knew about the house on Naples—Kirby insisted it be kept a secret."

"What about one of the fences he dealt with? Maybe he'd crossed one of them."

"I tend to doubt it. Fences don't operate that way."

"Well, you should know. Willie . . ."

"Yeah." I sipped my wine, feeling gloomy and frustrated.

Sharon asked, "Who else besides Adrian knew about that house?"

"Well, Waterson, but his alibi is firm. And Aunt June. Adrian called her from a pay phone at a store on the corner the day she walked in on Kirby and Waterson making a deal with a fence, and June drove over to the city and picked her up. Adrian had told June about the trouble she was in when she and Kirby went to Tomales for the autumnal equinox firing in late September, and June'd offered to take her in after she went to security about what was going on. I don't know how June thought Adrian could escape prosecution for her part in the scam, but then, she didn't strike me as a terribly realistic person."

"Caring, though," Sharon said. "Caring and controlling."

I nodded. "June, the fierce protectress. Who died with a fireplace poker in her hand. Waterson had a gun, and she still tried to go up against him."

"And Kirby had come out to her place. Had scared Adrian."

"Yes," I said.

Sharon got up, took our glasses, and went to the kitchen for refills. I stared moodily into the fire. When I'd taken this job, I'd assumed I'd be running skip traces and interviewing witnesses for lawsuits. Now I'd found two dead bodies, almost killed a man, almost gotten killed myself—all in the course of a few days. Add to that an ethical dilemma . . .

When Sharon came back I said, "If I suggest this to the police, and June really was innocent, I'll be smearing the memory of a basically good woman."

She was silent, framing her reply. "If June was innocent, the police won't find any evidence. If she was guilty, they may find a weapon with blood and hair samples that match Kirby's somewhere on the premises at Tomales, and be able to close the file."

"But what will that do to Adrian?"

"From what you tell me, she's a survivor. And you've got to think of Kirby's parents. You've got to think of justice."

Leave it to Sharon to bring up the J-word. She thinks about things like that all the time, but to me they're just abstractions.

"And you've got to think about the truth," she added.

Not fair—she knows how I feel about the truth. "All right," I finally said. "I'll call Adah back later."

"Good. By the way, how are Adrian and her mother doing?"

"Well, all of this has been tough on them. Will be tough for a while. But they'll make it. Adrian is a survivor, and Donna—maybe this will help her realize her 'potential to be.' "

We both smiled wryly. Sharon said, "Here's to our potential to be," and we toasted.

After a while I went into her home office and called Adah. Then I called All Souls and spoke with Willie, who was regaling the folks in the kitchen with stories about the days when he was on the wrong side of the law, and told him I'd be there soon.

"So," Sharon said as I was putting on my slicker. "How're *you* holding up?"

"I'm still rocky, but that'll pass."

"Nightmares?"

"Yeah. But tonight they won't bother me. I plan to scare them off by sleeping with my favorite gorilla."

Sharon grinned and toasted me again, but damned if she didn't look a little melancholy.

Maybe she *still* knew something that I didn't.

Forbidden Things

1894

All the years that I was growing up in a poor suburb of Los Angeles, my mother would tell me stories of the days I couldn't remember when we lived with my father on the wild north coast. She'd tell of a gray, misty land suddenly made brilliant by quicksilver flashes off the sea; of white sand beaches that would disappear in a storm, then emerge strewn with driftwood and treasures from foreign shores; of a deeply forested ridge of hills where, so the Pomo Indians claimed, spirits walked by night.

Our cabin nestled on that ridge, high above the little town of Camel Rock and the humpbacked offshore mass that inspired its name. The cabin, built to last by my handyman father, was of local redwood, its foundation sunk deep in bedrock. There was a woodstove and home-woven curtains. There were stained-glass windows and a sleeping loft; there was. . . .

Although I had no recollection of this place we'd left when I was two, it somehow seemed more real to me than our shabby pink bungalow with the cracked sidewalk out front and the packed-dirt yard out back. I'd lie in bed at night feeling the heat from the woodstove, watching the light as it filtered through the stained-glass panels, listening to the wind buffet our secure aerie. I was sure I could smell my mother's baking bread, hear the deep rumble of my father's voice. But no matter how hard I tried, I could not call up the image of my father's face, even though a stiff and formal portrait of him sat on our coffee table.

When I asked my mother why she and I had left a place of quicksilver days and night-walking spirits, she'd grow quiet. When I asked where my father was now, she'd turn away. As I grew older I realized there were shadows over our departure—shadows in which forbidden things stood, still and silent.

Is it any wonder that when my mother died—young, at forty-nine, but life hadn't been kind to her and heart trouble ran in the family—is it any wonder that I packed everything I cared about and went back to the place of my birth to confront those forbidden things?

I'd located Camel Rock on the map when I was nine, tracing the coast highway with my finger until it reached a jutting point of land north of Fort Bragg. Once this had been logging country—hardy men working the cross-cut saw and jackscrew in the forests, bull teams dragging their heavy loads to the coast, fresh-cut logs thundering down the chutes to schooners that lay at anchor in the coves below. But by the time I was born, lumbering was an endangered industry. Today, I knew, the voice of the chain saw was stilled and few logging trucks rumbled along the highway. Legislation to protect the environment, coupled with a severe construction slump, had all but killed the old economy. Instead, new enterprises had sprung up: wineries, mushroom, garlic, and herb farms, tourist shops, and bed-and-breakfasts. These were only marginally profitable, however; the north coast was financially strapped.

I decided to go anyway.

It was a good time for me to leave Southern California. Two failed attempts at college, a ruined love affair, a series of slipping-down jobs— all argued for radical change. I'd had no family except my mother; even my cat had died the previous October. As I gave notice at the coffee shop where I'd been waitressing, disposed of the contents of the bungalow, and turned the keys back to the landlord, I said no good-byes. Yet I left with hope of a welcome. Maybe there would be a place for me in Camel Rock.

Maybe someone would even remember my family and fill in the gaps in my early life.

I know now that I was really hoping for a reunion with my father.

Mist blanketed the coast the afternoon I drove my old Pinto over the bridge spanning the mouth of the Deer River and into Camel Rock. Beyond sandstone cliffs the sea lay, flat and seemingly motionless. The town—a strip of buildings on either side of the highway with dirt lanes straggling up toward the hills—looked deserted. A few drifting columns of wood smoke, some lighted signs in shop windows, a hunched and bundled figure walking along the shoulder—these were the only signs of life. I drove slowly, taking it all in: a supermarket, some bars, a little mall full of tourist shops. Post office, laundromat, defunct real estate agency, old sagging hotel that looked to be the only real lodging place. When I'd gone four blocks and passed the last gas station and the cable TV company, I ran out of town. I U-turned, went back to the hotel, and parked my car between two pickups out front.

For a moment I sat behind the wheel, feeling flat. The town didn't look like the magical place my mother had described; if anything, it was seedier than the suburb I'd left yesterday. I had to force myself to get out, and, when I did, I stood beside the Pinto, staring up at the hotel. Pale green with once white trim, all of it blasted and faded by the elements. An inscription above its front door gave the date it was built—1879, the height of last century's logging boom. Neon beer signs flashed in its lower windows; gulls perched along the peak of its roof, their droppings splashed over the steps and front porch. I watched as one soared in for a landing, crying shrilly, Sea breeze ruffled my short blond hair, and I smelled fish and brine.

The smell of the sea had always delighted me. Now it triggered a sense of connection to this place. I thought: *Home.*

The thought lent me the impetus to take out my overnight bag and carried me over the threshold of the hotel. Inside was a dim lobby that smelled of dust and cat. I peered through the gloom but saw no one. Loud voices came from a room to the left, underscored by the clink of glasses and the thump and clatter of dice rolling; I went over, looked in, and saw an old-fashioned tavern, peopled mainly by men in work clothes. The ship's clock that hung crooked behind the bar said 4:20. Happy hour got under way early in Camel Rock.

There was a public phone on the other side of the lobby. I crossed to it and opened the thin county directory, aware that my fingers were trembling. No listing for my father. No listing for anyone with my last name. More disappointed than I had any right to be, I replaced the book and turned away.

Just then a woman came out of a door under the steep staircase. She was perhaps in her early sixties, tall and gaunt, with tightly permed, gray curls and a face lined by weariness. When she saw me, her pale eyes registered surprise. "May I help you?"

I hesitated, the impulse to flee the shabby hotel and drive away from Camel Rock nearly irresistible. Then I thought: *Come on, give the place a chance.* "Do you have a room available?"

"We've got nothing but available rooms." She smiled wryly and got a card for me to fill out. Lacking any other, I put down my old address and formed the letters of my signature—Ashley Heikkinen—carefully. I'd always hated my last name; it seemed graceless and misshapen beside my first. Now I was glad it was unusual; maybe someone here in town would recognize it. The woman glanced disinterestedly at the card, however, then turned away and studied a rack of keys. "Front room or back room?"

"Which is more quiet?"

"Well, in front you've got the highway noise, but there's not much traffic at night. In the back you've got the boys"—she motioned at the door to the tavern—"scrapping in the parking lot at closing time."

Just what I wanted—a room above a bar frequented by quarrelsome drunks. "I guess I'll take the front."

The woman must have read my expression. "Oh, honey, don't you worry about them. They're not so bad, but there's nobody as contentious as an out-of-work logger who's had one over his limit."

I smiled and offered my Visa card. She shook her head and pointed to a cash only sign. I dug in my wallet and came up with the amount she named. It wasn't much, but I didn't have much to begin with. There had been a small life insurance policy on my mother, but most of it had gone toward burying her. If I was to stay in Camel Rock, I'd need a job.

"Are a lot of people around here out of work?" I asked as the woman wrote up a receipt.

"Loggers, mostly. The type who won't bite the bullet and learn another trade. But the rest of us aren't in much better shape."

"Have you heard of any openings for a waitress or a bartender?"

"For yourself?"

"Yes. If I can find a job, I may settle here."

Her hand paused over the receipt book. "Honey, why on earth would you want to do that?"

"I was born here. Maybe you knew my parents . . . Melinda and John Heikkinen?"

She shook her head and tore the receipt from the book. "My husband and me, we just moved down here last year from Del Norte County . . . things're even worse up there, believe me. We bought this hotel because it was cheap and we thought we could make a go of it."

"Have you?"

"Not really. We don't have the wherewithal to fix it up, so we can't compete with the new motels or bed-and-breakfasts. And we made the mistake of giving bar credit to the locals."

"That's too bad," I said. "There must be some jobs available, though. I'm a good waitress, a fair bartender. And I . . . like people," I added lamely.

She smiled, the lines around her eyes crinkling kindly. I guessed she'd presented meager credentials a time or two herself. "Well, I suppose you could try over at the mall. Barbie Cannon's been doing real good with her Beachcomber Shop, and the tourist season'll be here before we know it. Maybe she can use some help."

I thanked her and took the room key she offered, but, as I picked up my bag, I thought of something else. "Is there a newspaper in town?"

"As far as I know, there never has been. There's one of those little county shoppers, but it doesn't have ads for jobs, if that's what you're after."

"Actually I'm trying to locate . . . a family member. I thought if there was a newspaper, I could look through their back issues. What about longtime residents of the town? Is there anybody who's an amateur historian, for instance?"

"Matter of fact, there is. Gus Galick. Lives on his fishing trawler, the *Irma*, down at the harbor. Comes in here regular."

"How long has he lived here?"

"All his life."

Just the person I wanted to talk with.

The woman added: "Gus is away this week, took a charter party down the coast. I think he said he'd be back next Thursday."

Another disappointment. I swallowed it, told myself the delay would give me time to settle in and get to know the place of my birth. And I'd start by visiting the Beachcomber Shop.

The shop offered exactly the kind of merchandise its name implied: seashells, driftwood, inexpert carvings of gulls, grebes, and sea lions. Postcards and calendars and T-shirts and paperback guidebooks. Shell jewelry, paperweights, ceramic whales, and dolphins. Nautical toys and candles and wind chimes. All of which were totally predictable, but the woman who popped up from behind the counter was anything but.

She was very tall, well over six feet, and her black hair stood up in long, stiff spikes. A gold ring pierced her left nostril, and several others hung from either earlobe. She wore a black leather tunic with metal studs, over lacy black tights and calf-high boots. In L.A., I wouldn't have given her a second glance, but this was Camel Rock. Such people weren't supposed to happen here.

The woman watched my reaction, then threw back her head and laughed throatily. I felt a blush begin to creep over my face.

"Hey, don't worry about it," she told me. "You should see how I scare the little bastards who drag their parents in here, whining about how they absolutely *have* to have a blow-up Willie the Whale."

"Uh, isn't that bad for business?"

"Hell, no. Embarrasses the parents and they buy twice as much as they would've."

"Oh."

"So . . . what can I do for you?"

"I'm looking for Barbie Cannon."

"You found her." She flopped onto a stool next to the counter, stretching out her long legs.

"My name's Ashley Heikkinen." I watched her face for some sign of recognition. There wasn't any, but that didn't surprise me; Barbie Cannon was only a few years older than I—perhaps thirty—and too young to remember a family that had left so long ago. Besides, she didn't look as if she'd been born and raised here.

"I'm looking for a job," I went on, "and the woman at the hotel said you might need some help in the shop."

She glanced around at the merchandise that was heaped haphazardly on the shelves and spilled over onto the floor here and there. "Well, Penny's right . . . I probably do." Then she looked back at me. "You're not local."

"I just came up from L.A."

"Me, too, about a year ago. There're a fair number of us transplants, and the division between us and the locals is pretty clear-cut."

"How so?"

"A lot of the natives are down on their luck, resentful of the newcomers, especially ones like me, who're doing well. Oh, some of them're all right . . . they understand that the only way for the area to survive is to restructure the economy. But most of them are just sitting around the bars mumbling about how the spotted owl ruined their lives and hoping the timber industry'll make a comeback . . . and that ain't gonna happen. So why're *you* here?"

"I was born in Camel Rock. And I'm sick of Southern California."

"So you decided to get back to your roots."

"In a way."

"You alone?"

I nodded.

"Got a place to stay?"

"The hotel, for now."

"Well, it's not so bad, and Penny'll extend credit if you run short. As for a job. . . ." She paused, looking around again. "You know, I came up here thinking I'd work on my photography. The next Ansel Adams and all that." She grinned self-mockingly. "Trouble is, I got to be such a successful businesswoman that I don't even have time to load my camera. Tell you what . . . why don't we go over to the hotel tavern, tilt a few, talk it over?"

"Why not?" I said.

Mist hugged the tops of the sequoias and curled in tendrils around their trunks. The mossy ground under my feet was damp and slick. I hugged my hooded sweatshirt against the chill and moved cautiously up the incline from where I'd left the car on an overgrown logging road. My soles began to slip, and I crouched, catching at a stump for balance. The wet fronds of a fern brushed my cheek.

I'd been tramping through the hills for over two hours, searching every lane and dirt track for the burned-out cabin that Barbie Cannon had photographed shortly after her arrival in Camel Rock last year. Barbie had invited me to her place for dinner the night before, after we'd agreed on the terms of my new part-time job, and in the course of the evening she'd shown me her portfolio of photographs. One, a grimy black-and-white image of a ruin, so strongly affected me that I'd barely been able to sleep. This morning I'd dropped by the shop and gotten Barbie to draw me a map of where she'd found it, but her recollection was so vague that I might as well have had no map at all.

I pushed back to my feet and continued climbing. The top of the rise was covered by a dense stand of sumac and bay laurel; the spicy scent of the laurel leaves mixed with stronger odors of redwood and eucalyptus. The mixed bouquet triggered the same sense of connection that I'd felt as I stood in front of the hotel the previous afternoon. I breathed deeply, then elbowed through the dense branches.

From the other side of the thicket I looked down on a sloping meadow splashed with the brilliant yellow-orange of California poppies. More sequoias crowned the ridge on its far side, and through their branches I caught a glimpse of the flat, leaden sea. A stronger feeling of familiarity stole over me. I remembered my mother saying: "In the spring, the meadow was full of poppies, and you could see the ocean from our front steps . . ."

The mist was beginning to break up overhead. I watched a hawk circle against a patch of blue high above the meadow, then wheel and flap away toward the inland hills. He passed over my head, and I could feel the beating of his great wings. I turned, my gaze following his flight path . . .

And then I spotted the cabin, overgrown and wrapped in shadow, only yards away. Built into the downward slope of the hill, its moss-covered foundations were anchored in bedrock, as I'd been told. But the rest was only blackened and broken timbers, a collapsed shake roof on which vegetation had taken root, a rusted stove chimney about to topple, empty windows and doors.

I drew in my breath and held it for a long moment. Then I slowly moved forward.

Stone steps, four of them. I counted as I climbed. Yes, you could still see the Pacific from here, the meadow, too. And the opening was where the door had been. Beyond it, nothing but a concrete slab covered the debris. Plenty of evidence that picnickers had been here.

I stepped over the threshold.

One big empty room. Nothing left, not even the mammoth iron woodstove. Vines growing through the timbers, running across the floor. And at the far side, a collapsed heap of burned lumber—the sleeping loft?

Something crunched under my foot. I looked down, squatted, poked at it gingerly with my fingertip. Glass, green glass. It could have come from a picnicker's wine bottle. Or it could have come from a broken stained-glass window.

I stood, coldness upon my scalp and shoulder blades. Coldness that had nothing to do with the sea wind that bore the mist from the coast. I closed my eyes against the shadows and the ruin. Once again I could smell my mother's baking bread, hear my father's voice. Once again I thought: *Home.*

But when I opened my eyes, the warmth and light vanished. Now all I saw was the scene of a terrible tragedy.

"Barbie," I said, "what do you know about the Northcoast Lumber Company?"

She looked up from the box of wind chimes she was unpacking. "Used to be the big employer around here."

"Where do they have their offices? I couldn't find a listing in the county phone book."

"I hear they went bust in the eighties."

"Then why would they still own land up in the hills?"

"Don't know. Why?"

I hesitated. Yesterday, the day after I'd found the cabin, I'd driven down to the county offices at Fort Bragg and spent the entire afternoon poring over the land plats for this area. The place where the ruin stood appeared to belong to the lumber company. There was no reason I shouldn't confide in Barbie about my search, but something held me back. After a moment I said: "Oh, I saw some acreage that I might be interested in buying."

She raised her eyebrows; the extravagant white eye shadow and bright-red lipstick that she wore today made her look like an astonished clown. "On what I'm paying you for part-time work, you're buying land?"

"I've got some savings from my mom's life insurance." That much was true, but the small amount wouldn't buy even a square foot of land.

"Huh." She went back to her unpacking. "Well, I don't know for a fact that Northcoast did go bust. Penny told me that the owner's widow is still alive. Used to live on a big estate near here, but a long time ago she moved down the coast to that fancy retirement community at Timber Point. Maybe she could tell you about this acreage."

"What's her name, do you know?"

"No, but you could ask Penny. She and Crane bought the hotel from her."

"Madeline Carmichael," Penny said. "Lady in her late fifties. She and her husband used to own a lot of property around here."

"You know her, then."

"Nope, never met her. Our dealings were through a broker and her lawyer."

"She lives down at Timber Point?"

"Uhn-huh. The broker told us she's a recluse, never leaves her house, and has everything she needs delivered."

"Why, do you suppose?"

"Why not? She can afford it. Oh, the broker hinted that there's some tragedy in her past, but I don't put much stock in that. I'll tell you"— her tired eyes swept the dingy hotel lobby—"if I had a beautiful home and all that money, I'd never go out, either."

Madeline Carmichael's phone number and address were unlisted. When I drove down to Timber Point the next day, I found high grape-stake fences and a gatehouse; the guard told me that Mrs. Carmichael would see no one who wasn't on her visitor list. When I asked him to call her, he refused. "If she was expecting you," he said, "she'd have sent your name down."

Penny had given me the name of the broker who handled the sale of the hotel. He put me in touch with Mrs. Carmichael's lawyer in Fort Bragg. The attorney told me he'd check about the ownership of the land and get back to me. When he did, his reply was terse: The land was part of the original Carmichael estate; title was held by the nearly defunct lumber company; it was not for sale.

So why had my parents built their cabin on the Carmichael estate? Were my strong feelings of connection to the burned-out ruin in the hills false?

Maybe, I told myself, it was time to stop chasing memories and start building a life for myself here in Camel Rock. Maybe it was best to leave the past alone.

The following weekend brought the kind of quicksilver days my mother had told me about, and in turn they lured tourists in record numbers. We couldn't restock the Beachcomber Shop's shelves fast enough. On the next

Wednesday—Barbie's photography day—I was unpacking fresh merchandise and filling in where necessary while waiting for the woman Barbie bought her driftwood sculptures from to make a delivery. Business was slack in the late-afternoon hours. I moved slowly, my mind on what to wear to a dinner party being given that evening by some new acquaintances who ran an herb farm. When the bell over the door jangled, I started.

It was Mrs. Fleming, the driftwood lady. I recognized her by the big plastic wash basket of sculptures that she toted. A tiny white-haired woman, she seemed too frail for such a load. I moved to take it from her.

She resisted, surprisingly strong. Her eyes narrowed, and she asked: "Where's Barbie?"

"Wednesday's her day off."

"And who are you?"

"Ashley Heikkinen. I'm Barbie's part-time—"

"*What* did you say?"

"My name is Ashley Heikkinen. I just started here last week."

Mrs. Fleming set the basket on the counter and regarded me sternly, spots of red appearing on her cheeks. "Just what are you up to, young woman?"

"I don't understand."

"Why are you using that name?"

"Using . . . ? It's my name."

"It most certainly is not! This is a very cruel joke."

The woman had to be unbalanced. Patiently I said: "Look, my name really is Ashley Heikkinen. I was born in Camel Rock but moved away when I was two. I grew up outside Los Angeles, and when my mother died, I decided to come back here."

Mrs. Fleming shook her head, her lips compressed, eyes glittering with anger.

"I can prove who I am," I added, reaching under the counter for my purse. "Here's my identification."

"Of course, you have identification. Everyone knows how to obtain that under the circumstances."

"What circumstances?"

She turned and moved toward the door. "I can't imagine what you possibly hope to gain by this charade, young woman, but you can be sure I'll speak to Barbie about you."

"Please, wait!"

She pushed through the door, and the bell above it jangled harshly as it slammed shut. I hurried to the window and watched her cross the parking lot in a vigorous stride that belied her frail appearance. As she turned at the highway, I looked down and saw I had my wallet out, prepared to prove my identity.

Why, I wondered, *did I feel compelled to justify my existence to this obviously deranged stranger?*

The dinner party that evening was pleasant, and I returned to the hotel at a little after midnight with the fledgling sense of belonging that making friends in a strange place brings. The fog was in thick, drawn by hot inland temperatures. It put a gritty sheen on my face, and when I touched my tongue to my lips, I tasted the sea. I locked the Pinto and started across the rutted parking lot to the rear entrance. Heavy footsteps came up behind me.

Conditioned by many years in L.A., I already held my car key in my right hand, tip out, as a weapon. I glanced back and saw a stocky, bearded man bearing down on me. When I sidestepped and turned, he stopped, and his gaze moved to the key. He'd been drinking—beer, and plenty of it.

From the tavern, I thought. *Probably came out to the parking lot because the restroom's in use and he couldn't wait.* "After you," I said, opening the door for him.

He stepped inside the narrow, dim hallway. I let him get a ways ahead, then followed. The door stuck, and I turned to give it a tug. The man reversed, came up swiftly, and grasped my shoulder.

"Hey!" I said.

He spun me around and slammed me against the wall. "Lady, what the hell're you after?"

"Let go of me!" I pushed at him.

He pushed back, grabbed my other shoulder, and pinned me there. I stopped struggling, took a deep breath, told myself to remain calm.

"Not going to hurt you, lady," he said. "I just want to know what your game is."

Two lunatics in one day. "What do you mean . . . game?"

"My name is Ashley Heikkinen," he said in a falsetto, then dropped to his normal pitch. "Who're you trying to fool? And what's in it for you?"

"I don't—"

"Don't give me that! You might be able to stonewall an old lady like my mother—"

"Your mother?"

"Yeah, Janet Fleming. You expect her to believe you, for Christ's sake? What you did, you upset her plenty. She had to take one of the Valiums the doctor gave me for my bad back."

"I don't understand what your mother's problem is."

"Jesus, you're a cold bitch! Her own goddaughter, for Christ's sake, and you expect her to *believe* you?"

"Goddaughter?"

His face was close to mine now; hot beer breath touched my cheeks. "My ma's goddaughter was Ashley Heikkinen."

"That's impossible! I never had a godmother. I never met your mother until this afternoon."

The man shook his head. "I'll tell you what's impossible: Ashley Heikkinen appearing in Camel Rock after all these years. Ashley's dead. She died in a fire when she wasn't even two years old. My ma ought to know; she identified the body."

A chill washed over me from my scalp to my toes. The man stared, apparently recognizing my shock as genuine. After a moment I asked: "Where was the fire?"

He ignored the question, frowning. "Either you're a damned good actress or something weird's going on. Can't have two people born with that name. Not in Camel Rock."

"Where was the fire?"

He shook his head again, this time as if to clear it. His mouth twisted, and I feared he was going to be sick. Then he let go of me and stumbled through the door to the parking lot. I released my breath in a long sigh and slumped against the wall. A car started outside. When its tires had spun on the gravel and its engine revved on the highway, I pushed myself upright and went along the hall to the empty lobby. A single bulb burned in the fixture above the reception desk, as it did every night. The usual sounds of laughter and conversation came from the tavern.

Everything seemed normal. Nothing was. I ran upstairs to the shelter of my room.

After I'd double-locked the door, I turned on the overhead and crossed to the bureau and leaned across it toward the streaky mirror. My face was drawn and unusually pale.

Ashley Heikkinen dead?

Dead in a fire when she wasn't quite two years old?

I closed my eyes, picturing the blackened ruin in the hills above town. Then I opened them and stared at my frightened face. It was the face of a stranger.

"If Ashley Heikkinen is dead," I said, "then who am *I*?"

Mrs. Fleming wouldn't talk to me. When I got to her cottage on one of the packed-dirt side streets after nine the next morning, she refused to open the door, and threatened to run me off with her dead husband's shotgun. "And don't think I'm not a good markswoman," she added.

She must have gone straight to the phone, because Barbie was hanging up when I walked into the Beachcomber Shop a few minutes later. She frowned at me and said: "I just had the most insane call from Janet Fleming."

"About me?"

"How'd you guess? She was giving me all this stuff about you not being who you say you are and the 'real Ashley Heikkinen' dying in a fire when she was a baby. Must be going around the bend."

I sat down on the stool next to the counter. "Actually, there might be something to what she says." And then I told her all of it: my mother's stories, the forbidden things that went unsaid, the burned-out cabin in the hills, my encounters with Janet Fleming and her son. "I tried to talk with Missus Fleming this morning," I finished, "but she threatened me with a shotgun."

"And she's been known to use that gun, too. You must've really upset her."

"Yes. From something she said yesterday afternoon, I gather she thinks I got hold of the other Ashley's birth certificate and created a set of fake ID around it."

"You sound like you believe there *was* another Ashley."

"I saw that burned-out cabin. Besides, why would Missus Fleming make something like that up?"

"But you recognized the cabin, both from my photograph and when you went there. You said it felt like home."

"I recognized it from my mother's stories, that's true. Barbie, I've lived those stories for most of my life. You know how kids sometimes get the notion that they're so special they can't really belong to their parents, that they're a prince or princess who was given to a servant couple to raise?"

"Oh, sure, we all went through that stage. Only in my case, I was Mick Jagger's love child, and someday he was going to acknowledge me and give me all his money."

"Well, my mother's stories convinced me that I didn't really belong in a downscale tract in a crappy valley town. They made me special, some-body who came from a magical place. And I dreamed of it every night."

"So you're saying that you only recognized the cabin from the images your mother planted in your mind?"

"It's possible."

Barbie considered. "OK, I'll buy that. And here's a scenario that might fit: after the fire, your parents moved away. That would explain why your mom didn't want to talk about why they left Camel Rock. And they had another child . . . you. They gave you Ashley's name and her history. It wasn't right, but grief does crazy things to otherwise sane people."

It worked—but only in part. "That still doesn't explain what happened to my father and why my mother would never talk about him."

"Maybe she was the one who went crazy with grief, and after a while he couldn't take it anymore, so he left."

She made it sound so logical and uncomplicated. But I'd known the quality of my mother's silences; there was more to them than Barbie's scenario encompassed.

I bit my lip in frustration. "You know, Missus Fleming could shed a lot of light on this, but she refuses to deal with me."

"Then find somebody who will."

"Who?" I asked. And then I thought of Gus Galick, the man Penny had told me about who had lived in Camel Rock all his life. "Barbie, do you know Gus Galick?"

"Sure. He's one of the few old-timers around here that I've really connected with. Gus builds ships in bottles. I sold some on consignment for him last year. He used to be a rum-runner during Prohibition, has some great stories about bringing in cases of Canadian booze to the coves along the coast."

"He must be older than God."

"Older than God and sharp as a tack. I bet he could tell you what you need to know."

"Penny said he was away on some charter trip."

"Was, but he's back now. I saw the *Irma* in her slip at the harbor when I drove by this morning."

Camel Rock's harbor was a sheltered cove with a bait shack and a few slips for fishing boats. Of them, Gus Galick's *Irma* was by far the most shipshape, and her captain was equally trim, with a shock of silvery-gray hair and leathery tan skin. I didn't give him my name, just identified myself as a friend of Penny and Barbie. Galick seemed to take people at face value, though; he welcomed me on board, took me belowdecks, and poured me a cup of coffee in the cozy wood-paneled cabin. When we were seated on either side of the teak table, I asked my first question.

"Sure, I remember the fire on the old Carmichael estate," he said. "Summer of 'seventy-one. Both the father and the little girl died."

I gripped the coffee mug tighter. "The father died, too?"

"Yeah. Heikkinen, his name was Norwegian, maybe. I don't recall his first name, or the little girl's."

"John and Ashley."

"These people kin to you?"

"In a way. Mister Galick, what happened to Melinda, the mother?"

He thought. "Left town, I guess. I never did see her after the double funeral."

"Where are John and Ashley buried?"

"Graveyard of the Catholic church." He motioned toward the hills, where I'd seen its spire protruding through the trees. "Carmichaels paid for everything, of course. Guilt, I guess."

"Why guilt?"

"The fire started on their land. Was the father's fault . . . John Heikkinen's, I mean . . . but still, they'd sacked him, and that was why he was drinking so heavy. Fell asleep with the doors to the woodstove open, and before he could wake up, the place was a furnace."

The free-flowing information was beginning to overwhelm me. "Let me get this straight . . . John Heikkinen worked for the Carmichaels?"

"Was their caretaker. His wife looked after their house."

"Where was she when the fire started?"

"At the main house, washing up after the supper dishes. I heard she saw the flames, run down there, and tried to save her family. The Carmichaels held her back till the volunteer fire department could get there . . . they knew there wasn't any hope from the beginning."

I set the mug down, gripped the table's edge with icy fingers. Galick leaned forward, eyes concerned. "Something wrong, miss? Have I upset you?"

I shook my head. "It's just . . . a shock, hearing about it after all these years." After a pause, I asked: "Did the Heikkinens have any other children?"

"Only the little girl who died."

I took out a photograph of my mother and passed it over to him. It wasn't a good picture, just a snap of her on the steps of our stucco bungalow down south. "Is this Melinda Heikkinen?"

He took a pair of glasses from a case on the table, put them on, and looked closely at it. Then he shrugged and handed it back to me. "There's some resemblance, but . . . She looks like she's had a hard life."

"She did." I replaced the photo in my wallet. "Can you think of anyone who could tell me more about the Heikkinens?"

"Well, there's Janet Fleming. She was Missus Heikkinen's aunt and the little girl's godmother. The mother was so broken up that Janet had to identify the bodies, so I guess she'd know everything there is to know about the fire."

"Anyone else?"

"Well, of course there's Madeline Carmichael. But she's living down at Timber Point now, and she never sees anybody."

"Why not?"

"I've got my own ideas on that. It started after her husband died. Young man, only in his fifties. Heart attack." Galick grimaced. "Carmichael was one of these pillars of the community, never drank, smoked, or womanized. Keeled over at a church service in 'seventy-five. Me, I've lived a gaudy life, as they say. Even now I eat and drink all the wrong things, and I like a cigar after dinner. And I just go on and on. Tells you a lot about the randomness of it all."

I didn't want to think about that randomness; it was much too soon after losing my own mother to an untimely death for that. I asked: "About Missus Carmichael . . . It was her husband's death that turned her into a recluse?"

"No, miss." He shook his head firmly. "My idea is that his dying was just the last straw. The seeds were planted when their little girl disappeared three years before that."

"Disappeared?"

"It was in 'seventy-two, the year after the fire. The little girl was two years old, a change-of-life baby. Abigail, she was called. Abby, for short. Madeline Carmichael left her in her playpen on the verandah of their house, and she just plain vanished. At first they thought it was a kidnapping. The lumber company was failing, but the family still had plenty of money. But nobody ever made a ransom demand, and they never did find a trace of Abby or the person who took her."

The base of my spine began to tingle. As a child, I'd always been smaller than others of my age. Slower in school, too. The way a child might be if she was a year younger than the age shown on her birth certificate.

Abigail Carmichael, I thought. *Abby, for short.*

The Catholic churchyard sat tucked back against a eucalyptus grove; the trees' leaves caught the sunlight in a subtle shimmer, and their aromatic buds were thick under my feet. An iron fence surrounded the graves, and unpaved paths meandered among the mostly crumbling headstones. I meandered, too, shock gradually leaching away to depression. The foundations of my life were as tilted as the oldest grave marker, and I wasn't sure I had the strength to construct a new one.

But I'd come here with a purpose, so finally I got a grip on myself and began covering the cemetery in a grid pattern.

I found them in the last row, where the fence backed up against the eucalyptus. Two small headstones set side by side. John and Ashley. There was room to John's right for another grave, one that now would never be occupied.

I knelt and brushed a curl of bark from Ashley's stone. The carving was simple, only her name and the dates. She'd been born April 6, 1969, and died February 1, 1971.

I knelt there for a long time. Then I said good-bye and went home.

The old Carmichael house sat at the end of a chained-off drive that I'd earlier taken for a logging road. It was a wonder I hadn't stumbled across it in my search for the cabin. Built of dark timber and stone, with a wide verandah running the length of the lower story, it once might have been imposing. But now the windows were boarded, birds roosted in its eaves, and all around it the forest encroached. I followed a cracked flagstone path through a lawn long gone to weeds and wildflowers to the broad front steps. Stood at their foot, my hand on the cold wrought-iron railing.

Could a child of two retain memories? I'd believed so before, but mine had turned out to be false, spoon-fed to me by the woman who had taken me from this verandah twenty-four years earlier. All the same, something in this lonely place spoke to me; I felt a sense of peace and safety that I'd never before experienced.

I hadn't known real security; my mother's and my life together had been too uncertain, too difficult, too shadowed by the past. Those circumstances probably accounted for my long string of failures, my inability to make my way in the world. A life built on lies and forbidden things was bound to go nowhere.

And yet it hadn't had to be that way. All this could have been mine, had it not been for a woman unhinged by grief. I could have grown up in this once lovely home, surrounded by my real parents' love. Perhaps if I had, my father would not have died of an untimely heart attack, and my birth mother would not have become a recluse. A sickening wave of anger swept over me, followed by a deep sadness. Tears came to my eyes, and I wiped them away.

I couldn't afford to waste time crying. Too much time had been wasted already.

To prove my real identity, I needed the help of Madeline Carmichael's attorney, and he took a good deal of convincing. I had to provide documentation and witnesses to my years as Ashley Heikkinen before he would consent to check Abigail Carmichael's birth records. Most of the summer went by before he broached the subject to Mrs. Carmichael. But blood composition and the delicate whorls on feet and fingers don't lie; finally, on a bright September afternoon, I arrived at Timber Point—alone, at the invitation of my birth mother.

I was nervous and gripped the Pinto's wheel with damp hands as I followed the guard's directions across a rolling seaside meadow to the Carmichael house. Like the others in this exclusive development, it was of modern design, with a silvery wood exterior that blended with the sawgrass and Scotch broom. A glass wall faced the Pacific, reflecting sun glints on the water. Along the shoreline a flock of pelicans flew south in loose formation.

I'd worn my best dress—pink cotton, too light for the season, but it was all I had—and had spent a ridiculous amount of time on my hair and makeup. As I parked the shabby Pinto in the drive, I wished I could make it disappear. My approach to the door was awkward; I stumbled on the unlandscaped ground and almost turned my ankle. The uniformed maid who admitted me gave me the kind of glance that once, as a hostess at a coffee shop, I'd reserved for customers without shirt or shoes. She showed me to a living room facing the sea and went away.

I stood in the room's center on an Oriental carpet, unsure whether to sit or stand. Three framed photographs on a grand piano caught my attention; I went over and looked at them. A man and a woman, middle-aged and handsome. A child, perhaps a year old, in a striped romper. The child had my eyes.

"Yes, that's Abigail." The throaty voice—smoker's voice—came from behind me. I turned to face the woman in the photograph. Older now, but still handsome, with upswept creamy white hair and pale porcelain skin, she wore a long caftan in some sort of soft champagne-colored fabric. No reason for Madeline Carmichael to get dressed; she never left the house.

She came over to me and peered at my face. For a moment her eyes were soft and questioning, then they hardened and looked away. "Please," she said, "sit down over here."

I followed her to two matching brocade settees positioned at right angles to the seaward window. We sat, one on each, with a coffee table between us. Mrs. Carmichael took a cigarette from a silver box on the table and lit it with a matching lighter.

Exhaling and fanning the smoke away, she said: "I have a number of things to say to you that will explain my position in this matter. First, I believe the evidence you've presented. You are my daughter Abigail. Melinda Heikkinen was very bitter toward my husband and me. If we hadn't dismissed her husband, he wouldn't have been passed out from drinking when the fire started. If we hadn't kept her late at her duties that night, she would have been home and able to prevent it. If we hadn't stopped her from plunging into the conflagration, she might have saved her child. That, I suppose, served to justify her taking our child as a replacement."

She paused to smoke. I waited.

"The logic of what happened seems apparent at this remove," Mrs. Carmichael added, "but at the time we didn't think to mention Melinda as a potential suspect. She'd left Camel Rock the year before; even her aunt, Janet Fleming, had heard nothing from her. My husband and I had more or less put her out of our minds. And, of course, neither of us was thinking logically at the time."

I was beginning to feel uneasy. She was speaking so analytically and dispassionately—not at all like a mother who had been reunited with her long lost child.

She went on: "I must tell you about our family. California pioneers on both sides. The Carmichaels were lumber barons. My family were merchant princes engaging in the China trade. Abigail was the last of both lines, born to carry on our tradition. Surely you can understand why this matter is so . . . difficult."

She was speaking of Abigail as someone separate from me.

"What matter?" I asked.

"That rôle in life, the one Abigail was born to, takes a certain type of individual. My Abby, the child I would have raised had it not been for Melinda Heikkinen, would not have turned out so" She bit her lower lip, looked away at the sea.

"So what, Missus Carmichael?"

She shook her head, crushing out her cigarette.

A wave of humiliation swept over me. I glanced down at my cheap pink dress, at a chip in the polish on my thumbnail. When I raised my eyes, my birth mother was examining me with faint distaste.

I'd always had a temper; now it rose, and I gave in to it. "So what, Missus Carmichael?" I repeated. "So *common*?"

She winced but didn't reply.

I said: "I suppose you think it's your right to judge a person on her appearance or her financial situation. But you should remember that my life hasn't been easy . . . not like yours. Melinda Heikkinen could never make ends meet. We lived in a valley town east of L.A. She was sick a lot. I had to work from the time I was fourteen. There was trouble with gangs in our neighborhood."

Then I paused, hearing myself. No, I would not do this. I would not whine or beg.

"I wasn't brought up to complain," I continued, "and I'm not complaining now. In spite of working, I graduated high school with honors. I got a small scholarship, and Melinda persuaded me to go to college. She helped out financially when she could. I didn't finish, but that was my own fault. Whatever mistakes I've made are my own doing, not Melinda's. Maybe she told me lies about our life here on the coast, but they gave me something to hang on to. A lot of the time they were all I had, and now they've been taken from me. But I'm still not complaining."

Madeline Carmichael's dispassionate façade cracked. She closed her eyes, compressed her lips. After a moment she said: "How can you defend that woman?"

"For twenty-four years she was the only mother I knew."

Her eyes remained closed. She said: "Please, I will pay you any amount of money if you will go away and pretend this meeting never took place."

For a moment I couldn't speak. Then I exclaimed: "I don't want your money! This is not about money!"

"What, then?"

"What do I want? I thought I wanted my real mother."

"And now that you've met me, you're not sure you do." She opened her eyes, looked directly into mine. "Our feelings aren't really all that different, are they, Abigail?"

I shook my head in confusion.

Madeline Carmichael took a deep breath. "Abigail, you say you lived on Melinda's lies, that they were something to sustain you?"

I nodded.

"I've lived on lies, too, and they sustained *me*. For twenty-three years I've put myself to sleep with dreams of our meeting. I woke to them. No matter what I was doing, they were only a fingertip's reach away. And now they've been taken from me, as yours have. My Abby, the daughter I pictured in those dreams, will never walk into this room and make everything all right. Just as the things you've dreamed of are never going to happen."

I looked around the room—at the grand piano, the Oriental carpets, the antiques, and exquisite art objects. Noticed for the first time how stylized and sterile it was, how the cold expanse of glass beside me made the sea blinding and bleak.

"You're right," I said, standing up. "Even if you were to take me in and offer me all this, it wouldn't be the life I wanted."

Mrs. Carmichael extended a staying hand toward me.

I stepped back. "No. And don't worry . . . I won't bother you again."

As I went out into the quicksilver afternoon and shut the door behind me, I thought that even though Melinda Heikkinen had given me a different life, she'd also offered me dreams to soften the hard times and love to ease my passage. My birth mother hadn't even offered me coffee or tea.

On a cold, rainy December evening, Barbie Cannon and I sat at a table near the fireplace in the hotel's tavern, drinking red wine in celebration of my good fortune.

"I can't believe," she said for what must have been the dozenth time, "that old lady Carmichael up and gave you her house in the hills."

"Any more than you can believe I accepted it."

"Well, I thought you were too proud to take her money."

"Too proud to be bought off, but she offered the house with no strings attached. Besides, it's in such bad shape that I'll probably be fixing it up for the rest of my life."

"And she probably took a big tax write-off on it. No wonder rich people stay rich." Barbie snorted. "By the way, how come you're still calling yourself Ashley Heikkinen?"

I shrugged. "Why not? It's been my name for as long as I can remember. It's a good name."

"You're acting awfully laid back about this whole thing."

"You didn't see me when I got back from Timber Point. But I've worked it all through. In a way, I understand how Missus Carmichael feels. The house is nice, but anything else she could have given me isn't what I was looking for."

"So what *were* you looking for?"

I stared into the fire. Madeline Carmichael's porcelain face flashed against the background of the flames. Instead of anger I felt a tug of pity for her: a lonely woman waiting her life out, but really as dead and gone as the merchant princes, the lumber barons, the old days on this wild north coast. Then I banished the image and pictured, instead, the faces of the friends I'd made since coming to Camel Rock: Barbie, Penny and Crane, the couple who ran the herb farm, Gus Galick, and . . . now . . . Janet Fleming and her son, Stu. Remembered all the good times: dinners and walks on the beach, Penny and Crane's fortieth wedding anniversary party, Barbie's first photographic exhibit, a fishing trip on Gus's trawler. And thought of all the good times to come.

"What was I looking for?" I said. "Something I found the day I got here."

The Lost Coast

1995

California's Lost Coast is at the same time one of the most desolate and beautiful of shorelines. Northerly winds whip the sand into a dust-devil frenzy; eerie, stationary fogs hang in the trees and distort the driftwood until it resembles the bones of prehistoric mammals; bruised clouds hover above the peaks of the distant King Range, then blow down to sea level and dump icy torrents. But on a fair day the sea and sky show infinite shadings of blue, and the wildflowers are a riot of color. If you wait quietly, you can spot deer, peregrine falcons, foxes, otters, even black bears and mountain lions.

A contradictory and oddly compelling place, this seventy-three-mile stretch of coast southwest of Eureka, where—as with most worthwhile things or people—you must take the bad with the good.

Unfortunately, on my first visit there I was taking mostly the bad. Strong wind pushed my MG all over the steep, narrow road, making its hairpin turns even more perilous. Early October rain cut my visibility to a few yards. After I crossed the swollen Bear River, the road continued to twist and wind, and I began to understand why the natives had dubbed it The Wildcat.

Somewhere ahead, my client had told me, was the hamlet of Petrolia—site of the first oil well drilled in California, he'd irrelevantly added. The man was a conservative politician, a former lumber company attorney, and given what I knew of his voting record on the environment, I was certain we disagreed on the desirability of that event, as well as any number of similar issues. But the urgency of the current situation dictated that I keep my opinions to myself, so I'd simply written down the directions he gave me—omitting his traveloguelike asides—and gotten under way.

I drove through Petrolia—a handful of new buildings, since the village had been all but leveled in the disastrous earthquake of 1992—and turned toward the sea on an unpaved road. After two miles I began looking for the orange post that marked the dirt track to the client's cabin.

The whole time, I was wishing I was back in San Francisco. This wasn't my kind of case. I didn't like the client, Steve Shoemaker, and even though the fee was good, this was the week I'd scheduled to take off a few personal business days from All Souls Legal Cooperative, where I'm chief investigator. But Jack Stuart, our criminal specialist, had asked me to take on the job as a favor to him. Steve Shoemaker was Jack's old friend from college in Southern California, and he'd asked for a referral to a private detective. Jack owed Steve a favor; I owed Jack several, so there was no way I could gracefully refuse.

But I couldn't shake the feeling that something was wrong with this case. And I couldn't stop wishing that I'd come to the Lost Coast in summertime, with a backpack and in the company of my lover—instead of on a rainy fall afternoon, with a .38 Special, and soon to be in the company of Shoemaker's disagreeable wife, Andrea.

The rain was sheeting down by the time I spotted the orange post. It had turned the hard-packed earth to mud, and my MG's tires sank deep in the ruts, its undercarriage scraping dangerously. I could barely make out the stand of live oaks and sycamores where the track ended; no way to tell if another vehicle had traveled over it recently.

When I reached the end of the track, I saw one of those boxy four-wheel-drive wagons—Bronco? Cherokee?—drawn in under the drooping branches of an oak. Andrea Shoemaker's? I'd neglected to get a description from her husband of what she drove. I got out of the MG, turning the hood of my heavy sweater up against the downpour; the wind promptly blew it off. So much for what the catalog had described as "extra protection on those cold nights." I yanked the hood up again and held it there, went around and took my .38 from the trunk and shoved it into the outside flap of my purse. Then I went over and tried the door of the four-wheel drive. Unlocked. I opened it, slipped into the driver's seat.

Nothing identifying its owner was on the seats or in the side pockets, but in the glove compartment I found a registration in the name of Andrea Shoemaker. I rummaged around, came up with nothing else of interest. Then I got out and walked through the trees, looking for the cabin.

Shoemaker had told me to follow a deer track through the grove. No sign of it in this downpour, no deer, either. Nothing but wind-lashed trees, the oaks pelting me with acorns. I moved slowly through them, swiveling my head from side to side, until I made out a bulky shape tucked beneath the farthest of the sycamores.

As I got closer, I saw the cabin was of plain weathered wood, rudely constructed, with the chimney of a woodstove extending from its composition shingle roof. Small—two or three rooms—and no light showing in its windows. And the door was open, banging against the inside wall.

I quickened my pace, taking the gun from my purse. Alongside the door I stopped to listen. Silence. I had a flashlight in my bag; I took it out. Moved to where I could see inside, then turned the flash on and shone it through the door.

All that was visible was rough board walls, an oilcloth-covered table and chairs, an ancient woodstove. I stepped inside, swinging the light around. Unlit oil lamp on the table; flower-cushioned wooden furniture of the sort you always find in vacation cabins; rag rugs; shelves holding an assortment of tattered paperbacks, seashells, and driftwood. I shifted the light again, more slowly.

A chair on the far side of the table was tipped over, and a woman's purse lay on the edge of the woodstove, its contents spilling out. When I got over there, I saw a .32 Iver Johnson revolver lying on the floor.

Andrea Shoemaker owned a .32. She'd told me so the day before.

Two doors opened off the room. Quietly I went to one and tried it. A closet, shelves stocked with staples and canned goods and bottled water. I looked around the room again, listening. No sound but the wail of wind and the pelt of rain on the roof. I stepped to the other door.

A bedroom almost filled wall-to-wall by a king-size bed covered with a goose-down comforter and piled with colorful pillows. Old bureau pushed in one corner, another unlit oil lamp on the single nightstand. Small travel bag on the bed.

The bag hadn't been opened. I examined its contents. Jeans, a couple of sweaters, underthings, toilet articles. Package of condoms. Uhn-huh. She'd come here, as I'd found out, to meet a man. The affairs usually began with a casual pick-up; they were never of long duration; and they all seemed to culminate in a romantic week-end in the isolated cabin.

Dangerous game, particularly in these days when AIDS and the prevalence of disturbed individuals of both sexes threatened. But Andrea Shoemaker had kept her latest date with an even larger threat hanging over her: for the past six weeks, a man with a serious grudge against her husband had been stalking her. For all I knew, he and the date were one and the same.

And where was Andrea now?

This case had started on Wednesday, two days ago, when I'd driven up to Eureka, a lumbering and fishing town on Humboldt Bay. After I passed the Humboldt County line, I began to see huge logging trucks toiling through the mountain passes, shredded curls of redwood bark trailing in their wakes. Twenty-five miles south of the city itself was the company-owned town of Scotia, mill stacks belching white smoke and filling the air with the scent of freshly cut wood. Yards full of logs waiting to be fed to the mills lined the highway. When I reached Eureka itself, the downtown struck me as curiously quiet; many of the stores were out of business, and the sidewalks were mostly deserted. The recession had hit the lumber industry hard, and the earthquake hadn't helped the area's strapped economy.

I'd arranged to meet Steve Shoemaker at his law offices in Old Town, near the waterfront. It was a picturesque area full of renovated warehouses and interesting shops and restaurants, tricked out for tourists with the inevitable horse-and-carriage rides and T-shirt shops, but still pleasant. Shoemaker's offices were off a cobblestoned courtyard containing a couple of antique shops and a decorator's showroom.

When I gave my card to the secretary, she said Assemblyman Shoemaker was in conference and asked me to wait. The man, I knew, had lost his seat in the state legislature this past election, so the term of address seemed inappropriate. The appointments of the waiting room struck me as a bit much—brass and mahogany and marble and velvet, plenty of it, the furnishings all antiques that tended to the garish. I sat on a red velvet sofa and looked for something to read. *Architectural Digest, National Review, Foreign Affairs*—that was it, take it or leave it. I left it. My idea of waiting-room reading is *People;* I love it, but I'm too embarrassed to subscribe.

The minutes ticked by: ten, fifteen, twenty. I contemplated the issue of *Architectural Digest,* then opted instead for staring at a fake Rembrandt on the far wall. Twenty-five, thirty. I was getting irritated now. Shoemaker had asked me to be here by three; I'd arrived on the dot. If this was, as he'd claimed, a matter of such urgency and delicacy that he couldn't go into it on the phone, why was he in conference at the appointed time?

Thirty-five minutes. Thirty-seven. The door to the inner sanctum opened and a woman strode out. A tall woman, with long chestnut hair, wearing a raincoat and black leather boots. Her eyes rested on me in passing—a cool gray, hard with anger. Then she went out, slamming the door behind her.

The secretary—a trim blonde in a tailored suit—started as the door slammed. She glanced at me and tried to cover with a smile, but its edges were strained, and her fingertips pressed hard against the desk. The phone at her elbow buzzed; she snatched up the receiver. Spoke into it, then said to me: "Miz McCone, Assemblyman Shoemaker will see you now." As she ushered me inside, she again gave me her frayed-edge smile.

Tense situation in this office, I thought. Brought on by what? The matter Steve Shoemaker wanted me to investigate? The client who had just made her angry exit? Or something else entirely . . . ?

Shoemaker's office was even more pretentious than the waiting room:

more brass, mahogany, velvet, and marble; more fake Old Masters in heavy gilt frames; more antiques; more of everything. Shoemaker's demeanor was not as nervous as his secretary's, but, when he rose to greet me, I noticed a jerkiness in his movements, as if he were holding himself under tight control. I clasped his outstretched hand and smiled, hoping the familiar social rituals would set him more at ease.

Momentarily they did. He thanked me for coming, apologized for making me wait, and inquired after Jack Stuart. After I was seated in one of the client's chairs, he offered me a drink; I asked for mineral water. As he went to a wet bar tucked behind a tapestry screen, I took the opportunity to study him.

Shoemaker was handsome: dark hair, with the gray so artfully interwoven that it must have been professionally dyed. Chiseled features, nice, well-muscled body, shown off to perfection by an expensive blue suit. When he handed me my drink, his smile revealed white, even teeth that I—having spent the greater part of the previous month in the company of my dentist—recognized as capped. Yes, a very good-looking man, politician handsome. Jack's old friend or not, his appearance and manner called up my gut-level distrust.

My client went around his desk and reclaimed his chair. He held a drink of his own—something dark amber—and he took a deep swallow before speaking. The alcohol replenished his vitality some; he drank again, set the glass on a pewter coaster, and said: "Miz McCone, I'm glad you could come up here on such short notice."

"You mentioned on the phone that the case is extremely urgent . . . and delicate."

He ran his hand over his hair—lightly, so as not to disturb its styling. "Extremely urgent and delicate," he repeated, seeming to savor the phrase.

"Why don't you tell me about it?"

His eyes strayed to the half-full glass on the coaster. Then they moved to the door through which I'd entered. Returned to me. "You saw the woman who just left?" I nodded.

"My wife, Andrea."

I waited.

"She's very angry with me for hiring you."

"She did act angry. Why?"

Now he reached for the glass and belted down its contents. Leaned back and rattled the ice cubes as he spoke. "It's a long story. Painful to me. I'm not sure where to begin. I just . . . don't know what to make of the things that are happening."

"That's what you've hired me to do. Begin anywhere. We'll fill in the gaps later." I pulled a small tape recorder from my bag and set it on the edge of his desk. "Do you mind?"

Shoemaker eyed it warily, but shook his head. After a moment's hesitation, he said: "Someone is stalking my wife."

"Following her? Threatening her?"

"Not following, not that I know of. He writes notes, threatening to kill her. He leaves . . . things at the house. At her place of business. Dead things. Birds, rats, one time a cat. Andrea loves cats. She. . . ." He shook his head, went to the bar for a refill.

"What else? Phone calls?"

"No. One time, a floral arrangement . . . suitable for a funeral."

"Does he sign the notes?"

"John. Just John."

"Does Missus Shoemaker know anyone named John who has a grudge against her?"

"She says no. And I . . ." He sat down, fresh drink in hand. "I have reason to believe that this John has a grudge against me, is using this harassment of Andrea to get at me personally."

"Why do you think that?"

"The wording of the notes."

"May I see them?"

He looked around, as if he were afraid someone might be listening. "Later. I keep them elsewhere."

Something, then, I thought, that he didn't want his office staff to see. Something shameful, perhaps even criminal. "Okay," I said, "how long has this been going on?"

"About six weeks."

"Have you contacted the police?"

"Informally. A man I know on the force, Sergeant Bob Wolfe. But after he started looking into it, I had to ask him to drop it."

"Why?"

"I'm in a sensitive political position."

"Excuse me if I'm mistaken, Mister Shoemaker, but it's my understanding that you're no longer serving in the state legislature."

"That's correct, but I'm about to announce my candidacy in a special election for a senate seat that's recently been vacated."

"I see. So after you asked your contact on the police force to back off, you decided to use a private investigator, and Jack recommended me. Why not use someone local?"

"As I said, my position is sensitive. I don't want word of this getting out in the community. That's why Andrea is so angry with me. She claims I value my political career more than her life."

I waited, wondering how he'd attempt to explain that away.

He didn't even try, merely went on. "In our . . . conversation just prior to this, she threatened to leave me. This coming weekend she plans to go to a cabin on the Lost Coast that she inherited from her father to . . . as she put it . . . sort things through. Alone. Do you know that part of the coast?"

"I've read some travel pieces on it."

"Then you're aware how remote it is. The cabin's very isolated. I don't want Andrea going there while this John person is on the loose."

"Does she go there often?"

"Fairly often. I don't . . . it's too rustic for me . . . no running water, phone, or electricity. But Andrea likes it. Why do you ask?"

"I'm wondering if John . . . whoever he is . . . knows about the cabin. Has she been there since the harassment began?"

"No. Initially she agreed that it wouldn't be a good idea. But now. . . ." He shrugged.

"I'll need to speak with Missus Shoemaker. Maybe I can reason with her, persuade her not to go until we've identified John. Or maybe she'll allow me to go along as her bodyguard."

"You can speak with her if you like, but she's beyond reasoning with. And there's no way you can stop her or force her to allow you to accompany her. My wife is a strong-willed woman . . . that interior decorating firm across the courtyard is hers, she built it from the ground up. When Andrea decides to do something, she does it. And asks permission from no one."

"Still, I'd like to try reasoning. This trip to the cabin . . . that's the urgency you mentioned on the phone. Two days to find the man behind the harassment before she goes out there and perhaps makes a target of herself."

"Yes."

"Then I'd better get started. That funeral arrangement . . . what florist did it come from?"

Shoemaker shook his head. "It arrived at least five weeks ago, before either of us noticed a pattern to the harassment. Andrea just shrugged it off, threw the wrappings and card away."

"Let's go and look at the notes, then. They're my only lead."

Vengeance will be mine. The sudden blow. The quick attack.

Vengeance is the price of silence.

Mute testimony paves the way to an early grave. The rest is silence.

A freshly turned grave is silent testimony to an old wrong and its avenger.

There was more in the same vein—slightly Biblical-flavored and stilted. But chilling to me, even though the safe deposit booth at Shoemaker's bank was overly warm. If that was my reaction, what had these notes done to Andrea Shoemaker? No wonder she was thinking of leaving a husband who cared more for the electorate's opinion than his wife's life and safety.

The notes had been typed without error on an electric machine that had left no such obvious clues as chipped or skewed keys. The paper and envelopes were plain and cheap, purchasable at any discount store. They had been handled, I was sure, by nothing more than gloved hands. No signature—just the typed name *John*.

But the writer had wanted the Shoemakers—one of them, anyway—to know who he was. Thus the theme that ran through them all: silence and revenge.

I said: "I take it your contact at the E.P.D. had their lab go over these?"

"Yes. There was nothing. That's why he wanted to probe further . . . something I couldn't permit him to do."

"Because of this revenge-and-silence business. Tell me about it."

Shoemaker looked around furtively. My God, did he think bank employees had nothing better to do with their time than to eavesdrop on our conversation?

"We'll go have a drink," he said. "I know a place that's private."

We went to a restaurant a few blocks away, where Shoemaker had another bourbon and I toyed with a glass of iced tea. After some prodding, he told me his story; it didn't enhance him in my eyes.

Seventeen years ago Shoemaker had been interviewing for a staff attorney's position at a large lumber company. While on a tour of the mills, he witnessed an accident in which a worker named Sam Carding was severely mangled while trying to clear a jam in a bark-stripping machine. Shoemaker, who had worked in the mills summers to pay for his education, knew the accident was due to company negligence but accepted a handsome job offer in exchange for not testifying for the plaintiff in the ensuing lawsuit. The court ruled against Carding, confined to a wheelchair and in constant pain; a year later, while the case was still under appeal, Carding shot his wife and himself. The couple's three children were given token settlements in exchange for dropping the suit, and then were adopted by relatives in a different part of the country.

"It's not a pretty story, Mister Shoemaker," I said, "and I can see why the wording of the notes might make you suspect there's a connection between it and this harassment. But who do you think John is?"

"Carding's eldest boy. Carding and his family knew I'd witnessed the accident . . . one of his coworkers saw me watching from the catwalk and told him. Later, when I turned up as a senior counsel . . ." He shrugged.

"But why, after all this time . . . ?"

"Why not? People nurse grudges. John Carding was sixteen at the time of the lawsuit. There were some ugly scenes with him, both at my home and my office at the mill. By now he'd be in his forties. Maybe it's his way of acting out some sort of mid-life crisis."

"Well, I'll call my office and have my assistant run a check on all three Carding kids. And I want to speak with Missus Shoemaker . . . preferably in your presence."

He glanced at his watch. "It can't be tonight. She's got a meeting of her professional organization, and I'm dining with my campaign manager."

A potentially psychotic man was threatening Andrea's life, yet they both carried on as usual. Well, who was I to question it? Maybe it was their way of coping.

"Tomorrow, then," I said. "Your home. At the noon hour."

Shoemaker nodded. Then he gave me the address, as well as the names of John Carding's siblings.

I left him on the sidewalk in front of the restaurant—a handsome man whose shoulders now slumped inside his expensive suit coat, shivering in the brisk wind off Humboldt Bay. As we shook hands, I saw that shame made his gaze unsteady, the set of his mouth less than firm.

I knew that kind of shame. Over the course of my career, I'd committed some dreadful acts that years later woke me in the deep of the night to sudden panic. I'd also *not* committed certain acts—failures that woke me to regret and emptiness. My sins of omission were infinitely worse than those of commission, because I knew that if I'd acted, I could have made a difference. Could even have saved a life.

I wasn't able to reach Rae Kelleher, my assistant at All Souls, that evening, and by the time she got back to me the next morning—Thursday—I was definitely annoyed. Still, I tried to keep a lid on my irritation. Rae is young, attractive, and in love. I couldn't expect her to spend her evenings waiting to be of service to her workaholic boss.

I got her started on a computer check on all three Cardings, then took myself to the Eureka P.D. and spoke with Shoemaker's contact, Sergeant Bob Wolfe. Wolfe—a dark-haired, sharp-featured man whose appearance was a good match for his surname—told me he'd had the notes processed by the lab, which had turned up no useful evidence.

"Then I started to probe, you know? When you got a harassment case like this, you look into the victims' private lives."

"And that was when Shoemaker told you to back off?"

"Uhn-huh."

"When was this?"

"About five weeks ago."

"I wonder why he waited so long to hire me. Did he, by any chance, ask you for a referral to a local investigator?"

Wolfe frowned. "Not this time."

"Then you'd referred him to someone before?"

"Yeah, guy who used to be on the force . . . Dave Morrison. Last April."

"Did Shoemaker tell you why he needed an investigator?"

"No, and I didn't ask. These politicians, they're always trying to get something on their rivals. I didn't want any part of it."

"Do you have Morrison's address and phone number handy?"

Wolfe reached into his desk drawer, shuffled things, and flipped a business card across the blotter. "Dave gave me a stack of these when he set up shop," he said. "Always glad to help an old pal."

Morrison was out of town, the message on his answering machine said, but would be back tomorrow afternoon. I left a message of my own, asking him to call me at my motel. Then I headed for the Shoemakers' home, hoping I could talk some common sense into Andrea.

But Andrea wasn't having any common sense.

She strode around the parlor of their big Victorian—built by one of the city's lumber barons, her husband told me when I complimented them on it—arguing and waving her arms and making scathing statements punctuated by a good amount of profanity. And knocking back martinis, even though it was only a little past noon.

Yes, she was going to the cabin. No, neither her husband nor I was welcome there. No, she wouldn't postpone the trip; she was sick and tired of being cooped up like some kind of zoo animal because her husband had made a mistake years before she'd met him. All right, she realized this John person was dangerous. But she'd taken self-defense classes and owned a .32 revolver. Of course, she knew how to use it. Practiced frequently, too. Women had to be prepared these days, and she was.

But, she added darkly, glaring at her husband, she'd just as soon not have to shoot John. She'd rather send him straight back to Steve and let them settle this score. May the best man win—and she was placing bets on John.

As far as I was concerned, Steve and Andrea Shoemaker deserved each other.

I tried to explain to her that self-defense classes don't fully prepare you for a paralyzing, heart-pounding encounter with an actual violent stranger. I tried to warn her that the ability to shoot well on a firing range doesn't fully prepare you for pumping a bullet into a human being who is advancing swiftly on you.

I wanted to tell her she was being an idiot.

Before I could, she slammed down her glass and stormed out of the house.

Her husband replenished his own drink and said: "Now do you see what I'm up against?"

I didn't respond to that. Instead, I said: "I spoke with Sergeant Wolfe earlier."

"And?"

"He told me he referred you to a local private investigator, Dave Morrison, last April."

"So?"

"Why didn't you hire Morrison for this job?"

"As I told you yesterday, my—"

"Sensitive position, yes." Shoemaker scowled. Before he could comment, I asked: "What was the job last April?"

"Nothing to do with this matter."

"Something to do with politics?"

"In a way."

"Mister Shoemaker, hasn't it occurred to you that a political enemy may be using the Carding case as a smoke screen? That a rival's trying to throw you off balance before this special election?"

"It did, and . . . well, it isn't my opponent's style. My God, we're civilized people. But those notes . . . they're the work of a lunatic."

I wasn't so sure he was right—both about the notes being the work of a lunatic and politicians being civilized people—but I merely said: "OK, you keep working on Missus Shoemaker. At least persuade her to let me go to the Lost Coast with her. I'll be in touch." Then I headed for the public library.

After a few hours of ruining my eyes at the microfilm machine, I knew little more than before. Newspaper accounts of the Carding accident, lawsuit, and murder-suicide didn't differ substantially from what my client had told me. Their coverage of the Shoemakers' activities was only marginally interesting.

Normally I don't do a great deal of background investigation on clients, but, as Sergeant Wolfe had said, in a case like this, where one or both of them was a target, a thorough look at careers and lifestyles was mandatory. The papers described Steve as a straightforward, effective assemblyman who took a hard, conservative stance on such issues as welfare and the environment. He was strongly probusiness, particularly the lumber industry. He and his "charming and talented wife" didn't share many interests: Steve hunted and golfed; Andrea was a "generous supporter of the arts" and a "lavish party-giver." An odd couple, I thought, and odd people to be friends of Jack Stuart, a liberal who'd chosen to dedicate his career to representing the underdog.

Back at the motel, I put in a call to Jack. Why, I asked him, had he remained close to a man who was so clearly his opposite? Jack laughed. "You're trying to say politely that you think he's a pompous, conservative ass."

"Well . . ."

"OK, I admit it . . . he is. But back in college, he was a mentor to me. I doubt I would have gone into the law if it hadn't been for Steve. And we shared some good times, too. One summer we took a motorcycle trip around the country, like something out of *Easy Rider* without the tragedy. I guess we stay in touch because of a shared past."

I was trying to imagine Steve Shoemaker on a motorcycle; the picture wouldn't materialize. "Was he always so conservative?" I asked.

"No, not until he moved back to Eureka and went to work for that lumber company. Then I don't know. Everything changed. It was as if something happened that took all the fight out of him."

What had happened, I thought, was trading another man's life for a prestigious job.

Jack and I chatted for a moment longer, and then I asked him to transfer me to Rae. She hadn't turned up anything on the Cardings yet but was working on it. In the meantime, she added, she'd taken care of what correspondence had come in, dealt with seven phone calls, entered next week's must-dos in the call-up file she'd created for me, and found a remedy for the blight that was affecting my rubber plant.

With a pang, I realized that the office ran just as well—better, perhaps —when I wasn't there. It would keep functioning smoothly without me for weeks, months, maybe years.

Hell, it would probably keep functioning smoothly even if I were dead.

In the morning I opened the Yellow Pages to "florists" and began calling each that was listed. While Shoemaker had been vague on the date his wife received the funeral arrangement, surely a customer who wanted one sent to a private home, rather than a mortuary, would stand out in the order-taker's mind. The listing was long, covering a relatively wide area; it wasn't until I reached the Rs and my watch showed nearly eleven o'clock that I got lucky.

"I don't remember any order like that in the past six weeks," the clerk at Rainbow Florists said, "but we had one yesterday, was delivered this morning."

I gripped the receiver harder. "Will you pull the order, please?"

"I'm not sure I should—"

"Please. You could help save a woman's life." Quick intake of breath, then his voice filled with excitement; he'd become part of a real-life drama. "One minute. I'll check." When he came back on the line, he said: "Thirty-dollar standard condolence arrangement, delivered this morning to Mister Steven Shoemaker."

"*Mister?* Not Missus or Miz?"

"Mister, definitely. I took the order myself." He read off the Shoemakers' address.

"Who placed it?"

"A kid. Came in with cash and written instructions."

Standard ploy—hire a kid off the street so nobody can identify you. "Thanks very much."

"Aren't you going to tell me . . . ?"

I hung up and dialed Shoemaker's office. His secretary told me he was working at home today. I dialed the home number. Busy. I hung up, and the phone rang immediately. Rae, with information on the Cardings.

She'd traced Sam Carding's daughter and younger son. The daughter lived near Cleveland, Ohio, and Rae had spoken with her on the phone. John, his sister had told her, was a drifter and an addict; she hadn't seen him in more than ten years. When Rae reached the younger brother at his office in L.A., he told her the same, adding that he assumed John had died years ago.

I thanked Rae and told her to keep on it. Then I called Shoemaker's number again. Still busy; time to go over there.

Shoemaker's Lincoln was parked in the drive of the Victorian, a dusty Honda motorcycle beside it. As I rang the doorbell, I again tried to picture a younger, free-spirited Steve bumming around the country on a bike with Jack, but the image simply wouldn't come clear. It took Shoemaker a while to answer the door, and, when he saw me, his mouth pulled down in displeasure.

"Come in, and be quick about it," he told me. "I'm on an important conference call."

I was quick about it. He rushed down the hallway to what must be a study, and I went into the parlor where we'd talked the day before. Unlike his offices, it was exquisitely decorated, calling up images of the days of the lumber barons. Andrea's work, probably. Had she also done his offices? Perhaps their gaudy decor was her way of getting back at a husband who put his political life ahead of their marriage?

It was at least a half an hour before Shoemaker finished with his call. He appeared in the archway leading to the hall, somewhat disheveled, running his fingers through his hair. "Come with me," he said. "I have something to show you."

He led me to a large kitchen at the back of the house. A floral arrangement sat on a granite-topped center island: white lilies with a single red rose. Shoemaker handed me the card. *My sympathy on your wife's passing.* It was signed: *John.*

"Where's Missus Shoemaker?" I asked.

"Apparently she went out to the coast last night. I haven't seen her since she walked out on us at the noon hour."

"And you've been home the whole time?"

He nodded. "Mainly on the phone."

"Why didn't you call me when she didn't come home?"

"I didn't realize she hadn't until mid-morning. We have separate bedrooms, and Andrea comes and goes as she pleases. Then this arrangement arrived, and my conference call came through . . ." He shrugged, spreading his hands helplessly.

"All right," I said. "I'm going out there whether she likes it or not. And I think you'd better clear up whatever you're doing here and follow. Maybe your showing up there will convince her you care about her safety, make her listen to reason."

As I spoke, Shoemaker had taken a fifth of Tanqueray gin and a jar of Del Prado Spanish olives from a Lucky sack that sat on the counter. He opened a cupboard, reached for a glass.

"No," I said. "This is no time to have a drink."

He hesitated, then replaced the glass, and began giving me directions to the cabin. His voice was flat, and his curious traveloguelike digressions made me feel as if I were listening to a tape of a *National Geographic* special. Reality, I thought, had finally sunk in, and it had turned him into an automaton.

I had one stop to make before heading out to the coast, but it was right on my way. Morrison Investigations had its office in what looked to be a former motel on Highway 101, near the outskirts of the city. It was a neighborhood of fast-food restaurants and bars, thrift shops and marginal businesses. Besides the detective agency, the motel's cinder-block units housed an insurance brokerage, a secretarial service, two accountants, and a palm reader. Dave Morrison, who was just arriving as I pulled into the parking area, was a bit of a surprise: in his mid-forties, wearing one small gold earring, and a short ponytail. I wondered what Steve Shoemaker had made of him.

Morrison showed me into a two-room suite crowded with computer equipment and file cabinets and furniture that looked as if he might have hauled it down the street from the nearby Thrift Emporium. When he noticed me studying him, he grinned easily. "I know I don't look like a former cop. I worked undercover Narcotics my last few years on the force. Afterwards, I realized I was comfortable with the uniform." His gestures took in his lumberjack's shirt, work-worn jeans, and boots.

I smiled in return, and he cleared some files off a chair so I could sit.

"So you're working for Steve Shoemaker," he said.

"I understand you did, too."

He nodded. "Last April and again around the beginning of August."

"Did he approach you about another job after that?"

He shook his head.

"And the jobs you did for him were . . . ?"

"You know better than to ask that."

"I was going to ask, were they completed to his satisfaction?"

"Yes."

"Do you have any idea why Shoemaker would go to the trouble of bringing me up from San Francisco when he had an investigator here whose work satisfied him?"

Head shake.

"Shoemaker told me the first job you did for him had to do with politics."

The corner of his mouth twitched "In a matter of speaking." He paused, shrewd eyes assessing me. "How come you're investigating your own client?"

"It's that kind of case. And something feels wrong. Did you get that sense about either of the jobs you took on for him?"

"No." Then he hesitated, frowning. "Well, maybe. Why don't you just come out and ask what you want to? If I can, I'll answer."

"OK . . . did either of the jobs have to do with a man named John Carding?"

That surprised him. After a moment he asked a question of his own. "He's still trying to trace Carding?"

"Yes."

Morrison got up and moved toward the window, stopped and drummed his fingers on top of a file cabinet. "Well, I can save you further trouble. John Carding is untraceable. I tried every way I know . . . and that's every way there is. My guess is that hc's dead, years dead."

"And when was it you tried to trace him?"

"Most of August."

Weeks before Andrea Shoemaker had begun to receive the notes from "John." Unless the harassment had started earlier? No, I'd seen all the notes, examined their postmarks. Unless he'd thrown away the first ones, as she had the card that came with the funeral arrangement?

"Shoemaker tell you why he wanted to find Carding?" I asked.

"Uhn-uh."

"And your investigation last April had nothing to do with Carding?"

At first I thought Morrison hadn't heard the question. He was looking out the window, then he turned, expression thoughtful, and opened one of the drawers of the filing cabinet beside him. "Let me refresh my memory," he said, taking out a couple of folders. I watched as he flipped through them, frowning.

Finally he said: "I'm not gonna ask about your case. If something feels wrong, it could be because of what I turned up last spring . . . and that I don't want on my conscience." He closed one file, slipped it back in the cabinet, then glanced at his watch. "Damn! I just remembered I've got to make a call." He crossed to the desk, set the open file on it. "I better do it from the other room. You stay here, find something to read."

I waited until he'd left, then went over and picked up the file. Read it with growing interest and began putting things together. Andrea had been discreet about her extramarital activities, but not so discreet that a competent investigator like Morrison couldn't uncover them.

When Morrison returned, I was ready to leave for the Lost Coast.

"Hope you weren't bored," he said.

"No. I'm easily amused. And, Mister Morrison, I owe you a dinner."

"You know where to find me. I'll look forward to seeing you again."

And now that I'd reached the cabin, Andrea had disappeared. The victim of violence, all signs indicated. But the victim of whom? John Carding— a man no one had seen or heard from for over ten years? Another man named John, one of her cast-off lovers? Or . . . ?

What mattered now was to find her.

I retraced my steps, turning up the hood of my sweater again as I went outside. Circled the cabin, peering through the lashing rain. I could make out a couple of other small structures back there: outhouse and shed. The outhouse was empty. I crossed to the shed. Its door was propped open with a log, as if she'd been getting fuel for the stove.

Inside, next to a neatly stacked cord of wood, I found her.

She lay facedown on the hard-packed dirt floor, blue-jeaned legs splayed, plaid-jacketed arms flung above her head, chestnut hair cas- cading over her back. The little room was silent, the total silence that sur- rounds the dead. Even my own breath was stilled; when it came again, it sounded obscenely loud.

I knelt beside her, forced myself to perform all the checks I've made more times than I could have imagined. No breath, no pulse, no warmth to the skin. And the rigidity. . . .

On the average—although there's a wide variance—rigor mortis sets in to the upper body five to six hours after death; the whole body is usually affected within eighteen hours. I backed up and felt the lower part of her body. Rigid—rigor was complete. I straightened, went to stand in the doorway. She'd probably been dead since midnight. And the cause? I couldn't see any wounds, couldn't further examine her without disturbing the scene. What I should be doing was getting in touch with the sheriff's department.

Back to the cabin. Emotions tore at me: anger, regret, and—yes—guilt that I hadn't prevented this. But I also sensed that I *couldn't* have prevented it. I, or someone like me, had been an integral component from the first.

In the front room I found some kitchen matches and lit the oil lamp. Then I went around the table and looked down at where her revolver lay on the floor. More evidence—don't touch it. The purse and its spilled contents rested near the edge of the stove. I inventoried the items visually: the usual makeup, brush, comb, spray perfume, wallet, keys, roll of postage stamps, daily planner that flopped open to show pockets for business cards and receipts. And a loose piece of paper.

Lucky Food Center, it said at the top. Perhaps she'd stopped to pick up supplies before leaving Eureka, the date and time on this receipt might indicate how long she'd remained in town before storming out on her husband and me.

I picked it up. At the bottom I found yesterday's date and the time of purchase: 9:14 p.m.

KY   SERV DELI ... CRABS ... WINE ... DEL
PRADO OLIVE ... LG RED   DEL ... ROUGE
ET NOIR ... BAKERY ... TANQ GIN. . . .

A sound outside. Footsteps slogging through the mud. I stuffed the receipt into my pocket.

Steve Shoemaker came through the open door in a hurry, rain hat pulled low on his forehead, droplets sluicing down his chiseled nose. He stopped when he saw me, looked around. "Where's Andrea?"

I said: "I don't know."

"What do you mean, you don't know? Her Bronco's outside. That's her purse on the stove."

"And her bag's on the bed, but she's nowhere to be found."

Shoemaker arranged his face into lines of concern. "There's been a struggle here."

"Appears that way."

"Come on, we'll look for her. She may be in the outhouse or the shed. She may be hurt."

"It won't be necessary to look." I had my gun out of my purse now, and I leveled it at him. "I know you killed your wife, Shoemaker."

"What?"

"Her body's where you left it last night. What time did you kill her? How?"

His faked concern shaded into panic. "I didn't—"

"You did."

No reply. His eyes moved from side to side—calculating, looking for a way out.

I added: "You drove her here in the Bronco, with your motorcycle inside. Arranged things to simulate a struggle, put her in the shed, then drove back to town on the bike. You shouldn't have left the bike outside the house where I could see it. It wasn't muddy out here last night, but it sure was dusty."

"Where are these baseless accusations coming from? John Carding . . ."

"Is untraceable, probably dead, as you know from the check Dave Morrison ran."

"He told you. What about the notes, the flowers, the dead things . . . ?"

"Sent by you."

"Why would I do that?"

"To set the scene for getting rid of a chronically unfaithful wife who had potential to become a political embarrassment."

He wasn't cracking, though. "Granted, Andrea had her problems. But why would I rake up the Carding matter?"

"Because it would sound convincing for you to admit what you did all those years ago. God knows it convinced me. And I doubt the police would ever have made the details public. Why destroy a grieving widower and prominent citizen? Particularly when they'd never find Carding or bring him to trial. You've got one problem, though . . . me. You never should have brought me in to back up your scenario."

He licked his lips, glaring at me. Then he drew himself up, leaned forward aggressively—a posture the attorneys at All Souls jokingly refer to as their "litigator's mode."

"You have no proof of this," he said firmly, jabbing his index finger at me. "No proof whatsoever."

"Deli items, crabs, wine, apples," I recited. "Del Prado Spanish olives, Tanqueray gin."

"What the hell are you talking about?"

"I have Andrea's receipt for the items she bought at Lucky yesterday, before she stopped home to pick up her weekend bag. None of these things is here in the cabin."

"So?"

"I know that at least two of them . . . the olives and the gin . . . are at your house in Eureka. I'm willing to bet they all are."

"What if they are? She did some shopping for me yesterday morning. . . ."

"The receipt is dated yesterday *evening*, nine-fourteen p.m. I'll quote you, Shoemaker. 'Apparently she went out to the coast last night. I haven't seen her since she walked out on us at the noon hour.' But you claim you didn't leave home after noon."

That did it; that opened the cracks. He stood for a moment, then half collapsed into one of the chairs and put his head in his hands.

The next summer, after I testified at the trial in which Steve Shoemaker was convicted of the first-degree murder of his wife, I returned to the Lost Coast—with a backpack, without the .38, and in the company of my lover. We walked sand beaches under skies that showed infinite shadings of blue; we made love in fields of wildflowers; we waited quietly for the deer, falcons, and foxes.

I'd already taken the bad from this place; now I could take the good.

The Holes In the System

1996

There are some days that just ought to be called off. Mondays are always hideous: The trouble starts when I dribble toothpaste all over my clothes or lock my keys in the car and doesn't let up till I stub my toe on the bedstand at night. Tuesdays are usually when the morning paper doesn't get delivered. Wednesdays are better, but if I get to feeling optimistic and go to aerobics class at the Y, chances are ten to one that I'll wrench my back. Thursdays—forget it. And by five on Friday, all I want to do is crawl under the covers and hide.

You can see why I love weekends.

The day I got assigned to the Boydston case was a Tuesday.

Cautious optimism, that was what I was nursing. The paper lay folded tidily on the front steps of All Souls Legal Cooperative—where I both live and work as a private investigator. I read it and drank my coffee, not even burning my tongue. Nobody I knew had died, and there was even a cheerful story below the fold in the Metro section. By the time I'd looked at the comics and found that all five strips I bother to read were funny, I was feeling downright perky.

Well, why not? I wasn't making a lot of money, but my job was secure.

The attic room I occupied was snug and comfy. I had a boyfriend, and even if the relationship was about as deep as a desert stream on the Fourth of July, he could be taken most anyplace. And to top it off, this wasn't a bad-hair day.

All that smug reflection made me feel charitable toward my fellow humans—or at least my coworkers and their clients—so I refolded the paper and carried it from the kitchen of our big Victorian to the front parlor and waiting room so others could partake. A man was sitting on the shabby maroon sofa: bald and chubby, dressed in lime-green polyester pants and a strangely patterned green, blue, and yellow shirt that reminded me of drawings of sperm cells. One thing for sure, he'd never get run over by a bus while he was wearing that getup.

He looked at me as I set the paper on the coffee table and said, "How ya doin', little lady?"

Now, there's some contention that the word "lady" is demeaning. Frankly, it doesn't bother me: when I hear it I know I'm looking halfway presentable and haven't got something disgusting caught between my front teeth. No, what rankled was the word "little." When you're five foot three the word reminds you of things you'd just as soon not dwell on—like being unable to see over people's heads at parades, or the little-girly clothes that designers of petite sizes are always trying to foist on you. "Little," especially at nine in the morning, doesn't cut it.

I glared at the guy. Unfortunately, he'd gotten to his feet and I had to look up.

He didn't notice I was annoyed; maybe he was nearsighted. "Sure looks like it's gonna be a fine day," he said.

Now I identified his accent—pure Texas. Another strike against him, because of Uncle Roy, but that's another story.

"It *would've* been a nice day," I muttered.

"Ma'am?"

That did it! The first—and last—time somebody had gotten away with calling me "Ma'am" was on my twenty-eighth birthday two weeks before, when a bag boy tried to help me out of Safeway with my two feather-light sacks of groceries. It was not a precedent I wanted followed.

Speaking more clearly, I said, "It would've been a nice day, except for you."

He frowned. "What'd I do?"

"Try 'little,' a Texas accent, and 'ma'am'!"

"Ma'am, are you all right?"

"Aaargh!" I fled the parlor and ran up the stairs to the office of my boss, Sharon McCone.

Sharon is my friend, mentor, and sometimes—heaven help me—custodian of my honesty. She's been all those things since she hired me a few years ago to assist her at the co-op. Not that our association is always smooth sailing: She can be a stern taskmaster, and she harbors a devilish sense of humor that surfaces at inconvenient times. But she is always been there for me, even during the death throes of my marriage to my pig-selfish, perpetual-student husband, Doug Grayson. And ever since I've stopped referring to him as "that bastard Doug," she's decided I'm a grown-up who can be trusted to manage her own life—within limits.

That morning she was sitting behind her desk with her chair swiveled around so she could look out the bay window at the front of the Victorian. I've found her in that pose hundreds of times: sunk low on her spine, long legs crossed, dark eyes brooding. The view is of dowdy houses across the triangular park that divides the street, and usually hazed by San Francisco fog, but it doesn't matter; whatever she's seeing is strictly inside her head, and she says she gets her best insights into her cases that way.

I stepped into the office and cleared my throat. Slowly Shar turned, looking at me as if I were a stranger. Then her eyes cleared. "Rae, hi. Nice work on closing the Anderson file so soon."

"Thanks. I found the others you left on my desk; they're pretty routine. You have anything else for me?"

"As a matter of fact, yes." She smiled slyly and slid a manila folder across the desk. "Why don't you take this client?"

I opened the folder and studied the information sheet stapled inside.

All it gave was a name—Darrin Boydston—and an address on Mission Street. Under the job description Shar had noted "background check."

"Another one?" I asked, letting my voice telegraph my disappointment.

"Uh-huh. I think you'll find it interesting."

"Why?"

She waved a slender hand at me. "Go! It'll be a challenge."

Now, that *did* make me suspicious. "If it's such a challenge, how come you're not handling it?"

For an instant her eyes sparked. She doesn't like it when I hint that she skims the best cases for herself—although that's exactly what she does, and I don't blame her. "Just go see him."

"He'll be at this address?"

"No. He's downstairs. I got done talking with him ten minutes ago."

"Downstairs? *Where* downstairs?"

"In the parlor."

Oh, God!

She smiled again. "Lime-green, with a Texas accent."

"So," Darrin Boydston said, "Did y'all come back down to chew me out some more?"

"I'm sorry about that." I handed him my card. "Ms. McCone has assigned me to your case."

He studied it and looked me up and down. "You promise to keep a civil tongue in your head?"

"I said I was sorry."

"Well, you damn near ruint my morning."

How many more times was I going to have to apologize?

"Let's get goin', little lady." He started for the door.

I winced and asked, "Where?"

"My place. I got somebody I want you to meet."

Boydston's car was a white Lincoln Continental—beautiful machine, except for the bull's horns mounted on the front grille. I stared at them in horror.

"Pretty, aren't they?" he said, opening the passenger's door.

"I'll follow you in my car," I told him.

He shrugged. "Suit yourself."

As I got into the Ramblin' Wreck—my ancient, exhaust-belching Rambler American—I looked back and saw Boydston staring at *it* in horror.

Boydston's place was a storefront on Mission a few blocks down from my Safeway—an area that could do with some urban renewal and just might get it, if the upwardly mobile ethnic groups that're moving into the neighborhood get their way. It shared the building with a Thai restaurant and a Filipino travel agency. In its front window, red neon tubing spelled out THE CASH COW, but the neon graphic below was a bull. I imagined Boydston trying to reach a decision: call it The Cash Cow and have a good name but a dumb graphic; call it The Cash Bull and have a dumb name and a good graphic; or just say the hell with it and mix genders.

But what kind of establishment was this?

My client took the first available parking space, leaving me to fend for myself. When I finally found another and walked back two blocks he'd already gone inside.

Chivalry is dead. Sometimes I think common courtesy's obit is about to be published, too.

When I went into the store, the first thing I noticed was a huge potted barrel cactus, and the second was dozens of guitars hanging from the ceiling. A rack of worn cowboy boots completed the picture.

Texas again. The state that spawned the likes of Uncle Roy was going to keep getting in my face all day long.

The room was full of glass showcases that displayed an amazing assortment of stuff: rings, watches, guns, cameras, fishing reels, kitchen gadgets, small tools, knickknacks, silverware, even a metronome. There was a whole section of electronic equipment like TVs and VCRs, a jumble of probably obsolete computer gear, a fleet of vacuum cleaners poised to roar to life and tidy the world, enough exercise equipment to trim down half the population, and a jukebox that just then was playing a country song by Shar's brother-in-law, Ricky Savage. Delicacy prevents me from describing what his voice does to my libido.

Darrin Boydston stood behind a high counter, tapping on a keyboard. On the wall behind him a sign warned CUSTOMERS MUST PRESENT TICKET TO CLAIM MERCHANDISE. I'm not too quick most mornings, but I did manage to figure out that The Cash Cow was a pawnshop.

"Y'all took long enough," my client said. "You gonna charge me for the time you spent parking?"

I sighed. "Your billable hours start now." Then I looked at my watch and made a mental note of the time.

He turned the computer off, motioned for me to come around the counter, and led me through a door into a warehouse area. Its shelves were crammed with more of the kind of stuff he had out front. Halfway down the center aisle he made a right turn and took me past small appliances: blenders, food processors, toasters, electric woks, pasta makers, even an ancient pressure cooker. It reminded me of the one the grandmother who raised me used to have, and I wrinkled my nose at it, thinking of those sweltering late-summer days when she'd make me help her with the yearly canning. No wonder I resist the womanly household arts!

Boydston said, "They buy these gizmos 'cause they think they need 'em. Then they find out they don't need and can't afford 'em. And then it all ends up in my lap." He sounded exceptionally cheerful about this particular brand of human folly, and I supposed he had good reason.

He led me at a fast clip toward the back of the warehouse—so fast that I had to trot to keep up with him. One of the other problems with being short is that you're forever running along behind taller people. Since I'd already decided to hate Darrin Boydston, I also decided he was walking fast to spite me.

At the end of the next-to-last aisle we came upon a thin man in a white T-shirt and black work pants who was moving boxes from the shelves to a dolly. Although Boydston and I were making plenty of noise, he didn't hear us come up. My client put his hand on the man's shoulder, and he stiffened. When he turned I saw he was only a boy, no more than twelve or thirteen, with the fine features and thick black hair of a Eurasian. The look in his eyes reminded me of an abused kitten my boyfriend Willie had taken in: afraid and resigned to further terrible experiences. He glanced from me to Boydston, and when my client nodded reassuringly, the fear faded to remoteness.

Boydston said to me, "Meet Daniel."

"Hello, Daniel." I held out my hand. He looked at it, then at Boydston. He nodded again, and Daniel touched my fingers, moving back quickly as if they were hot.

"Daniel," Boydston said, "doesn't speak or hear. Speech therapist I know met him, says he's prob'ly been deaf and mute since he was born."

The boy was watching his face intently. I said, "He reads lips or understands signing, though."

"Does some lip reading, yeah. But no signing. For that you gotta have schooling. Far as I can tell, Daniel hasn't. But him and me, we worked out a personal kind of language to get by."

Daniel tugged at Boyston's sleeve and motioned at the shelves, eyebrows raised. Boydston nodded, then pointed to his watch, held up five fingers, and pointed to the front of the building. Daniel nodded and turned back to his work. Boydston said, "You see?"

"Uh-huh. You two communicate pretty well. How'd he come to work for you?"

My client began leading me back to the store—walking slower now. "The way it went, I found him all huddled up in the back doorway one morning 'bout six weeks ago when I opened up. He was damn near froze but dressed in clean clothes and a new jacket. Was in good shape, 'cept for some healed-over cuts on his face. And he had this laminated card . . . wait, I'll show you." He held the door for me, then rummaged through a drawer below the counter.

The card was a blue three-by-five—encased in clear plastic; on it somebody had typed I WILL WORK FOR FOOD AND A PLACE TO SLEEP. I DO NOT SPEAK OR HEAR, BUT I AM A GOOD WORKER. PLEASE HELP ME.

"So you gave him a job?"

Boydston sat down on a stool. "Yeah. He sleeps in a little room off the warehouse and cooks on a hot plate. Mostly stuff outta cans. Every week I give him cash; he brings back the change—won't take any more than what his food costs, and that's not much."

I turned the card over. Turned over my opinion of Darrin Boydston, too. "How d'you know his name's Daniel?"

"I don't. That's just what I call him."

"Why Daniel?"

He looked embarrassed and brushed at a speck of lint on the leg of his pants. "Had a best buddy in high school down in Amarillo. Daniel Atkins. Got killed in 'Nam." He paused. "Funny, me giving his name to a slope kid when they were the ones that killed him." Another pause. "Of course, this Daniel wasn't even born then, none of that business was his fault. And there's something about him . . . I don't know, he must reminds me of my buddy. Don't suppose old Danny would mind none."

"I'm sure he wouldn't." Damn, it was getting harder and harder to hate Boydston! I decided to let go of it. "Okay," I said, "my casefile calls for a background check. I take it you want me to find out who Daniel is."

"Yeah. Right now he doesn't exist—officially, I mean. He hasn't got a birth certificate, can't get a Social Security number. That means I can't put him on the payroll, and he can't get government help. No classes where he can learn the stuff I can't teach him. No SSI payments either. My therapist friend says he's one of the people that slip through the cracks in the system."

The cracks are more like yawning holes, if you ask me. I said, "I've got to warn you, Mr. Boydston: Daniel may be in the country illegally."

"You think I haven't thought of that? Hell, I'm one of the people that voted for Prop One Eighty-seven. Keep those foreigners from coming here and taking jobs from decent citizens. Don't give 'em nothin' and maybe they'll go home and quit using up my tax dollar. That was before I met Daniel." He scowled. "*Damn*, I hate moral dilemmas! I'll tell you one thing, though: This is a good kid, he deserves a chance. If he's here illegally . . . well, I'll deal with it somehow."

I liked his approach to his moral dilemma; I'd used it myself a time or ten. "Okay," I said, "tell me everything you know about him."

"Well, there're the clothes he had on when I found him. They're in this sack; take a look." He hauled a grocery bag from under the counter and handed it to me.

I pulled the clothing out: rugby shirt in white, green, and navy; navy cords; navy-and-tan down jacket. They were practically new, but the labels had been cut out.

"Lands' End?" I said. "Eddie Bauer?"

"One of those, but who can tell which?"

I couldn't, but I had a friend who could. "Can I take these?"

"Sure, but don't let Daniel see you got 'em. He's real attached to 'em, cried when I took 'em away to be cleaned the first time."

"Somebody cared about him, to dress him well and have this card made up. Laminating like that is a simple process, though; you can get it done in print shops."

"Hell, you could get it done *here*. I got in one of those laminating gizmos a week ago; belongs to a printer who's having a hard time of it, checks his shop equipment in and out like this was a lending library."

"What else can you tell me about Daniel? What's he like?"

Boydston considered. "Well, he's proud—the way he brings back the change from the money I give him tells me that. He's smart; he picked up on the warehouse routine easy, and he already knew how to cook. Whoever his people are, they don't have much; he knew what a hot plate was, but when I showed him a microwave it scared him. And he's got a tic about labels—cuts 'em out of the clothes I give him. There's more, too." He looked toward the door; Daniel was peeking hesitantly around its jamb. Boydston waved for him to come in and added, "I'll let Daniel do the telling."

The boy came into the room, eyes lowered shyly—or fearfully. Boydston looked at him till he looked back. Speaking very slowly and mouthing the words carefully, he asked, "Where are you from?

Daniel pointed at the floor.

"San Francisco?"

Nod.

"This district?"

Frown.

"Mission district? Mis-sion?"

Nod.

"Your momma, where is she?"

Daniel bit his lip.

"Your momma?"

He raised his hand and waved.

"Gone away?" I asked Boydston.

"Gone away or dead. How long, Daniel?" When the boy didn't respond, he repeated, "How long?"

Shrug.

"Time confuses him." Boydston said. "Daniel, your daddy—where is he?"

The boy's eyes narrowed and he made a sudden violent gesture toward the door.

"Gone away?"

Curt nod.

"How long?"

Shrug.

"How long, Daniel?"

After a moment he held up two fingers.

"Days?"

Headshake.

"Weeks?"

Frown.

"Months?"

Another frown.

"Years?"

Nod.

"Thanks, Daniel." Boydston smiled at him and motioned to the door. "You can go back to work now." He watched the boy leave, eyes troubled, then asked me, "So what d'you think?"

"Well—he's got good linguistic abilities; somebody bothered to teach him—probably the mother. His recollections seem scrambled. He's fairly sure when the father left, less sure about the mother. That could mean she went away or died recently and he hasn't found a way to mesh it with the rest of his personal history. Whatever happened, he was left to fend for himself."

"Can you do anything for him?"

"I'm sure going to try."

My best lead on Daniel's identity was the clothing. There had to be a reason for the labels being cut out—and I didn't think it was because of a tic on the boy's part. No, somebody had wanted to conceal the origins of the duds, and when I found out where they'd come from I could pursue my investigation from that angle. I left The Cash Cow, got in the Ramblin' Wreck, and when it finally stopped coughing, drove to the six-story building on Brannan Street south of Market where my friend Janie labors in what she calls the rag trade. Right now she works for a T-shirt manufacturer—and there've been years when I would've gone naked without her gifts of overruns—but during her career she's touched on every area of the business; if anybody could steer me toward the manufacturer of Daniel's clothes, she was the one. I gave them to her and she told me to call later. Then I set out on the trail of a Mission district printer who had a laminating machine.

Print and copy shops were in abundant supply there. A fair number of them did laminating work, but none recognized—or would own up to recognizing—Daniel's three-by-five card. It took me nearly all day to canvass them, except for the half hour when I had a beer and a burrito at La Tacquería, and by four o'clock I was totally discouraged. So I stopped at my favorite ice cream shop, called Janie, and found she was in a meeting, and to ease my frustration had a double-scoop caramel swirl in a chocolate-chip-cookie cone.

No wonder I'm usually carrying five spare pounds!

The shop had a section of little plastic tables and chairs, and I rested my weary feet there, planning to check in at the office and then call it a day. If turning the facts of the case over and over in my mind all evening could be considered calling it a day . . .

Shar warned me about that right off the bat. "If you like this business and stick with it," she'd said, "you'll work twenty-four hours a day, seven days a week. You'll think you're not working because you'll be at a party or watching TV or even in bed with your husband. And then all of a sudden you'll realize that half your mind's thinking about your current case and searching for a solution. Frankly, it doesn't make for much of a life."

Actually it makes for more than one life. Sometimes I think the time I spend on stake-outs or questioning people or prowling the city belongs to another Rae, one who has no connection to the Rae who goes to parties and watches TV and—now—sleeps with her boyfriend. I'm divided, but I don't mind it. And if Rae-the-investigator intrudes on the off-duty Rae's time, that's okay. Because the off-duty Rae gets to watch Rae-the-investigator make her moves—fascinated and a little envious.

Schizoid? Maybe. But I can't help but live and breathe the business. By now that's as natural as breathing air.

So I sat on the little plastic chair savoring my caramel swirl and chocolate chips and realized that the half of my mind that wasn't on sweets had come up with a weird little coincidence. Licking ice cream dribbles off my fingers, I went back to the phone and called Darrin Boydston. The printer who had hocked his laminating machine was named Jason Hill, he told me, and his shop was Quik Prints, on Mission near Geneva.

I'd gone there earlier this afternoon. When I showed Jason Hill the laminated card he'd looked kind of funny but claimed he didn't do that kind of work, and there hadn't been any equipment in evidence to brand him a liar. Actually, he wasn't a liar; he didn't do that kind of work *anymore*.

Hill was closing up when I got to Quik Prints, and he looked damned unhappy to see me again. I took the laminated card from my pocket and slapped it into his hand. "The machine you made this on is living at The Cash Cow right now," I said. "You want to tell me about it?"

Hill—one of those bony-thin guys that you want to take home and fatten up—sighed. "You from Child Welfare or what?"

"I'm working for your pawn broker, Darrin Boydston." I showed him the ID he hadn't bothered to look at earlier. "Who had the card made up?"

"I did."

"Why?"

"For the kid's sake." He switched the Open sign in the window to Closed and came out onto the sidewalk. "Mind if we walk to my bus stop while we talk?"

I shook my head and fell in next to him. The famous San Francisco fog was in, gray and dirty, making the gray and dirty Outer Mission even more depressing than usual. As we headed toward the intersection of Mission and Geneva, Hill told me his story.

"I found the kid on the sidewalk about seven weeks ago. It was five in the morning—I'd come in early for a rush job—and he was dazed and banged up and bleeding. Looked like he'd been mugged. I took him into the shop and was going to call the cops, but he started crying—upset about the blood on his down jacket. I sponged it off, and by the time I got back from the restroom, he was sweeping the print-room floor. I really didn't have time to deal with the cops, so I just let him sweep. He kind of made himself indispensable."

"And then?"

"He cried when I tried to put him outside that night, so I got him some food and let him sleep in the shop. He had coffee ready the next morning and helped me take out the trash. I still thought I should call the cops, but I was worried: He couldn't tell them who he was or where he lived; he'd end up in some detention center or a foster home and his folks might never find him. I grew up in foster homes myself; I know all about the system. He was a sweet kid and deserved better than that. You know?"

"I know."

"Well, I couldn't figure *what* to do with him. I couldn't keep him at the shop much longer—the landlord's nosy and always on the premises. And I couldn't take him home—I live in a tiny studio with my girlfriend and three dogs. So after a week I got an idea: I'd park him someplace with a laminated card asking for a job; I knew he wouldn't lose it or throw it away because he loved the laminated stuff and saved all of the discards."

"Why'd you leave him at The Cash Cow?"

"Mr. Boydston has a reputation for taking care of people. He's helped me out plenty of times."

"How?"

"Well, when he sends out the sixty-day notices saying you should claim your stuff or it'll be sold, as long as you go in and make a token payment, he'll hang on to it. He sees you're hurting, he'll give you more than the stuff's worth. He bends over backward to make a loan." We got to the bus stop and Hill joined the rush-hour line. "And I was right about Mr. Boydston helping the kid, too. When I took the machine in last week, there he was, sweeping the sidewalk."

"He recognize you?"

"Didn't see me. Before I crossed the street, Mr. Boydston sent him on some errand. The kid's in good hands."

Funny how every now and then, when you think the whole city's gone to hell, you discover there're a few good people left . . .

Wednesday morning: cautious optimism again, but I wasn't going to push my luck by attending an aerobics class. Today I'd put all my energy into the Boydston case.

First, a call to Janie, whom I hadn't been able to reach at home the night before.

"The clothes were manufactured by a company called Casuals, Incorporated," she told me. "They only sell by catalog, and their offices and factory are on Third Street."

"Any idea why the labels were cut out?"

"Well, at first I thought they might've been overstocks that were sold through one of the discounters like Ross, but that doesn't happen often with the catalog outfits. So I took a close look at the garments and saw they've got defects—nothing major, but they wouldn't want to pass them off as first quality."

"Where would somebody get hold of them?"

"A factory store, if the company has one. I didn't have time to check."

It wasn't much of a lead, but even a little lead's better than nothing at all. I promised Janie I'd buy her a beer sometime soon and headed for the industrial corridor along Third Street.

Casuals, Inc. didn't have an on-site factory store, so I went into the front office to ask if there was one in another location. No, the receptionist told me, they didn't sell garments found to be defective.

"What happens to them?"

"Usually they're offered at a discount to employees and their families."

That gave me an idea, and five minutes later I was talking with a Mr. Fong in personnel. "A single mother with a deaf-mute son? That would be Mae Jones. She worked here as a seamstress for . . . let's see . . . a little under a year."

"But she's not employed here anymore?"

"No. We had to lay off a number of people, and those with the least seniority are the first to go."

"Do you know where she's working now?"

"Sorry, I don't."

"Mr. Fong, is Mae Jones a documented worker?"

"Green card was in order. We don't hire illegals."

"And you have an address for her?"

"Yes, but I'm afraid I can't give that out."

"I understand, but I think you'll want to make an exception in this case. You see, Mae's son was found wandering the Mission seven weeks ago, the victim of a mugging. I'm trying to reunite them."

Mr. Fong didn't hesitate to fetch Mae's file and give me the address, on Lucky Street in the Mission. Maybe, I thought, this was my lucky break.

The house was a Victorian that had been sided with concrete block and painted a weird shade of purple. Sagging steps led to a porch where six mailboxes hung. None of the names on them was Jones. I rang all the bells and got no answer. Now what?

"Can I help you?" an Asian-accented voice said behind me. It belonged to a stooped old woman carrying a fishnet bag full of vegetables. Her eyes, surrounded by deep wrinkles, were kind.

"I'm looking for Mae Jones." The woman had been taking out a keyring. Now she jammed it into the pocket of her loose-fitting trousers and backed up against the porch railing. Fear made her nostrils flare.

"What?" I asked. "What's wrong?"

"You are from them!"

"Them? Who?"

"I know nothing."

"Please don't be scared. I'm trying to help Mrs. Jones's son."

"Tommy? Where is Tommy?"

I explained about Jason Hill finding him and Darrin Boydston taking him in.

When I finished the woman had relaxed a little. "I am so happy one of them is safe."

"Please, tell me about the Joneses."

She hesitated, looking me over. Then she nodded as if I'd passed some kind of test and took me inside to a small apartment furnished with things that made the thrift-shop junk in my nest at All Souls look like Chippendale. Although I would've rather she tell her story quickly, she insisted on making tea. When we were finally settled with little cups like the ones I'd bought years ago at Bargain Bazaar in Chinatown, she began.

"Mae went away eight weeks ago today. I thought Tommy was with her. When she did not pay her rent, the landlord went inside the apartment. He said they left everything."

"Has the apartment been rented to someone else?"

She nodded. "Mae and Tommy's things are stored in the garage. Did you say it was seven weeks ago that Tommy was found?"

"Give or take a few days."

"Poor boy. He must have stayed in the apartment waiting for his mother. He is so quiet and can take care of himself."

"What d'you suppose he was doing on Mission Street near Geneva, then?"

"Maybe looking for her." The woman's face was frightened again.

"Why there?" I asked.

She stared down into her teacup. After a bit she said, "You know Mae lost her job at the sewing factory?"

I nodded.

"It was a good job, and she is a good seamstress, but times are bad and she could not find another job."

"And then?"

"There is a place on Geneva Avenue. It looks like an apartment house, but it is really a sewing factory. The owners advertise by word of mouth among the Asian immigrants. They say they pay high wages, give employees meals and a place to live, and do not ask questions. They hire many who are here illegally."

"Is Mae an illegal?"

"No. She was married to an American serviceman and has her permanent green card. Tommy was born in San Francisco. But a few years ago her husband divorced her and she lost her medical benefits. She is in poor health—she has tuberculosis. Her money was running out, and she was desperate. I warned her, but she wouldn't listen."

"Warned her against what?"

"There is talk about that factory. The building is fenced and the fences are topped with razor wire. The windows are boarded and barred. They say that once a worker enters she is not allowed to leave. They say workers are forced to sew eighteen hours a day for very low wages. They say that the cost of food is taken out of their pay, and that ten people sleep in a room large enough for two."

"That's slavery! Why doesn't the city do something?"

The old woman shrugged. "The city has no proof and does not care. The workers are only immigrants. They are not important."

I felt a real rant coming on and fought to control it. I've lived in San Francisco for seven years, since I graduated from Berkeley, a few miles and light-years across the Bay, and I'm getting sick and tired of the so-called important people. The city is beautiful and lively and tolerant, but there's a core of citizens who think nobody and nothing counts but them and their concerns. Someday when I'm in charge of the world (an event I fully expect to happen, especially when I've had a few beers), they'll have to answer to *me* for their high-handed behavior.

"Okay," I said, "tell me exactly where this place is, and we'll see what we can do about it."

"Slavery, plain and simple," Shar said.

"Right."

"Something's got to be done about it."

"Right."

We were sitting in a booth at the Remedy Lounge, our favorite tavern down the hill from All Souls on Mission Street. She was drinking white wine, I was drinking beer, and it wasn't but three in the afternoon. But McCone and I have found that some of our best ideas come to us when we tilt a couple. I'd spent the last four hours casing—oops, I'm not supposed to call it that—conducting a surveillance on the building on Geneva Avenue. Sure looked suspicious—trucks coming and going, but no workers leaving at lunchtime.

"But what can be done?" I asked. "Who do we contact?"

She considered. "Illegals? U.S. Immigration and Naturalization Service. False imprisonment? City police and district attorney's office. Substandard working conditions? OSHA, Department of Labor, State Employment Development Division. Take your pick."

"Which is best to start with?"

"None—yet. You've got no proof of what's going on there."

"Then we'll just have to get proof, won't we?"

"Uh-huh."

"You and I both used to work in security. Ought to be a snap to get into that building."

"Maybe."

"All we need is access. Take some pictures. Tape a statement from one of the workers. Are you with me?"

She nodded. "I'm with you. And as backup, why don't we take Willie?"

"*My* Willie? The diamond king of Northern California? Shar, this is an investigation, not a date!"

"Before he opened those discount jewelry stores Willie was a professional fence, as you may recall. And although he won't admit it, I happen to know he personally stole a lot of the items he moved. Willie has talents we can use."

"My tennis elbow hurts! Why're you making me do this?"

I glared at Willie. "Shh! You've never played tennis in your life."

"The doc told me most people who've got it have never played."

"Just be quiet and cut the wire."

"How d'you know there isn't an alarm?"

"Shar and I have checked. Trust us."

"I trust you two, I'll probably end up in San Quentin."

"Cut!"

Willie snipped a fair segment out of the razor wire topping the chain-link fence. I climbed over first, nearly doing myself grievous personal injury as I swung over the top. Shar followed, and then the diamond king—making unseemly grunting noises. His tall frame was encased in dark sweats tonight, and they accentuated the beginnings of a beer belly.

As we each dropped to the ground, we quickly moved into the shadow of the three-story frame building and flattened ourselves against its wall. Willie wheezed and pushed his longish hair out of his eyes. I gave Shar a look that said, *Some asset you invited along.* She shrugged apologetically.

According to plan, we began inching around the building, searching for a point of entry. We didn't see any guards. If the factory employed them, it would be for keeping people in; it had probably never occurred to the owners that someone might actually *want* in.

After about three minutes Shar came to a stop and I bumped into her. She steadied me and pointed down. A foot off the ground was an opening that had been boarded up; the plywood was splintered and coming loose. I squatted and took a look at it. Some kind of duct—maybe people-size. Together we pulled the board off.

Yep. A duct. But not very big. Willie wouldn't fit through it—which was fine by me, because I didn't want him alerting everybody in the place with his groaning. I'd fit, but Shar would fit better still.

I motioned for her to go first.

She made an after-you gesture.

I shook my head.

It's your case, she mouthed.

I sighed, handed her the camera loaded with infrared film that I carried, and started squeezing through, headfirst.

I've got to admit that I have all sorts of mild phobias. I get twitchy in crowds, and I'm not fond of heights, and I hate to fly, and small places make my skin crawl. This duct was a *very* small space. I pushed onward, trying to keep my mind on other things—such as Tommy and Mae Jones.

When my hands reached the end of the duct I pulled hard, then moved them around till I felt a concrete floor about two feet below. I wriggled forward, felt my foot kick something, and heard Shar grunt. *Sorry.* The room I slid down into was pitch black. I waited till Shar was crouched beside me, then whispered, "D'you have your flashlight?"

She handed me the camera, fumbled in her pocket, and then I saw streaks of light bleeding around the fingers she placed around its bulb. We waited, listening. No one stirred, no one spoke. After a moment, Shar took her hand away from the flash and began shining its beam around. A storage room full of sealed cardboard boxes, with a door at the far side. We exchanged glances and began moving through the stacked cartons.

When we got to the door I put my ear to it and listened. No sound. I turned the knob slowly. Unlocked. I eased the door open. A dimly lighted hallway. There was another door with a lighted window set into it at the far end. Shar and I moved along opposite walls and stopped on either side of the door. I went up on tiptoe and peeked through the corner of the glass.

Inside was a factory: row after row of sewing machines, all making jittery up-and-down motions and clacking away. Each was operated by an Asian woman. Each woman slumped wearily as she fed the fabric through.

It was twelve-thirty in the morning, and they still had them sewing!

I drew back and motioned for Shar to have a look. She did, then turned to me, lips tight, eyes ablaze.

Pictures? she mouthed.

I shook my head. *Can't risk being seen.*

Now what?

I shrugged.

She frowned and started back the other way, slipping from door to door and trying each knob. Finally she stopped and pointed to one with a placard that said STAIRWAY. I followed her through it and we started up. The next floor was offices—locked up and dark. "We went back to the stairwell, climbed another flight. On the landing I almost tripped over a small, huddled figure.

It was a tiny gray-haired woman, crouching there with a dirty thermal blanket wrapped around her. She shivered repeatedly. Sick, and hiding from the foreman. I squatted beside her.

The woman started and her eyes got big with terror. She scrambled backwards toward the steps, almost falling over. I grabbed her arm and steadied her; her flesh felt as if it was burning up. "Don't be scared," I said.

Her eyes moved from me to Shar. Little cornered bunny-rabbit eyes, red and full of the awful knowledge that there's no place left to hide. She babbled something in a tongue that I couldn't understand. I put my arms around her and patted her back—universal language. After a bit she stopped trying to pull away.

I whispered, "Do you know Mae Jones?"

She drew back and blinked.

"Mae Jones?" I repeated.

Slowly she nodded and pointed to the door off the next landing.

So Tommy's mother *was* here. If we could get her out, we'd have an English-speaking witness who, because she had her permanent green card, wouldn't be afraid to go to the authorities and file charges against the owners of this place. But there was no telling who or what was beyond that door. I glanced at Shar. She shook her head.

The sick woman was watching me. I thought back to yesterday morning and the way Darrin Boydston had communicated with the boy he called Daniel. It was worth a try.

I pointed to the woman. Pointed to the door. "Mae Jones." I pointed to the door again, then pointed to the floor.

The woman was straining to understand. I went through the routine twice more. She nodded and struggled to her feet. Trailing the ratty blanket behind her, she climbed the stairs and went through the door.

Shar and I released sighs at the same time. Then we sat down on the steps and waited.

It wasn't five minutes before the door opened. We both ducked down, just in case. An overly thin woman of about thirty-five rushed through so quickly that she stumbled on the top step and caught herself on the railing. She would have been beautiful, but lines of worry and pain cut deep into her face; her hair had been lopped off short and stood up in dirty spikes. Her eyes were jumpy, alternately glancing at us and behind her. She hurried down the stairs.

"You want me?"

"If you're Mae Jones." Already I was guiding her down the steps.

"I am. Who are—"

"We're going to get you out of here, take you to Tommy."

"Tommy! Is he—"

"He's all right, yes."

Her face brightened, but then was taken over by fear. "We must hurry. Lan faked a faint, but they will notice I'm gone very soon."

We rushed down the stairs, along the hall toward the storage room. We were at its door when a man called out behind us. He was coming from the sewing room at the far end.

Mae froze. I shoved her, and then we were weaving through the stacked cartons. Shar got down on her knees, helped Mae into the duct, and dove in behind her. The door banged open.

The man was yelling in a strange language. I slid into the duct, pulling myself along on its riveted sides. Hands grabbed for my ankles and got the left one. I kicked out with my right foot. He grabbed for it and missed. I kicked upward, hard, and heard a satisfying yelp of pain. His hand let go of my ankle and I wriggled forward and fell to the ground outside. Shar and Mae were already running for the fence.

But where the hell was Willie?

Then I saw him: a shadowy figure, motioning with both arms as if he were guiding an airplane up to the jetway. There was an enormous hole in the chain-link fence. Shar and Mae ducked through it.

I started running. Lights went on at the corners of the building. Men came outside, shouting. I heard a whine, then a crack.

Rifle, firing at us!

Willie and I hurled ourselves to the ground. We moved on elbows and knees through the hole in the fence and across the sidewalk to the shelter of a van parked there. Shar and Mae huddled behind it. Willie and I collapsed beside them just as sirens began to go off.

"Like 'Nam all over again," he said.

I stared at him in astonishment. Willie had spent most of the war hanging out in a bar in Cam Ranh Bay.

Shar said, "Thank God you cut the hole in the fence!"

Modestly he replied, "Yeah, well, you gotta do something when you're bored out of your skull."

Because a shot had been fired, the SFPD had probable cause to search the building. Inside they found some sixty Asian women—most of them illegals—who had been imprisoned there, some as long as five years, as well as evidence of other sweatshops the owners were running, both here and in Southern California. The INS was called in, statements were taken, and finally at around five that morning Mae Jones was permitted to go with us to be reunited with her son.

Darrin Boydston greeted us at The Cash Cow, wearing electric-blue pants and a western-style shirt with the bucking-bull emblem embroidered over its pockets. A polyester cowboy. He stood watching as Tommy and Mae hugged and kissed, wiped a sentimental tear from his eye, and offered Mae a job. She accepted, and then he drove them to the house of a friend who would put them up until they found a place of their own. I waited around the pawnshop till he returned.

When Boydston came through the door he looked down in the mouth. He pulled up a stool next to the one I sat on and said, "Sure am gonna miss that boy."

"Well, you'll probably be seeing a lot of him, with Mae working here."

"Yeah." He brightened some. "And I'm gonna help her get him into classes. Stuff like that. After she lost her navy benefits when that skunk of a husband walked out on her, she didn't know about all the other stuff that's available." He paused, then added, "So what's the damage?"

"You mean, what do you owe us? We'll bill you."

"Better be an honest accounting, little lady," he said. "Ma'am, I mean," he added in his twangiest Texas accent. And smiled.

I smiled, too.

Up at the Riverside

1999

Duck if you see a cop, Ted."

And so we were off on our mission: my boss, Sharon McCone; my partner, Neal Osborn; and me, Ted Smalley. She, the issuer of my orders, drove her venerable MG convertible. He sat slouched and rumpled beside her. I was perched on the backseat, if you could call it that, which you really can't because it's nothing more than a shelf for carrying one's groceries and such. And illegal for passengers, which is why I had to keep a keen eye out for the law.

I think our minor vehicular transgression made Shar feel free—far away from her everyday concerns about clients and caseloads at the investigative agency she owns. I knew our excursion was taking Neal's mind off the rising rent and declining profits of his used bookstore. And even though I entertained an image of myself as a sack from Safeway, my thinning hair ruffling like the leaves of a protruding bunch of celery, I still felt like a kid cutting school. A kid who had freed himself from billing and correspondence, to say nothing of keeping five private investigators and the next-door law firm in number two pencils and scratch pads.

Soon we were across the Golden Gate Bridge and speeding north on Highway 101. It was a summer Friday and traffic was heavy, but Shar made the MG zip from lane to lane and we outdistanced them all. Our mission was a pleasurable one: a stop along the Russian River to look at and perhaps purchase the jukebox of Neal's and my dreams, then a picnic on the beach at Jenner.

Our plans had been formulated that morning when Shar called us at the ungodly hour of six, all excited. "One of those jukeboxes you guys want is advertised in today's classified," she said. "Seeburg Trashcan, and you won't believe this: It's almost within your price range."

While I primed my brain into running order, Neal went to fetch our copy of the paper. "Phone number's in the 707 area code," he said into the downstairs extension. "Sonoma County."

"Nice up there," Shar said wistfully.

"Maybe Ted and I can take a drive on Sunday, check it out."

I issued a Neanderthal grunt of agreement. Till I have at least two cups of coffee, I'm not verbal. "I've a feeling somebody'll snap it up before then," she said.

"Well, if you'll give Ted part of the day off, I can ask my assistant to mind the store."

"I . . . oh, hell, why don't the three of us take the whole day off? I'll pack a picnic. You know that sourdough loaf I make, with all the melted cheese and stuff?"

"Say no more."

Shar exited the freeway at River Road and we sped through vineyards toward the redwood forest. When we rolled into the town of Guerneville, its main street mirrored our holiday spirits. People roamed the sidewalks in shorts and T-shirts, many eating ice cream cones or by-the-slice pizza; a flea market in the parking lot of a supermarket was doing a brisk business; rainbow flags flapped in the breeze outside gay-owned businesses.

The town has been the hub of the resort area for generations; rustic cabins and summer homes line the riverbank and back up onto the hillsides. In the seventies it became a vacation-time mecca for gays, and the same wide-open atmosphere as in San Francisco's Castro district prevailed, but by the late eighties the AIDS epidemic, a sagging economy, and a succession of disastrous floods had taken away the magic. Now it appeared that Guerneville was bouncing back as an eclectic and bohemian community of hardy folk who are willing to risk yearly cresting floodwaters and mud slides. I, the grocery sack, smiled benevolently as we cruised along.

Outside of town the road wound high above the slow-moving river. At the hamlet of Monte Rio, we crossed the bridge and turned down a narrow lane made narrower by encroaching redwoods and vehicles pulled close to the walls of the mainly shabby houses. Neal began squinting at the numbers. "Dammit, why don't they make them bigger?" he muttered.

I refrained from reminding him that he was overdue for his annual checkup at the optometrist's.

Shar was the one who spotted the place: a large sagging three-story dirty-white clapboard structure with a parking area out front. The roof was missing a fair number of its shingles, the windows were hopelessly crusted with grime, and one column of the wide front porch leaned alarmingly. On the porch, to either side of the double front door, sat identical green wicker rockers, and in each sat a scowly-looking man. Between them, extending from the door and down the steps, was a series of orange cones such as highway department crews use. A yellow plastic tape strung from cone to cone bore the words DANGER DO NOT CROSS DANGER DO NOT CROSS DANGER DO NOT CROSS . . .

In as reverent a tone as I'd ever heard him use, Neal said, "Good God, it's the old Riverside Hotel!"

While staring at it, Shar had overshot the parking area. As she drove along looking for a place to turn around she asked, "You know this place?"

"From years ago. Was built as a fancy resort in the twenties. People would come up from the city and spend their entire vacations here. Then in the seventies the original owner's family sold it to a guy named Tom Atwater, who turned it into a gay hotel. Great restaurant and bar, cottages with individual hot tubs scattered on the grounds leading down to the beach, anything-goes atmosphere."

"You stayed there?" I asked.

Neal heard the edge in my voice. He turned his head and smiled at me, laugh lines around his eyes crinkling. It amuses and flatters him that I'm jealous of his past. "I had dinner there. Twice."

Shar turned the MG in a driveway and we coasted back toward the hotel. The men were watching us. Both were probably in their mid fifties, dressed in shorts and T-shirts, but otherwise—except for the scowls—they were total opposites. The one on our left was a scarecrow with a shock of long gray-blond hair; the one on the right reminded me of Elmer Fudd, and had just as bald a pate.

When we climbed out of the car—the grocery sack needing a firm tug—Neal called, "I phoned earlier about the jukebox."

The scarecrow jerked his thumb at Fudd and kept scowling. Fudd arranged his face into more pleasant lines and got up from the rocker.

"I'm Chris Fowler," he said. "You Neal and Ted?"

"I'm Neal, this is Ted, and that's Sharon."

"Come on in, I'll show you the box."

" 'Come on in, I'll show you the box,' " the scarecrow mimicked in a high nasal whine.

"Jesus!" Chris Fowler exclaimed. He led us through his side of the double front door.

Inside was a reception area that must've been magnificent before the Oriental carpets faded and the flocked wallpaper became water-stained and peeling. In its center stood a mahogany desk backed by an old-fashioned pigeonhole arrangement, and wide stairs on either side led up to the second story. The yellow tape continued, from the door to the pigeonholes, neatly bisecting the room.

Shar stopped and stared at it, frowning. I tugged her arm and shook my head. Sometimes the woman can be so rude. Chris Fowler didn't notice though, just turned right into a dimly lighted barroom. "There's your jukebox," he said.

A thing of beauty, it was. Granted, a particular acquired-taste kind of beauty: shaped like an enormous trash can of fake blond wood, with two flaring red plastic side panels and a gaudy gilt grille studded with plastic gems. Tiny mirrored squares surrounded the grille, and the whole thing was decked out with as much chrome as a 1950s Cadillac. I went up to it and touched the coin slot. Five plays for a quarter, two for a dime, one for a nickel. Those were the days.

Instantly I fell in love.

When I looked at Neal, his eyes were sparkling. "Can we play it?" he asked Chris.

"Sure." He took a nickel from his pocket and dropped it into the slot. Whirrs, clicks, and then voices crooned in mellow tones, "See the pyramids along the Nile . . ."

Shar shook her head, rolled her eyes, and wandered off to inspect a pinball machine. She despairs of Neal's and my campy tendencies.

"So what d'you think?" Chris asked.

I said, "Good sound tone."

Neal said, "The price is kind of steep for us, though."

Chris said, "I'll throw in a box of extra seventy-eights."

Neal said, "I don't know . . ."

And then Shar wandered back over. "What's with the tape?" she asked Chris. "And what's with the guy on the other side of it?"

Neal looked as if he wanted to strangle her. I stifled a moan. A model of subtlety, Shar, and right when we were trying to strike a deal.

Chris grimaced. "That's my partner of many years, Ira Sloan. We've agreed to disagree. The tape's my way of indicating my displeasure with him."

"Disagree over what?"

"This hotel. We jointly inherited it six months ago from Tom Atwater. Did either of you guys know him?"

I shook my head, but Neal nodded. He said, "I met him." Grinned at me and added, "Twice."

"Well," Chris said, "Tom was an old friend. In fact, he introduced Ira and me, nearly twenty years ago. When he left the place to us we thought, what a great way to get out of the city, have our own business in an area that's experiencing a renaissance. So we sold our city house, moved up here, called in the contractors, and got estimates of what it would take to go upscale and reopen. The building's run-down, but the construction's solid. All it needs outside is a new roof and paint job. The cottages were swept away in the floods, but eventually they can be rebuilt. Inside here, all it would take is redecorating, a new chimney and fireplace in the common room on the other side, and updated kitchen equipment. So then what does my partner decide to do?"

All three of us shook our heads, caught up in his breathless monologue.

"My loving partner decides we're to do nothing. Even though we've got more than enough money to fix the place up, he wants to leave it as is and live out our golden years here in Faulkneresque splendor while it falls down around us!"

Neal and I looked properly horrified, but Shar asked, "So why'd you put up the tape?" Maybe a singleminded focus is an asset in a private investigator, but it seems to me it plays hell with interpersonal relations.

Chris wanted to talk about the tape, however. "Ira and I divided the place, straight down the middle. He took the common room, utility room, and the area on the floors above it. I took the restaurant, kitchen, bar, and above. I prepare the meals and slip his under the tape on the reception desk. He washes our clothes and pushes mine over here to me. I'll tell you, it's quite a life!"

"And in the meantime, you're selling off the fixtures in your half?"

"Only the ones that won't fit the image I want to create here."

"How can you create it in half a hotel?"

"I can't, but I'm hoping Ira'll come around eventually. I wish I knew why he has this tic about keeping the place the way it is. If I did, I know I could talk him out of the notion."

Shar was looking thoughtful now. She walked around the jukebox, examining its lovely lines and gnawing at her lower lip. She peered through the glass at the turntable where the 78 of "You Belong to Me" now rested silently. She glanced through the archway at the yellow plastic tape.

"Chris," she said, "what would it be worth to you to find out what Ira's problem is?"

"A lot."

"A reduction of price on this jukebox to one my friends can afford?"

I couldn't believe it! Yes, she was offering out of the goodness of her heart, because she'd seen how badly Neal and I wanted the jukebox, and she knew the limits of our budget. But she was also doing it because she never can resist a chance to play detective.

Chris looked surprised, then grinned. "A big reduction, but I don't see how—"

She took one of her business cards from her purse and handed it to him. Said to me, "Come on, Watson. The game's afoot."

"Mr. Sloan?" Shar was standing at the tape on the porch. I was trying to hide behind her.

Ira Sloan's eyes flicked toward us, then straight ahead.

"Oh, Mr. Sloan!" Now she was waving, for heaven's sake, as if he wasn't sitting a mere five feet away!

His scowl deepened.

Shar stepped over the tape. "Mr. Sloan, d'you suppose you could give Ted and me a tour of your side of the hotel? We love old places like this, and we both think it's a shame your partner wants to spoil it."

He turned his head, looking skeptical but not as ferocious.

Shar reached back and yanked on my arm so hard that I almost tripped over the tape. "Ted's partner, Neal, is in there with Chris, talking upscale. I had to remove Ted before they end up with a tape down the middle of their apartment."

Ira Sloan ran his hand through his longish hair and stood up. He was very tall—at least six-four—and so skinny he seemed to have no ass at all. Had he always been so thin, or was it the result of too many cooling meals shoved across the reception desk?

He said, "The tape was his idea."

"So he told us."

"Thinks it's funny."

"It's not."

"I like people who appreciate old things. It'll be a pleasure to show you around."

The common room was full of big maple furniture with wide wooden arms and thick floral chintz-covered cushions, faded now. The chairs and sofas would've been fashionable in the thirties and forties, campy in the seventies. Now they just looked tired. Casement windows overlooked the lawn and the river, and on the far side of the room was a deep stone fireplace whose chimney showed chinks where the mortar had crumbled. Against the stones hung an oval stained-glass panel in muddy-looking colors. It reminded me of the stone in one of those mood rings that were popular in the seventies.

By the time we'd inspected the room, Shar and Ira Sloan were chattering up a storm. By the time we got upstairs to the guestrooms, they were old friends.

The guestrooms were furnished with waterbeds, another cultural icon of the sybaritic decade. Now their mattresses were shriveled like used condoms. The suites had Jacuzzi tubs set before the windows, once brightly colored porcelain but now rust-stained and grimy. The balconies off the third-story rooms were narrow and cobwebby, and the webbing on their lounge chairs had been stripped away, probably by nesting birds.

Shar asked, "How long was the hotel in operation?"

"Tom closed it in 'eighty-three."

"Why?"

"Declining business. By then . . . well, a lot of things were over."

It made me so sad. The Riverside Hotel's brief time in the sun had been a wild, tumultuous, drug-hazed era—but also curiously innocent. A time of experimentation and newfound freedom. A time to adopt new lifestyles without fear of reprisal. But now the age of innocence was over, and harsh reality had set in. Many of the men who had stayed here were dead, many others decaying like this structure.

Why would Ira Sloan want to keep intact this monument to the death of happiness?

Back downstairs Shar whispered to me, "Stay here. Talk with him." Then she was gone into the reception room and over the tape.

I turned, trying to think of something to say to Ira Sloan, but he'd vanished into some dark corner of the haunted place, possibly to commune with his favorite ghost. I sat down on one of the chairs amid a cloud of rising dust to see if he'd return. Against the chimney, the stained-glass mood-ring stone seemed to have darkened. My mood darkened with it. I wanted out of this place and into the sun.

In about ten minutes Ira Sloan still hadn't reappeared. I heard a rustling behind the reception desk. Shar—who else? She was removing a ledger from a drawer under the warning tape and spreading it open.

"Well, that's interesting," she muttered after a couple of minutes. "Very interesting."

A little while more and she shut the ledger and stuffed it into her tote bag. Smiled at me and said, "Let's go now. You look as though you can use some of my famous sourdough loaf and a walk by the sea."

When we were ensconced on the sand with our repast spread before us, I asked Shar, "What'd you take from the desk?"

"The guest register." She pulled it from her tote and handed it to me.

"You stole it?"

Her mouth twitched—a warning sign. "Borrowed it, with Chris's permission."

"Why?"

"Well, when I went back to talk with him some more, I asked how the two of them decided who got what. He said Ira insisted on his side of the hotel, and Chris was glad to divide it that way because he likes to cook."

Neal poured wine into plastic glasses and handed them around. "Bizarre arrangement, if you ask me."

Shar was cutting the sourdough loaf, in imminent danger of sawing off a finger as well. I took the knife from her and performed culinary surgery.

"Anyway," she went on, "then I asked Chris if Ira had insisted on getting anything else. He said only the guest register. But by then Chris'd gotten his back up, and he pointed out that the ledger was kept in a drawer of the desk that's bisected by the tape. So they agreed to leave it there and hold it in common. Ira wasn't happy with the arrangement."

I filled paper plates with slices of the loaf. Its delicious aroma was quickly dispelling my hotel-induced funk.

"And did the register tell you anything?" Neal asked.

"Only that somebody—I assume Ira—tore the pages out for the week of August 13, 1978. Recently."

"How d'you know it was recent?"

"Fresh tears look different from old ones. The edges of these aren't browning." She flipped the book open to where the pages were missing.

"So now what?"

"I try to find out who was there and what happened that week. Maybe somebody well known who was still in the closet stayed there. Or somebody who was with a person he wasn't supposed to be with."

I asked, "How're you going to find out, if the pages're missing?"

She stabbed her finger at the first column on the ledger page, then at the last. "Date checked in, date checked out. Five individuals who checked in before the thirteenth checked out on the eighteenth. My job for this weekend is to try to locate and talk with them."

"Hey, Ted, come along with me!"

Shar was in the driver's seat of the agency van parked on the floor of Pier 24½, where we have our offices. I was dragging tail down the iron stairway from the second level, intent on heading home after a perfectly outlandish Monday. I went over to the van and leaned in the open window. "What's happening?"

"With any luck, you and I are going to collect your jukebox this evening and have it back at your place by the time Neal closes the store." Anachronism, Neal's used bookstore, is open till nine on Mondays.

I jumped into the van, the day's horrors forgotten. "You find out what Ira Sloan's problem is?"

"Some of it. The rest is about to unfold."

I got my seatbelt on just as she swerved into traffic on the waterfront boulevard outside the pier. Thanked God I was firmly strapped in, a grocery sack no longer.

—⚏—

The house was on a quiet street on the west side of Petaluma, a small city some forty minutes north of the Golden Gate. It used to be called the Egg Basket of the World, before the chicken boom went bust. From what I hear lately, it's turning into Yuppie Heaven.

As we got out of the van I looked up at the gray Victorian. It had a wide porch, high windows, and a fanlike pediment over the door that was painted in the colors of the rainbow. This, Shar had told me, was the home of Mark Curry, one of the men who had stayed at the Riverside during the second week of August 1978. Surprisingly, given the passage of time, she'd managed to locate three of the five who'd signed the register before the missing week, and to interview two so far.

"Ted," she said, "how long have gays been doing that rainbow thing?"

"You mean the flags and all? Funny—since 1978. The first rainbow flag was designed by a San Francisco artist, Gilbert Baker, as a sign of the gay community's solidarity. A version of it was flown in the next year's Pride Parade."

"I didn't realize it went back that far." She started up the walk, and I followed.

The man who answered the door was slender and handsome, with a fine-boned face, a diamond stud in one nostril, and a full head of wavy gray hair that threatened to turn me green with envy. His wood-paneled parlor made me envious, too: full of Chippendale furniture, with a gilt harp in the front window. Mark Curry seated us there, offered coffee, and went to fetch it.

Shar saw the way I was looking at the room. "It's not you," she said. "In a room like this that jukebox would look—"

"Like a wart on the face of an angel. But in our place—"

"It'll still look like a trashcan."

Mark Curry came back with a silver coffee service and got down to business while he poured. "After you phoned, Ms. McCone, I got in touch with Chris Fowler. He's an old friend, from the time we worked as volunteers at an AIDS hospice. He vouched for you, so I dug out my journal for 1978 and refreshed my memory about August's stay at the Riverside."

"You arrived there August eleventh?"

"Yes."

"Alone?"

"No, with my then partner, Dave Howell. He's been dead . . . do you believe nearly sixteen years now?"

"I'm sorry."

"Thanks. Sometimes it seems like yesterday."

"Were you and Mr. Howell staying in a cottage or the main building?"

"Main building, third floor, river side. Over the bar."

"D'you recall who else was there?"

"Well, the place was always full in the summertime, and a lot of the men I didn't know. And even more people came in over the weekend. There was to be a canoeing regatta on Wednesday the sixteenth, with a big barbecue on the beach that evening, and they were gearing up for it.

I said, "*Canoeing* regatta?"

Mark Curry winked at me. "A bunch of guys, stoned and silly, banging into each other and capsizing and having a great time of it."

"Sounds like fun."

Shar said, "So who do you remember?"

"Well, Tom Atwater, of course. His lover, Bobby Gardena, showed up on Tuesday. Bobby had a house in the city, divided his time between there and the river. Ira Sloan, one of Tom's best friends, and the guy who inherited that white elephant along with Chris. He was alone, had just broken off a relationship, and seemed pretty unhappy, but a few months later Tom introduced him to Chris, and they've been together ever since. Then there was Sandy Janssen. Darryl Williams. And of course there was . . ."

Shar dutifully noted the names, but I sensed she'd lost interest in them. Nobody well known who customarily hid in the closet, no scandalous mispairing. When Mark Curry ran out of people, she said, "Tell me about the week of the thirteenth. Did anything out of the ordinary happen?"

Mark Curry laughed. "Out of the ordinary was de rigueur at the Riverside."

"More out of the ordinary than usual."

Her serious—and curiously intense—tone sobered him. He stared into his coffee cup, recapturing his memories. When he spoke, his voice was subdued.

"The night of the regatta, you know? Everybody was on the beach, carrying on till all hours. A little before two, Dave and I decided we wanted to have a couple of quiet drinks alone, so we slipped away from the party. I remember walking up the slope from the beach and across the lawn to the hotel. Everything was so quiet. I suppose it was just the contrast to the commotion on the beach, but it gave me the shivers. Dave, too. And when we went inside, it was still quiet, but . . ."

"But what, Mr. Curry?"

"There was a . . . an undercurrent. A sense of whispers and footfalls, but you couldn't really identify whose or where they were. Like something was going on, but not really. You know how that can be?"

Shar's face was thoughtful. She's had a lot of unusual experiences in her life, and I was sure she did know how that could be.

Mark Curry added, "Dave and I went into the bar and sat down. Nobody came. We were about to make our own drinks—you could do that, so long as you signed a chit—when Ira Sloan stepped out of the kitchen and told us the bar was closed."

"But this was after legal closing time."

He shook his head. "The bar at the Riverside never closed. It was immune to the dictates of the state lawmakers—some of whom were its frequent patrons."

"I see. Did Ira give you any explanation?"

"No. He asked if we wanted to buy a bottle, so we did, and took it up to our room and consumed it on our balcony. And all night the noisy party on the beach went on. But the quiet in the hotel was louder than any cacophony I've ever experienced."

When we got back to the van, Shar took out her phone and made a call. "Hi, Mick," she said. "Anything?"

Mick Savage, her nephew, computer specialist, and fastest skiptracer in the west.

"I see . . . Uh-huh . . . Right . . . No evidence about a gas leak on Friday the eighteenth? . . . Yes, I thought as much . . . No, nothing else. And thanks."

She broke the connection, stuffed the phone back into her bag, and looked at me. Her expression was profoundly sad.

"You've got yourself a jukebox," she said.

"Before I go into this," Shar said to Chris Fowler, "there's something I ought to say."

The three of us were seated at a table in the bar at the Riverside. The dim lighting made Chris look curiously young and hopeful.

"Secrets," Shar went on, "are not necessarily harmful, so long as they remain secrets. But once you put them into words, they can't be taken back. Ever."

Chris nodded. "I understand what you're trying to tell me, but I need to know."

"All right, then. I spoke with three men who were present at the hotel on Wednesday, August 16, 1978. Each gave me bits and pieces of a story that led me to suspect what happened. A check I had run on a fourth man pretty much confirmed my suspicions.

"On August sixteenth of that year, a canoeing regatta was held at this hotel—a big yearly event. The cottages and rooms were all full, but we're only concerned with a few people: Tom Atwater and his lover, Bobby Gardena. Ira. And my witnesses: Mark Curry, Darryl Williams, and Sandy Janssen.

"All three witnesses came up here the Friday before the regatta. Ira arrived on Sunday, Bobby Gardena on Tuesday. It soon became apparent to everybody that Tom and Bobby weren't getting on. Bobby was baiting Tom. They quarreled frequently and publicly. Bobby confided to Sandy Janssen that he'd told Tom he'd quit his job and put his San Francisco house up for sale, with the intention of moving to New Orleans. Tom accused him of being involved with somebody else, and Bobby wouldn't confirm or deny it. He taunted Tom with the possibility.

"After the regatta there was a barbecue on the beach. Everybody was there except for Tom, Bobby, and Ira. Bobby had told Darryl Williams he planned to pack and head back to the city that night. Ira was described by Mark Curry as alone and unhappy."

I heard a noise in the reception area and looked that way. A thin scarecrow's shape stood deep in shadow on the other side of the desk. Ira Sloan. I started to say something, then thought, No. Shar and Chris are discussing him. He has a right to hear, doesn't he?

"Something unusual happened that night," Shar continued. "Mark Curry noticed it when he returned to the hotel around two. Sandy Janssen described a strange atmosphere that kept him from sleeping well. Darryl Williams talked about hearing whispers in the corridors. The next morning Tom told everybody that Bobby had left early for the city, but Darryl claims he saw Bobby's car in the lot when he looked out his window around nine. An hour later it was gone. None of my three witnesses ever heard from or saw Bobby again. The skip trace I had run on him turned up nothing. The final closing on the sale of his city house was handled by Tom, who had his power-of-attorney."

Chris Fowler started to say something, but Shar held up her hand. "And here's the most telling point: On Thursday night, all the guests received notice that they had to vacate the premises on Friday morning, due to a potentially dangerous gas leak that needed to be worked on. A leak that PG&E has no record of. The only men who remained behind were Tom and Ira."

Chris sat very still, breathing shallowly. I looked at the reception area. The scarecrow figure in the shadows hadn't moved.

"I think you can draw your own conclusions," Shar added. She spoke gently and sadly—not the usual trumpeting and crowing that I hear from her when she solves a case.

Slowly Chris said, "God, I can't believe Tom killed Bobby! He was a gentle man. I never saw him raise his hand to anybody."

"It may have been self-defense," Shar said. "Darryl Williams told me one of his friends had an earlier relationship with Bobby, an abusive one. Bobby always threw the first punches."

"So an argument, a moment of violence . . ."

"Is all it takes."

"Naturally he would've turned to Ira to help him cover up. They were best friends, had been since grade school. But that doesn't make Ira a murderer."

"No, it doesn't."

"Anyway, you can't prove it."

"Not without Bobby's remains—which are probably somewhere in this hotel."

Chris glanced around, shivering slightly. "And as long as they're here, Ira and I will be at a stalemate, estranged for the rest of our lives. That's how long he'll guard them."

I was still staring at Ira Sloan's dark figure, but now I looked beyond it, into the common room. The stained-glass oval hanging on the fireplace chimney, that I'd fancifully thought of as the stone in a mood ring, gleamed in the rays from a nearby floor lamp: pink, red, orange, yellow, green, blue, indigo. The seven colors of the rainbow.

I said, "I know where Bobby's buried."

"When I saw this stained-glass yesterday," I said, "I couldn't tell the colors, on account of it being hung where no light could pass through. A strange place, and that should've told Shar or me something right then. Tonight, with the lamp on, I see that it's actually the seven colors of the rainbow."

We—Shar, Chris, and I—were standing in front of the fireplace. I could feel Ira Sloan's presence in the shadows behind us.

"It's the only rainbow symbol in the hotel," I went on, "and it was probably commissioned by Tom Atwater sometime in 1978."

"Why then?" Shar asked.

"Remember I told you that the first rainbow flag was designed in 'seventy-eight? And that a version of it was flown in the 'seventy-nine Pride Parade?"

She nodded.

"The 'seventy-eight flag was seven colors, like this panel. Respectively, they symbolized sexuality, life, healing, sun, nature, art, harmony, and spirit. But the flag that was flown at the parade only had six colors. They dropped indigo so there would be exactly three stripes on either side of the street. That's the one that's become popular and is recognized by the International Congress of Flag Makers."

Chris said, "So Tom and Ira put Bobby's body someplace temporary the night of the murder—maybe the walk-in freezer—and after Tom closed the hotel, they walled him in behind the fireplace. But Tom was a sentimental guy, and he loved Bobby. He'd've wanted some monument."

Behind us there was a whisper of noise, such as I imagined had filled this hotel the night of August 16, 1978. Shar heard it—I could tell from the way she cocked her head—but Chris didn't.

Bitterly he said, "It couldn't've been self defense. If it was, Tom or Ira would've called the county sheriff."

"It wasn't self-defense," Ira's voice said. "It was an accident. I was there. I saw it."

Slowly we turned toward the reception area. Ira Sloan had come out of the shadows and was backed up against the warning tape, his face twisted with the despair of one who expects not to be believed.

"Bobby was leaving to go back to the city," he added. "He was taunting Tom about how he'd be seeing his new lover. They were at the top of the stairs. Tom called Bobby an ugly name, and Bobby went to hit him. Tom ducked, Bobby lost his balance. He fell, rolled over and over, and hit his head on the base of the reception desk." He motioned at the sharp corner near the stairway.

Shar asked, "Why didn't you call the sheriff?"

"Tom had been outspoken about gay rights. Outspoken and abrasive. He had enemies on the county board of supervisors and in the sheriff's department. They'd have seen to it that he was charged with murder. Tom was afraid, so I did what any friend would do."

Chris said, "For God's sake, Ira, why didn't you tell me this when we inherited the hotel?"

"I wanted to preserve Tom's memory. And I was afraid what you might think of me. What you might do about it."

His partner was silent for a moment. Then he said, "I should've let you keep your secret."

"Maybe not," Shar told him. "Secrets that tear two people apart are destructive and potentially dangerous."

"But—"

"The fact is, Chris, that secrets come in all varieties. What you do about them, too. You can expose them, and then everybody gets hurt. You can make a tacit agreement to keep them, and by the time they come out, nobody cares, but keeping them's still exacted its toll on you. Or you can share them with a select group of trusted people and agree to do something about them."

"What're you trying to tell me?"

"The group of people in this room is a small and closed-mouthed one. We all know Ira can keep his own counsel. Bobby Gardena's been in his tomb a long time, but I doubt he's rested easily. Perhaps it would release him if you moved his remains to a more suitable place on the property, and created a better monument to him."

I said, "A better monument, like a garden in the colors of the rainbow."

Chris nodded. A faint ray of hope touched Ira's tortured features.

I added, "Of course, a fitting monument to both Bobby and Tom would be if you renovated this hotel like you planned and reopened it to the living."

Chris nodded again. Then he went to Ira, grasped the warning tape, and tore it free from where it was anchored to the pigeonholes.

I rode in the back of the van on our way home to the city, making sure the Seeburg Trashcan didn't slip its moorings. Both Shar and I were quiet as we maneuvered it up my building's elevator and into the apartment.

Later, after Neal promised to become the fifth party to a closely held secret, I told him the story of August 16, 1978. He was quiet, too.

But still later, when we'd jockeyed the Trashcan into position in our living room and plugged it in, the nostalgic tunes of happier times played long into the night, heralding happy times to come.

Season of Sharing

2001 (with Bill Pronzini)

McCone

I stepped out of my office and looked over the garland-laden railing of the upstairs catwalk at the floor of Pier 24½. Six o'clock, and the annual charity Christmas party for staff members of the various businesses housed there had just begun.

The cars that we customarily parked downstairs had been removed to the street; a buffet table and bar in the center of the huge space was already surrounded; the loving cup for the best decorations—nonecumenical, as many of us practiced Judaism, Buddhism, Islam, or no religion at all—sat on its pedestal, to be awarded at the end of the festivities. We called this event the Season of Sharing party, because we solicited cash and noncash donations for a designated charity, with one firm handling the collection and disbursement on a rotating basis. This year's cause was a group called Home for the Holidays, dedicated to housing and feeding homeless people during the season.

A party with a serious purpose, but that didn't mean we hadn't enjoyed preparing for it and wouldn't have a great time celebrating. The decorations this year were exceptional all around. My office manager, Ted Smalley, had opted for a galactic theme in this time of worldwide dissension, hanging from the garland silver stars, moons, planets, and crystal beads to represent the Milky Way. The architects on the opposite catwalk, Chandler & Santos, had fashioned a cityscape of colored lights and neon tubing; and their neighbors, a group of certified public accountants, had suspended cardboard cutouts of people of all races and genders holding hands. Below was a miniature Santa's Village, complete with electric tram (marketing consultants); a forest of small live fir trees dusted in realistic-looking snow, where replicas of various endangered animals took refuge (ecological nonprofit); swirls of rich, colorful cloth that a fan moved in a kaleidoscopic pattern (fashion designer); a Model T Ford with Santa at the wheel and presents in the rumbleseat (car leasing agency). One of these would win the big loving cup perched on the high pedestal for best of show.

I sighed with pleasure—both at the prospect of an enjoyable evening with good friends and at the knowledge that we would be bringing happy holidays to at least a few of the city's many homeless. Already the barrels of canned goods, new toys, and warm clothing were filled.

As I glanced at the one for cash offerings, I spotted my colleague and friend Wolf approaching with his wife Kerry. The party was limited to Pier 24½ workers and their guests, but for the past month Wolf had been on my payroll, assisting on a complex fraud case that I hadn't had time to attend to myself, so I'd urged him to attend. It had taken a lot of urging. Wolf hated large gatherings, and I was certain he'd only agreed to come as a favor to me and his outgoing advertising-executive wife.

It wasn't the only way I was going to reward him for saving my butt, I thought with some anticipation. The job he'd done for me was an important one, for a client who threw a lot of business my agency's way. I'd been tied up on a long investigation into improprieties in the city's building-inspection department, which had revealed that a senior official was taking kickbacks in exchange for speeding up the permit process.

Only half an hour ago Ted had given me a disk containing my report, which I would deliver to the mayor's office on Monday—the only copy, as the deputy mayor who was my contact there had insisted on total confidentiality. It currently rested under a stack of files in my in box, unimportant looking and labeled "Expenses, November 2001," rather than in the office safe, which had been broken into a few days ago.

Wolf was already looking overwhelmed by the crowd down below. I donned my fuzzy Santa Claus hat and went to try to put him at ease.

Wolf

Kerry said, "Doesn't the pier look nice? So festive."

"Yeah," I said. "Festive."

"Look at all the different displays. Some are really clever."

I looked. "At least they don't have some poor jerk dressed up in a Santa Claus suit."

"I suppose that's a reference to the Christmas Charity Benefit. You're never going to let me forget that, are you?"

"Ho, ho, ho."

She poked me in the ribs. "Don't be grumpy."

"I'm not grumpy."

"If you're going to be grumpy . . ."

I said again, grumpily, that I wasn't grumpy. It was the truth. What I was was ill at ease. Parties of any kind have that effect on me. Large groups of people, no matter how festive the occasion, make me feel claustrophobic; I don't mix well, I'm not good at small talk even with people I know. Kerry keeps trying to socialize me and it keeps not working. The quiet of home and hearth is what I prefer, particularly during the Christmas season. The one other time I'd let her talk me into attending a Yuletide party, the infamous Gala Family Christmas Charity Benefit a few years back, had been an unmitigated disaster. And only partly because I'd allowed myself to be stuffed into a Santa Claus suit, little kiddies to make dents on my knees and share with me their innermost, toy-laden desires.

"Let's make a donation," Kerry said.

She'd hauled me into the midst of the Pier 24½ party and we were now stopped in front of a red, white, and blue barrel in the center of the concrete floor. Propped up in front was a sign: HOME FOR THE HOLIDAYS. *Season of Sharing Fund, Be Generous!*

Kerry put a folded twenty-dollar bill into the barrel. I took a five out of my wallet.

"For heaven's sake," she said, "don't be a Scrooge. Read the sign."

I said, "Be generous, Mr. Spade."

"What's that?"

"Never mind." I exchanged the five for two twenties and slotted them into the barrel.

"That's better. Oh, here's Sharon."

McCone came bustling up. The furred Santa Claus cap she wore over her black hair made my scalp itch. She hugged Kerry, waved some green plant stuff over my head, and then kissed me on the mouth.

"Hey," I said, "I'm a married man. And you're young enough to be my daughter."

"Don't mind him," Kerry said. "He's in one of his grumpy moods."

"I am not grumpy!"

McCone said, "Well, whatever you are, I'm glad you're here. Both of you."

"Where's Ripinsky?" I asked her.

"He had to fly down to RKI headquarters in San Diego. Urgent business. But he'll be back in time for us to spend Christmas together."

She and Kerry proceeded to jabber about how festive the pier looked, how innovative the displays were, particularly McCone Investigations' galactic theme, how all the businesses here were hoping to raise at least five thousand dollars for the homeless. It never ceases to amaze me how adaptable women are. Put two of them together, even a pair of strangers, into any social situation and they're not only immediately comfortable with each other and their surroundings, they never seem at a loss for words.

While they were chattering, I looked around some more. What galactic theme? I thought.

Pretty soon Kerry paused long enough to suggest I go and get us something to drink. "I'd like white wine," she said. "Sharon?"

"The same."

So I waded through the partygoers to the bar. The noise level in there, enhanced by a loud-speakered version of "Deck the Hall," was such that I had to raise my voice to a near-shout to put in my order. Two white wines, nothing more. My brain gets fuzzy enough at parties as it is.

Somebody came up and tapped my arm while I was waiting. McCone's office manager, Ted Smalley, and his bookseller partner, Neal Osborn, both of them wearing red stocking caps with tassels. Neal said, "Great party, isn't it? Didn't Ted do a terrific job of coordinating the decorations and displays?"

"Terrific," I said. "Great, uh, galactic theme, Ted."

He beamed at me. "Everyone cooperated beautifully."

Neal ordered for the two of them. When he was done he said to Ted, "Shall we tell him now or wait until later?"

"Now. I can't wait to see his face."

"Do you want to do the honors or shall I?"

"You go ahead. It was your idea."

"No, it was your idea. The surprise itself was mine. Mine and Sharon's."

I said, "What're you two talking about?"

"You'll find out," Neal said, "if you go upstairs to Sharon's office. There's something on her desk for you."

"A present? Why would you get me a present?"

"For all your help on the Patterson case," Ted said. "Do you still have the spare key Sharon gave you?"

I didn't know what to say, except "Yes" and "Thanks." I'm not used to getting presents from anyone other than Kerry and my assistant, Tamara Corbin.

"Don't open it up there," Neal said. "Bring it down so we can all watch."

Oh, boy. Being the center of attention is something I like about as much as parties. Even so, I felt touched and pleased.

I delivered the glasses of wine, told Kerry where I was going—Sharon grinned when I mentioned the present—and then went upstairs. As I approached McCone's private office, I had the spare key in my hand. But I didn't need it. The door was closed but not locked.

That in itself didn't make me suspicious, but what I saw when I opened the door and walked in set off alarm bells in my head. A man spun around from in front of Sharon's desk—a blond man who didn't work for McCone Investigations, who gave me a frightened-deer look and seemed to teeter briefly on the edge of panic. Then he got a grip on himself, put on a weak smile. He was familiar—I'd seen him around the pier before. An employee of one of the other firms, the architects on the opposite catwalk. His name was Kennett or Bennett.

"You startled me," he said. "What're you doing here?"

"I'll ask you the same question."

"Sharon asked me to get something for her. If you'll excuse me . . ."

He edged past where I stood, not making eye contact, one hand squeezed into the pocket of a pair of very tight leather pants. In other circumstances, or if he'd lingered a few more seconds, I would've restrained him; but I hesitated just long enough for him to get past me and out the door.

I followed as he hurried along the catwalk, close to the garland-festooned railing, his hand still in his pocket. Only fifty feet separated us when he reached the stairs; I had a clear look at him all the way down, but then the Model T Ford display cut off my view and the party swirl swallowed him.

I clambered down until I could once more see all of the pier floor. It was no more than fifteen seconds before I picked him out again. He stopped near some kind of trophy on a pedestal and joined a small group of people, making a gesture with the hand that had been in his pocket. Sharon McCone wasn't one of the group.

I spotted her nearby and made straight for her myself, keeping my eye on Leather Pants all the way.

McCone

I was standing with Ted and Neal when Wolf came hurrying up, a frown darkening his rugged Italian features. He wasn't carrying his present.

"How could he not find the package?" Ted said. "It's right in the middle of your desk."

Something told me the frown had nothing to do with being unable to locate a package. Quickly I moved to meet him.

"Did you send somebody up to your office besides me?" He was looking past me at something or someone.

"No. Why?"

"Well, I just surprised a man inside. Five-ten or so, blond hair, dressed in black leather pants and a thin-ribbed black sweater. I think he works for the architects—Bennett? Kennett?"

Now it was my turn to frown. "Tony Kennett." He was a draftsman for Chandler & Santos, had taken to hanging around our offices lately, trying to persuade my newest hire, Julia Rafael, to go out with him. Julia, who at twenty-five had been through more bad relationships than most women experience in a lifetime, had so far resisted. "Did you talk with him? Ask him what he was doing there?"

"He claimed you'd sent him up to get something. But he had a guilty, scared look. He all but ran out, and came down here. He's over by that trophy."

I looked around, spotted Kennett. He was talking to some people, but even at a distance he looked nervous.

One of my operatives, Craig Morland, had just joined us. He said, "Kennett's been in Julia's and my office damn near every day this week, dying to put the moves on her."

"I don't like or trust him," Ted added.

"Ted, you and Craig keep an eye on him. Make sure he doesn't leave the pier."

They nodded, and Craig said to Neal, "Find Julia, Mick, and Charlotte. Just in case we need them."

A good man, the former FBI agent; he didn't waste time with unnecessary questions.

I turned to Wolf. "Let's go upstairs, see what Kennett might've been after." My voice was heavy with foreboding; I had a good suspicion what it was.

"Grandma Got Run Over by a Reindeer" was playing as we climbed to the catwalk. The irreverent novelty song had always been a favorite of mine, but now I took no pleasure in it. We went along to my office. The door was slightly ajar, but Wolf had indicated he'd left it that way. We went in. The brightly wrapped package for Wolf still sat in the center of my desk, but the papers and files in my in box had been disturbed.

"Dammit!" I exclaimed. I felt through the box's contents to where the disk containing the report on the building-inspection department should be.

Gone. My only copy.

"I knew it!"

"What's missing?" Wolf asked.

"Final report on that political case I've been working."

"The high-confidentiality one for City Hall?"

"Uh-huh. Kennett must've taken it. Unless we can get it back, it'll go straight into the wrong hands, and then there'll be a cover-up like this city's seldom seen."

"And we've seen some spectacular ones. How is Kennett involved?"

I didn't reply, because I'd spotted a key on the floor by my desk. Shiny-new, as if it had just been cut by a machine at a hardware store. I picked it up, took my own office key out. They were a match.

"Now I'm sure it's Kennett," I said, holding up the key. "I run a pretty open shop here; the same key operates all the doors so staff members will have access to the other offices in case they need something. We trust each other, so we tend to trust the other tenants of the pier. Kennett's become something of a fixture here in the past week; simple enough for him to snag a key and have a copy made. And I think he's used it before, because three days ago our creaky old office safe was broken into."

"Anything taken?" Wolf asked.

I shook my head. "Not even my gun, which would be a natural for a common thief."

"You report it?"

"Ted did. There were no fingerprints on it except his and mine."

"Okay, but why was Kennett after the confidential report?"

I considered that, and then the answer came to me, filtered through a dim memory of an event nearly a year past. "Because he's a close friend of the city official I've been investigating—he was at the official's fortieth birthday party last January. Kennett's buddy must've found out there was an ongoing investigation and asked him to find out what I knew."

"Kennett must still have the disk on him."

"And we're going to get it back."

I led Wolf from my office, locking it after us like the proverbial barn door. We paused on the catwalk, surveying the crowd below. Kennett now stood near the bar, drink in hand, talking to someone else.

By the time we got down there, Kennett had moved to Santa's Village and was apparently admiring it. When he saw us he fidgeted and his eyes took on a flat, glassy look.

I said, "Where's the disk, Tony?"

"What disk?"

"The one you took from my office."

"I . . . don't know what you're talking about."

"Do you deny you were in my office around half an hour ago?"

"I certainly do."

I indicated Wolf. "Do you deny you told this man I'd asked you to go up there and get something?"

"I've never seen him before."

Beside me, I felt Wolf tense; a growly sound came from deep in his throat. "You're a liar and a thief both, Kennett," he said.

Kennett gulped what liquor remained in his plastic cup, seemed fortified by it. He set the cup on the display table, extended his arms dramatically. "So search me," he said loudly. "Go ahead!"

People were looking at us now. I studied Kennett's clothing. The leather pants were skin tight; the outline of a disc would have shown clearly. The same with the sweater. Somehow he'd gotten rid of it—somewhere in this cavernous pier that was honeycombed with hiding places.

"That won't be necessary," I said. "Maybe we made a mistake. Enjoy the party."

When we were out of earshot of Kennett, Wolf grasped my elbow. "A mistake? Enjoy the party? What's that about?"

I said, "He's going to have to stay till the end—my people will see to that. In the meantime, we'll let him think he's getting away with the disk."

"Now all we have to do is find it before the party's over."

"That's all," I said grimly.

Wolf

McCone is as efficient an investigator as I've known in thirty-some years in the business. Doubly so in a crisis. She sought out and briefed the members of her staff, individually and in pairs, designating Craig Morland to stay close to Kennett, and her nephew, Mick, and Julia Rafael to watch the exits. The rest of us went upstairs to her office—Neal Osborn and Kerry included, Neal because we might need an extra hand and Kerry because she'd seen Kennett come downstairs with me in his wake.

When we were all settled, McCone behind her desk, the rest of us sitting or standing, she said, "What we need to do is brainstorm this, see if we can get some idea of what Kennett did with the disk. Wolf and I will do most of the talking, but if anybody has anything to contribute, jump in any time."

The others nodded silently. That was another thing about Sharon: She ran a fairly loose ship, delegating a good deal of authority to her operatives, but when she took command she did it forcefully and got complete cooperation in return.

She asked me to go over again, in detail, what had happened earlier. When I was done, she said, "So Kennett didn't go around to the opposite catwalk before he went downstairs. That means he couldn't have hidden the disk in his own office."

"Right."

"And you had him in sight the whole time, except for those few seconds in the crowd. How many seconds, would you say?"

"No more than fifteen. That's probably when he got rid of the disk. First thing that occurs to me is that he passed it to someone else."

"Not likely. This feels like a one-man operation to me."

"Besides," Ted said, "I know all the other people at Chandler and Santos. He's the only one I wouldn't trust."

"Let's eliminate one other unlikely possibility," I said. "That Kennett hid the disk somewhere in here before I came in. The old purloined letter trick."

McCone shook her head. "He didn't expect to get caught and he'd be a fool to risk sneaking into my office another time. He had to've had it on him when he left."

"Okay. Next thing is whether he had any chance at all to hide it while I had him in sight. I'd say no, but I can't be a hundred percent certain. He did walk close to the railing all the way to the stairs. It's remotely possible he slipped the disk in among the decorations."

"I doubt it. All the ones on this side are ours, so again, he couldn't be sure of getting his hands on it later. Ted, go check and make sure."

As Ted went out, I said, "Something else I just remembered. Kennett had one hand in his pocket when I surprised him. It was still in his pocket on the catwalk, on the stairs, and when I lost sight of him. But when I picked him up again, the hand was out—he made a gesture with it when he joined the group by the trophy. That's another point in favor of a hiding place somewhere on the pier floor."

"Did he turn straight into the crowd when he came off the stairs?"

"Hard left turn, yeah."

"That means he passed right by the Model T Ford display."

"Good possibility. And right next to the Ford . . ."

Charlotte Keirn said, "The ecological nonprofit display."

"Also possible. Among the branches of one of the fir trees."

"The only problem with that is, the way the little forest is set up, he'd have had to go into the display itself. That would be inviting attention."

"Have a look anyway."

Ted came in just then, shaking his head. "Nothing among the galactic decorations."

"Check the Model T next. Inside and out."

Neal said, "I'll go with him."

The three of them left together. I said to Kerry, "You also lost sight of Kennett for a time. Where was he when you spotted him again?"

"Over by Santa's Village, on his way toward the loving cup."

"The village is too small to hide anything," Sharon said, "even something as small as a computer disk."

"What about the cup? If it's hollow, he could've dropped it inside."

"It's hollow, but Kennett isn't very tall and the way the cup sits on the pedestal, he'd've had to stretch up on his toes. Too conspicuous. People would've noticed and wondered."

"Then it's got to be either the Model T or the fir trees."

But it was neither one. We waited restlessly until first Charlotte and then Ted and Neal returned empty-handed. Neal said, "I even got down on my hands and knees and checked underneath the car, just in case. You should've seen the looks I got."

I'd been ruminating. Now I said, "We've been going on the assumption that if I hadn't come in unexpectedly and caught him, Kennett would've kept the disk on his person until the party ended. But remember how he's dressed. If he'd had it in his pocket, as tight as those leather pants are, the outline would've showed."

"You're right," McCone said. "He wouldn't run that kind of risk. If he'd intended to keep it on him, he'd've worn looser clothing."

"Which means he planned to hide it all along. Someplace he'd picked out in advance, someplace he'd be sure to have easy access to later." I looked at Kerry. "You said Kennett was walking by Santa's Village. Straight past it toward the trophy?"

"Come to think of it, no. He was moving at an angle."

"From which direction, left or right?"

"Right. An angle from the right."

"So he didn't go more or less on a straight line through the crowd. He veered off to the right first, then veered back again."

"The bar and buffet are in the center, but farther back. What else is over that way?"

"Nothing, except—"

Mick said, "Home for the Holidays."

I said, "Be generous."

Ted said, "And this year it's Chandler and Santos's turn to disburse the donations."

McCone said, "That's it! That's where the disk has to be."

That was where, all right. Kennett's unfunny private joke, his own personal donation to the homeless. Right through that little slot into the Season of Sharing Fund barrel as he passed by.

McCone

I wanted to go straight down and retrieve the disk, but Wolf persuaded me not to. This was a highly sensitive matter, and it wouldn't do to bring it to the attention of everyone in the pier. In the end I sent Ted, Charlotte, and Neal out to keep an eye on Kennett, and Wolf, Kerry, and I settled down to wait till the end of the party.

The minutes, and then the hours, dragged by. Kerry went downstairs to fetch us food from the buffet, but after nibbling on a canapé, I pushed my portion aside and let Wolf finish it off. He is one of the calmest men I know in tense situations, patiently waiting it out until the proper time to take action. He once told me how he chafes while on long surveillances, but from his manner that night I never would have guessed it. Of course, the current situation had given him the perfect excuse not to mingle with the crowd.

Neal stuck his head through the door at a few minutes after eleven. "The pier's locked down and the cleanup crews're assembling."

Downstairs, party wreckage was everywhere: dirty plates and glasses, a sprinkling of confetti, balled-up napkins, spills and splotches. The decorations—even Santa's Village, next to which the trophy sat—looked as tired as the people who had volunteered to remain to deal with the mess. I spotted Nat Chandler and Harvey Santos, partners in the architectural firm, hauling a barrel full of canned goods up the stairs to their offices. Tony Kennett wasn't in sight.

Mick was leaning casually on the cash-donations barrel—standing guard without being too obvious about it. I went over to him, asked, "Where's Kennett?"

"He went up to Chandler and Santos's offices about ten minutes ago. Probably waiting inside, planning to liberate the disk after the partners lock up and go home."

Nat and Harvey were coming back downstairs now. I signaled to them.

"I want you to witness this," I said when they came over.

Wolf lifted the slotted lid of the barrel. It was three-quarters full of cash, coins, and checks. I plunged my hand into the donations and felt around.

"What're you doing?" Harvey asked.

"You'll see."

My fingers touched a flat, round object encased in a thin plastic pouch. "Got it!" I said to Wolf and pulled it from the barrel.

As Nat and Harvey exchanged puzzled glances, I looked up at the catwalk in front of their offices. Kennett stood at the rail watching us. I held up the disk. Even at that distance I could see his shoulders sag and his face crumple.

Wolf

After the police had been summoned and Tony Kennett hauled off to jail, McCone invited her staff and Neal and Kerry and me back up to her office for a celebratory libation. I'd forgotten all about my Christmas present, which Sharon had slipped into a desk drawer during our earlier session. But she and the others hadn't forgotten. She brought the package out and handed it to me with a little flourish.

"With thanks and love from all of us," she said.

Embarrassed, I said, "I haven't gotten anything for any of you yet."

"Never mind that. Open your present, Wolf."

I hefted it first. Not very heavy. I stripped off the paper, took the lid off the gift box—and inside was another, smaller box sealed with half a pound of Scotch tape. Ted's doing; I could tell from his expression. So I used my pocket knife to slice through the tape, opened the second box, rifled through a wad of tissue paper, and found—

Two plastic-bagged issues of *Black Mask*. And not just any two issues: rare, fine-condition copies of the September 1929 and February 1930 numbers, each containing an installment of the original six-part serial version of Hammett's *The Maltese Falcon*.

When I looked up, they were all grinning at me. I said, "How'd you know these were the only two *Falcon* issues I didn't have?" Funny, but my voice sounded a little choked up.

"I told them," Kerry said. "I checked your pulp collection to make sure."

"And I found the copies through one of my friends in the antiquarian book trade," Neal said.

"They must've cost a small fortune."

McCone waved that away. "What they cost doesn't matter. You not only helped close the Patterson case, and to get the disk back tonight, but you've been a good friend for a long time. It's the Season of Sharing with friends, too."

I just sat there.

Kerry said, "Aren't you going to say something?"

Only one thing came to mind. It didn't seem to be enough, but Kerry told me later that it was all that was needed.

"Happy holidays, everybody."

The Cyaniders

2003

Historians claim that we were the people who broke the wild spirit of the American gold mining frontier, and I suppose in a way it's true. We came west armed not with picks and shovels but with university degrees in engineering; we rode into the moribund camps and towns not on mules or horses but in hired coaches. And we staged a quiet revolution that changed the mining world forever.

I changed my particular part of that world—the Knob mineral district in Soledad County, California—more than most of my colleagues. I, you see, was the lone woman among the four men who came there.

The Knob is exactly what its name implies: a bald, rounded outcropping rising above thick piney slopes, which in the 1860s was host to one of the richest veins of gold in the northwestern part of the state. But when I first came there, it stood as a monument to played-out mines, waste dumps, and near-deserted towns. Its desolation cast a pall over the verdant forest and canons that then, in autumn, were choked with golden-leafed aspen. Its shadow darkened the nearby town of Seven Wells, giving its few remaining citizens pause about spending another hard winter there.

None of that mattered to me, not then. As I stood looking up at the

Knob, far from the mountains of my native Colorado, I saw not the rot-
ting timbers of the mine adits and sluices, but the richness of the autumn
foliage and the festiveness of the red berries that hung in abundance on
the thorny pyracantha shrubs. Where others saw ruin, I saw opportunity
for rejuvenation. The tailings that spilled down the hillside to a nearby
creek were a blight, of course, as was the mill, which had not been
stripped of its equipment, but soon the Knob would once more bustle
with activity. I took great breaths of the crisp air and knew that I'd come
to a special place that would own a part of me forever.

It was the tailings and the remaining poor-quality veins of ore that had
brought the five of us to Soledad County. Some dozen years before, in the
late 1880s, three Scotsmen had developed a method by which cyanide was
used to leech gold from such unlikely sources. In 1889 the Forrest-
MacArthur process was first used on a production basis at the Crown
Mine at Karangahake, New Zealand, and now, in 1900, various United
States metallurgical teams had reported varying degrees of success with it.
The proprietors of the firm for which I worked, Denver Precious Metals,
were men who detested being bested by their competitors; they had
quickly acquired title to most of the defunct mines in the Knob district
and dispatched their cyaniders, as we came to be known, on an
exploratory mission.

I speak with authority about Matthew and Peter Lazarus, co-owners of
Denver Precious Metals. They were, respectively, my father and my uncle.
Both a love of mining and an unflinching desire to be the biggest and the
best runs thickly in the veins of all our family members.

The town of Seven Wells, so named for its abundant underground springs,
lay in a narrow meadow between Soledad County's thickly forested coastal
ridgeline, where logging was king, and the rugged, sparsely inhabited
foothills of the Eel River Forest. It once numbered nearly ten thousand in
population, and housed two hotels, two general stores, various shops,
twelve boarding houses, fifteen saloons, and seventeen brothels. Of these,
only the general store, a few shops, and a hotel-and-saloon of dubious
repute remained. Small homes fanned out from the town center, but most

were abandoned and deteriorating; as we drove along the main street, I saw the same was the case with those buildings that lined it. A few old men sat on benches in front of the store, and three children played ball in the park-like grounds surrounding the stone-walled public well across from it, but foot traffic on the sidewalks was light.

It had been decided that during our initial stay in Wells I was to board at the home of one Widow Collins; I was delivered there while my colleagues went on to settle into their quarters at the hotel. My father and mother had indulged me in many ways, but they stood firm on the issue of my residing in an establishment that was a former brothel, with four mining engineers who, in my father's words, were no better than they should be. So up onto the front porch of the Widow Collins's neat little house I went, carrying a full load of rather dire preconceptions. Fortunately they were all disproved by the pretty, plump woman who greeted me, with a small boy peering out from behind her blue skirts.

Dora Collins was only a few years older than I, twenty-eight at most. Her brown eyes were warm and lively, her cheeks flushed with excitement at the prospect of a visitor. Her dark hair was in rebellion, exuberant curls escaping from the bun at the nape of her neck. She took my grip and ushered me inside her home, setting the bag down and clasping both my hands in hers.

"Miss Lazarus," she said, "you have no idea how honored I am to make your acquaintance."

"Please call me Elizabeth."

"If you'll call me Dora. And this"—she nodded at the boy, who was now peering from around a doorjamb—"is Noah."

Noah's response to the introduction was to scamper away.

"He's shy," his mother said, "but in no time he'll take to you. Now, let me show you to your room, and then we'll have a cup of tea. I'm ever so anxious to hear about the business that brings you to Seven Wells."

It was the beginning of a firm friendship.

Dora Collins, I learned in the course of our conversation over tea and scones, had been born and raised in the logging town of Talbot's Mills, some thirty miles to the southwest. She had married her childhood sweet-heart, a manager with Seven Wells Mining, and moved there with him in 1890. Three years later, when they were beginning to despair of having a child, the boy, Noah, was born. And the year after that William Collins was killed in a freak accident at the mine site. "Why did you stay on?" I asked her.

"I thought I would do some good here. You see, the mine had been operating at minimal capacity ever since we arrived, the town shrinking year by year. But there were still children who needed educating, and before my marriage I had trained to be a schoolteacher. For the past five years I've been conducting classes in my parlor, but now I have only three pupils. Their families will soon be leaving, and so will Noah and I."

"To go where?"

"Back to my family in Talbot's Mills." Her eyes clouded. "I don't really wish to do that. We haven't been on good terms since my marriage, but a woman in my position has no other choice. But enough about me. How did you come to be an engineer?"

It was a question I was often asked, so I had a ready response. "My father claims mining is in the family blood. Since I am an only child, it was my duty to carry on the tradition. My mother is herself an educated woman, and felt her daughter should enjoy the same advantages. I attended Colorado School of Mines with their blessing, and, after thoroughly reviewing my academic record, my father hired me."

"You must have visited so many interesting places and seen so many wonderful things."

"Actually, this is the first time I've set foot outside Colorado."

"And you've never . . . ?" She hesitated. "Forgive me if I ask too personal a question."

"Please, ask freely." I knew what her question was.

"You've never married?"

"No. There was someone, and we had planned . . . But he was killed in an accident similar to your husband's."

Her eyes moistened with understanding, and she touched my arm. "I am so sorry."

"It's a long time past," I replied, although the day four years ago that my fiancé had died still seemed like yesterday. "And I have my work, as you have your son."

The next morning I met with the others at the former assay office on Main Street that was to be our headquarters in town. As we unpacked the record-keeping supplies and laboratory equipment that would enable us to test the strengths of the sodium-cyanide solutions and later the quality of the gold it would precipitate, the men told me about their evening.

"The saloonkeeper at the hotel says there's a good bit of resentment over us coming to town," Adams Horton said. Hort, as he was known, had worked for Denver Precious Metals from the beginning. The big, ruddy-faced, white-haired man was as much of an uncle to me as Peter Lazarus, and he had promised my parents to look out for me during our stay in California.

"Because we've bought up title to most of the mines?" I asked.

"And because we're able to extract the gold with relative ease, while the few remaining miners must struggle for theirs. We are outsiders, and the townspeople are afraid we'll leave the town poorer."

"Poorer!" Tod Schuyler snorted. "After the sum we parted with in that saloon last night?"

Tod was in his thirties, married, but said to have an eye for the ladies. Indeed, he was handsome, but his overly friendly manner and lack of seriousness, to say nothing of his heavy indulgence in drink, did not endear him to me.

John Estes, a childless widower with a thin, angular frame and sparse gray hair, spoke. "You know what Hort means, Tod. Seven Wells is a dying community. Everyone, from the shopkeepers to the miners with small claims, is bound to resent us." John was a senior engineer at the company and knew the mining culture well. He was also a kind man who had helped me refine many of the techniques I had learned at the School of Mines.

"What was the name of that Cornishman?" Uncle Hort, as I called him, asked.

John Estes paused to think. "Trevelyan. Andrew Trevelyan. He and his brothers came over from Cornwall in 'forty-nine. Did well in the Mother Lode . . . the Cornish are talented miners. Trevelyan is old now, and bitter. Angry, too. The saloonkeeper says he's made threats."

"Against us?" I asked.

"Among others."

"Are you worried about them?"

"No." He shook his head. "As I said, Trevelyan's old, and an idle talker. There's nothing to be afraid of."

I glanced at the fifth member of our team, Lionel Eliot. He was my age and had joined the company only three months before. A bachelor, he had revealed little of himself on our journey to Seven Wells. Now his lightly freckled face—a suitable companion to his thick reddish hair— was thoughtful. His pale blue eyes met my gaze levelly, and, in the few seconds before he looked away, I saw they were deeply disturbed.

"What do you know of a man called Andrew Trevelyan?" I asked Dora. It was late in the afternoon, and we were having tea.

"Trevelyan? What makes you ask?"

"My colleagues have heard that he's made threats against us."

Dora compressed her lips, frowning. "I would have caution, then. He's a brutish man."

"But old."

"And still dangerous. He beat his wife for years, until one of their grown sons took her off to live with his family in Sacramento. And there is a rumor that he killed his own brother in a dispute over their mining claim."

"Killed him? How?"

"No one knows. The brother, Conrad, disappeared. No trace of him has ever been found. And a week later the other brother, Wesley, left town and never returned. They say Wesley witnessed the murder and was afraid for his own life."

"But this is only rumor."

"Rumor has a way of attaching itself to the proper object. When you see Andrew Trevelyan, you will understand what I mean."

—〰—

I had that dubious privilege three days later, returning to the assay office after spending a morning at the Knob supervising the unloading of steel drums of cyanide from I. G. Farben and milling equipment from the Krupp Works. Dora had arrived, bringing me a surprise meal of bread and cheese and hard-cooked eggs, and, after we had finished, she suddenly drew me to the window fronting on Main Street. Motioning to a man striding along the opposite sidewalk, she said: "Andrew Trevelyan."

He was brutish-looking and, while old, showed no signs of weakness. Well over six feet, he towered above the people he passed, his barrel chest thrust out, big fists pumping the air as if to punish it. His hair was a wild grayish-white tangle, his thick-featured face coarsely textured and wrinkled. His clothing—flannel shirt, leather vest, denim trousers—looked none too clean even at a distance, and his heavy boots were caked in mud. Both women and men gave him wide berth as he strode along, casting what I assumed were evil looks at all he encountered.

"I now understand what you meant by rumor attaching itself to the proper object," I said to Dora.

"And why I told you to have caution."

"I wish the men were here so we could point him out to them."

"He will point himself out to them before very long, I assure you."

The next week passed quietly and productively. We collected our samples from the tailings and waste dumps, and adjusted our cyanide solutions to achieve maximum recovery of the gold. Dora had asked me if I were not discomforted by working with such a deadly poison, and I had explained that in its diluted state it was quite benign. Gold, and silver, too, had an affinity for cyanide and would attach itself to it; later we would run the resultant solution through zinc shavings, which would precipitate the precious metal. The Forrest-MacArthur process was a simple one, and rendered safe because cyanide was neither unstable nor corrosive, or explosive.

In the quiet of the former assay office Lionel Eliot and I performed our tests and recorded our results, while the others supervised the setting up of the mill at the Knob and hiring of miners to extract the low-grade ore that remained in the earth. During those hours we spent together, Lionel and I seldom spoke, but it was not an uncomfortable silence. In fact, after a day spent conducting tests, I emerged as refreshed as if it had been devoted not to work but to sleep. And that was fortunate because, as Dora had predicted, young Noah had taken to me with the energetic zeal of a seven-year-old, constantly entreating me to join in his games and read him stories. Dora was disconcerted and cautioned him to leave me be, but Noah had found a willing playmate in "Auntie Elizabeth." It had been four years since I felt such simple joy, and now I began to delight in the rhythm of my days.

That rhythm was broken at the beginning of our third week in Seven Wells. It was late afternoon, and, feeling a stiffness in my back, I had risen from my chair and gone to the window overlooking Main Street. A figure on the far sidewalk drew my attention: Andrew Trevelyan leaning against the wall of the abandoned building behind him, his large arms folded across his chest, a peaked cap pulled low on his brow. Distance and shadow could not disguise the malice on his coarse-featured face as he stared at me. Quickly I stepped back from the window and said: "Mister Eliot?"

Lionel Eliot looked up from the logbook in which he was recording the results of a test we had completed earlier on a sample of low-grade ore. Before he could speak, I motioned for him to join me. When he saw me, his breath escaped in a hiss.

"Do you think we have something to fear from him?" I asked.

He hesitated, then shook his head. "No. I've been talking with people about Trevelyan . . . the shopkeepers, the men who sit in front of the general store. To a man, they fear Trevelyan, but they say he seldom engages in confrontation unless provoked. Still . . ."

"Yes?"

"I would rather you did not walk back to your lodgings alone today. If I may, I'll escort you.

"I would be pleased." Very much, in fact. During the hours we had spent in one another's presence, I had come to like and respect Lionel

Eliot. Although he was a quiet and unassuming man, I sensed that a deep and rich vein of strength ran through his core.

Andrew Trevelyan was across the street the next day, and the next. Lionel Eliot escorted me both to and from our office and one of the other men was always with me when my presence was required at the Knob. The mill was nearly ready to operate, and initial tests of the equipment were being made.

On the afternoon of the third day of Trevelyan's presence, Uncle Hort returned from the Knob earlier than usual for the purpose of having a talk with Trevelyan. Lionel Eliot and I watched as he crossed the street and approached the big Cornishman. After a few moments of discussion, Uncle Hort turned and came back to the office.

"Mister Trevelyan," he said, "claims he has taken a fancy to that particular spot because the sun shines upon it in a manner that pleases him."

"The sun!" I exclaimed. "That side of the street is mainly in shade."

Uncle Hort nodded. "He also claims that he bears us no ill will. 'If I'd gotten myself an education like you people, I'd be more than a dirt-poor miner,' he told me. 'You people were smart to look to the future.'"

"Was he sincere?" I asked.

He snorted. "Sincere? Lizzie, you may be a grown-up lady with an engineer's degree, but sometimes I question your good sense."

I felt the blood rush to my face and could find no suitable response.

Lionel Eliot, however, surprised me. "On the contrary, Hort," he said, "I think Miss Lazarus has excellent instincts. There may be more to this Cornishman than any of us realizes."

Uncle Hort erupted with laughter. "If you discover his good side, you must be certain to inform me of it. And what is this 'Miss Lazarus' nonsense? Formality isn't necessary among us. She's Lizzie to John, Tod, and me, and should be Lizzie to you as well." With that embarrassing pronouncement, he moved to the back of the room, where he began pawing through the test logs.

Lionel Eliot smiled sympathetically at me. "Do you like to be called Lizzie?"

"Not really. It makes me sound twelve years old."

"Then may I call you Elizabeth?"

"You may. But what shall I call you?"

"Not Ly, as the others do. It makes me sound untruthful, I prefer Lionel. It means lionlike."

"Lionel," I said. The name suited him perfectly.

Three days later, days in which Andrew Trevelyan kept his vigil in the sunless patch on the opposite side of Main Street, Lionel and I entered the office in the morning to find the others already assembled. Uncle Hort and John Estes looked grave. Tod Schuyler seemed subdued, and he had a dark, knotted bruise on his high cheek bone. His eyes were reddened, his complexion pale. Too much whiskey the night before, I supposed.

Before I could ask what the trouble was, Uncle Hort said: "There has been a confrontation with the Cornishman, Lizzie. I will spare you the more sordid details"—this with a meaningful glance at Tod Schuyler—"but I feel that from now on a man should stay under the roof with you and Missus Collins. On our way to the Knob, we will stop there and ask if John may rent a room from her."

"This confrontation. . . ."

"Ly will tell you about it. We must go now."

I watched as they filed out, noting that Tod walked stiffly, cradling one arm to his ribs. "Lionel," I said, "exactly what are these 'sordid details'?"

He smiled. "Hort said that would be the first thing you would ask. And, unlike him, I feel you are woman enough to hear them. Yesterday evening Tod was drinking in the hotel saloon with a woman whose reputation is not above reproach. The kind of woman who—"

"I know what kind of woman frequents saloons, Lionel."

"Of course. Her name is Addie Lawton, and she is a good deal older than Tod. Her husband deserted her a number of years ago, and since then she's made her living by . . ." Lionel looked so discomforted that I had to smile.

"I am not easily shocked," I told him. "And I am aware of what goes on when a woman is left penniless and a man like Tod is far from home. Please continue with your story."

As the hours went by, Lionel said, the whiskey flowed. Tod and his companion became loudly intoxicated, so they scarcely noticed when Andrew Trevelyan strode into the saloon. The Cornishman went directly to their table and pulled Tod from his chair, shouting that no sissified mining engineer from Denver was going to steal his woman. As he began to drag Tod toward the door, Addie Lawton followed, urging Tod to stand up to Trevelyan. But Tod went limp in Trevelyan's grasp, and, when they reached the street, the Cornishman hit him on the face. After he fell to the ground, Trevelyan kicked him several times in the ribs."

"And then?" I asked when Lionel paused.

"Then Addie Lawton called Tod a coward and left with Trevelyan."

I did not care for Tod Schuyler, but I regretted that he had been humiliated in such a fashion. Men like Lionel or John or Uncle Hort could tolerate such insult, but it must have dealt a crushing blow to Tod.

As if he knew what I was thinking, Lionel said: "Yes. I'm afraid that Schuyler may have difficulty showing his face on the streets after this incident. Hort has offered to allow him to return home."

"But he's essential to the team."

"No one is that essential."

Tod Schuyler remained in Seven Wells, but as a changed man. He no longer frequented the saloon, and spent many hours brooding in his room. Gone was his jocular and overly familiar manner. He performed his work silently, his mouth set in grim lines. Often he absented himself from town and the mill for hours, riding about the countryside. And he did not join in at the gatherings that occurred several times a week at Dora's house, now that John was boarding there. Dora and Noah had taken to John much as they had to me. When he asked if he might invite Lionel and Uncle Hort to supper one night, Dora readily agreed. Other suppers followed.

Andrew Trevelyan had withdrawn from our lives as well, and it was a relief not to find him staring from across the street every time I looked out the office window. The townspeople said that, since the night he beat Tod, he had stayed close to his cabin on Drinkwater Creek, and the woman, Addie Lawton, stayed with him.

As autumn turned to winter and Thanksgiving approached, my days resumed their pleasant rhythm. Operations had begun at the mill, and Uncle Hort began to speak of returning to Denver for Christmas. John and Lionel said they would prefer to remain in Seven Wells. As for myself, I welcomed the opportunity to spend my first California Christmas in Dora Collins's cozy home, with the people who I was beginning to regard as family.

Then, the day before Thanksgiving, all the windows in our office were smashed. No one had seen or would admit to having seen the culprit, who had struck sometime after Uncle Hort had left there at six in the evening. We had the windows boarded over, and got on with our work as best we could, but all of us, even the usually unshakeable John Estes, were nervous and irritable. Tod Schuyler became even more withdrawn, and Lionel said that he had taken to drinking alone in his room. The incident cast a shadow over the Thanksgiving feast Dora and I prepared, and shortly after that Uncle Hort cancelled his plans to spend Christmas with his grown children in Denver.

Finally, the next Monday, John Estes was shot.

It happened in the morning at the Knob. A shot rang out in a thick copse of trees along the creek, and a bullet struck him in the shoulder, its force knocking him back into a waste dump. No one saw the shooter, although later Tod Schuyler discovered some broken branches that showed where he must have stood. Quickly two workers loaded John into a wagon and brought him to Dora's house, unconscious and bleeding profusely. Uncle Hort arrived behind them on horseback and spoke grimly of transporting him to a doctor.

Dora said: "The nearest doctor is thirty miles away, over bad roads. A journey of that sort could kill him. Bring him inside."

"Bring him inside to die?" Uncle Hort exclaimed.

Her eyes flashed both annoyance and amusement. "I can doctor him as well as anyone. In the mining camps, we women quickly learn such skills."

A chastened Uncle Hort motioned for the workers to carry John inside.

Dora asked my assistance, and we went upstairs to John's room. The wound, she found, was not as serious as the profuse bleeding had led her to believe, and the bullet had not lodged there. While she cleaned and bandaged it, we heard Lionel arrive, and then Uncle Hort's voice rose from the parlor, loud and strident.

"We know the identity of our shooter, Ly. It is that Cornishman. A coward, hiding in the trees with his rifle! Tomorrow morning I am riding to Talbot's Mills to inform the deputy sheriff there about these incidents."

Lionel said something in a low voice.

"You're right that we have no concrete proof of his involvement, but circumstances support it," Uncle Hort replied. "The man killed his own brother."

"Again, there's no proof."

"Nevertheless, I am determined to talk with the sheriff without further delay."

While Lionel and I walked to our office the next morning, he informed me that Uncle Hort had left for Talbot's Mills at first light. After we were seated at our desks, he grew silent, and, although he made a show of paging through his logbooks and notes, I sensed he was troubled. By noon, when I decided to return to Dora's house to see how John was mending, he still hadn't spoken and paid me little attention as I gathered my things and went out the door.

I found Dora in the kitchen making a soup stock. John was resting comfortably, she told me. "He is all for getting out of bed and going after the Cornishman himself," she added. "I fear that John will not be an easy patient."

I noted her use of John's first name; up to now she had referred to him as Mr. Estes. "How long will he be bedridden?" I asked.

"As long as I can persuade him to remain there. Perhaps a day."

"I've never known him to be troublesome."

She smiled mysteriously. "Men are always troublesome when they seek to impress."

A knock came at the kitchen door, and a woman's voice called out Dora's name. There was a frantic quality to it that made my friend raise her eyebrows in alarm. Quickly she set aside her wooden spoon, and went to see who was there.

It was Millicent Wilson, a neighbor whose son Tommy frequently played with Noah. Her eyes were round and frightened, her face pale. She grasped Dora's arm, exclaiming: "You must come!"

Dora reached for her cloak where it hung on a peg inside the door. "What is it?"

"My Tommy and your Noah. They're very ill."

I followed the two women outside as Dora asked: "How ill? In what way?"

"They're dizzy and breathing with difficulty. Noah's limbs are twitching."

Now Dora paled. "When did these symptoms start?"

"They were playing near the well in the park across from the general store when I did my marketing. Tommy says they both drank of it and immediately became sick. This was perhaps fifteen minutes ago."

Dora hurried toward Millicent's small white house. "I'll need warm soapy water to begin. And afterward, salt water, also warm. Wood ashes from your stove and vinegar will also help."

Recognizing the course of treatment she planned to follow, I asked in a low voice: "Poison?"

She nodded grimly. "I'll force them to regurgitate the stomach contents, and then neutralize what remains. In the meantime, I need you to go to the general store and ask them to close off the well."

"Of course." But before it was closed, I would take a sample of the water.

"Cyanide," I said, looking up from the laboratory table at Lionel. "We are fortunate that the well water diluted it so much. Otherwise, we would have had two dead boys."

His face was deeply troubled. "We should also take samples at the other public wells and close them until we can make an analysis."

"And then we should inventory our supplies of cyanide at the mill."

—⁓—

The six other public wells in town were tainted, and an entire drum of cyanide was missing from our stores. While Lionel rode about warning the owners of private wells about possible contamination, I looked in on Noah and Tommy and found that Dora's doctoring had been successful. Thanks to her quick assessment of their symptoms, their discomfort had been shortened.

By the time I returned to our office, a crowd was gathering—an angry crowd demanding we take our poison and return to Denver. I urged them to remain calm, assured them the trouble was well in hand, but they only became louder and more enraged, so I locked the office door and withdrew to the rear, wishing for a steadying presence. But Uncle Hort was in Talbot's Mills by now; John was in his invalid's bed at Dora's house; Tod was at the mill; and Lionel was probably taking samples at the private wells. The job of defending the office and reputation of Denver Precious Metals had fallen to me, and I felt a poor champion at best.

After perhaps an hour, the noise outside, which had fallen off to a murmur, again rose to a din. Above the townspeople's voices I heard that of Tod Schuyler. I went to the front of the office and pressed my ear to the still-boarded window, trying to hear what he was saying.

"Yes, it was our cyanide!" he shouted. "But if you want to place the blame, look to the Cornishman, Andrew Trevelyan. He's held a grudge against Denver Precious Metals since we arrived here, and I caught him skulking around the shed where the cyanide drums are stored on the night one of them disappeared."

The crowd's noise grew louder, an ugly, ominous growl that made the skin on my arms prickle.

"The Cornishman has no regard for human life," Tod went on. "Ours, yours, or your children's."

He spoke on in that vein, inciting the crowd. Perhaps the Cornishman deserved retribution, I thought, but not at the hands of an angry mob. And what of his woman, Addie Lawton? She could also become their victim.

I knew what I must do. After fetching my cloak, I slipped out the rear door of the office into the alleyway and hurried to the stable where we kept our horses.

Drinkwater Creek had been a mere trickle when we arrived in early autumn, but recent rains had swelled it to a fast-moving stream. I followed its banks some five miles from town through thick woods, my horse stepping gingerly over rocks and tree roots, until I came to a lightning-split eucalyptus that Lionel had once told me marked the boundary of the Cornishman's claim. Then I turned east, away from the creek, toward a plume of wood smoke that drifted above the pines. Emerging from the trees, I found a clearing where a rough board shack stood. As I approached, a woman stepped out, a rifle cradled in her arms. Her hair was disheveled, her long skirts dirty and torn, her face bore deep lines that told of long exposure to the harsh elements.

"Addie Lawton?" I asked.

"I am. And you are that woman from the mining company."

Of course, in a town as small as Seven Wells she would know who I was. "Elizabeth Lazarus," I told her. "May I speak to you?"

"If you must."

"And Mister Trevelyan, if he is at home."

Her lips twisted mirthlessly. "He is at home, yes. But can you speak to him? I think not."

"This is a matter of life or death."

Again, the strange humorless smile. "Then come in."

Addie Lawton and I were waiting outside the cabin when the mob arrived, Tod in the lead. He drew his horse to a halt when he saw us, rifles in our arms. The others followed suit.

"So," he said, "the coward sends out women to defend him. What are you doing here, Lizzie? This is no affair of yours."

"It is my affair when unjust accusations are flung about."

"Then you should be with us, and against them." He motioned at Addie Lawton, then the cabin. To her, he added: "Go inside and send out the Cornishman."

She stared at him, her eyes hard.

I said: "I'm afraid she can't do that."

"Why? He's here, isn't he?"

"He is, in a fashion."

The crowd was silent now, listening closely. Tod glanced back at them. "You speak in riddles, Lizzie."

"Very well, I'll speak plainly. Andrew Trevelyan died this morning. Of pneumonia. He became ill two weeks ago and has been bedridden ever since. It's quite impossible that he smashed our office windows, shot John Estes, stole our cyanide, or poisoned those wells."

Tod's face reddened. "Did she"—again motioning at Addie Lawton—"tell you that?"

"I saw his body with my own eyes. He could not have done those things. But an enemy of his could. An enemy who had access to our office . . . and to the cyanide at the Knob. And who claims he saw Andrew Trevelyan 'skulking' around the mill the night the cyanide was taken. Yet the same person was unsure earlier today as to when the drum disappeared."

The men with Tod were beginning to cast suspicious glances at him. He saw their expressions and, without another word, whirled his horse and galloped off into the woods. A murmur of unrest traveled through the crowd. One man shouted: "He's the one she's talking about!"

Fearing the mob would now turn its rage upon Tod, I said: "Leave him be. Mister Horton has gone into Talbot's Mills for the sheriff's deputy."

"But he'll escape before the deputy arrives!" another man cried.

"Mister Schuyler won't go far. Men like him are unaccustomed to fleeing on horseback, particularly in a snowstorm."

A few flakes had touched my cheeks in the past minute. The men in the crowd turned their faces to the sky and watched the snow begin to fall more thickly. Then, in silence, they turned their horses toward town.

—⁂—

Tod Schuyler was apprehended while struggling through the high drifts near Talbot's Mills the next morning, after being thrown by his horse and spending the frigid night in an abandoned cabin. Although there was no substantial proof of my allegations against him, and formal charges were never brought, his career with Denver Precious Metals was over. Early in the new year, he abandoned his family and disappeared into Mexico.

The poison in the wells diluted quickly, and, with the spring runoff, they were pure once more. The memory of the incident so remained in the consciousness of Soledad County's populace, however, that they took to calling Seven Wells Cyanide Wells. Several years later, it became the official appellation.

The Forrest-MacArthur process proved very successful for us, and eventually earned great profit for the company. In April, John Estes was appointed mill manager at the Knob. He and his wife, the former Dora Collins, and their son Noah still live in Cyanide Wells.

Uncle Hort went back to Denver, but within a year he was off to Montana's copper country. A restless man with an insatiable appetite for new places, he nevertheless stays in contact with those he holds dear.

In July of that fortuitous New Year, Lionel and I boarded a stage for Virginia City, Nevada, and the Comstock Lode. There we became known as the first husband-and-wife cyaniders—a title that might sound ominous to many, but to us signifies a sharing of the life we love.

The Indian Witch

2001

From the Santa Carla, California, *Observer*
January 1, 1900

W e called her the Indian Witch, even though her name was really Mrs. Morrissey. Her husband, Thad Morrissey, ran the only saloon in town, and they lived, just the two of them, in a big clapboard house on Second Avenue a few doors down from Main Street. In 1884 Santa Carla was a small town where everybody knew everybody else's business, but no one knew the Morrisseys'.

No one even knew where they had come from. They arrived in town in the fall of 1863: a big, fair-haired, red-faced Irishman and his small, dark Indian wife. Within the week Thad Morrissey bought the saloon and they moved from their rooming house to Second Avenue. Every day at exactly quarter to noon he would walk to the saloon, open up, and spend the hours between then and midnight pouring drinks for loggers who had come into town from the heavily forested ridge that separates Santa Carla from the rugged northern California coastline. He was a genial host, always willing to listen to a man's troubles or extend credit, but he spoke little of himself.

Mrs. Morrissey was even more of a puzzle. From the day she and her husband moved into the house on Second Avenue she never once left it. It was thought she feared shunning by the townswomen, as marriages between whites and Indians were generally viewed as repugnant, but that did not explain why she dared not venture so far as her own yard or deep front porch. A servant girl from one of the town's poorer families did her shopping and presumably was paid well enough that she was reluctant to talk about what she saw and heard inside the big, shadowy house. And so the Morrisseys lived for over twenty years.

In 1882 my family moved to the end of Second Avenue, where grass-land spread to the eastern hills. Often my younger brothers and I would play with our friends in the vacant lot across from the Morrissey house. We boys would see Thad Morrissey leave for the saloon, and the servant girl come and go, but we never set eyes upon Mrs. Morrissey until one hot July day in 1884, when a curtain moved in an upstairs window and a stern, dark face looked down at us. I was close to the house at the time, having run into the street to retrieve a ball my brother had thrown, and when I looked up, her gaze met mine.

I shall never forget her eyes: black and implacable—although I would not have known what such a word meant at age twelve—with a flatness that bespoke knowledge of many terrible things. They frightened me so badly that I dropped the ball and fled back to the safety of the lot. And on that day we christened Mrs. Morrissey the Indian Witch.

Every day for the rest of July and August we would wait for her to appear in the window. Every day she obliged us on the stroke of three. She would remain there, unmoving, watching us at play for exactly ten minutes. When school began in September, she would watch us as we walked home. By then it seemed to me that I was the object of her gaze.

September passed quickly, and then it was October: lemon-yellow days with a chill on the evening air. But shortly before Halloween, as if nature were angry at the passage of summer, heat enveloped our inland valley. On the coast, the dog-hole ports, where logging companies sent their timber down chutes to schooners at anchor in the coves, were unnavigable because of fog, but Santa Carla experienced no such relief. And on one of those still, blazing afternoons Thad Morrissey toppled forward as he reached across his bar to pour whisky for a logger and died at the age of sixty-two.

Word of his death spread quickly through town. We boys gathered at the vacant lot after school to see what would transpire at the Morrissey house. A delegation of men, including Doc Bolton and Mayor Drew, arrived. They were met by the servant girl, who spoke briefly with them. The next day we learned the Indian Witch had sent instructions through her that her husband was to be buried without ceremony in a plot he had purchased in the graveyard. The townsfolk were shocked to hear it was a single plot. Thad Morrissey had made no provision for his wife, and not even a funeral wreath adorned the forbidding house's door. The Indian Witch continued to appear at the upstairs window, but now she seemed to study me more intensely.

The heat wave finally broke, and November turned chilly. Our thoughts moved forward to Thanksgiving and Christmas. One evening, nearly three weeks after Thad Morrissey's passing, I was walking by his widow's house on the way to visit a friend when a voice spoke to me.

"Young man, come here!"

I stopped, my blood suddenly colder than the air, and peered into the shadows. She was on the porch, wrapped in a black shawl, her hand beckoning to me. My first impulse was to run, but curiosity overcame it and I moved closer.

"Come up on the porch, please."

The voice was refined with scarcely a trace of an accent, not at all as I had imagined it. Or perhaps I had not imagined her as possessing any sort of voice, so stony and silent had she seemed as she stood at the window. I ascended the steps slowly.

The Indian Witch looked me up and down, taking my measure. Then she nodded as if satisfied with what she saw. "I want you to do something for me," she said.

"Ma'am?" The word came out a croak.

She brought out her other hand from beneath the shawl and extended a folded sheet of paper. "I have here a list of things to be purchased. I will reward you for doing so."

"But your girl—"

"Martha cannot perform these errands. No one is to know these things are for me. Will you do this?"

I looked into her eyes and saw both pride and pleading. Then I nodded and held out my hand for the paper, which was thick with money tucked into its fold.

"Why did you choose me?" I asked.

"I have watched you. I know you are trustworthy. Bring the things tomorrow night." Then she turned and went into the house.

I forgot about my visit to my friend and ran home, clutching the Indian Witch's list. My brothers were in the bedroom we three shared and my parents in the parlor, so I took the list to the kitchen, where a kerosene lamp burned low, and examined it.

The items puzzled me: a pair of sturdy boots in the smallest available size, heavy socks, a warm jacket, a small pack, dried meat, and other portable foodstuffs. It appeared to me as if she were about to embark upon a long hike, except in those days respectable matrons of our town did not walk great distances (and, so far as I know, still do not).

I saved my errands for late the next afternoon, as I was sure they would attract notice and I wanted my father to return from his work at the grain mill before anyone could question him about his son's unusual purchases. By the time he heard about them, the deed would be done, and I would have quite a story to tell. My father loved nothing more than a good story.

By suppertime my shopping was completed, and the bundles, along with some extra money, stowed behind our outhouse. I could barely taste my food for my excitement. As soon as I could, I slipped out, retrieved the bundles, and carried them to the Indian Witch's house. She was waiting on the porch, wearing the same black shawl, but on this night she beckoned me inside.

To my surprise, the house was quite ordinary, not much different from my own. She motioned for me to deposit the bundles beside the front door, then bent to look through them. When she straightened, she had the extra money in her hand.

"Yes, I was right about your trustworthiness," she said. "I always could judge a good man."

A good *man*. My heart swelled at the compliment.

She handed me the money. "I want you to have this."

My reward! I had thought perhaps a piece of pie or cake. But this was too much money, five dollars.

"I cannot accept—"

"You can and you will. Come into the parlor, please."

I followed, clutching the money, wondering what else she had in store for me.

A fire burned on the hearth, strong and steady. She had laid and lighted it herself, which impressed me, as my father always proclaimed women incapable of such acts. The Indian Witch motioned me toward a large chair that must have been Thad Morrissey's, and claimed a cushioned rocker for herself. She gripped its arms with long-fingered hands, and, when she looked into my eyes, the firelight made hers glitter fiercely.

She said: "I know what you call me, you and your friends. 'The Indian Witch'."

I gulped and could say nothing.

"It is because I am different. You need to put a name to that difference, so you imagine I have evil powers."

"Ma'am—"

"Be quiet! I have decided to tell you my story. Perhaps it will teach you not to judge others until you know the reasons behind their differences. But first you must promise to tell no one.

"Promise!"

I promised. And then she began.

My story begins in the winter of eighteen fifty-six. My tribe— I am Pomo—had always lived on Cape Perdido, at the northwestern boundary of this county. The rains were bad for two years, the sea worse. Fish and game were scarce, the wild plants even more so. My father could not feed our family.

There was a man who ran a saloon in the logging town on the ridge who was known to be charitable. My father went to ask his help, taking me along. My father was proud. He did not want to beg, and the man knew that. So he bargained. He would give food in exchange for me, Wonena. I was fourteen years of age, the man thirty-four. His name was Thaddeus Morrissey.

My father had no choice but to agree to this proposition. The family would have starved otherwise. For myself, I was not afraid to stay. As I said before, I could always judge a good man. A lesser man than Thaddeus Morrissey would have made me his slave and turned me out when he tired of me. But instead he married me and gave me my Christian name, Emma. He moved me into his rooms above the saloon and asked a neighbor woman to teach me to cook and bake bread and keep house. In the mornings, before he went downstairs, my husband taught me English. He laughed at my mistakes, but gently. He in turn learned words and phrases from my language. In time I came to love him, and he to love me. I think perhaps he had loved me from the first, although we never spoke of it. I became more white than Indian.

In eighteen sixty-one we began to hear rumors. A white man had discovered oil on my tribe's land on Cape Perdido. Now the big companies wanted to drill wells there, but the tribal council said they would never permit it. Those lands were their hunting and gathering grounds. Their ancestors' spirits dwelled there. Cape Perdido was sacred to them.

The government, of course, was on the side of the big companies. They sent troops to force the Pomos off their land. This, of course, was happening to Indians everywhere when valuable things were found on their lands, and some fought back. My tribe decided to fight back, also.

Do you know Perdido means something not easily tamed? In those days it was even more rugged and wild than now. The Pomos knew that cape, but the government soldiers did not. For over a year they stumbled into the ravines and got lost in the forests and fell from the steep cliffs, while the Pomos hid in natural shelters and moved invisibly across the land, killing the intruders one by one.

Finally the government agreed to peace talks with the Pomo leaders. They were three: my uncle, my cousin, and my brother. I remembered my uncle and cousin as violent men, my brother as easily led by them.

The army officers had heard of me, Emma Morrissey, who used to be Wonena. They knew I could speak both English and my own language, and that these leaders were my people. The officers conscripted me to accompany them to the talks.

My husband was against my going. He feared my tribesmen would harm me, or the officers abandon me should trouble arise. But the officers were insistent, and I wanted to help bring about peace. As I said before, I had become more white than Indian.

At dawn on the day of the talks, my husband and I met the officers at a stage stop at the foot of the ridge. They also were three: General Shelby, Commander Bramwell, and Indian Agent Avery. My husband cautioned them to protect me. He said he would wait at the stage stop for no more than four hours, and then follow us. General Shelby said we would return long before then.

We set out for the meeting place, an ancient clearing in the forest that was sacred to the tribe. There, three boulders stood in a row, as if cast down by the heavens, as no rocks similar to them existed for miles. I rode astride my horse, trying to remember the faces of my brother, uncle, and cousin, but it had been too many years since I had parted from them. All I could see was stone. Three great stones, hiding three stone faces. And with that vision, the knowledge of what was to happen grew upon me.

I reined in my horse, called for the others to halt. I told them that, if they went to the clearing, they would surely be killed. They scoffed at the notion, refused to believe me. The Pomos had given their word to the government, the general said. They would not dare break it. I pleaded with the men, told them of my vision. I wept. Nothing I could do or say would stay them. We rode on.

When we arrived, the clearing was empty. The boulders stood before us . . . massive, gray, misshapen. All around us redwood trees towered, the sun shining through their misted branches. Nothing moved or breathed. The clearing no longer felt sacred, because death waited behind those boulders.

General Shelby was angry. "These savages have no time-pieces," he complained. He dismounted, began pacing about.

It was then I saw the barrel of the rifle move from behind the boulder nearest us. It was then I shouted.

The shot boomed, and a bullet pierced General Shelby's chest. Blood stained his uniform.

As the general fell, Commander Bramwell wheeled his horse and galloped from the clearing. He was abandoning me, as my husband had feared the soldiers would.

Indian Agent Avery was confused. A second bullet from behind a second boulder brought him down before he could take shelter or flee.

From behind the third boulder my brother, Kientok, stepped. He aimed his rifle at me, but he did not fire. After a moment he lowered it and said in our language: "Another day, Wonena." Then all three were gone into the forest.

Weak and weeping, I made my way back to the stage stop where my husband waited. When I told him what had happened, his lips went white, but he said nothing, simply took the reins of my horse and led me home. By the next afternoon he had sold the saloon and loaded all our belongings into our wagon. We journeyed inland, and, when we moved into this house, I found that I could not leave it. If my whereabouts were discovered, soldiers would come for me. Surely Commander Bramwell would want to destroy an Indian woman who could brand him a coward. Men from my tribe might come to exact retribution. I believed that so long as I remained indoors with my loaded pistol at hand I would be safe. But I was not safe from the fear. It became my constant companion. It ate at our lives, as did my husband's knowledge of what I would surely do after his passing.

Shortly after my husband and I came to Santa Carla, my tribe was defeated. My uncle and cousin, upon the testimony of Commander Bramwell, were hanged for the murders of General Shelby and Indian Agent Avery. My brother and a number of other men escaped to the ridge, but most of the tribe was removed by the government to a reserve in Oregon. The oil companies drilled their wells on Cape Perdido. Like the wells at Petrolia in Humboldt County, they soon went dry. Oilville, the town that had grown around them, fell into ruins.

Few of the Pomos returned to their lands after they were abandoned by the white man. The Oregon reserve had become home to them. My brother and his renegade band dwell on the cape, however, and now, my duty to my husband fulfilled, I must return to them and take up the threads of my life. My husband knew I would do so, and this is why he made no provision for my burial at Santa Carla.

This, young man, is the story of Emma Morrissey. Now the story of Wonena will begin.

After I left Emma Morrissey's house that November night, I waited, cold and cramped, behind a manzanita bush in the vacant lot. I was aware that by now my parents had discovered my absence and would punish me upon my return, but it seemed small price to pay to view the conclusion of Mrs. Morrissey's story.

I was rewarded when, at half past midnight, a small, shadowy figure emerged from the house and moved down the porch steps. It wore a warm jacket and sturdy boots and carried a small pack that I knew to be filled with provisions for a long journey. Emma Morrissey did not look back at the place that had been her prison for the past twenty years, but merely slipped down the street and disappeared into the darkness as invisibly as her tribesmen had moved across Cape Perdido over two decades before.

I remained where I was, shivering and wondering if Mrs. Morrissey believed the lies she had told me. Her self-imposed confinement to the house had not been out of fear, but in penance for betraying her own people. And she was not making her journey to Cape Perdido to take up the threads of her former life. Instead, this woman who had become more white than Indian would return to face the retribution that her brother, Kientok, had promised with his final words to her: "Another day, Wonena."

The boy to whom Emma Morrissey told her story is, of course, I, Phineas Garry, editor of this newspaper. You know me as a serious, middle-aged man of many words and opinions, most of which have inflamed the more conservative elements of our population. For nearly a decade, outraged readers have asked me why I espouse certain causes, particularly those I support of the rights of our natives.

I have chosen the dawning of this new century to break my long-kept promise and tell the tale that has shaped my life, in order that Wonena should not have lived—and died—in vain.

The Cracks
in the Sidewalk
1996

Gracie

I'm leaning against my mailbox and the sun's shining on my face and my pigeons are coming round. Storage box number 27368. The mail carrier's already been here—new one, because he didn't know my name and kind of shied away from me like I smell bad. Which I probably do. I'll have him trained soon, though, and he'll say "Hi, Gracie" and pass the time of day and maybe bring me something to eat. Just the way the merchants in this block do. It's been four years now, and I've got them all trained. Box 27368—it's gotten to be like home.

Home . . .

Nope, I can't think about that. Not anymore.

Funny how the neighborhood's changed since I started taking up space on this corner with my cart and my pigeons, on my blanket on good days, on plastic in the rain. Used to be the folks who lived in this part of San Francisco were Mexicans and the Irish ran the bars and used-furniture stores. Now you see a lot of Chinese or whatever, and there're all these new restaurants and coffeehouses. Pretty fancy stuff. But that's okay; they draw a nice class of people, and the waiters bring

me the leftovers. And my pigeons are still the same—good company.
They're sort of like family.

Family...

No, I can't think about that anymore.

Cecily

I've been watching the homeless woman they call Gracie for two years
now, ever since I left my husband and moved into the studio over the
Lucky Shamrock and started to write my novel. She shows up every
morning promptly at nine and sits next to the mail-storage box and holds
court with the pigeons. People in the neighborhood bring her food, and
she always shares it with the birds. You'd expect them to flock all over her,
but instead they hang back respectfully, each waiting its turn. It's as if
Gracie and they speak the same language, although I've never heard her
say a word to them.

How to describe her without relying on the obvious stereotypes of
homeless persons? Not that she isn't stereotypical: She's ragged and she
smells bad and her gray-brown hair is long and tangled. But in spite of
the wrinkles and roughness of her skin, she seems ageless, and on days
like this when she smiles and turns her face up to the sun she has a strange
kind of beauty. Beauty disrupted by what I take to be flashes of pain. Not
physical, but psychic pain—the reason, perhaps, that she took up residence on the cracked sidewalk of the Mission District.

I wish I knew more about her.

All I know are these few things: She's somewhere in her late thirties, a
few years older than I. She told the corner grocer that. She has what she
calls a "hidey-hole" where she goes to sleep at night—someplace safe, she
told the mailman, where she won't be disturbed. She guards her shopping
cart full of plastic bags very carefully; she'd kill anyone who touched it, she
warned my landlord. She's been coming here nearly four years and hasn't
missed a single day; Deirdre, the bartender at the Lucky Shamrock, has
kept track. She was born in Oroville, up in the foothills of the Sierras; she
mentioned that to my neighbor when she saw him wearing a sweatshirt
saying OROVILLE—BEST LITTLE CITY BY A DAM SITE.

And that's it.

Maybe there's a way to find out more about her. Amateur detective work. Call it research, if I feel a need to justify it. Gracie might make a good character for a story. Anyway, it would be something to fool around with while I watch the mailbox and listen for the phone, hoping somebody's going to buy my damn novel. Something to keep my mind off this endless cycle of hope and rejection. Something to keep my mind off my regrets.

Yes, maybe I'll try to find out more about Gracie.

Gracie

Today I'm studying on the cracks in the sidewalk. They're pretty complicated, running this way and that, and on the surface they look dark and empty. But if you got down real close and put your eye to them there's no telling what you might see. In a way the cracks're like people. Or music.

Music . . .

Nope, that's something else I can't think about.

Seems the list of what I can't think on is getting longer and longer. Bits of the past tug at me, and then I've got to push them away. Like soft summer nights when it finally cools and the lawn sprinklers twirl on the grass. Like the sleepy eyes of a little boy when you tuck him into bed. Like the feel of a guitar in your hands.

My hands.

My little boy.

Soft summer nights up in Oroville.

No.

Forget the cracks, Gracie. There's that woman again—the one with the curly red hair and green eyes that're always watching. Watching *you*. Talking about you to the folks in the stores and the restaurants. Wonder what she wants?

Not my cart—it better not be my cart. My gold's in there.

My gold . . .

No. That's at the top of the list.

Cecily

By now I've spoken with everybody in the neighborhood who's had any contact with Gracie, and they've only added a few details to what I already know. She hasn't been back to Oroville for over ten years, and she never will go back; somebody there did a "terrible thing" to her. When she told that to my neighbor, she became extremely agitated and made him a little afraid. He thought she might be about to tip over into a violent psychotic episode, but the next time he saw her she was as gentle as ever. Frankly, I think he's making too much of her rage. He ought to see the heap of glass I had to sweep off my kitchenette floor yesterday when yet another publisher returned my manuscript.

Gracie's also quite familiar with the Los Angeles area—she demonstrated that in several random remarks she made to Deirdre. She told at least three people that she came to San Francisco because the climate is mild and she knew she'd have to live on the street. She sings to the pigeons sometimes, very low, and stops right away when she realizes somebody's listening. My landlord's heard her a dozen times or more, and he says she's got a good voice. Oh, yes—she doesn't drink or do drugs. She told one of the waiters at Gino's that she has to keep her mind clear so she can control it—whatever that means.

Not much to go on. I wish I could get a full name for her; I'm not even sure Gracie is her name. God, I'm glad to have this little project to keep me occupied! Disappointments pile on disappointments lately, and sometimes I feel as if I were trapped in one of those cracks in the sidewalk that obviously fascinate Gracie. As if I'm being squeezed tighter and tighter . . .

Enough of that. I think I'll go to the library and see if they have that book on finding people that I heard about. Technically, Gracie isn't lost, but her identity's missing. Maybe the book would give me an idea of how to go about locating it.

Gracie

Not feeling so good today, I don't know why, and that red-haired woman's snooping around again. Who the hell is she? A fan?

Yeah, sure. A fan of old Gracie. Old Gracie, who smells bad and has got the look of a loser written all over her.

House of cards, he used to say. It can all collapse at any minute, and then how'll you feel about your sacrifices? *Sacrifices.* The way he said it, it sounded like a filthy word. But I never gave up anything that mattered. Well, one thing, one person—but I didn't know I was giving him up at the time.

No, no, *no!*

The past's tugging at me more and more, and I don't seem able to push it away so easy. Control, Gracie. But I'm not feeling good, and I think it's gonna rain. Another night in my hidey-hole with the rain beating down, trying not to remember the good times. The high times. The times when—

No.

Cecily

What a joke my life is. Three thanks-but-no-thanks letters from agents I'd hoped would represent me, and I can't even get the Gracie project off the ground. The book I checked out of the library was about as helpful—as my father used to say—as tits on a billygoat. Not that it wasn't informative and thorough. Gracie's just not a good subject for that kind of investigation.

I tried using the data sheet in the appendix. Space at the top for name: Gracie. Also known as: ? Last known address: Oroville, California—but that was more than ten years ago. Last known phone number: ? Automobiles owned, police record, birth date, Social Security number, real estate owned, driver's license number, profession, children, relatives, spouse: all blank. Height: five feet six, give or take. Weight: too damn thin. Present location: divides time between postal storage box 27368 and hidey-hole, location unknown.

Some detective, me.

Give it up, Cecily. Give it up and get on with your life. Take yourself downtown to the temp agency and sign on for a three-month job before your cash all flows out. Better yet, get yourself a real, permanent job and give up your stupid dreams. They aren't going to happen.

But they might. Wasn't I always one of the lucky ones? Besides, they tell you that all it takes is one editor who likes your work. They tell you all it takes is keeping at it. A page a day, and in a year you'll have a novel. One more submission, and soon you'll see your name on a book jacket. And there's always the next manuscript. This Gracie would make one hell of a character, might even make the basis for a good novel. If only I could find out . . .

The cart. Bet there's something in that damned cart that she guards so carefully. Tomorrow I think I'll try to befriend Gracie.

Gracie

Feeling real bad today, even my pigeons sense it and leave me alone. That red-haired woman's been sneaking around. This morning she brought me a bagel slathered in cream cheese just the way I like them. I left the bagel for the pigeons, fed the cream cheese to a stray cat. I know a bribe when I see one.

Bribes. There were plenty: a new car if you're a good girl. A new house, too, if you cooperate. And there was the biggest bribe of all, the one they never came through with.

No.

Funny, things keep misting over today, and I'm not even crying. Haven't cried for years. No, this reminds me more of the smoky neon haze and the flashing lights. The sea of faces that I couldn't pick a single individual out of. Smoky sea of faces, but it didn't matter. The one I wanted to see wasn't there.

Bribes, yeah. Lies, really. *We'll make sure everything's worked out. Trust us. It's taking longer than we thought. He's making it difficult. Be patient. And by the way, we're not too sure about this new material.*

Bribes . . .

The wall between me and the things on my list of what not to remember is crumbling. Where's my control? That wall's my last defense.

Cecily

Deirdre's worried about Gracie. She's looking worse than usual and has been refusing food. She fed the bagel I brought her to the pigeons, even though Del at Gino's said bagels with cream cheese are one of her favorite things. Deirdre thinks we should do something—but what?

Notify her family? Not possible. Take her to a hospital? She's not likely to have health insurance. I suppose there's always a free clinic, but would she agree to go? I doubt it. There's no doubt she's shutting out the world, though. She barely acknowledges anyone.

I think I'll follow her to her hidey-hole tonight. We ought to know where it is, in case she gets seriously ill. Besides, maybe there's a clue to who she is secreted there.

Gracie

The pigeons've deserted me, guess they know I'm not really with them anymore. I'm mostly back there in the smoky neon past and the memories're really pulling hard now. The unsuspecting look on my little boy's face and the regret in my heart when I tucked him in, knowing it was the last time. The rage on his father's face when I said I was leaving. The lean times that weren't really so lean because I sure wasn't living like I am today. The high times that didn't last. The painful times when I realized they weren't going to keep their promises.

It'll be all right. We'll arrange everything.

But it wasn't all right and nothing got arranged. It'll never be all right again.

Cecily

Gracie's hidey-hole is an abandoned trash Dumpster behind a condemned building on 18th Street. I had quite a time finding it. The woman acts like a criminal who's afraid she's being tailed, and it took three nights of ducking into doorways and hiding behind parked cars to follow her there. I watched through a hole in the fence while she unloaded the plastic bags from her cart to the Dumpster, then climbed in after them. The clang when she pulled the lid down was deafening, and I can imagine how noisy it is in there when it rains, like it's starting to right now. Anyway, Gracie's home for the night.

Tomorrow morning after she leaves I'm going to investigate that Dumpster.

Gracie

Rain thundering down hard, loud and echoing like applause. It's the only applause old Gracie's likely to hear anymore.

Old Gracie, that's how I think of myself. And I'm only thirty-nine, barely middle-aged. But I crammed a lot into those last seventeen years, and life catches up with some of us faster than others. I don't know as I'd have the nerve to look in a mirror anymore. What I'd see might scare me.

That red-haired woman was following me for a couple of nights—after my gold, for sure—but today I didn't see her. How she knows about the gold, I don't know. I never told anybody, but that must be it, it's all I've got of value. I'm gonna have to watch out for her, but keeping on guard is one hell of a job when you're feeling like I do.

It must be the rain. If only this rain'd stop, I'd feel better.

Cecily

Checking out that Dumpster was about the most disgusting piece of work I've done in years. It smelled horrible, and the stench is still with me—in my hair and on my clothing. The bottom half is covered with construction debris like two-by-fours and Sheetrock, and on top of it Gracie's made a nest of unbelievably filthy bedding. At first I thought there wasn't anything of hers there and, frankly, I wasn't too enthusiastic about searching thoroughly. But then, in a space between some planking beneath the wad of bedding, I found a cardboard gift box—heart-shaped and printed with roses that had faded almost to white. Inside it were some pictures of a little boy.

He was a chubby little blond, all dressed up to have his photo taken, and on the back of each somebody had written his name—Michael Joseph—and the date. In one he wore a party hat and had his hand stuck in a birthday cake, and on its back was the date—March 8, 1975—and his age—two years.

Gracie's little boy? Probably. Why else would she have saved his pictures and the lock of hair in the blue envelope that was the only other thing in the box?

So now I have a lead. A woman named Gracie (if that's her real name) had a son named Michael Joseph on March 8, 1973, perhaps in Oroville. Is that enough information to justify a trip up to Butte County to check the birth records? A trip in my car, which by all rights shouldn't make it to the San Francisco County line?

Well, why not? I collected yet another rejection letter yesterday. I need to get away from here.

Gracie

I could tell right away when I got back tonight—somebody's been in my hidey-hole. Nothing looked different, but I could smell whoever it was, the way one animal can smell another.

I guess that's what it all boils down to in the end: We're not much different from the animals.

I'll stay here tonight because it's raining again and I'm weary from the walk and unloading my cart. But tomorrow I'm out of here. Can't stay where it isn't safe. Can't sleep in a place somebody's defiled.

Well, they didn't find anything. Everything I own was in my cart. Everything except the box with the pictures of Mikey. They disappeared a few years ago, right about the time I moved in here. Must've fallen out of the cart, or else somebody took them. Doesn't matter, though; I remember him as clear as if I'd tucked him in for the last time only yesterday. Remember his father, too, cursing me as I went out the door, telling me I'd never see my son again.

I never did.

I remember all the promises, too; my lawyer and my manager were going to work it all out so I could have Mikey with me. But his father made it difficult and then things went downhill and then there was the drug bust and all the publicity—

Why am I letting the past suck me in? All those years I had such good control. No more drink, no more drugs, just pure, strong control. A dozen years on the street, first down south, then up here, and I always kept my mind on the present and its tiny details. My pigeons, the people passing by, the cracks in the sidewalk . . .

It's like I've tumbled into one of those cracks. I'm falling and I don't know what'll happen next.

Cecily

Here I am in Oroville, in a cheap motel not far from the Butte County Courthouse. By all rights I shouldn't have made it this far. The car tried to die three times—once while I was trying to navigate the freeway maze at Sacramento—but I arrived before the vital statistics department closed. And now I know who Gracie is!

Michael Joseph Venema was born on March 8, 1973, to Michael William and Grace Ann Venema in Butte Hospital. The father was thirty-five at the time, the mother only sixteen. Venema's not a common name here; the current directory lists only one—initial M—on Lark Lane. I've already located it on the map, and I'm going there tomorrow morning. It's a Saturday, so somebody's bound to be at home. I'll just show up and maybe the element of surprise will help me pry loose the story of my neighborhood bag lady.

God, I'm good at this! Maybe I should scrap my literary ambitions and become an investigative reporter.

Gracie

I miss my Dumpster. Was noisy when it rained, that's true, but at least it was dry. The only shelter I could find tonight was this doorway behind Gino's, and I had to wait for them to close up before I crawled into it, so I got plenty wet. My blankets're soaked, but the plastic has to go over my cart to protect my things. How much longer till morning?

Well, how would I know? Haven't had a watch for years. I pawned it early on. That was when I was still sleeping in hotel rooms, thinking things would turn around for me. Then I was sleeping in my car and had to sell everything else, one by one. And then it was a really cheap hotel, and I turned some tricks to keep the money coming, but when a pimp tried to move in on me, I knew it was time to get my act together and leave town. So I came here and made do. In all the years I've lived on the street in different parts of this city, I've never turned another trick and I've never panhandled. For a while before I started feeling so bad I picked up little jobs, working just for food. But lately I've had to rely on other people's kindnesses.

It hurts to be so dependent.

There's another gust of wind, blowing the rain at me. It's raining like a son of a bitch tonight. It better let up in the morning.

I miss my Dumpster. I miss . . .

No. I've still got *some* control left. Not much, but a shred.

Cecily

Now I know Gracie's story, and I'm so distracted that I got on the wrong freeway coming back through Sacramento. There's a possibility I may be able to reunite her with her son Mike—plus I've got my novel, all of it, and it's going to be terrific! I wouldn't be surprised if it changed my life.

I went to Mike's house this morning—a little prefab on a couple of acres in the country south of town. He was there, as were his wife and baby son. At first he didn't believe his mother was alive, then he didn't want to talk about her. But when I told him Gracie's circumstances he opened up and agreed to tell me what he knew. And he knew practically everything, because his father finally told him the truth when he was dying last year.

Gracie was a singer. One of those bluesy-pop kind like Linda Ronstadt, whom you can't categorize as either country or Top 40. She got her start singing at their church and received some encouragement from a friend's uncle who was a sound engineer at an L.A. recording studio. At sixteen she'd married Mike's father—who was nearly twenty years her senior—and they'd never been very happy. So on the strength of that slim encouragement, she left him and their son and went to L.A. to try to break into the business.

And she did, under the name Grace Ventura. The interesting thing is, I remember her first hit, "Smoky Neon Haze," very clearly. It was romantic and tragic, and I was just at the age when tragedy is an appealing concept rather than a harsh reality.

Anyway, Mike's father was very bitter about Gracie deserting them— the way my husband was when I told him I was leaving to become a writer. After Gracie's first album did well and her second earned her a gold record, she decided she wanted custody of Mike, but there was no way his father would give him up. Her lawyer initiated a custody suit, but while that was going on Gracie's third album flopped. Gracie started drinking and doing drugs and couldn't come up with the material for a fourth album; then she was busted for possession of cocaine, and Mike's father used that against her to gain permanent custody. And then the record company dropped her. She tried for a couple of years to make a comeback, then finally disappeared. She had no money; she'd signed a contract that gave most of her earnings to the record label, and what they didn't take, her manager and lawyer did. No wonder she ended up on the streets.

I'm not sure how Mike feels about being reunited with his mother; he was very noncommittal. He has his own life now, and his printing business is just getting off the ground. But he did say he'd try to help her, and that's the message I'm to deliver to Gracie when I get back to the city.

I hope it works out. For Gracie's sake, of course, and also because it would make a perfect upbeat ending to my novel.

Gracie

It's dry and warm here in the storage room. Deirdre found me crouched behind the garbage cans in the alley a while ago and brought me inside. Gave me some blankets she borrowed from one of the folks upstairs. They're the first clean things I've had next to my skin in years.

Tomorrow she wants to take me to the free clinic. I won't go, but I'm grateful for the offer.

Warm and dry and dark in here. I keep drifting—out of the present, into the past, back and forth. No control now. In spite of the dark I can see the lights—bright colors, made hazy by the smoke. Just like in that first song . . . what was it called? Don't remember. Doesn't matter.

It was a good one, though. Top of the charts. Didn't even surprise me. I always thought I was one of the lucky ones.

I can see the faces, too. Seems like acres of them, looking up at me while I'm blinded by the lights. Listen to the applause! For me. And that didn't surprise me, either. I always knew it would happen. But where was that? When?

Can't remember. Doesn't matter.

Was only one face that ever mattered. Little boy. Who was he?

Michael Joseph. Mikey.

Funny, for years I've fought the memories. Pushed them away when they tugged, kept my mind on the here and now. Then I fell into the crack in the sidewalk, and it damn near swallowed me up. Now the memories're fading, except for one. Michael Joseph. Mikey.

That's a good one. I'll hold on to it.

Cecily

Gracie died last night in the storeroom at the Lucky Shamrock. Deirdre brought her in there to keep her out of the rain, and when she looked in on her after closing, she was dead. The coroner's people said it was pneumonia; she'd probably been walking around with it for a long time, and the soaking finished her.

I cried when Deirdre told me. I haven't cried in years, and there I was, sobbing over a woman whose full name I didn't even know until two days ago.

I wonder why she wasn't in her hidey-hole. Was it because she realized I violated it and didn't feel safe anymore? God, I hope not! But how could she have known?

I wish I could've told her about her son, that he said he'd help her. But maybe it's for the best, after all. Gracie might have wanted more than Mike was willing to give her—emotionally, I mean. Besides, she must've been quite unbalanced toward the end.

I guess it's for the best, but I still wish I could've told her.

This morning Deirdre and I decided we'd better go through the stuff in her cart, in case there was anything salvageable that Mike might want. Some of the plastic bags were filled with ragged clothing, others with faded and crumbling clippings that chronicled the brief career of Grace Ventura. There was a Bible, some spangled stage costumes, a few paperbacks, a bundle of letters about the custody suit, a set of keys to a Mercedes, and other mementos that were in such bad shape we couldn't tell what they'd been. But at the very bottom of the cart, wrapped in rags and more plastic bags, was the gold record awarded to her for her second album, "Soft Summer Nights."

On one hand, not much to say for a life that once held such promise. On the other hand, it says it all.

It gives me pause. Makes me wonder about my own life. Is all of this worth it? I really don't know. But I'm not giving up—not now, when I've got Gracie's story to tell. I wouldn't be the least bit surprised if it changed my life.

After all, aren't I one of the lucky ones?

Aren't I?

Dust to Dust

1982

T he dust was particularly bad on Monday, July sixth. It rose from the
second floor where the demolition was going on and hung in the
dry air of the photo lab. The trouble was, it didn't stay suspended. It settled on the Formica countertops, in the stainless steel sink, on the plastic
I'd covered the enlarger with. And worst of all, it settled on the negatives
drying in the supposedly airtight cabinet.

The second time I checked the negatives I gave up. They'd have to be
soaked for hours to get the dust out of the emulsion. And when I rehung
them they'd only be coated with the stuff again.

I turned off the orange safelight and went into the studio. A thick film
of powder covered everything there, too. I'd had the foresight to put my
cameras away, but somehow the dust crept into the cupboard, through the
leather cases and onto the lenses themselves. The restoration project was
turning into a nightmare, and it had barely begun.

I crossed the studio to the Victorian's big front windows. The city of
Phoenix sprawled before me, skyscrapers shimmering in the heat. Camel-
back Mountain rose out of the flat land to the right, and the oasis of
Encanto Park beckoned at the left. I could drive over there and sit under

a tree by the water. I could rent a paddlewheel boat. Anything to escape the dry grit-laden heat.

But I had to work on the photos for the book.

And I couldn't work on them because I couldn't get the negatives to come out clear.

I leaned my forehead against the window frame, biting back my frustration.

"Jane!" My name echoed faintly from below. "Jane! Come down here!"

It was Roy, the workman I'd hired to demolish the rabbit warren of cubicles that had been constructed when the Victorian was turned into a rooming house in the thirties. The last time he'd shouted for me like that was because he'd discovered a stained-glass window preserved intact between two false walls. My spirits lifting, I hurried down the winding stairs.

The second floor was a wasteland heaped with debris. Walls leaned at crazy angles. Piles of smashed plaster blocked the hall. Rough beams and lath were exposed. The air was even worse down there—full of powder that caught in my nostrils and covered my clothing whenever I brushed against anything.

I called back to Roy, but his answering shout came from further below, in the front hall.

I descended the stairs into the gloom, keeping to the wall side because the banister was missing. Roy stood, crowbar in hand, at the rear of the stairway. He was a tall, thin man with a pockmarked face and curly black hair, a drifter who had wandered into town willing to work cheap so long as no questions were asked about his past. Roy, along with his mongrel dog, now lived in his truck in my driveway. In spite of his odd appearance and stealthy comings and goings, I felt safer having him around while living in a half-demolished house.

Now he pushed up the goggles he wore to keep the plaster out of his eyes and waved the crowbar toward the stairs.

"Jane, I've really found something this time." His voice trembled. Roy had a genuine enthusiasm for old houses, and this house in particular.

I hurried down the hall and looked under the stairs. The plaster-and-lath had been partially ripped off and tossed onto the floor. Behind it, I could see only darkness. The odor of dry rot wafted out of the opening.

Dammit, now there was debris in the downstairs hall too. "I thought I told you to finish the second floor before you started here."

"But take a look."

"I am. I see a mess."

"No, here. Take the flashlight. Look."

I took it and shone it through the hole. It illuminated gold-patterned wallpaper and wood paneling. My irritation vanished. "What is it, do you suppose?"

"I think it's what they call a 'cozy.' A place where they hung coats and ladies left their outside boots when they came calling." He shouldered past me. "Let's get a better look."

I backed off and watched as he tugged at the wall with the crowbar, the muscles in his back and arms straining. In minutes, he had ripped a larger section off. It crashed to the floor and when the dust cleared I shone the light once more.

It was a paneled nook with a bench and ornate brass hooks on the wall. "I think you're right—it's a cozy."

Roy attacked the wall once more and soon the opening was clear. He stepped inside, the leg of his jeans catching on a nail. "It's big enough for three people." His voice echoed in the empty space.

"Why do you think they sealed it up?" I asked.

"Fire regulations, when they converted to a rooming house. They—what's this?"

I leaned forward.

Roy turned, his hand outstretched I looked at the object resting on his palm and recoiled.

"God!"

"Take it easy." He stepped out of the cozy. "It's only a dead bird."

It was small, probably a sparrow, and like the stained-glass window Roy had found last week, perfectly preserved.

"Ugh!" I said. "How did it get in there?"

Roy stared at the small body in fascination. "It's probably been there since the wall was constructed. Died of hunger, or lack of air."

I shivered. "But it's not rotted."

"In this dry climate? It's like mummification. You could preserve a body for decades."

"Put it down. It's probably diseased."

He shrugged. "I doubt it." But he stepped back into the cozy and placed it on the bench. Then he motioned for the flashlight. "The wallpaper's in good shape. And the wood looks like golden oak. And . . . hello."

"Now what?"

He bent over and picked something up. "It's a comb, a mother-of-pearl comb like ladies wore in their hair." He held it out. The comb had long teeth to sweep up heavy tresses on a woman's head.

"This place never ceases to amaze me." I took it and brushed off the plaster dust. Plaster . . . "Roy, this wall couldn't have been put up in the thirties."

"Well, the building permit shows the house was converted then."

"But the rest of the false walls are fireproof Sheetrock, like regulations required. This one is plaster-and-lath. This cozy has been sealed off longer than that. Maybe since ladies wore this kind of comb."

"Maybe." His eyes lit up. "We've found an eighty-year-old bird mummy."

"I guess so." The comb fascinated me, as the bird had Roy. I stared at it.

"You should get shots of this for your book," Roy said.

"What?"

"Your book."

I shook my head, disoriented. Of course—the book. It was defraying the cost of the renovation, a photo essay on restoring one of Phoenix's grand old ladies.

"You haven't forgotten the book?" Roy's tone was mocking.

I shook my head again. "Roy, why did you break down this wall? When I told you to finish upstairs first?"

"Look, if you're pissed off about the mess—"

"No, I'm curious. Why?"

Now he looked confused. "I . . ."

"Yes?"

"I don't know."

"Don't know?"

He frowned, his pockmarked face twisting in concentration. "I really *don't* know. I had gone to the kitchen for a beer and I came through here and . . . I don't know."

I watched him thoughtfully, clutching the mother-of-pearl comb. "Okay," I finally said, "just don't start on a new area again without checking with me."

"Sorry. I'll clean up this mess."

"Not yet. Let me get some photos first." Still holding the comb, I went up to the studio to get a camera.

In the week that followed, Roy attacked the second floor with a vengeance and it began to take on its original floor plan. He made other discoveries—nothing as spectacular as the cozy, but interesting—old newspapers, coffee cans of a brand not sold in decades, a dirty pair of baby booties. I photographed each faithfully and assured my publisher that the work was going well.

It wasn't, though. As Roy worked, the dust increased and my frustration with the book project—not to mention the commercial jobs that were my bread and butter—deepened. The house, fortunately, was paid for, purchased with a bequest from my aunt, the only member of my family who didn't think it dreadful for a girl from Fairmont, West Virginia, to run off and become a photographer in a big western city. The money from the book, however, was what would make the house habitable, and the first part of the advance had already been eaten up. The only way I was going to squeeze more cash out of the publisher was to show him some progress, and so far I had made none of that.

Friday morning I told Roy to take the day off. Maybe I could get some work done if he wasn't raising clouds of dust. I spent the morning in the lab developing the rolls I'd shot that week, then went into the studio and looked over what prints I had ready to show to the publisher.

The exterior shots, taken before the demolition had begun, were fine. They showed a three-story structure with square bay windows and rough peeling paint. The fanlight over the front door had been broken and replaced with plywood, and much of the gingerbread trim was missing. All in all, she was a bedraggled old lady, but she would again be beautiful— if I could finish the damned book.

The early interior shots were not bad either. In fact, they evoked a nice sense of gloomy neglect. And the renovation of this floor, the attic, into studio and lab was well documented. It was with the second floor that my problems began.

At first the dust had been slight, and I hadn't noticed it on the negatives. As a result the prints were marred with white specks. In a couple of cases the dust had scratched the negatives while I'd handled them and the fine lines showed up in the pictures. Touching them up would be painstaking work but it could be done.

But now the dust had become more active, taken over. I was forced to soak and resoak the negatives. A few rolls of film had proven unsalvageable after repeated soakings. And, in losing them, I was losing documentation of a very important part of the renovation.

I went to the window and looked down at the driveway where Roy was sunning himself on the grass beside his truck. The mongrel dog lay next to a tire in the shade of the vehicle. Roy reached under there for one of his everpresent beers, swigged at it and set it back down.

How, I wondered, did he stand the heat? He took to it like a native, seemingly oblivious to the sun's glare. But then, maybe Roy *was* a native of the Sun Belt. What did I know of him, really?

Only that he was a tireless worker and his knowledge of old houses was invaluable to me. He unerringly sensed which were the original walls and which were false, what should be torn down and what should remain. He could tell whether a fixture was the real thing or merely a good copy. I could not have managed without him.

I shrugged off thoughts of my handyman and lifted my hair from my shoulders. It was wheat-colored, heavy, and, right now, uncomfortable. I pulled it on top of my head, looked around, and spotted the mother-of-pearl comb we'd found in the cozy. It was small, designed to be worn as half of a pair on one side of the head. I secured the hair on my left with it, then pinned up the right side with one of the clips I used to hang negatives. Then I went into the darkroom.

The negatives were dry. I took one strip out of the cabinet and held it to the light. It seemed relatively clear. Perhaps, as long as the house wasn't disturbed the dust ceased its silent takeover. I removed the other strips. Dammit, some were still spotty, especially those of the cozy and the objects we'd discovered in it. Those could be reshot, however. I decided to go ahead and make contact prints of the lot.

I cut the negatives into strips of six frames each, then inserted them in plastic holders. Shutting the door and turning on the safelight, I removed photographic paper from the small refrigerator, placed it and the negative holders under the glass in the enlarger, and set my timer. Nine seconds at f/8 would do nicely.

When the first sheet of paper was exposed, I slipped it into the developer tray and watched, fascinated as I had been the first time I'd done this, for the images to emerge. Yes, nine seconds had been right. I went to the enlarger and exposed the other negatives.

I moved the contact sheets along, developer to stop bath to fixer, then put them into the washing tray. Now I could open the door to the darkroom and let some air in. Even though Roy had insulated up here, it was still hot and close when I was working in the lab. I pinned my hair more securely on my head and took the contact sheets to the print dryer.

I scanned the sheets eagerly as they came off the roller. Most of the negatives had printed clearly and some of the shots were quite good. I should be able to assemble a decent selection for my editor with very little trouble. Relieved, I reached for the final sheet.

There were the pictures I had shot the day we'd discovered the cozy. They were different from the others. And different from the past dust-damaged rolls. I picked up my magnifying loupe and took the sheet out into the light.

Somehow the dust had gotten to this set of negatives. Rather than leaving speckles, though, it had drifted like a sandstorm. It clustered in iridescent patches, as if an object had caught the light in a strange way. The effect was eerie; perhaps I could put it to use. I circled the oddest-looking frames and went back into the darkroom, shutting the door securely. I selected the negative that corresponded to one circled on the sheet, routinely sprayed it with canned air for surface dirt and inserted it into the holder of the enlarger. Adjusting the height, I shone the light through the negative, positioning the image within the paper guides. Yes, I had something extremely odd here. Quickly I snapped off the light, set the timer and slipped a piece of unexposed paper into the guides. The light came on again, the timer whirred and then all was silent and dark. I slid the paper into the developer tray and waited.

The image was of the cozy with the bird mummy resting on the bench. That would have been good enough, but the effect of the dust made it spectacular. Above the dead bird rose a white-gray shape, a second bird in flight, spiraling upward.

Like a ghost. The ghost of a trapped bird, finally freed.

I shivered.

Could I use something like this in the book? It was perfect. But what if my editor asked how I'd done it? Photography was not only art but science. You strove for images that evoked certain emotions. But you had damn well better know how you got those images.

Don't worry about that now, I told myself. See what else is here.

I replaced the bird negative with another one and exposed it. The image emerged slowly in the developing tray: first the carved arch of the cozy, then the plaster-and-lath heaped on the floor, finally the shimmering figure of a man.

I leaned over the tray. Roy? A double exposure perhaps? It looked like Roy, yet it didn't. And I hadn't taken any pictures of him anyway. No, this was another effect created by the dust, a mere outline of a tall man in what appeared to be an old-fashioned frock coat.

The ghost of a man? That was silly. I didn't believe in such things. Not in *my* house.

Still, the photos had a wonderful eeriness. I could include them in the book, as a novelty chapter. I could write a little explanation about the dust.

And while on the subject of dust, wasn't it rising again? Had Roy begun work, even though I'd told him not to?

I crossed the studio to the window and looked down. No, he was still there by the truck, although he was now dappled by the shade of the nearby tree. The sun had moved; it was getting on toward midafternoon.

Back in the darkroom I continued to print from the dust-damaged group of negatives. Maybe I was becoming fanciful, or maybe the chemicals were getting to me after being cooped up in here all day, but I was seeing stranger and stranger images. One looked like a woman in a long, full-skirted dress, standing in the entrance to the cozy. In another the man was reaching out—maybe trying to catch the bird that had invaded his home?

Was it his home? Who were these people? What were they doing in my negatives?

As I worked the heat increased. I became aware of the dust which, with or without Roy's help, had again taken up its stealthy activity. It had a life all its own, as demonstrated by these photos. I began to worry that it would damage the prints before I could put them on the dryer and went into the studio.

Dust lay on every surface again. What had caused it to rise? I went to the window and looked down. Roy was sitting on the bed of the truck with the mongrel, drinking another beer. Well, if he hadn't done anything, I was truly stumped. Was I going to be plagued by dust throughout the restoration, whether work was going on or not?

I began to pace the studio, repinning my hair and securing the mother-of-pearl comb as I went. The eerie images had me more disturbed than I was willing to admit. And this dust . . . dammit, this *dust!*

Anger flaring, I headed down the stairs. I'd get to the bottom of this. There had to be a perfectly natural cause, and if I had to turn the house upside down I'd find it.

The air on the second floor was choking, but the dust seemed to rise from the first. I charged down the next flight of stairs, unheedful for the first time since I'd lived here of the missing banister. The dust seemed thickest by the cozy. Maybe opening the wall had created a draft. I hurried back there.

A current of air, cooler than that in the hall, emanated from the cozy. I stepped inside and felt around with my hand. It came from a crack in the bench. A crack? I knelt to examine it. No, it wasn't a crack. It looked like the seat of the bench was designed to be lifted. Of course it was— there were hidden hinges which we'd missed when we'd first discovered it.

I grasped the edge of the bench and pulled. It was stuck. I tugged harder. Still it didn't give. Feeling along the seat I found the nails that held it shut.

This called for Roy's strength. I went to the front door and called him. "Bring your crowbar. We're about to make another discovery."

He stood up in the bed of the truck and rummaged through his tools, then came toward me, crowbar in hand. "What now?"

"The cozy. That bench in there has a seat that raises. Some sort of woodbox, maybe."

Roy stopped inside the front door. "Now that you mention it, I think you're right. It's not a woodbox, though. In the old days, ladies would change into house shoes from outdoor shoes when they came calling. The bench was to store them in."

"Well, it's going to be my woodbox. And I think it's what's making the dust move around so much. There's a draft coming from it." I led him back to the cozy. "How come you know so much about old houses anyway?"

He shrugged. "When you've torn up as many as I have, you learn fast. I've always had an affinity for the Victorians. What do you want me to do here?"

"It's nailed shut. Pry it open."

"I might wreck the wood."

"Pry gently."

"I'll try."

I stepped back and let him at the bench. He worked carefully, loosening each nail with the point of the bar. It seemed to take a long time. Finally he turned.

"There. All the nails are out."

"Then open it."

"No, it's your discovery. You do it." He stepped back.

The draft was stronger now. I went up to the bench, then hesitated.

"Go on," Roy said. His voice shook with excitement.

My palms were sweaty. Grit stuck to them. I reached out and lifted the seat.

My sight was blurred by a duststorm like those on the negatives. Then it cleared. I leaned forward. Recoiled. A scream rose in my throat, but it came out as a croak.

It was the lady of my photographs.

She lay on her back inside the bench. She wore a long, full-skirted dress of some beaded material. Her hands were crossed on her breasts. Like the bird mummy, she was perfectly preserved—even to the heavy wheat-colored hair, with the mother-of-pearl comb holding it up on the left side.

I put my hand to *my* wheat-colored hair. To my mother-of-pearl comb. Then, shaken, I turned to Roy.

He had raised the arm that held the crowbar—just like the man had had his hand raised in the last print, the one I'd forgotten to remove from the dryer. Roy's work shirt billowed out, resembling an old-fashioned frock coat. The look in his eyes was eerie.

And the dust was rising again . . .

Cattails

1982

We came around the lake, Frances and I, heading toward the picnic ground. I was lugging the basket and when the going got rough, like where the path narrowed to a ledge of rock, I would set it down a minute before braving the uneven ground.

All the while I was seeing us as if we were in a movie—something I do more and more the older I get.

They come around the lake, an old couple of seventy, on a picnic. The woman strides ahead, still slender and active, her red scarf fluttering in the breeze. He follows, carrying the wicker basket, a stooped gray-headed man who moves hesitantly, as if he is a little afraid.

Drama, I thought. We're more and more prone to it as the real thing fades from our lives. We make ourselves stars in scenarios that are at best boring. Ah, well, it's a way to keep going. I have my little dramas; Frances has her spiritualism and séances. And, thinking of keeping going, I must or Frances will tell me I'm good for nothing, not even carrying the basket to the picnic ground.

Frances had already arrived there by the time I reached the meadow. I set the basket down once more and mopped my damp brow. She motioned impatiently to me and, with a muttered "Yes, dear," I went on. It was the same place we always came for our annual outing. The same sunlight glinted coldly on the water; the same chill wind blew up from the shore; the same dampness saturated the ground.

January. A hell of a time for a picnic, even here in the hills of Northern California. I knew why she insisted on it. Who would know better than I? And yet I wondered—was there more to it than that? Was the fool woman trying to kill me with these damned outings?

She spread the plaid blanket on the ground in front of the log we always used as a backrest. I lowered myself onto it, groaning. Yes, the ground was damp as ever. Soon it would seep through the blanket and into my clothes. Frances unpacked the big wicker basket, portioning out food like she did at home. It was a nice basket, with real plates and silverware, all held in their own little niches. Frances had even packed cloth napkins—leave it to her not to forget. The basket was the kind you saw advertised nowadays in catalogs for rich people to buy, but it hadn't cost us very much. I'd made the niches myself and outfitted it with what was left of our first set of dishes and flatware. That was back in the days when I liked doing handy projects, before . . .

"Charles, you're not eating." Frances thrust my plate into my hands.

Ham sandwich. On rye. With mustard. Pickle, garlic dill. Potato salad, Frances's special recipe. The same as always.

"Don't you think next year we could have something different?"

Frances looked at me with an expression close to hatred. "You know we can't."

"Guess not." I bit into the sandwich.

Frances opened a beer for me. Bud. I'm not supposed to drink, not since the last seizure, and I've been good, damned good. But on these yearly picnics it's different. It's got to be.

Frances poured herself some wine. We ate in silence, staring at the cattails along the shore of the lake.

When we finished what was on our plates, Frances opened another beer for me and took out the birthday cake. It was chocolate with darker chocolate icing. I knew that without looking.

"He would have been twenty-nine," she said.

"Yes."

"Twenty-nine. A man."

"Yes," I said again, with mental reservations.

"Poor Richie. He was such a beautiful baby."

I was silent, watching the cattails.

"Do you remember, Charles? What a beautiful baby he was?"

"Yes."

That had been in Detroit. Back when the auto industry was going great guns and jobs on the assembly line were a dime a dozen. We'd had a redbrick house in a suburb called Royal Oak. And a green Ford—that's where I'd worked, Ford's, the River Rouge plant—and a yard with big maple trees. And, unexpectedly, we'd had Richie.

"He was such a good baby, too. He never cried."

"No, he didn't."

Richie never cried. He'd been unusually silent, watching us. And I'd started to drink more. I'd come home and see them, mother and the change-of-life baby she'd never wanted, beneath the big maple trees. And I'd go to the kitchen for a beer.

I lost the job at Ford's. Our furniture was sold. The house went on the market. And then we headed west in the green car. To Chicago.

Now Frances handed me another beer.

"I shouldn't." I wasn't used to drinking anymore and I already felt drunk.

"Drink it."

I shrugged and tilted the can.

Chicago had been miserable. There we'd lived in a railroad flat in an old dark brick building. It was always cold in the flat, and in the Polish butcher shop where I clerked. Frances started talking about going to work, but I wouldn't let her. Richie needed her. Needed watching.

The beer was making me feel sleepy.

In Chicago, the snow had drifted and covered the front stoop. I would come home in the dark, carrying meat that the butcher shop was going to throw out—chicken backs and nearly spoiled pork and sometimes a soup bone. I'd take them to the kitchen, passing through the front room where

Richie's playpen was, and set them on the drainboard. And then I'd go to the pantry for a shot or two of something to warm me. It was winter when the green Ford died. It was winter when I lost the job at the butcher shop. A snowstorm was howling in off Lake Michigan when we got on the Greyhound for Texas. I'd heard of work in Midland.

Beside me, Frances leaned back against the log. I set my empty beer can down and lay on my side.

"That's right, Charles, go to sleep." Her voice shook with controlled anger, as always.

I closed my eyes, traveling back to Texas.

Roughnecking the oil rigs hadn't been easy. It was hard work, dirty work, and for a newcomer, the midnight shift was the only one available. But times hadn't been any better for Frances and Richie. In the winter, the northers blew through every crack in the little box of a house we'd rented. And summer's heat turned the place into an oven. Frances never complained. Richie did, but then, Richie complained about everything.

Summer nights in Midland were the only good times. We'd sit outside, sometimes alone, sometimes with neighbors, drinking beer and talking. Once in a while we'd go to a roadhouse, if we could find someone to take care of Richie. That wasn't often, though. It was hard to find someone to stay with such a difficult child. And then I fell off the oil rig and broke my leg. When it healed, we boarded another bus, this time for New Mexico.

I jerked suddenly. Must have dozed off. Frances sat beside me, clutching some cattails she'd picked from the edge of the lake while I slept. She set them down and took out the blue candles and started sticking them on the birthday cake.

"Do you remember that birthday of Richie's in New Mexico?" She began lighting the candles, all twenty-nine of them.

"Yes."

"We gave him that red plastic music box? Like an organ grinder's? With the fuzzy monkey on top that went up and down when you turned the handle?"

"Yes." I looked away from the candles to the cattails and the lake beyond. The monkey had gone up and down when you turned the handle—until Richie had stomped on the toy and smashed it to bits.

In Roswell we'd had a small stucco house, nicer than the one in Midland. Our garden had been westernized—that's what they call pebbles instead of grass, cacti instead of shrubs. Not that I spent a lot of time there. I worked long hours in the clothing mill.

Frances picked up the cattails and began pulling them apart, scattering their fuzzy insides. The breeze blew most of the fluff away across the meadow, but some stuck to the icing on the cake.

"He loved that monkey, didn't he?"

"Yes," I lied.

"And the tune the music box played—what was it?"

" 'Pop Goes the Weasel.' " But she knew that.

"Of course. 'Pop Goes the Weasel.' " The fuzz continued to drift through her fingers. The wind from the lake blew some of it against my nose. It tickled.

"Roswell was where I met Linda," Frances added. "Do you remember her?"

"There's nothing wrong with my memory."

"She foretold it all."

"Some of it."

"All."

I let her have the last word. Frances was a stubborn woman.

Linda. Roswell was where Frances had gotten interested in spiritualism, foretelling the future, that sort of stuff. I hadn't liked it, but, hell, it gave Frances something to do. And there was little enough to do, stuck out there in the desert. I had to hand it to Linda—she foretold my losing the job at the clothing mill. And our next move, to Los Angeles.

Frances was almost done with the cattails. Soon she'd ask me to get her some more.

Los Angeles. A haze always hanging over the city. Tall palms that were nothing but poles with sickly wisps of leaves at the top. And for me, job after job, each worse, until I was clerking at the Orange Julius for minimum wage. For Frances and Richie it wasn't so bad, though. We lived in Santa Monica, near the beach. Nothing fancy, but she could take him there and he'd play in the surf. It kept him out of trouble—he'd taken to stealing candy and little objects from the stores. When they went to the beach on weekends I stayed home and drank.

"I need some more cattails, Charles."

"Soon."

Was the Orange Julius the last job in L.A.? Funny how they all blended together. But it had to be—I was fired from there after Richie lifted twenty dollars from the cash register while visiting me. By then we'd scraped together enough money from Frances's babysitting wages to buy an old car—a white Nash Rambler. It took us all the way to San Francisco and these East Bay hills where we were sitting today.

"Charles, the cattails."

"Soon."

The wind was blowing off the lake. The cattails at the shore moved, beckoning me. The cake was covered with white fuzz. The candles guttered, dripping blue wax.

"Linda," Frances said. "Do you remember when she came to stay with us in Oakland?"

"Yes."

"We had the séance."

"Yes."

I didn't believe in the damned things, but I'd gone along with it. Linda had set up chairs around the dining room table in our little shingled house. The room had been too small for the number of people there and Linda had made cutting remarks. That hurt. It was all we could afford. I was on disability then because of the accident at the chemical plant. I'd been worrying about Richie's adjustment problems in school and my inattention on the job had caused an explosion.

"That was my first experience with those who have gone beyond," Frances said now.

"Yes."

"You didn't like it."

"No, I didn't."

There had been rapping noises. And chill drafts. A dish had fallen off a shelf. Linda said afterward it had been a young spirit we had contacted. She claimed young spirits were easier to raise.

I still didn't believe in any of it. Not a damned bit!

"Charles, the cattails."

I stood up.

Linda had promised to return to Oakland the next summer. We would all conduct more "fun" experiments. By the time she did, Frances was an expert in those experiments. She'd gone to every charlatan in town after that day in January, here at the lake. She'd gone because on that unseasonably warm day, during his birthday picnic at this very meadow, Richie had drowned while fetching cattails from the shore. Died by drowning, just as Linda had prophesied in New Mexico. Some said it had been my fault because I'd been drunk and had fallen asleep and failed to watch him. Frances seemed to think so. But Frances had been wandering around in the woods or somewhere and hadn't watched him either.

I started down toward the lake. The wind had come up and the over-ripe cattails were breaking open, their white fuzz trailing like fog.

Funny. They had never done that before.

I looked back at Frances. She motioned impatiently.

I continued down to the lakeside.

Frances had gone to the mediums for years, hoping to make contact with Richie's spirit. When that hadn't worked, she went less and spiritualism became merely a hobby for her. But one thing she still insisted on was coming here every year to reenact the fatal picnic. Even though it was usually cold in January, even though others would have stayed away from the place where their child had died, she came and went through the ritual. Why? Anger at me, I supposed. Anger because I'd been drunk and asleep that day.

The cattail fuzz was thicker now. I stopped. The lake was obscured by it. Turning, I realized I could barely see Frances.

Shapes seemed to be forming in the mist.

The shape of Richie. A bad child.

The shape of Frances. An unhappy mother.

"Daddy, help!"

The cry seemed to come out of the mist at the water's edge. I froze for a moment, then started down there. The mist got thicker. Confused, I stopped. Had I heard something? Or was it only in my head?

Drama, I thought. Drama.

The old man stands enveloped in the swirling mist, shaking his gray head. Gradually his sight returns. He peers around, searching far the shapes. He cocks his head, listening for another cry. There is no sound, but the shapes emerge . . .

A shape picking cattails. And then another, coming through the mist, arm outstretched. Then pushing. Then holding the other shape down. Doing the thing the old man has always suspected but refused to accept.

The mist began to settle. I turned, looked back up the slope. Frances was there, coming at me. Her mouth was set; I hadn't returned with the cattails.

Don't come down here, Frances, I thought. It's dangerous down here now that I've seen those shapes and the mist has cleared. Don't come down.

Frances came on toward me. She was going to bawl me out for not bringing the cattails. I waited.

One of these days, I thought, it might happen. Maybe not this year, maybe not next, but someday it might. Someday I might drown *you*, Frances, just as—maybe—you drowned our poor, unloved son Richie that day so long ago . . .

Cave of Ice

1986 (with Bill Pronzini)

On the hottest day of summer in the year 1901, Will Reese disobeyed his father's orders and returned to the ice cave. He just couldn't stay away any longer. He had thought about little else but the cave for the past week.

The entrance was at the bottom of a deep, rock-strewn depression on his folks' sheep ranch, one of many such pits in this section of the southern Idaho plain. His father had told him they were collapsed lava cones that had been formed by long-ago flows from the extinct volcano nearby. As Will climbed down into the depression, the temperature dropped with amazing swiftness. At the bottom, near the cave opening, the air had a wintry feel. The coldness was what had led him to the cave that day last week, after he had come here on the trail of a stray Hampshire yearling.

Will donned his sheepskin coat, lit the lantern he had brought, and wedged his tall, lank frame through the fissure into the cave's main chamber. When he stood up, the light reflected in dazzling pinpoints from a hundred icy surfaces.

Ice filled the cave, from frozen pools along its floor to huge crystals suspended from its ceiling twenty feet above. A massive glacial wall bulked up directly ahead, a wall that might have been a few feet or many yards thick. Several natural stone steps, sheeted with ice, led up to a narrow ledge nearby. On the ledge's far side was an icefall, a natural slide that dropped fifteen feet into an arched lava tube. At the bottom of the slide was a jumble of gleaming bones, probably those of a large animal that had fallen down the slide and been unable to climb out.

Will could see his breath misting frostily into the lamplight. He could hear water dripping into the cave from underground streams, water that would soon be frozen. He felt the same excitement he had the first time he'd stood here. An ice cave! He hadn't known such things existed. But his father had; Clay Reese had an unquenchable thirst for knowledge, which he tried to slake by reading and rereading mail-order books on many different subjects. He had told Will about the caves, after Will had raced home with news of his find and brought his father back.

There were two kinds of ice caves, one type found in glaciers and the other in volcanic fissures such as this one. Usually the ice in both types melted in warm weather, but this was one of the rare exceptions. No one knew for sure how or why such caves acted as natural icehouses. Perhaps it had something to do with air pressure and wind flow. The phenomenon was very rare, which made Will's discovery all the more special to him.

His father, however, hadn't seemed to understand this. "I don't want you coming back here again," he'd said. "Now don't argue, Son. It's not safe in a cave like this . . . all kinds of things can happen. Stay clear."

Will had tried in vain to get his father to change his mind. Clay Reese was sometimes difficult to talk to, and lately he had been even more reticent than usual, as if something were weighing on his mind. A fiercely proud man, he had once dreamed of attending college, a dream that had ended with the death of his own father when he was Will's age, fifteen. Disappointment and hard work had turned him into a private person. Yet he and Will had always shared a closeness based on fairness and understanding. Until now, he had always listened to Will's side of things. Will just didn't understand the sudden change in him.

Will spent the better part of an hour exploring. Between the ice wall and the near lava wall was a passage that led more than fifty yards deeper under the volcanic rock, before it ended finally in a glacial barrier that completely filled the cave. Small chambers formed by arches and broken-rock walls opened off the passage. The cave was enormous, no telling yet just how large.

But an hour was all he could spare. He would be missed if he stayed much longer, and he had already been reprimanded more than once this week for neglecting his chores. He made his way back to the main chamber and slipped outside, shrugging out of his coat.

The summer heat was intense after the cave's chill; Will was sweating by the time he reached the rim of the pit. He started toward where he had left his roan horse picketed in the shade of a lava overhang. But then he stopped and stood shading his eyes, peering out over the flat, sun-blasted plain.

Billows of dust rose in a long line, hazing the bright blue sky. Wagons, four of them, were coming from the direction of Volcano, the only settlement within twenty miles. They weren't traveling on the road that led out among the sheep ranches in the area; they were coming at an angle through the sagebrush. And they seemed to be heading toward Will.

Frowning, he moved over next to his horse and waited there, hidden, holding the animal's muzzle to keep him still. The wagons clattered ahead without changing course, and finally drew to a halt at the far end of the pit, where it was easiest to scale the rocky wall. Close to a dozen men clambered down and began to unload lumber, a keg of nails, coils of rope, axes, picks, shovels, and other tools.

Stunned, Will saw that one of the men was his father. Clay Reese, in fact, seemed to be directing the activities of the others. Will also recognized Jess Lacy, proprietor of the Volcano Mercantile, and Harmon Bennett, president of the bank. The other men were laborers.

"First thing to do," Will heard his father say, "is clear a path into the pit so we can take the wagons down there. We'll also have to enlarge the cave opening."

"Dynamite, Clay?" one of the men asked.

"No. Picks and shovels should do it. Then we can start building the ramps and cutting the ice into blocks."

Along with Jess Lacy and Harmon Bennett, Clay Reese disappeared inside the cave. The other men began clearing away rocks, grading a pathway for the wagons.

Will had seen enough. He led the roan away quietly, then mounted and rode out across the plain. His shock had given way to a sense of betrayal.

The town could use ice on these scorching summer days, when cellars weren't able to preserve meat and other perishables; Will understood that. But what he didn't understand was why his father had kept secret his decision to sell the ice. The cave belonged to Will more than to anybody, because he had found it. So why hadn't his father told him about what he intended to do?

Will decided to ask him at dinner.

He rode out to the ranch's north boundary fence to make one of three repairs he had been asked to attend to. By the time he finished, it was too late to make the others; the sun was just starting to wester. He rode on home.

The ranch wagon stood in front of the weathered barn when he arrived, but his father's saddle horse was gone. So were two of the family's three sheep dogs. The other dog followed him into the barn, its barks mingling with the bleating of the sheep in the pens that flanked the shearing shed. He unsaddled his roan, fed it some hay, then crossed to the small sod house under the cottonwoods and went inside.

His mother, in spite of it being the hottest day of the year, was stirring a stew pot on the black iron stove. She turned, her eyes stern. "Will, where have you been all day?"

"I . . . Where's Pa?"

"Out east. A ewe and her lamb got through that fence you were supposed to mend and fell into one of the lava pits. Honestly, Will, I don't know what's the matter with you lately. Your father shouldn't have to attend to your chores."

Clay Reese returned an hour before sundown. Immediately he called Will outside and reprimanded him for neglecting to mend the east fence. "The ewe and her lamb weren't badly hurt," he said, "but they might have been killed."

"I'm sorry, Pa."

His father grunted and started to turn away.

"Pa," Will said, "I was at the ice cave today. I saw you come out with the men from town."

"What? I thought I told you not to go there."

"Yes, sir, you did. But why didn't you tell me you planned to sell the ice?"

"Because it's not your business, that's why."

"Pa, it *is* my business. I found that cave. And we've always talked about things before."

"That's enough!" Clay Reese's lean face was flushed. "We won't discuss it. You stay away from that cave. Understood?"

"Yes, sir."

Baffled and hurt, Will tried to bring the subject up again the next day. But his father once more refused to discuss it. Will went about his chores, a sad, empty feeling growing inside him.

Ever since he'd been small, his father had treated him as an adult. The ranch was not a prosperous one, and all three Reeses worked in partnership to keep it going. Yet now his father was shutting him out, and it hurt; it was making him lose respect for a man he had always looked up to. Will couldn't bear that. He began to think of leaving the ranch, striking out on his own.

He could go to a city—Boise, perhaps—and find work. Then, later on, he could enter college, for his father's thirst for knowledge had been instilled in him, too, and Clay Reese's dream had become his dream. He knew that leaving home would be a form of betrayal, but no more of one than his father's.

He determined to try one more time to talk to the man. It was Saturday noon, and thunderclouds were piling up in the east, when Will approached his father again. Clay Reese was hitching up the wagon for a drive somewhere.

"Pa," he said, "I have to talk to you about the ice cave."

His father's face seemed to cloud as darkly as the sky. "How many times do I have to tell you, Will? There's nothing to discuss. I can't talk now, anyway. I have business to attend to." He climbed into the wagon seat, flicked the reins, and drove off.

Resigned, Will went to his room and packed a bundle. He would leave that night, after his parents were asleep.

The storm broke around 4 p.m., with thunder and lightning and gusty winds. Clay Reese did not return for supper, and finally Will and his mother ate without him. He had probably decided to wait out the storm in town.

Will spent a restless night as thunder grumbled and rain pelted. It would have been foolish to start his journey in this storm, and, until his father returned, he didn't feel right leaving his mother alone.

Sometime toward morning the storm passed, and he fell into a heavy sleep. It was well past dawn, with the sun blazing again, when his mother awoke him. "Get up, Will," she said. Her voice was anxious. "Your father still isn't home, and I'm worried. You'd best ride into town and try to find him."

"Right away, Ma."

Will dressed quickly, saddled his roan, and rode into the clear, rain-fresh morning. He'd only gone half a mile toward Volcano, however, when he thought of the cave. His father could have gone there yesterday, instead of to town; the ice might have been the business he'd referred to. And it wouldn't take long to check. Will turned his horse off the road and pointed him across open land.

He saw his father's wagon as soon as he came in sight of the lava pit. He sent the roan into a hard run, reined up beside the wagon, and jumped off. There was no sign of Clay Reese, or of any of the laborers, this being Sunday. Will scrambled down the newly graded wagon ramp and ran to the cave opening. It had been enlarged considerably, shored up with timbers. He entered, rumbling in the pocket of his pants for matches.

In the flare of the first match he struck, he saw a jumble of equipment piled to one side; among the axes and picks and coiled rope was a lantern. He used a second match to light the lantern's wick. Now he could see more of the cave—gouges and holes in the once-smooth walls where ice blocks had been cut away; narrow wooden ramps built into the passageway, close to the floor, so that the blocks could be easily dragged out. But there was no sign of his father.

Carrying the lantern, Will hurried deeper into the cave. He went all the way to the solid barrier, then came back and checked some of the smaller chambers. All of them were empty.

He had to fight down panic as he ran back into the main chamber. His father *must* have come into the cave; where could he be? Then Will's gaze picked up the stone steps, the ledge at their top, and the chill air seemed to grow even colder. He climbed the steps, moving as fast as he dared on the slippery surface ice. When he reached the top, he leaned into the fall with the lantern extended.

Down at the bottom of the slide, a huddled form lay alongside the bones of the long-dead animal.

"Pa!" Will shouted the word, shouted it again. But the huddled figure didn't move.

Will half ran, half slid, down the steps and got one of the coils of rope. Back on the ledge, he found a projection of rock and tied one end of the rope securely around it. He played the other end down the fall, tested the fastening, then swung his body onto the slide and let himself down to where his father lay.

Clay Reese was unconscious, but still alive. Will's relief didn't last long, however. Try as he might, he couldn't revive his father. The man had been here all night, lying on the ice. He seemed half frozen. If he did regain consciousness, Will knew, he wouldn't have the strength to climb out by himself.

Will swiftly tied the rope around his father, under the arms. When he struggled back up to the ledge, he tried to pull his father out, but he didn't have the strength to move the inert figure more than a foot or so. He had to have help, yet if he left, his father might die before he could bring men back.

Then another idea came to him, and he wasted no time putting it into action. He got a second coil of rope from below, unfastened the first rope from the projection, and tied the two ropes together to make one long one. When he took the free end down across the cave and outside, he had ten feet left.

He climbed to where the roan stood, caught the bridle, and urged the animal to the cave's entrance. He tied the rope to the saddle horn, mounted, and backed the roan until the rope was taut. Then he and the horse began to pull.

It took agonizing minutes, the roan stumbling a time or two, almost losing balance. But finally the rope slackened somewhat, and this told Will his father had at last been drawn to the top of the fall. Dismounting, he raced back into the cave.

Clay Reese lay sprawled across the ledge. He was starting to regain consciousness when Will reached his side.

He managed to get his father to his feet, then down the steps, out of the cave, and to the far end of the pit where the day's heat penetrated. Exhausted, they both sank to the rocky ground. Clay Reese gave his son a weak smile.

"You saved my life," he said when the sun began to take away the chill. "I thought I was a dead man for sure."

"What happened, Pa?"

"I climbed those steps out of curiosity, slipped on the ice, and fell down the slide. I couldn't get back out again." His expression turned rueful. "I told you it could be dangerous in there, Will . . . that you shouldn't go in alone. I should have obeyed my own orders."

"Why did you go in alone?"

"To do some exploring, see if I could tell how big the cave really is. If there's enough ice to last another couple of summers, I reckon we'll start making some money."

"*Start* making money?" Will asked, surprised.

"Will, you have a right to know the truth." His father spoke slowly, the words coming hard for him. "The reason I didn't talk to you about selling the ice is that I was afraid to face up to you. I didn't want anyone to know how close we were to losing the ranch. Until you found the cave, I hadn't been able to make the mortgage payments for some time . . . the bank was getting ready to foreclose."

"So that's why you've been so troubled lately."

"Yes. I worked out an arrangement with Jess Lacy and with Harmon Bennett at the bank. Jess buys the ice at a fair price, and I turn the money over to Mister Bennett. The mortgage will be paid off by next summer. Then we can start saving for your college education."

Will was silent for a time; he felt ashamed at having doubted his father. Finally he said: "Pa, I understand now. But I wish you'd told me all of this before."

"I guess I should have," his father admitted. "But my foolish pride wouldn't let me. I'm sorry, Son."

"I'm sorry, too," Will said. "I . . . well . . . I felt like you didn't need me anymore. I was going to leave, go off to Boise and hunt work. I'd be gone now if it hadn't stormed last night."

His father grimaced, his face etched with pain. "This has been a bad misunderstanding, Will. From now on, we'll both be honest with each other. As for the cave, well, we'll explore it together next time. And work together on our ice business, too."

"I'd like that, Pa."

Will stood and began to help his father up the ramp to the wagon. As he did, he glanced over at the mouth of the cave—not his cave, but their cave, the family's cave. Then his eyes met his father's, and they both smiled.

Deceptions

1987

San Francisco's Golden Gate Bridge is deceptively fragile-looking, especially when fog swirls across its high span. But from where I was standing, almost underneath it at the south end, even the mists couldn't disguise the massiveness of its concrete piers and the taut strength of its cables. I tipped my head back and looked up the tower to where it disappeared into the drifting grayness, thinking about the other ways the bridge is deceptive.

For one thing, its color isn't gold, but rust red, reminiscent of dried blood. And though the bridge is a marvel of engineering, it is also plagued by maintenance problems that keep the Bridge District in constant danger of financial collapse. For a reputedly romantic structure, it has seen more than its fair share of tragedy: Some eight hundred–odd lost souls have jumped to their deaths from its deck.

Today I was there to try to find out if that figure should be raised by one. So far I'd met with little success.

I was standing next to my car in the parking lot of Fort Point, a historic fortification at the mouth of San Francisco Bay. Where the pavement stopped, the land fell away to jagged black rocks; waves smashed

against them, sending up geysers of salty spray. Beyond the rocks the
water was choppy, and Angel Island and Alcatraz were mere humpbacked
shapes in the mist. I shivered, wishing I'd worn something heavier than
my poplin jacket, and started toward the fort.

This was the last stop on a journey that had taken me from the toll
booths and Bridge District offices to Vista Point at the Marin County
end of the span, and back to the National Park Service headquarters down
the road from the fort. None of the Park Service or bridge personnel—
including a group of maintenance workers near the north tower—had
seen the slender dark-haired woman in the picture I'd shown them,
walking south on the pedestrian sidewalk at about four yesterday afternoon. None of them had seen her jump.

It was for that reason—plus the facts that her parents had revealed
about twenty-two-year-old Vanessa DiCesare—that made me tend to
doubt she actually had committed suicide, in spite of the note she'd left
taped to the dashboard of the Honda she'd abandoned at Vista Point.
Surely at four o'clock on a Monday afternoon, *someone* would have
noticed her. Still, I had to follow up every possibility, and the people at
the Parks Service station had suggested I check with the rangers at Fort
Point.

I entered the dark-brick structure through a long, low tunnel—called a
sally port, the sign said—which was flanked at either end by massive
wooden doors with iron studding. Years before, I'd visited the fort, and
now I recalled that it was more or less typical of harbor fortifications built
in the Civil War era: a ground floor topped by two tiers of working and
living quarters, encircling a central courtyard.

I emerged into the court and looked up at the west side; the tiers were
a series of brick archways, their openings as black as empty eyesockets,
each roped off at waist level by a narrow strip of yellow plastic. There was
construction gear in the courtyard; the entire west side was under renovation and probably off limits to the public.

As I stood there trying to remember the layout of the place and wondering which way to go, I became aware of a hollow metallic clanking that
echoed in the circular enclosure. The noise drew my eyes upward to the

wooden watchtower atop the west tiers, and then to the red arch of the bridge's girders directly above it. The clanking seemed to have something to do with the cars passing over the roadbed, and it was underlaid by a constant grumbling rush of tires on pavement. The sounds, coupled with the soaring height of the fog-laced girders, made me feel small and insignificant. I shivered again and turned to my left, looking for one of the rangers.

The man who came out of a nearby doorway startled me, more because of his costume than the suddenness of his appearance. Instead of the Park Service uniform I remembered the rangers wearing on my previous visit, he was clad in what looked like an old Union Army uniform: a dark blue frock coat, lighter blue trousers, and a wide-brimmed hat with a red plume. The long saber in a scabbard that was strapped to his waist made him look thoroughly authentic.

He smiled at my obvious surprise and came over to me, bushy eyebrows lifted inquiringly. "Can I help you, ma'am?"

I reached into my bag and took out my private investigator's license and showed it to him. "I'm Sharon McCone, from All Souls Legal Cooperative. Do you have a minute to answer some questions?"

He frowned, the way people often do when confronted by a private detective, probably trying to remember whether he'd done anything lately that would warrant investigation. Then he said, "Sure," and motioned for me to step into the shelter of the sally port.

"I'm investigating a disappearance, a possible suicide from the bridge," I said. "It would have happened about four yesterday afternoon. Were you on duty then?"

He shook his head. "Monday's my day off."

"Is there anyone else here who might have been working then?"

"You could check with Lee—Lee Gottschalk, the other ranger on this shift."

"Where can I find him?"

He moved back into the courtyard and looked around. "I saw him taking a couple of tourists around just a few minutes ago. People are crazy; they'll come out in any kind of weather."

"Can you tell me which way he went?"

The ranger gestured to our right. "Along this side. When he's done down here, he'll take them up that iron stairway to the first tier, but I can't say how far he's gotten yet."

I thanked him and started off in the direction he'd indicated.

There were open doors in the cement wall between the sally port and the iron staircase. I glanced through the first and saw no one. The second led into a narrow dark hallway; when I was halfway down it, I saw that this was the fort's jail. One cell was set up as a display, complete with a mannequin prisoner; the other, beyond an archway that was not much taller than my own five-foot-six, was unrestored. Its waterstained walls were covered with graffiti, and a metal railing protected a two-foot-square iron grid on the floor. A sign said that it was a cistern with a forty-thousand-gallon capacity. Well, I thought, that's interesting, but playing tourist isn't helping me catch up with Lee Gottschalk. Quickly I left the jail and hurried up the iron staircase the first ranger had indicated. At its top, I turned to my left and bumped into a chain-link fence that blocked access to the area under renovation. Warning myself to watch where I was going, I went the other way, toward the east tier. The archways there were fenced off with similar chain link so no one could fall, and doors opened off the gallery into what I supposed had been the soldiers' living quarters. I pushed through the first one and stepped into a small museum.

The room was high-ceilinged, with tall, narrow windows in the outside wall. No ranger or tourists were in sight. I looked toward an interior door that led to the next room and saw a series of mirror images: one door within another leading off into the distance, each diminishing in size until the last seemed very tiny. I had the unpleasant sensation that if I walked along there, I would become progressively smaller and eventually disappear.

From somewhere down there came the sound of voices. I followed it, passing through more museum displays until I came to a room containing an old-fashioned bedstead and footlocker. A ranger, looking much the same as the man downstairs except for a beard and granny glasses, stood beyond the bedstead lecturing to a man and a woman who were bundled to their chins in bulky sweaters.

"You'll notice that the fireplaces are very small," he was saying, motioning to the one on the wall next to the bed, "and you can imagine how cold it could get for the soldiers garrisoned here. They didn't have a heated employees' lounge like we do." Smiling at his own little joke, he glanced at me. "Do you want to join the tour?"

I shook my head and stepped over by the footlocker. "Are you Lee Gottschalk?"

"Yes." He spoke the word a shade warily.

"I have a few questions I'd like to ask you. How long will the rest of the tour take?"

"At least half an hour. These folks want to see the unrestored rooms on the third floor."

I didn't want to wait around that long, so I said, "Could you take a couple of minutes and talk with me now?"

He moved his head so the light from the windows caught his granny glasses and I couldn't see the expression in his eyes, but his mouth tightened in a way that might have been annoyance. After a moment he said, "Well, the rest of the tour on this floor is pretty much self-guided." To the tourists, he added, "Why don't you go on ahead and I'll catch up after I talk with this lady."

They nodded agreeably and moved on into the next room. Lee Gottschalk folded his arms across his chest and leaned against the small fireplace. "Now what can I do for you?"

I introduced myself and showed him my license. His mouth twitched briefly in surprise, but he didn't comment. I said, "At about four yesterday afternoon, a young woman left her car at Vista Point with a suicide note in it. I'm trying to locate a witness who saw her jump. I took out the photograph I'd been showing to people and handed it to him. By now I had Vanessa DiCesare's features memorized: high forehead, straight nose, full lips, glossy wings of dark-brown hair curling inward at the jawbone. It was a strong face, not beautiful but striking—and a face I'd recognize anywhere.

Gottschalk studied the photo, then handed it back to me. "I read about her in the morning paper. Why are you trying to find a witness?"

"Her parents have hired me to look into it."

"The paper said her father is some big politician here in the city."

"I didn't see any harm in discussing what had already appeared in print. "Yes, Ernest DiCesare—he's on the Board of Supes and likely to be our next mayor."

"And she was a law student, engaged to some hotshot lawyer who ran her father's last political campaign."

"Right again."

He shook his head, lips pushing out in bewilderment. "Sounds like she had a lot going for her. Why would she kill herself? Did that note taped inside her car explain it?"

I'd seen the note, but its contents were confidential. "No. Did you happen to see anything unusual yesterday afternoon?"

"No. But if I'd seen anyone jump, I'd have reported it to the bridge offices so they could send out a suicide prevention team." He stared at me almost combatively, as if I'd accused him of some kind of wrongdoing, then seemed to relent a little. "Come outside," he said, "and I'll show you something."

We went through the door to the gallery, and he guided me to the chain-link barrier in the archway and pointed up. "Look at the angle of the bridge, and the distance we are from it. You couldn't spot anyone standing at the rail from here, at least not well enough to tell if they were acting upset. And a jumper would have to hurl herself way out before she'd be noticeable."

"And there's nowhere else in the fort from where a jumper would be clearly visible?"

"Maybe from one of the watchtowers or the extreme west side. But they're off limits to the public, and we only give them one routine check at closing."

Satisfied now, I said, "Well, that about does it. I appreciate your taking the time."

He nodded and we started along the gallery. When we reached the other end, where an enclosed staircase spiraled up and down, I thanked him again and we parted company.

The way the facts looked to me now, Vanessa DiCesare had faked this suicide and just walked away—away from her wealthy old-line Italian family, from her up-and-coming liberal lawyer, from a life that either had become too much or just hadn't been enough. Vanessa was over twenty-one; she had a legal right to disappear if she wanted to. But her parents and her fiancé loved her, and they also had a right to know she was alive and well. If I could locate her and reassure them without ruining whatever new life she planned to create for herself, I would feel I'd performed the job I'd been hired to do. But right now I was weary, chilled to the bone, and out of leads. I decided to go back to All Souls and consider my next moves in warmth and comfort.

All Souls Legal Cooperative is housed in a ramshackle Victorian on one of the steeply sloping side streets of Bernal Heights, a working-class district in the southern part of the city. The co-op caters mainly to clients who live in the area: people with low to middle incomes who don't have money for expensive lawyers. The sliding fee scale allows them to obtain quality legal assistance at reasonable prices—a concept that is probably outdated in the self-centered 1980s, but which is kept alive by the people who staff All Souls. It's a place where the lawyers care about their clients, and a good place to work.

I left my MG at the curb and hurried up the front steps through the blowing fog. The warmth inside was almost a shock after the chilliness at Fort Point; I unbuttoned my jacket and went down the long deserted hallway to the big country kitchen at the rear. There I found my boss, Hank Zahn, stirring up a mug of the navy grog he often concocts on cold November evenings like this one.

He looked at me, pointed to the rum bottle, and said, "Shall I make you one?" When I nodded, he reached for another mug.

I went to the round oak table under the windows, moved a pile of newspapers from one of the chairs, and sat down. Hank added lemon juice, hot water, and sugar syrup to the rum, dusted it artistically with nutmeg, and set it in front of me with a flourish. I sampled it as he sat down across from me, then nodded my approval.

He said, "How's it going with the DiCesare investigation?"

Hank had a personal interest in the case; Vanessa's fiancé, Gary Stornetta, was a longtime friend of his, which was why I, rather than one of the large investigative firms her father normally favored, had been asked to look into it. I said, "Everything I've come up with points to it being a disappearance, not a suicide."

"Just as Gary and her parents suspected."

"Yes. I've covered the entire area around the bridge. There are absolutely no witnesses, except for the tour bus driver who saw her park her car at four and got suspicious when it was still there at seven and reported it. But even he didn't see her walk off toward the bridge." I drank some more grog, felt its warmth, and began to relax. Behind his thick horn-rimmed glasses, Hank's eyes became concerned. "Did the DiCesares or Gary give you any idea why she would have done such a thing?"

"When I talked with Ernest and Sylvia this morning, they said Vanessa had changed her mind about marrying Gary. He's not admitting to that, but he doesn't speak of Vanessa the way a happy husband-to-be would. And it seems an unlikely match to me—he's close to twenty years older than she."

"More like fifteen," Hank said. "Gary's father was Ernest's best friend, and after Ron Stornetta died, Ernest more or less took him on as a protégé. Ernest was delighted that their families were finally going to be joined."

"Oh, he was delighted all right. He admitted to me that he'd practically arranged the marriage. 'Girl didn't know what was good for her,' he said. 'Needed a strong older man to guide her.'" I snorted.

Hank smiled faintly. He's a feminist, but over the years his sense of outrage has mellowed; mine still has a hair trigger.

"Anyway," I said, "when Vanessa first announced she was backing out of the engagement, Ernest told her he would cut off her funds for law school if she didn't go through with the wedding."

"Jesus, I had no idea he was capable of such . . . Neanderthal tactics."

"Well, he is. After that, Vanessa went ahead and set the wedding date. But Sylvia said she suspected she wouldn't go through with it. Vanessa talked of quitting law school and moving out of their home. And she'd been seeing other men; she and her father had a bad quarrel about it just last week. Anyway, all of that, plus the fact that one of her suitcases and some clothing are missing, made them highly suspicious of the suicide."

Hank reached for my mug and went to get us more grog. I began thumbing through the copy of the morning paper that I'd moved off the chair, looking for the story on Vanessa. I found it on page three.

> The daughter of Supervisor Ernest DiCesare apparently committed suicide by jumping from the Golden Gate Bridge late yesterday afternoon.
>
> Vanessa DiCesare, 22, abandoned her 1985 Honda Civic at Vista Point at approximately four p.m., police said. There were no witnesses to her jump, and the body has not been recovered. The contents of a suicide note found in her car have not been disclosed.
>
> Ms. DiCesare, a first-year student at Hastings College of Law, is the only child of the supervisor and his wife, Sylvia. She planned to be married next month to San Francisco attorney Gary R. Stometta, a political associate of her father.

Strange how routine it all sounded when reduced to journalistic language. And yet how mysterious—the "undisclosed contents" of the suicide note, for instance.

"You know," I said as Hank came back to the table and set down the fresh mugs of grog, "that note is another factor that makes me believe she staged this whole thing. It was so formal and controlled. If they had samples of suicide notes in etiquette books, I'd say she looked one up and copied it."

He ran his fingers through his wiry brown hair. "What I don't understand is why she didn't just break off the engagement and move out of the house. So what if her father cut off her money? There are lots worse things than working your way through law school."

"Oh, but this way she gets back at everyone, and has the advantage of being alive to gloat over it. Imagine her parents' and Gary's grief and guilt—it's the ultimate way of getting even."

"She must be a very angry young woman."

"Yes. After I talked with Ernest and Sylvia and Gary, I spoke briefly with Vanessa's best friend, a law student named Kathy Graves. Kathy told me that Vanessa was furious with her father for making her go through with the marriage. And she'd come to hate Gary because she'd decided he was only marrying her for her family's money and political power."

"Oh, come on. Gary's ambitious, sure. But you can't tell me he doesn't genuinely care for Vanessa."

"I'm only giving you her side of the story."

"So now what do you plan to do?"

"Talk with Gary and the DiCesares again. See if I can't come up with some bit of information that will help me find her."

"And then?"

"Then it's up to them to work it out."

The DiCesare home was mock-Tudor, brick and half-timber, set on a corner knoll in the exclusive area of St. Francis Wood. When I'd first come there that morning, I'd been slightly awed; now the house had lost its power to impress me. After delving into the lives of the family who lived there, I knew that it was merely a pile of brick and mortar and wood that contained more than the usual amount of misery.

The DiCesares and Gary Stornetta were waiting for me in the living room, a strangely formal place with several groupings of furniture and expensive-looking knickknacks laid out in precise patterns on the tables. Vanessa's parents and fiancé—like the house—seemed diminished since my previous visit: Sylvia huddled in armchair by the fireplace, her gray-blonde hair straggling from its elegant coiffure; Ernest stood behind her, haggard-faced, one hand protectively on her shoulder. Gary paced, smoking, and clawing at his hair with his other hand. Occasionally he dropped ashes on the thick wall-to-wall carpeting, but no one called it to his attention.

They listened to what I had to report without interruption. When I finished, there was a long silence. Then Sylvia put a hand over her eyes and said, "How she must hate us to do a thing like this!"

Ernest tightened his grip on his wife's shoulder. His face was a conflict of anger, bewilderment, and sorrow.

There was no question about which emotion had hold of Gary; he smashed out his cigarette in an ashtray, lit another, and resumed pacing. But while his movements before had merely been nervous, now his tall, lean body was rigid with thinly controlled fury. "Damn her!" he said. "Damn her anyway!"

"Gary." There was a warning note in Ernest's voice. Gary glanced at him, then Sylvia. "Sorry."

I said, "The question now is, do you want me to continue looking for her?"

In shocked tones, Sylvia said, "Of course we do!" Then she tipped her head back and looked at her husband.

Ernest was silent, his fingers pressing hard against the black wool of her dress.

"Ernest?" Now Sylvia's voice held a note of panic.

"Of course we do," he said. But the words somehow lacked conviction.

I took out my notebook and pencil, glancing at Gary. He had stopped pacing and was watching the DiCesares. His craggy face was still mottled with anger, and I sensed he shared Ernest's uncertainly.

Opening the notebook, I said, "I need more details about Vanessa, what her life was like the past month or so. Perhaps something will occur to one of you that didn't this morning."

"Ms. McCone," Ernest said, "I don't think Sylvia's up to this right now. Why don't you and Gary talk, and then if there's anything else, I'll be glad to help you."

"Fine." Gary was the one I was primarily interested in questioning, anyway. I waited until Ernest and Sylvia had left the room, then turned to him.

When the door shut behind them, he hurled his cigarette into the empty fireplace. "Goddamn little bitch!"

I said, "Why don't you sit down."

He looked at me for a few seconds, obviously wanting to keep on pacing, then flopped into the chair Sylvia had vacated. When I'd first met with Gary this morning, he'd been controlled and immaculately groomed, and he had seemed more solicitous of the DiCesares than concerned with his own feelings. Now his clothing was disheveled, his graying hair tousled, and he looked to be on the brink of a rage that would flatten anyone in its path.

Unfortunately, what I had to ask him would probably fan that rage. I braced myself and said, "Now tell me about Vanessa. And not all the stuff about her being a lovely young woman and a brilliant student. I heard all that this morning—but we both know it isn't the whole truth, don't we?"

Surprisingly he reached for a cigarette and lit it slowly, using the time to calm himself. When he spoke, his voice was as level as my own. "All right, it's not the whole truth. Vanessa *is* lovely and brilliant. She'll make a top-notch lawyer. There's a hardness in her; she gets it from Ernest. It took guts to fake this suicide."

"What do you think she hopes to gain from it?"

"Freedom. From me. From Ernest's domination. She's probably taken off somewhere for a good time. When she's ready she'll come back and make her demands."

"And what will they be?"

"Enough money to move into a place of her own and finish law school. And she'll get it, too. She's all her parents have."

"You don't think she's set out to make a new life for herself?"

"Hell, no. That would mean giving up all this." The sweep of his arm encompassed the house and all of the DiCesares' privileged world.

But there was one factor that made me doubt his assessment. I said, "What about the other men in her life?"

He tried to look surprised, but an angry muscle twitched in his jaw.

"Come on, Gary," I said, "you know there were other men. Even Ernest and Sylvia were aware of that."

"Ah, Christ!" He popped out of the chair and began pacing again. "All right, there were other men. It started a few months ago. I didn't understand it; things had been good with us; they still *were* good physically. But I thought, okay, she's young; this is only natural. So I decided to give her some rope, let her get it out of her system. She didn't throw it in my face, didn't embarrass me in front of my friends. Why shouldn't she have a last fling?"

"And then?"

"She began making noises about breaking off the engagement. And Ernest started that shit about not footing the bill for law school. Like a fool I went along with it, and she seemed to cave in from the pressure. But a few weeks later, it all started up again—only this time it was purposeful, cruel."

"In what way?"

"She'd know I was meeting political associates for lunch or dinner, and she'd show up at the restaurant with a date. Later she'd claim he was just a friend, but you couldn't prove it from the way they acted. We'd go to a party and she'd flirt with every man there. She got sly and secretive about where she'd been, what she'd been doing."

I had pictured Vanessa as a very angry young woman; now I realized she was not a particularly nice one, either.

Gary was saying, ". . . the last straw was on Halloween. We went to a costume party given by one of her friends from Hastings. I didn't want to go—costumes, a young crowd, not my kind of thing—and so she was angry with me to begin with. Anyway, she walked out with another man, some jerk in a soldier outfit. They were dancing—"

I sat up straighter. "Describe the costume."

"An old-fashioned soldier outfit. Wide-brimmed hat with a plume, frock coat, sword."

"What did the man look like?"

"Youngish. He had a full beard and wore granny glasses."

Lee Gottschalk.

The address I got from the phone directory for Lee Gottschalk was on California Street not far from Twenty-fifth Avenue and only a couple of miles from where I'd first met the ranger at Fort Point. When I arrived there and parked at the opposite curb, I didn't need to check the mailboxes to see which apartment was his; the corner windows on the second floor were ablaze with light, and inside I could see Gottschalk, sitting in an armchair in what appeared to be his living room. He seemed to be alone but expecting company, because frequently he looked up from the book he was reading and checked his watch.

In case the company was Vanessa DiCesare, I didn't want to go barging in there. Gottschalk might find a way to warn her off, or simply not answer the door when she arrived. Besides, I didn't yet have a definite connection between the two of them; the "jerk in a soldier outfit" *could* have been someone else, someone in a rented costume that just happened to resemble the working uniform at the fort. But my suspicions were strong enough to keep me watching Gottschalk for well over an hour. The ranger *had* lied to me that afternoon.

The lies had been casual and convincing, except for two mistakes—such small mistakes that I hadn't caught them even when I'd later read the newspaper account of Vanessa's purported suicide. But now I recognized them for what they were: The paper had called Gary Stornetta a "political associate" of Vanessa's father, rather than his former campaign manager, as Lee had termed him. And while the paper mentioned the suicide note, it had not said it was *taped* inside the car. While Gottschalk conceivably could know about Gary managing Ernest's campaign for the Board of Supes from other newspaper accounts, there was no way he could have known how the note was secured—except from Vanessa herself.

Because of those mistakes, I continued watching Gottschalk, straining my eyes as the mist grew heavier, hoping Vanessa would show up or that he'd eventually lead me to her. The ranger appeared to be nervous. He got up a couple of times and turned on a TV, flipped through the channels, and turned it off again. For about ten minutes, he paced back and forth. Finally, around twelve-thirty, he checked his watch again, then got up and drew the draperies shut. The lights went out behind them.

I tensed, staring through the blowing mist at the door of the apartment building. Somehow Gottschalk hadn't looked like a man who was going to bed. And my impression was correct. In a few minutes he came through the door onto the sidewalk carrying a suitcase—pale leather like the one of Vanessa's Sylvia had described to me—and got into a dark-colored Mustang parked on his side of the street. The car started up and he made a U-turn, then went right on Twenty-fifth Avenue. I followed. After a few minutes, it became apparent that he was heading for Fort Point.

When Gottschalk turned into the road to the fort, I kept going until I could pull over on the shoulder. The brake lights of the Mustang flared, and then Gottschalk got out and unlocked the low iron bar that blocked the road from sunset to sunrise; after he'd driven through he closed it again, and the car's lights disappeared down the road.

Had Vanessa been hiding at drafty, cold Fort Point? It seemed a strange choice of place, since she could have used a motel or Gottschalk's apartment. But perhaps she'd been afraid someone would recognize her in a public place, or connect her with Gottschalk and come looking, as I had. And while the fort would be a miserable place to hide during the hours it was open to the public—she'd have had to keep to one of the off-limits areas, such as the west side—at night she could probably avail herself of the heated employees' lounge.

Now I could reconstruct most of the scenario of what had gone on: Vanessa meets Lee; they talk about his work; she decides he is the person to help her fake her suicide. Maybe there's a romantic entanglement, maybe not; but for whatever reason, he agrees to go along with the plan. She leaves her car at Vista Point, walks across the bridge, and later he drives over there and picks up the suitcase. . . . But then why hadn't he delivered it to her at the fort? And to fetch the suitcase after she'd abandoned the car was too much of a risk; he might have been seen, or the people at the fort might have noticed him leaving for too long a break. Also, if she'd walked across the bridge, surely at least one of the people I'd talked with would have seen her—the maintenance crew near the north tower, for instance.

There was no point in speculating on it now, I decided. The thing to do was to follow Gottschalk down there and confront Vanessa before she disappeared again. For a moment I debated taking my gun out of the glovebox, but then decided against it. I don't like to carry it unless I'm going into a dangerous situation, and neither Gottschalk nor Vanessa posed any particular threat to me. I was merely here to deliver a message from Vanessa's parents asking her to come home. If she didn't care to respond to it, that was not my business—or my problem.

I got out of my car and locked it, then hurried across the road and down the narrow lane to the gate, ducking under it and continuing along toward the ranger station. On either side of me were tall, thick groves of eucalyptus; I could smell their acrid fragrance and hear the fog-laden wind rustle their brittle leaves. Their shadows turned the lane into a black winding alley, and the only sound besides distant traffic noises was my tennis shoes slapping on the broken pavement. The ranger station was dark, but ahead I could see Gottschalk's car parked next to the fort. The area was illuminated only by small security lights set at intervals on the walls of the structure. Above it the bridge arched, washed in fog-muted yellowish light; as I drew closer I became aware of the grumble and clank of traffic up there.

I ran across the parking area and checked Gottschalk's car. It was empty, but the suitcase rested on the passenger seat. I turned and started toward the sally port, noticing that its heavily studded door stood open a few inches. The low tunnel was completely dark. I felt my way along it toward the courtyard, one hand on its icy stone wall.

The doors to the courtyard also stood open. I peered through them into the gloom beyond. What light there was came from the bridge and more security beacons high up on the wooden watchtowers; I could barely make out the shapes of the construction equipment that stood near the west side. The clanking from the bridge was oppressive and eerie in the still night.

As I was about to step into the courtyard, there was a movement to my right. I drew back into the sally port as Lee Gottschalk came out of one of the ground-floor doorways. My first impulse was to confront him, but then I decided against it. He might shout, warn Vanessa, and she might escape before I could deliver her parents' message.

After a few seconds I looked out again, meaning to follow Gottschalk, but he was nowhere in sight. A faint shaft of light fell through the door from which he had emerged and rippled over the cobblestone floor. I went that way, through the door and along the narrow corridor to where an archway was illuminated. Then, realizing the archway led to the unre-stored cell of the jail I'd seen earlier, I paused. Surely Vanessa wasn't hiding in there . . .

I crept forward and looked through the arch. The light came from a heavy-duty flashlight that sat on the floor. It threw macabre shadows on the water-stained walls, showing their streaked paint and graffiti. My gaze followed its beams upward and then down, to where the grating of the cistern lay out of place on the floor beside the hole. Then I moved over to the railing, leaned across it, and trained the flashlight down into the well.

I saw, with a rush of shock and horror, the dark hair and once hand-some features of Vanessa DiCesare.

She had been hacked to death. Stabbed and slashed, as if in a frenzy. Her clothing was ripped; there were gashes on her face and hands; she was covered with dark smears of blood. Her eyes were open, staring with that horrible flatness of death.

I came back on my heels, clutching the railing for support. A wave of dizziness swept over me, followed by an icy coldness. I thought: He killed her. And then I pictured Gottschalk in his Union Army uniform, the saber hanging from his belt, and I knew what the weapon had been.

"God!" I said aloud.

Why had he murdered her? I had no way of knowing yet. But the answer to why he'd thrown her into the cistern instead of just putting her into the bay was clear: She was supposed to have committed suicide; and while bodies that fall from the Golden Gate Bridge sustain a great many injuries, slash and stab wounds aren't among them. Gottschalk could not count on the body being swept out to sea on the current; if she washed up somewhere along the coast, it would be obvious she had been murdered—and eventually an investigation might have led back to him. To him and his soldier's saber.

It also seemed clear that he'd come to the fort tonight to move the body. But why not last night, why leave her in the cistern all day? Probably he'd needed to plan, to secure keys to the gate and fort, to check the schedule of the night patrols for the best time to remove her. Whatever his reason,

I realized now that I'd walked into a very dangerous situation. Walked right in without bringing my gun. I turned quickly to get out of there . . .

And came face-to-face with Lee Gottschalk.

His eyes were wide, his mouth drawn back in a snarl of surprise. In one hand he held a bundle of heavy canvas. "You!" he said. "What the hell are you doing here?"

I jerked back from him, bumped into the railing, and dropped the flashlight. It clattered on the floor and began rolling toward the mouth of the cistern. Gottschalk lunged toward me, and as I dodged, the light fell into the hole and the cell went dark. I managed to push past him and ran down the hallway to the courtyard.

Stumbling on the cobblestones, I ran blindly for the sally port. Its doors were shut now—he'd probably taken that precaution when he'd returned from getting the tarp to wrap her body in. I grabbed the iron hasp and tugged but couldn't get it open. Gottschalk's footsteps were coming through the courtyard after me now. I let go of the hasp and ran again.

When I came to the enclosed staircase at the other end of the court, I started up. The steps were wide at the outside wall, narrow at the inside. My toes banged into the risers of the steps; a couple of times I teetered and almost fell backward. At the first tier I paused, then kept going. Gottschalk had said something about unrestored rooms on the second tier; they'd be a better place to hide than in the museum.

Down below I could hear him climbing after me. The sound of his feet—clattering and stumbling—echoed in the close space. I could hear him grunt and mumble; low, ugly sounds that I knew were curses.

I had absolutely no doubt that if he caught me, he would kill me. Maybe do to me what he had done to Vanessa . . .

I rounded the spiral once again and came out on the top-floor gallery, my heart beating wildly, my breath coming in pants. To my left were archways, black outlines filled with dark-gray sky. To my right was blackness. I went that way, hands out, feeling my way. My hands touched the rough wood of a door. I pushed, and it opened. As I passed through it, my shoulder bag caught on something; I yanked it loose and kept going. Beyond the door I heard Gottschalk curse loudly, the sound filled with surprise and pain; he must have fallen on the stairway. And that gave me a little more time. The tug at my shoulder bag had reminded me of the small flashlight I keep there. Flattening myself against the wall next to the door, I rummaged through the bag and brought out the flash. Its beam showed high walls and arching ceilings, plaster-and-lath pulled away to expose dark brick. I saw cubicles and cubbyholes opening into dead ends, but to my right was an arch. I made a small involuntary sound of relief, then thought *Quiet!* Gottschalk's footsteps started up the stairway again as I moved through the archway.

The crumbling plaster walls beyond the archway were set at odd angles—an interlocking funhouse maze connected by small doors. I slipped through one and found an irregularly shaped room heaped with debris. There didn't seem to be an exit, so I ducked back into the first room and moved toward the outside wall, where gray outlines indicated small, high-placed windows. I couldn't hear Gottschalk any more—couldn't hear anything but the roar and dank from the bridge directly overhead.

The front wall was brick and stone, and the windows had wide, waist-high sills. I leaned across one, looked through the salt-caked glass, and saw the open sea. I was at the front of the fort, the part that faced beyond the Golden Gate; to my immediate right would be the unrestored portion. If I could slip over into that area, I might be able to hide until the other rangers came to work in the morning.

But Gottschalk could be anywhere. I couldn't hear his footsteps above the infernal noise from the bridge. He could be right here in the room with me, pinpointing me by the beam of my flashlight. Fighting down panic, I switched the light off and continued along the wall, my hands recoiling from its clammy stone surface. It was icy cold in the vast, echoing space, but my own flesh felt colder still. The air had a salt tang, underlaid by odors of rot and mildew. For a couple of minutes the darkness was unalleviated, but then I saw a lighter rectangular shape ahead of me.

When I reached it I found it was some sort of embrasure, about four feet tall, but only a little over a foot wide. Beyond it I could see the edge of the gallery where it curved and stopped at the chain-link fence that

barred entrance to the other side of the fort. The fence wasn't very high—
only five feet or so. If I could get through this narrow opening, I could
climb it and find refuge.

The sudden noise behind me was like a firecracker popping. I whirled,
and saw a tall figure silhouetted against one of the seaward windows. He
lurched forward, tripping over whatever he'd stepped on. Forcing back a
cry, I hoisted myself up and began squeezing through the embrasure.

Its sides were rough brick. They scraped my flesh clear through my
clothing. Behind me I heard the slap of Gottschalk's shoes on the
wooden floor.

My hips wouldn't fit through the opening. I gasped, grunted, pulling
with my arms on the outside wall. Then I turned on my side, sucking in
my stomach. My bag caught again, and I let go of the wall long enough
to rip its strap off my elbow. As my hips squeezed through the embrasure,
I felt Gottschalk grab at my feet. I kicked out frantically, breaking his
hold, and fell off the sill to the floor of the gallery.

Fighting for breath, I pushed off the floor, threw myself at the fence,
and began climbing. The metal bit into my fingers, rattled and clashed
with my weight. At the top, the leg of my jeans got hung up on the spiky
wires. I tore it loose and jumped down the other side.

The door to the gallery burst open and Gottschalk came through it.
I got up from a crouch and ran into the darkness ahead of me. The
fence began to rattle as he started up it. I raced, half stumbling, along
the gallery, the open archways to my right. To my left was probably a
warren of rooms similar to those on the east side. I could lose him in
there . . .

Only I couldn't. The door I tried was locked. I ran to the next one and
hurled my body against its wooden panels. It didn't give. I heard myself
sob in fear and frustration.

Gottschalk was over the fence now, coming toward me, limping. His
breath came in erratic gasps, loud enough to hear over the noise of the
bridge. I twisted around, looking for shelter, and saw a pile of lumber
lying across one of the open archways.

I dashed toward it and slipped behind, wedged between it and the pillar of the arch. The courtyard lay two dizzying stories below me. I grasped the end of the top two-by-four. It moved easily, as if on a fulcrum.

Gottschalk had seen me. He came on steadily, his right leg dragging behind him. When he reached the pile of lumber and started over it toward me, I yanked on the two-by-four. The other end moved and struck him on the knee.

He screamed and stumbled back. Then he came forward again, hand outstretched toward me. I pulled back further against the pillar. His clutching hands missed me, and when they did he lost his balance and toppled onto the pile of lumber. And then the boards began to slide toward the open archway.

He grabbed at the boards, yelling and flailing his arms. I tried to reach for him, but the lumber was moving like an avalanche now, pitching over the side and crashing down into the courtyard two stories below. It carried Gottschalk's thrashing body with it, and his screams echoed in its wake. For an awful few seconds the boards continued to crash down on him, and then everything was terribly still. Even the thrumming of the bridge traffic seemed muted.

I straightened slowly and looked down into the courtyard. Gottschalk lay unmoving among the scattered pieces of lumber. For a moment I breathed deeply to control my vertigo; then I ran back to the chain-link fence, climbed it, and rushed down the spiral staircase to the courtyard.

When I got to the ranger's body, I could hear him moaning. I said, "Lie still. I'll call an ambulance."

He moaned louder as I ran across the courtyard and found a phone in the gift shop, but by the time I returned, he was silent. His breathing was so shallow that I thought he'd passed out, but then I heard mumbled words coming from his lips. I bent closer to listen.

"Vanessa," he said. "Wouldn't take me with her . . ."

I said, "Take you where?"

"Going away together. Left my car . . . over there so she could drive across the bridge. But when she . . . brought it here she said she was going alone . . ."

So you argued, I thought. And you lost your head and slashed her to death.

"Vanessa," he said again. "Never planned to take me . . . tricked me . . ."

I started to put a hand on his arm, but found I couldn't touch him. "Don't talk any more. The ambulance'll be here soon."

"Vanessa," he said. "Oh God, what did you do to me?"

I looked up at the bridge, rust red through the darkness and mist. In the distance, I could hear the wail of a siren.

Deceptions, I thought.

Deceptions . . .

Time of the Wolves

1988

I t was in the time of the wolves that my grandmother came to Kansas."
The old woman sat primly on the sofa in her apartment in the senior
citizens' complex. Although her faded blue eyes were focused on the
window, the historian, who sat opposite her, sensed Mrs. Clark was not
seeing the shopping malls and used-car lots that had spilled over into
what once was open prairie. As she'd begun speaking, her gaze had turned
inward—and into the past.

The historian—who was compiling an oral account of the Kansas pioneers—adjusted the volume button on her tape recorder and looked
expectantly at Mrs. Clark. But the descendant of those pioneers was in no
hurry; she waited a moment before resuming her story.

"The time of the wolves . . . that's the way I thought of it as a child,
and I speak of it that way to this very day. It's fitting . . . those were perilous times, in the eighteen seventies. Vicious packs of wolves and coyotes
roamed . . . fires would sweep the prairie without warning . . . there were
disastrous floods . . . and, of course, blizzards. But my grandmother was a
true pioneer woman . . . she knew no fear. One time in the winter of
eighteen seventy-two . . ."

—∞—

Alma Heusser stood in the doorway of the sod house, looking north over the prairie. It was gone four in the afternoon now, and storm clouds were bulking on the horizon. The chill in the air penetrated even her heavy buffalo-skin robe; a hush had fallen, as if all the creatures on the barren plain were holding their breath, waiting for the advent of the snow.

Alma's hand tightened on the rough door frame. Fear coiled in her stomach. Every time John was forced to make the long trek into town she stood like this, awaiting his return. Every moment until his horse appeared in the distance she imagined that some terrible event had taken him from her. And on this night, with the blizzard threatening . . .

The shadows deepened, purpled by the impending storm. Alma shivered and hugged herself beneath the enveloping robe. The land stretched before her: flat, treeless, its sameness mesmerizing. If she looked at it long enough, her eyes would begin to play tricks on her—tricks that held the power to drive her mad.

She'd heard of a woman who had been driven mad by the prairie: a timid, gentle woman who had traveled some miles east with her husband to gather wood. When they had finally stopped their wagon at a grove, the woman had gotten down and run to a tree—the first tree she had touched in three years. It was said they had had to pry her loose, because she refused to stop hugging it.

The sound of a horse's hoofs came from the distance. Behind Alma, ten-year-old Margaret asked: "Is that him? Is it Papa?"

Alma strained to see through the rapidly gathering dusk. "No," she said, her voice flat with disappointment. "No, it's only Mister Carstairs."

The Carstairses, William and Sarah, lived on a claim several miles east of there. It was not unusual for William to stop when passing on his way from town. But John had been in town today, too; why had they not ridden back together?

The coil of fear wound tighter as she went to greet him.

"No, I won't dismount," William Carstairs said in response to her invitation to come inside and warm himself. "Sarah doesn't know I am here, so I must be home swiftly. I've come to ask a favor."

"Certainly. What is it?"

"I'm off to the East in the morning. My mother is ill and hasn't much longer . . . she's asked for me. Sarah is anxious about being alone. As you know, she's been homesick these past two years. Will you look after her?"

"Of course." Alma spoke the words with a readiness she did not feel. She did not like Sarah Carstairs. There was something mean-spirited about the young woman, a suspicious air in the way she dealt with others that bordered on the hostile. But looking after neighbors was an inviolate obligation here on the prairie, essential to survival.

"Of course, we'll look after her," she said more warmly, afraid her reluctance had somehow sounded in her voice. "You need not worry."

After William Carstairs had ridden off, Alma remained in the doorway of the sod house until the horizon had receded into darkness. She would wait for John as long as was necessary, hoping that her hunger for the sight of him had the power to bring him home again.

"Neighbors were the greatest treasure my grandparents had," Mrs. Clark explained. "The pioneer people were a warm-hearted lot, open and giving, closer than many of today's families. And the women in particular were a great source of strength and comfort to one another. My grandmother's friendship with Sarah Carstairs, for example . . ."

"I suppose I must pay a visit to Sarah," Alma said. It was two days later. The snowstorm had never arrived, but even though it had retreated into Nebraska, another seemed to be on the way. If she didn't go to the Carstairses' claim today, she might not be able to look in on Sarah for some time to come.

John grunted noncommittally and went on trimming the wick of the oil lamp. Alma knew he didn't care for Sarah, either, but he was a taciturn man, slow to voice criticism. And he also understood the necessity of standing by one's neighbors.

"I promised William. He was so worried about her." Alma waited, hoping her husband would forbid her to go because of the impending storm. No such dictum was forthcoming, however. John Heusser was not one to distrust his wife's judgment; he would abide by whatever she decided.

So, driven by a promise she wished she had not been obligated to make, Alma set off on horseback within the hour.

The Carstairses' claim was a poor one, although to Alma's way of thinking it need not have been. In the hands of John Heusser it would have been bountiful with wheat and corn, but William Carstairs was an unskilled farmer. His crops had parched even during the past two summers of plentiful rain; his animals fell ill and died of unidentifiable ailments; the house and outbuildings grew ever more ramshackle through his neglect. If Alma were a fanciful woman—and she preferred to believe she was not—she would have said there was a curse on the land. Its appearance on this grim February day did little to dispel the illusion.

In the foreground stood the house, its roof beam sagging, its chimney askew. The barn and other outbuildings behind it looked no better. The horse in the enclosure was bony and spavined; the few chickens seemed too dispirited to scratch at the hard-packed earth. Alma tied her sorrel to the fence and walked toward the house, her reluctance to be there asserting herself until it was nearly a foreboding. There was no sign of welcome from within, none of the flurry of excitement that the arrival of a visitor on the isolated homesteads always occasioned. She called out, knocked at the door. And waited.

After a moment the door opened slowly and Sarah Carstairs looked out. Her dark hair hung loosely about her shoulders; she wore a muslin dress dyed the rich brown of walnut bark. Her eyes were deeply circled—haunted, Alma thought.

Quickly she shook off the notion and smiled. "We've heard that Mister Carstairs had to journey East," she said. "I thought you might enjoy some company."

The younger woman nodded. Then she opened the door wider and motioned Alma inside.

The room was much like Alma's main room at home, with narrow, tall windows, a rough board floor, and an iron stove for both cooking and heating. The curtains at the windows were plain burlap grain sacks, not at all like Alma's neatly stitched muslin ones, with their appliqués of flowers. The furnishings—a pair of rockers, pine cabinet, sideboard, and table—had been new when the Carstairses arrived from the East two years before, but their surfaces were coated with the grime that accumulated from cooking.

Sarah shut the door and turned to face Alma, still not speaking. To cover her confusion Alma thrust out the cornbread she had brought. The younger woman took it, nodding thanks. After a slight hesitation, she set it on the table and motioned somewhat gracelessly at one of the rockers. "Please," she said.

Alma undid the fastenings of her heavy cloak and sat down, puzzled by the strange reception. Sarah went to the stove and added a log, in spite of the room already being quite warm.

"He sent you to spy on me, didn't he?"

The words caught Alma by complete surprise. She stared at Sarah's narrow back, unable to make a reply.

Sarah turned, her sharp features pinched by what might have been anger. "That is why you're here, is it not?" she asked.

"Mister Carstairs did ask us to look out for you in his absence, yes."

"How like him," Sarah said bitterly.

Alma could think of nothing to say to that.

Sarah offered her coffee. As she prepared it, Alma studied the young woman. In spite of the heat in the room and her proximity to the stove, she rubbed her hands together; her shawl slipped off her thin shoulders, and she quickly pulled it back. When the coffee was ready—a bitter, nearly unpalatable brew— she sat cradling the cup in her hands, as if to draw even more warmth from it.

After her earlier strangeness Sarah seemed determined to talk about the commonplace: the storm that was surely due, the difficulty of obtaining proper cloth, her hope that William would not forget the bolt of calico she had requested he bring. She asked Alma about making soap. Had she ever done so? Would she allow her to help the next time so she might learn? As they spoke, she began to wipe beads of moisture from her brow. The room remained very warm; Alma removed her cloak and draped it over the back of the rocker.

Outside, the wind was rising, and the light that came through the narrow windows was tinged with gray. Alma became impatient to be off for home before the storm arrived, but she also became concerned with leaving Sarah alone. The young woman's conversation was rapidly growing erratic and rambling; she broke off in the middle of sentences to laugh irrelevantly. Her brow continued moist, and she threw off her shawl, fanning herself. Alma, who like all frontier women had had considerable experience at doctoring the sick, realized Sarah had been taken by a fever.

Her first thought was to take Sarah to her own home, where she might look after her properly, but one glance out the window discouraged her. The storm was nearing quickly now; the wind gusted, tearing at the dried cornstalks in William Carstairs's uncleared fields, and the sky was streaked with black and purple. A ride of several miles in such weather would be the death of Sarah, do Alma no good, either. She was here for the duration, with only a sick woman to help her make the place secure.

She glanced at Sarah, but the other woman seemed unaware of what was going on outside. Alma said: "You're feeling poorly, aren't you?"

Sarah shook her head vehemently. A strand of dark brown hair fell across her forehead and clung there damply. Alma sensed she was not a woman who would give in easily to illness, would fight any suggestion that she take to her bed until she was near collapse. She thought over the remedies she had administered to others in such a condition, wondered whether Sarah's supplies included the necessary sassafras tea or quinine. Sarah was rambling again—about the prairie, its loneliness and desolation, "... listen to that wind! It's with us every moment. I hate the wind and the cold, I hate the nights when the wolves prowl ..."

A stealthy touch of cold moved along Alma's spine. She, too, feared the wolves and coyotes. John told her it came from having Germanic blood. Their older relatives had often spoken in hushed tones of the wolf packs in the Black Forest. Many of their native fairy tales and legends concerned the cruel cunning of the animals, but John was always quick to point out that these were only stories. "Wolves will not attack a human unless they sense sickness or weakness," he often asserted. "You need only take caution."

But all of the settlers, John included, took great precautions against the roaming wolf packs; no one went out onto the prairie unarmed. And the stories of merciless and unprovoked attacks could not all be unfounded. "I hear wolves at night," Sarah said. "They scratch on the door and the sod. They're hungry. Oh, yes, they're hungry."

Alma suddenly got to her feet, unable to sit for the tautness in her limbs. She felt Sarah's eyes on her as she went to the sideboard and lit the oil lamp. When she turned to Sarah again, the young woman had tilted her head against the high back of the rocker and was viewing her through slitted lids. There was a glitter in the dark crescents that remained visible that struck Alma as somehow malicious.

"Are you afraid of the wolves, Alma?" she asked slyly.

"Anyone with good sense is."

"And you in particular?"

"Of course, I'd be afraid if I met one face-to-face!"

"Only if you were face-to-face with it? Then you won't be afraid staying here with me when they scratch at the door. I tell you, I hear them every night. Their claws go *snick, snick* on the boards."

The words were baiting. Alma felt her dislike for Sarah Carstairs gather strength. She said calmly: "Then you've noticed the storm is fast approaching."

Sarah extended a limp arm toward the window. "Look at the snow."

Alma glanced over there, saw the first flakes drifting past the wavery pane of glass. The sense of foreboding she'd felt upon her arrival intensified, sending little prickles over the surface of her skin.

Firmly she reined in her fear and met Sarah's eyes with a steady gaze. "You're right . . . I must stay here. I'll be as little trouble to you as possible."

"Why should you be trouble? I'll be glad of your company." Her tone mocked the meaning of the words. "We can talk. It's a long time since I've had anyone to talk to. We'll talk of my William."

Alma glanced at the window again, anxious to put her horse into the barn, out of the snow. She thought of the revolver she carried in her saddlebag as defense against the dangers of the prairie; she would feel safer if she brought it inside with her.

"We'll talk of my William," Sarah repeated "You'd like that, wouldn't you, Alma?"

"Of course. But first I must tend to my horse."

"Yes, of course, you'd like talking of William. You like talking to him. All those times when he stops at your place on his way home to me. On his way home, when your John isn't there. Oh, yes, Alma, I know about those visits." Sarah's eyes were wide now, the malicious light shining brightly.

Alma caught her breath. She opened her mouth to contradict the words, then shut it. It was the fever talking, she told herself, exaggerating the fears and delusions that life on the frontier could sometimes foster. There was no sense trying to reason with Sarah. What mattered now was to put the horse up and fetch her weapon. She said briskly, "We'll discuss this when I've returned," donned her cloak, and stepped out into the storm.

The snow was sheeting along on a northwesterly gale. The flakes were small and hard; they stung her face like hailstones. The wind made it difficult to walk; she leaned into it, moving slowly toward the hazy outline of her sorrel. He stood by the rail, his hoofs moving skittishly. Alma grasped his halter, clung to it a moment before she began leading him toward the ramshackle barn. The chickens had long ago fled to their coop. Sarah's bony bay was nowhere in sight.

The doors to the barn stood open, the interior in darkness. Alma led the sorrel inside and waited until her eyes accustomed themselves to the gloom. When they had, she spied a lantern hanging next to the door, matches and flint nearby. She fumbled with them, got the lantern lit, and looked around.

Sarah's bay stood in one of the stalls, apparently accustomed to looking out for itself. The stall was dirty, and the entire barn held an air of neglect. She set the lantern down, unsaddled the sorrel, and fed and watered both horses. As she turned to leave, she saw the dull gleam of an axe lying on top of a pile of wood. Without considering why she was doing so, she picked it up and carried it, along with her gun, outside. The barn doors were warped and difficult to secure, but with some effort she managed.

Back in the house, she found Sarah's rocker empty. She set down the axe and the gun, calling out in alarm. A moan came from beyond the rough burlap that curtained off the next room. Alma went over and pushed aside the cloth.

Sarah lay on a brass bed, her hair fanned out on the pillows. She had crawled under the tumbled quilts and blankets. Alma approached and put a hand to her forehead; it was hot, but Sarah was shivering.

Sarah moaned again. Her eyes opened and focused unsteadily on Alma. "Cold," she said. "So cold . . ."

"You've taken a fever." Alma spoke briskly, a manner she'd found effective with sick people. "Did you remove your shoes before getting into bed?"

Sarah nodded.

"Good. It's best you keep your clothes on, though . . . this storm is going to be a bad one . . . you'll need them for warmth."

Sarah rolled onto her side and drew herself into a ball, shivering violently. She mumbled something, but her words were muffled.

Alma leaned closer. "What did you say?"

"The wolves . . . they'll come tonight, scratching . . ."

"No wolves are going to come here in this storm. Anyway, I've a gun and the axe from your woodpile. No harm will come to us. Try to rest now, perhaps sleep. When you wake, I'll bring some tea that will help break the fever."

Alma went toward the door, then turned to look back at the sick woman. Sarah was curled on her side, but she had moved her head and was watching her. Her eyes were slitted once more, and the light from the lamp in the next room gleamed off them—hard and cold as the icicles that must be forming on the eaves.

Alma was seized by an unreasoning chill. She moved through the door, out into the lamplight, toward the stove's warmth. As she busied herself with finding things in the cabinet, she felt a violent tug of home.

Ridiculous to fret, she told herself. John and Margaret would be fine. They would worry about her, of course, but would know she had arrived here well in advance of the storm. And they would also credit her with the good sense not to start back home on such a night.

She rummaged through the shelves and drawers, found the herbs and tea and some roots that would make a healing brew. Outside, there was a momentary quieting of the wind; in the bedroom Sarah, also, lay quiet. Alma put on the kettle and sat down to wait for it to boil. It was then that she heard the first wolf howls, not far away on the prairie.

"The bravery of the pioneer women has never been equaled," Mrs. Clark told the historian. "And there was a solidarity, a sisterhood among them that you don't see any more. That sisterhood was what sustained my grandmother and Sarah Carstairs as they battled the wolves."

For hours the wolves howled in the distance. Sarah awoke, throwing off the covers, complaining of the heat. Alma dosed her repeatedly with the herbal brew and waited for the fever to break. Sarah tossed about on the bed, raving about wolves and the wind and William. She seemed to have some fevered notion that her husband had deserted her, and nothing Alma would say would calm her. Finally she wore herself out and slipped into a troubled sleep.

Alma prepared herself some tea and pulled one of the rockers close to the stove. She was bone-tired, and the cold was bitter now, invading the little house through every crack and pore in the sod. Briefly she thought she should bring Sarah into the main room, prepare a pallet on the floor nearer the heat source, but she decided it would do the woman more harm than good to be moved. As she sat warming herself and sipping the tea, she gradually became aware of an eerie hush and realized the wind had ceased.

Quickly she set down her cup and went to the window. The snow had stopped, too. Like its sister storm of two days before, this one had retreated north, leaving behind a barren white landscape. The moon had appeared, near to full, and its stark light glistened off the snow.

And against the snow moved the black silhouettes of the wolves.

They came from the north, rangy and shaggy, more like ragged shadows than flesh and blood creatures. Their howling was silenced now, and their gait held purpose. Alma counted five of them, all of a good size yet bony. Hungry.

She stepped back from the window and leaned against the wall beside it. Her breathing was shallow, and she felt strangely light-headed. For a moment she stood, one hand pressed to her midriff, bringing her senses under control. Then she moved across the room, to where William Carstairs's Winchester rifle hung on the wall. When she had it in her hands, she stood looking resolutely at it.

Of course, Alma knew how to fire a rifle; all frontier women did. But she was only a fair shot with it, a far better shot with her revolver. She could use a rifle to fire at the wolves at a distance, but the best she could hope for was to frighten them. Better to wait and see what transpired.

She set the rifle down and turned back to the window. The wolves were still some distance away. And what if they did come to the house, scratch at the door as Sarah had claimed? The house was well built; there was little harm the wolves could do it.

Alma went to the door to the bedroom. Sarah still slept, the covers pushed down from her shoulders. Alma went in and pulled them up again. Then she returned to the main room and the rocker.

The first scratchings came only minutes later. *Snick, snick* on the boards, just as Sarah had said.

Alma gripped the arms of the rocker with icy fingers. The revolver lay in her lap.

The scratching went on. Snuffling noises, too. In the bedroom, Sarah cried out in protest. Alma got up and looked in on her. The sick woman was writhing on the bed. "They're out there! I know they are!"

Alma went to her. "Hush, they won't hurt us." She tried to rearrange Sarah's covers, but she only thrashed harder.

"They'll break the door, they'll find a way in, they'll—" Alma pressed her hand over Sarah's mouth. "Stop it! You'll only do yourself harm."

Surprisingly, Sarah calmed. Alma wiped sweat from her brow and waited. The young woman continued to lie quietly.

When Alma went back to the window, she saw that the wolves had retreated. They stood together, several yards away, as if discussing how to breech the house.

Within minutes they returned. Their scratchings became bolder now, their claws ripped and tore at the sod. Heavy bodies thudded against the door, making the boards tremble.

In the bedroom, Sarah cried out. This time Alma ignored her.

The onslaught became more intense. Alma checked the load on William Carstairs's rifle, then looked at her pistol. Five rounds left. Five rounds, five wolves . . .

The wolves were in a frenzy now—incited, perhaps, by the odor of sickness within the house. Alma remembered John's words: "They will not attack a human unless they sense sickness or weakness." There was plenty of both here.

One of the wolves leapt at the window. The thick glass creaked but did not shatter. There were more thumps at the door; its boards groaned.

Alma took her pistol in both hands, held it ready, moved toward the door.

In the bedroom, Sarah cried out for William. Once again Alma ignored her.

The coil of fear that was so often in the pit of Alma's stomach wound taut. Strangely it gave her strength. She trained the revolver's muzzle on the door, ready should it give.

The attack came from a different quarter: The window shattered, glass smashing on the floor. A gray head appeared, tried to wiggle through the narrow casement. Alma smelled its foul odor, saw its fangs. She fired once . . . twice.

The wolf dropped out of sight.

The assault on the door ceased. Cautiously Alma moved forward. When she looked out the window, she saw the wolf lying dead on the ground—and the others renewing their attack on the door.

Alma scrambled back as another shaggy gray head appeared in the window frame. She fired. The wolf dropped back, snarling.

It lunged once more. Her finger squeezed the trigger. The wolf fell.

One round left. Alma turned, meaning to fetch the rifle. But Sarah stood behind her.

The sick woman wavered on her feet. Her face was coated with sweat, her hair tangled. In her hands she held the axe that Alma had brought from the woodpile.

In the instant before Sarah raised it above her head, Alma saw her eyes. They were made wild by something more than fever. The woman was totally mad.

Disbelief made Alma slow. It was only as the blade began its descent that she was able to move aside.

The blade came down, whacked into the boards where she had stood.

Her sudden motion nearly put her on the floor. She stumbled, fought to steady herself.

From behind her came a scrambling sound. She whirled, saw a wolf wriggling halfway through the window casement.

Sarah was struggling to lift the axe.

Alma pivoted and put her last bullet into the wolf's head.

Sarah had raised the axe. Alma dropped the revolver and rushed at her. She slammed into the young woman's shoulder, sent her spinning toward the stove. The axe crashed to the floor.

As she fell against the hot metal Sarah screamed—a sound more terrifying than the howls of the wolves.

"My grandmother was made of stronger cloth than Sarah Carstairs," Mrs. Clark said. "The wolf attack did irreparable damage to poor Sarah's mind. She was never the same again."

Alma was never sure what had driven the two remaining wolves off—whether it was the death of the others or the terrible keening of the sick and injured woman in the sod house. She was never clear on how she managed to do what needed to be done for Sarah, nor how she got through the remainder of that terrible night. But in the morning when John arrived—so afraid for her safety that he had left Margaret at home and braved the drifted snow alone—Sarah was bandaged and put to bed. The fever had broken, and they were able to transport her to their own home after securing the battered house against the elements.

If John sensed that something more terrible than a wolf attack had transpired during those dark hours, he never spoke of it. Certainly he knew Sarah was in grave trouble, though, because she never said a word throughout her entire convalescence, save to give her thanks when William returned—summoned by them from the East—and took her home. Within the month the Carstairses had deserted their claim and left Kansas, to return to their native state of Vermont. There, Alma hoped, the young woman would somehow find peace.

As for herself, fear still curled in the pit of her stomach as she waited for John on those nights when he was away. But no longer was she shamed by the feeling. The fear, she knew now, was a friend—something that had stood her in good stead once, would be there should she again need it. And now, when she crossed the prairie, she did so with courage, for she and the lifesaving fear were one.

Her story done, Mrs. Clark smiled at the historian. "As I've said, my dear," she concluded, "the women of the Kansas frontier were uncommon in their valor. They faced dangers we can barely imagine today. And they were fearless, one and all."

Her eyes moved away to the window, and to the housing tracts and shoddy commercial enterprises beyond it. "I can't help wondering how women like Alma Heusser would feel about the way the prairie looks today," she added. "I should think they would hate it, and yet . . ."

The historian had been about to shut off her recorder, but now she paused for a final comment. "And yet?" she prompted.

"And yet I think that somehow my grandmother would have understood that our world isn't as bad as it appears on the surface. Alma Heusser has always struck me as a woman who knew that things aren't always as they seem."

The Place That Time Forgot

1990

In San Francisco's Glen Park district there is a small building with the words GREENGLASS 5 & 10¢ STORE painted in faded red letters on its wooden facade. Broadleaf ivy grows in planter boxes below its windows and partially covers their dusty panes. Inside is a counter with jars of candy and bubble gum on top and cigars, cigarettes, and pipe tobacco down below. An old-fashioned jukebox—the kind with colored glass tubes—hulks against the opposite wall. The rest of the room is taken up by counters laden with merchandise that has been purchased at fire sales and manufacturers' liquidations. In a single shopping spree, it is possible for a customer to buy socks, playing cards, off-brand cosmetics, school supplies, kitchen utensils, sports equipment, toys, and light bulbs—all at prices of at least ten years ago.

It is a place forgotten by time, a fragment of yesterday in the midst of today's city.

I have now come to know the curious little store well, but up until one rainy Wednesday last March, I'd done no more than glance inside while passing. But that morning Hank Zahn, my boss at All Souls Legal Cooperative, had asked me to pay a call on its owner, Jody Greenglass.

Greenglass was a client who had asked if Hank knew an investigator who could trace a missing relative for him. It didn't sound like a particularly challenging assignment, but my assistant, who usually handles routine work, was out sick. So at ten o'clock, I put on my raincoat and went over there.

When I pushed open the door I saw there wasn't a customer in sight. The interior was gloomy and damp; a fly buzzed fitfully against one of the windows. I was about to call out, thinking the proprietor must be beyond the curtained doorway at the rear, when I realized a man was sitting on a stool behind the counter. That was all he was doing—just sitting, his eyes fixed on the wall above the jukebox.

He was a big man, elderly, with a belly that bulged out under his yellow shirt and black suspenders. His hair and beard were white and luxuriant, his eyebrows startlingly black by contrast. When I said, "Mr. Greenglass?" he looked at me, and I saw an expression of deep melancholy.

"Yes?" he asked politely.

"I'm Sharon McCone, from All Souls Legal Cooperative."

"Ah, yes. Mr. Zahn said he would send someone."

"I understand you want to locate a missing relative."

"My granddaughter."

"If you'll give me the particulars, I can get on it right away." I looked around for a place to sit but didn't see any chairs.

Greenglass stood. "I'll get you a stool." He went toward the curtained doorway, moving gingerly, as if his feet hurt him. They were encased in floppy slippers.

While I waited for him, I looked up at the wall behind the counter and saw it was plastered with faded pieces of slick paper that at first I took to be paybills. Upon closer examination I realized they were sheet music, probably of forties and fifties vintage. Their artwork was of that era anyway: formally dressed couples performing intricate dance steps; showgirls in extravagant costumes; men with patent leather hair singing their hearts out; perfectly coiffed women showing plenty of even, pearly white teeth. Some of the song titles were vaguely familiar to me: "Dreams of You," "The Heart Never Lies," "Sweet Mystique." Others I had never heard of.

Jody Greenglass came back with a wooden stool and set it on my side of the counter. I thanked him and perched on it, then took a pencil and notebook from my bag. He hoisted himself onto his own stool, sighing heavily.

"I see you were looking at my songs," he said.

"Yes. I haven't really seen any sheet music since my piano teacher gave up on me when I was about twelve. Some of those are pretty old, aren't they?"

"Not nearly as old as I am." He smiled wryly. "I wrote the first in 'thirty-nine, the last in 'fifty-three. Thirty-seven of them in all. A number were hits."

"*You* wrote them?"

He nodded and pointed to the credit line on the one closest to him: "Words and Music by Jody Greenglass."

"Well, for heaven's sake," I said. "I've never met a songwriter before. Were these recorded, too?"

"Sure. I've got them all on the jukebox. Some good singers performed them—Como, Crosby." His smile faded. "But then, in the fifties, popular music changed. Presley, Holly, those fellows—that's what did it. I couldn't change with it. Luckily, I'd always had the store; music was more of a hobby for me. 'My Little Girl' "—he indicated a sheet with a picture-pretty toddler on it—"was the last song I ever sold. Wrote it for my granddaughter when she was born in 'fifty-three. It was *not* a big hit."

"This is the granddaughter you want me to locate?"

"Yes. Stephanie Ann Weiss. If she's still alive, she's thirty-seven now."

"Let's talk about her. I take it she's your daughter's daughter."

"My daughter Ruth's. I only had the one child."

"Is your daughter still living?"

"I don't know." His eyes clouded. "There was a . . . an estrangement. I lost track of them both a couple of years after Stephanie was born."

"If it's not too painful, I'd like to hear about that."

"It's painful, but I can talk about it." He paused, thoughtful. "It's funny. For a long time it didn't hurt, because I had my anger and disappointment to shield myself. But those kinds of emotions can't last without fuel. Now that they're gone, I hurt as much as if it happened yesterday. That's what made me decide to try to make amends to my granddaughter."

"But not your daughter, too?"

He made a hand motion as if to erase the memory of her. "Our parting was too bitter; there are some things that can't be atoned for, and frankly, I'm afraid to try. But Stephanie—if her mother hasn't completely turned her against me, there might be a chance for us."

"Tell me about this parting."

In a halting manner that conveyed exactly how deep his pain went, he related his story.

Jody Greenglass had been widowed when his daughter was only ten and had raised the girl alone. Shortly after Ruth graduated from high school, she married the boy next door. The Weiss family had lived in the house next to Greenglass's Glen Park cottage for close to twenty years, and their son, Eddie, and Ruth were such fast childhood friends that a gate was installed in the fence between their adjoining backyards. Jody, in fact, thought of Eddie as his own son.

After their wedding the couple moved north to the small town of Petaluma, where Eddie had found a good job in the accounting department of one of the big egg hatcheries. In 1953, Stephanie Ann was born. Greenglass didn't know exactly when or why they began having marital problems; perhaps they hadn't been ready for parenthood, or perhaps the move from the city to the country didn't suit them. But by 1955, Ruth had divorced Eddie and taken up with a Mexican national named Victor Rios.

"I like to think I'm not prejudiced," Greenglass said to me. "I've mellowed with the years, I've learned. But you've got to remember that this was the mid-fifties. Divorce wasn't all that common in my circle. And people like us didn't even marry outside our faith, much less form relationships out of wedlock with those of a different race. Rios was an illiterate laborer, not even an American citizen. I was shocked that Ruth was living with this man, exposing her child to such a situation."

"So you tried to stop her."

He nodded wearily. "I tried. But Ruth wasn't listening to me anymore. She'd always been such a good girl. Maybe that was the problem—she'd been *too* good and it was her time to rebel. We quarreled bitterly, more than once. Finally I told her that if she kept on living with Rios, she and her child would be dead to me. She said that was just fine with her. I never saw or heard from her again."

"Never made any effort to contact her?"

"Not until a couple of weeks ago. I nursed my anger and bitterness, nursed them well. But then in the fall I had some health problems—my heart—and realized I'd be leaving this world without once seeing my grown-up granddaughter. So when I was back on my feet again, I went up to Petaluma, checked the phone book, asked around their old neighborhood. Nobody remembered them. That was when I decided I needed a detective."

I was silent, thinking of the thirty-some years that had elapsed. Locating Stephanie Ann Weiss—or whatever name she might now be using—after all that time would be difficult. Difficult, but not impossible, given she was still alive. And certainly more challenging than the job I'd initially envisioned.

Greenglass seemed to interpret my silence as pessimism. He said, "I know it's been a very long time, but isn't there something you can do for me? I'm seventy-eight years old; I want to make amends before I die."

I felt a prickle of excitement that I often experience when faced with an out-of-the-ordinary problem. I said, "I'll try to help you. As I said before, I can get on it right away."

I gathered more information from him—exact spelling of names, dates—then asked for the last address he had for Ruth in Petaluma. He had to go in the back of the store where, he explained, he now lived, to look it up. While he did so, I wandered over to the jukebox and studied the titles of the 78s. There was a basket of metal slugs on the top of the machine, and on a whim I fed it one and punched out selection E-3, "My Little Girl." The somewhat treacly lyrics boomed forth in a swarmy baritone; I could understand why the song hadn't gone over in the days when America was gearing up to feverishly embrace the likes of Elvis Presley. Still, I had to admit the melody was pleasing—downright catchy, in fact. By the time Greenglass returned with the address, I was humming along.

—∞—

Back in my office at All Souls, I set a skip trace in motion, starting with an inquiry to my friend Tracy at the Department of Motor Vehicles regarding Ruth Greenglass, Ruth Weiss, Ruth Rios, Stephanie Ann Weiss, Stephanie Ann Rios, or any variant thereof. A check with directory assistance revealed that neither woman currently had a phone in Petaluma or the surrounding communities. The Petaluma Library had nothing on them in their reverse street directory. Since I didn't know either woman's occupation, professional affiliations, doctor, or dentist, those avenues were closed to me. Petaluma High School would not divulge information about graduates, but the woman in Records with whom I spoke assured me that no one named Stephanie Weiss or Stephanie Rios had attended during the mid- to late sixties. The county's voter registration had a similar lack of information. The next line of inquiry to pursue while waiting for a reply from the DMV was vital statistics—primarily marriage licenses and death certificates—but for those I would need to go to the Sonoma County Courthouse in Santa Rosa. I checked my watch, saw it was only a little after one, and decided to drive up there.

Santa Rosa, some fifty miles north of San Francisco, is a former country town that has risen to the challenge of migrations from the crowded communities of the Bay Area and become a full-fledged city with a population nearing a hundred thousand. Testimony to this is the new County Administration Center on its outskirts, where I found the Recorder's Office housed in a building on the aptly named Fiscal Drive.

My hour-and-a-half journey up there proved well worth the time: the clerk I dealt with was extremely helpful, the records easily accessed. Within half an hour, for a nominal fee, I was in possession of a copy of Ruth Greenglass Weiss's death certificate. She had died of cancer at Petaluma General Hospital in June of 1974; her next of kin was shown as Stephanie Ann Weiss, at an address on Bassett Street in Petaluma. It was a different address from the last one Greenglass had had for them.

The melody of "My Little Girl" was still running through my head as

I drove back down the freeway to Petaluma, the southernmost community in the county. A picturesque river town with a core of nineteenth-
century business buildings, Victorian homes, and a park with a
bandstand, it is surrounded by little hills—which is what the Indian word
petaluma means. The town used to be called the Egg Basket of the World,
because of the proliferation of hatcheries such as the one where Eddie
Weiss worked, but since the decline of the egg- and chicken-ranching
businesses, it has become a trendy retreat for those seeking to avoid the
high housing costs of San Francisco and Marin. I had friends there—
people who had moved up from the city for just that reason—so I knew
the lay of the land fairly well.

Bassett Street was on the older west side of town, far from the bland,
treeless tracts that have sprung up to the east. The address I was seeking
turned out to be a small white-frame bungalow with a row of lilac bushes
planted along the property line on either side. Their branches hung heavy
with the unopened blossoms; in a few weeks the air would be sweet with
their perfume.

When I went up on the front porch and rang the bell, I was greeted by
a very pregnant young woman. Her name, she said, was Bonita Clark; she
and her husband Russ had bought the house two years before from some
people named Berry. The Berrys had lived there for at least ten years and
had never mentioned anyone named Weiss.

I hadn't really expected to find Stephanie Weiss still in residence, but
I'd hoped the present owner could tell me where she had moved. I said,
"Do you know anyone on the street who might have lived here in the early
seventies?"

"Well, there's old Mrs. Caubet. The pink house on the corner with all
the rosebushes. She's lived here forever."

I thanked her and went down the sidewalk to the house she'd indicated. Its front yard was a thicket of rosebushes whose colors ranged from
yellows to reds to a particularly beautiful silvery purple.

Mrs. Caubet turned out to be a tall, slender woman with sleek gray
hair, vigorous-looking in a blue sweatsuit and athletic shoes. I felt a flicker
of amusement when I first saw her, thinking of how Bonita Clark had

called her "old," said she'd lived there "forever." Interesting, I thought, how one's perspective shifts.

Yes, Mrs. Caubet said after she'd examined my credentials, she remembered the Weisses well. They'd moved to Bassett Street in 1970. "Ruth was already ill with the cancer that killed her," she added. "Steff was only seventeen, but so grown-up, the way she took care of her mother."

"Did either of them ever mention a man named Victor Rios?"

The woman's expression became guarded. "You say you're working for Ruth's father?"

"Yes."

She looked thoughtful, then motioned at a pair of white wicker chairs on the wraparound porch. "Let's sit down."

We sat. Mrs. Caubet continued to look thoughtful, pleating the ribbing on the cuff of her sleeve between her fingers. I waited.

After a time she said, "I wondered if Ruth's father would ever regret disowning her."

"He's in poor health. It's made him realize he doesn't have much longer to make amends."

"A pity that it took him until now. He's missed a great deal because of his stubbornness. I know; I'm a grandparent myself. And I'd like to put him in touch with Steff, but I don't know what happened to her. She left Petaluma six months after Ruth died."

"Did she say where she planned to go?"

"Just something about getting in touch with relatives. By that I assumed she meant her father's family in the city. She promised to write, but she never did, not even a Christmas card."

"Will you tell me what you remember about Ruth and Stephanie? It may give me some sort of lead, and besides, I'm sure my client will want to know about their lives after his falling-out with Ruth."

She shrugged. "It can't hurt. And to answer your earlier question, I have heard of Victor Rios. He was Ruth's second husband; although the marriage was a fairly long one, it was not a particularly good one. When she was diagnosed as having cancer, Rios couldn't deal with her illness, and he left her. Ruth divorced him, took back her first husband's name. It was either that, she once told me, or Greenglass, and she was even more bitter toward her father than toward Rios."

"After Victor Rios left, what did Ruth and Stephanie live on? I assume Ruth couldn't work."

"She had some savings—and, I suppose, alimony."

"It couldn't have been much. Jody Greenglass told me Rios was an illiterate laborer."

Mrs. Caubet frowned. "That's nonsense! He must have manufactured the idea, out of prejudice and anger at Ruth for leaving her first husband. He considered Eddie Weiss a son, you know. It's true that when Ruth met Rios, he didn't have as good a command of the English language as he might, but he did have a good job at Sunset Lane and Twine. They weren't rich, but I gather they never lacked for the essentials."

It made me wonder what else Greenglass had manufactured. "Did Ruth ever admit to living with Rios before their marriage?"

"No, but it wouldn't have surprised me. She always struck me as a nonconformist. And that, of course, would better explain her father's attitude."

"One other thing puzzles me," I said. "I checked with the high school, and they have no record of Stephanie attending."

"That's because she went to a parochial school. Rios was Catholic, and that's what he wanted. Ruth didn't care either way. As it was, Steff dropped out in her junior year to care for her mother. I offered to arrange home care so she might finish her education—I was once a social worker and knew how to go about it—but Steff said no. The only thing she really missed about school, she claimed, was choir and music class. She had a beautiful singing voice."

So she'd inherited her grandfather's talent, I thought. A talent I was coming to regard as considerable, since I still couldn't shake the lingering melody of "My Little Girl."

"How did Stephanie feel about her grandfather? And Victor Rios?" I asked.

"I think she was fond of Rios, in spite of what he'd done to her mother. Her feelings toward her grandfather I'm less sure of. I do remember that toward the end Steff had become very like her mother; observing that alarmed me somewhat."

"Why?"

"Ruth was a very bitter woman, totally turned in on herself. She had no real friends, and she seemed to want to draw Steff into a little circle from which the two of them could fend off the world together. By the time Steff left Petaluma she'd closed off, too, withdrawn from what few friends she'd been permitted. I'd say such bitterness in so young a woman is cause for alarm, wouldn't you?"

"I certainly would. And I suspect that if I do find her, it's going to be very hard to persuade her to reconcile with her grandfather."

Mrs. Caubet was silent for a moment, then said, "She might surprise you."

"Why do you say that?"

"It's just a feeling I have. There was a song Mr. Greenglass wrote in celebration of Steff's birth. Do you know about it?"

I nodded.

"They had a record of it. Ruth once told me that it was the only thing he'd ever given them, and she couldn't bear to take that away from Steff. Anyway, she used to play it occasionally. Sometimes I'd go over there, and Steff would be humming the melody while she worked around the house."

That didn't mean much, I thought. After all, I'd been mentally humming it since that morning.

When I arrived back in the city I first checked at All Souls to see if there had been a response to my inquiry from my friend at the DMV. There hadn't. Then I headed for Glen Park to break the news about his daughter's death to Jody Greenglass, as well as to get some additional information.

This time there were a few customers in the store: a young couple poking around in Housewares; an older woman selecting some knitting yarn. Greenglass sat at his customary position behind the counter. When I gave him a copy of Ruth's death certificate, he read it slowly, then folded it carefully and placed it in his shirt pocket. His lips trembled inside his nest of fluffy white beard, but otherwise he betrayed no emotion. He said, "I take it you didn't find Stephanie Ann at that address."

"She left Petaluma about six months after Ruth died. A neighbor thought she might have planned to go to relatives. Would that be the Weisses, do you suppose?"

He shook his head. "Norma and Al died within months of each other in the mid-sixties. They had a daughter, name of Sandra, but she married and moved away before Eddie and Ruth did. To Los Angeles, I think. I've no idea what her husband's name might be."

"What about Eddie Weiss—what happened to him?"

"I didn't tell you?"

"No."

"He died a few months after Ruth divorced him. Auto accident. He'd been drinking. Damned near killed his parents, following so close on the divorce. That was when Norma and Al stopped talking to me; I guess they blamed Ruth. Things got so uncomfortable there on the old street that I decided to come live here at the store."

The customer who had been looking at the yarn came up, her arms piled high with heather-blue skeins. I stepped aside so Greenglass could ring up the sale, glanced over my shoulder at the jukebox, then went up to it and played "My Little Girl" again. As the mellow notes poured from the machine, I realized that what had been running through my head all day was not quite the same. Close, very close, but there were subtle differences.

And come to think of it, why should the song have made such an impression, when I'd only heard it once? It was catchy, but there was no reason for it to haunt me as it did.

Unless I'd heard something like it. Heard it more than once. And recently . . .

I went around the counter and asked Greenglass if I could use his phone. Dialed the familiar number of radio KSUN, the Light of the Bay. My former lover, Don Del Boccio, had just come into the studio for his six-to-midnight stint as disk jockey, heartthrob, and hero to half a million teenagers who have to be either hearing-impaired or brain-damaged, and probably both. Don said he'd be glad to provide expert assistance, but not until he got off work. Why didn't I meet him at his loft around twelve-thirty?

I said I would and hung up, thanking the Lord that I somehow manage to remain on mostly good terms with the men from whom I've parted.

Don said, "Hum it again."

"You know I'm tone-deaf."

"You have no vocal capabilities. You can distinguish tone, though. I can interpret your warbling. Hum it."

We were seated in his big loft in the industrial district off Third Street, surrounded by his baby grand piano, drums, sound equipment, books, and—a recent acquisition—a huge aquarium of tropical fish. I'd taken a nap after going home from Greenglass's and felt reasonably fresh. Don—a big, easygoing man who enjoys his minor celebrity status and also keeps up his serious musical interests—was reasonably wired. We were drinking red wine and picking at a plate of antipasto he'd casually thrown together.

"Hum it," he said again.

I hummed, badly, my face growing hot as I listened to myself. He imitated me—on key. "It's definitely not rock, not with that tempo. Soft rock? Possibly. There's something about it . . . that sextolet—"

"That what?"

"An irregular rhythmic grouping. One of the things that makes it stick in your mind. Folk? Maybe country. You say you think you've been hearing it recently?"

"That's the only explanation I can come up with for it sticking in my mind the way it has."

"Hmm. There's been some new stuff coming along recently, out of L.A. rather than Nashville, that might—You listen to a country station?"

"KNEW, when I'm driving sometimes."

"Disloyal thing."

"I never listened to KSUN much, even when we . . ."

Our eyes met and held. We were both remembering, but I doubted if the mental images were the same. Don and I are too different; that was what ultimately broke us up.

After a moment he grinned and said, "Well, no one over the mental age of twelve does. Listen, what I guess is that you've been hearing a song that's a variation on the melody of the original one. Which is odd, because it's an uncommon one to begin with."

"Unless the person who wrote the new song knew the old one."

"Which you tell me isn't likely, since it wasn't very popular. What are you investigating—a plagiarism case?"

I shook my head. If Jody Greenglass's last song had been plagiarized, I doubted if it was intentional—at least not on the conscious level. I said, "Is it possible to track down the song, do you suppose?"

"Sure. Care to run over to the studio? I can do a scan on our library, see what we've got."

"But KSUN doesn't play anything except hard rock."

"No, but we get all sorts of promos, new releases. Let's give it a try."

"There you are," Don said. " 'It Never Stops Hurting.' Steff Rivers. Atlas Records. Released last November."

I remembered it now, half heard as I'd driven the city streets with my old MG's radio tuned low. Understandable that for her professional name she'd Anglicized that of the only father figure she'd ever known.

"Play it again," I said.

Don pressed the button on the console and the song flooded the sound booth, the woman's voice soaring and clean. The lyrics were about grieving for a lost lover, but I thought I knew other experiences that had gone into creating the naked emotion behind them: the scarcely known father who had died after the mother left him; the grandfather who had rejected both mother and child; the stepfather who had been unable to cope with fatal illness and had run away.

When the song ended and silence filled the little booth, I said to Don, "How would I go about locating her?"

He grinned. "One of the Atlas reps just happens to be a good friend of mine. I'll give her a call in the morning, see what I can do."

—⁓—

The rain started again early the next morning. It made the coastal road that
wound north on the high cliffs above the Pacific dangerously slick. By the
time I arrived at the village of Gualala, just over the Mendocino County
line, it was close to three, and the cloud cover was beginning to break up.

The town, I found, was just a strip of homes and businesses between
the densely forested hills and the sea. A few small shopping centers, some
unpretentious eateries, the ubiquitous realty offices, a new motel, and a
hotel built during the logging boom of the late 1800s—that was about it.
It would be an ideal place, I thought, for retirees or starving artists, as well
as a young woman seeking frequent escape from the pressures of a career
in the entertainment industry.

Don's record-company friend had checked with someone she knew in
Steff Rivers's producer's office to find out her present whereabouts, had
sworn me to secrecy about where I'd received the information and given
me an address. I'd pinpointed the turnoff from the main highway on a
county map. It was a small lane that curved off toward the sea about a half
mile north of town; the house at its end was actually a pair of A-frames,
weathered gray shingle, connected by a glassed-in walkway. Hydrangeas
and geraniums bloomed in tubs on either side of the front door; a stained-
glass oval depicting a sea gull in flight hung in the window. I left the MG
next to a gold Toyota sports car parked in the drive.

There was no answer to my knock. After a minute I skirted the house
and went around back. The lawn there was weedy and uneven; it sloped
down toward a low grapestake fence that guarded the edge of the ice
plant–covered bluff. On a bench in front of it sat a small figure wearing a
red rain slicker, the hood turned up against the fine mist. The person was
motionless, staring out at the flat, gray ocean.

When I started across the lawn, the figure turned. I recognized Steff
Rivers from the publicity photo Don had dug out of KSUN's files the
night before. Her hair was black and cut very short, molded to her head
like a bathing cap; her eyes were large, long-lashed, and darkly luminous.
In her strong features I saw traces of Jody Greenglass's.

She called out, "Be careful there. Some damn rodent has dug the
yard up."

I walked cautiously the rest of the way to the bench.

"I don't know what's wrong with it," she said, gesturing at a hot tub on a deck opening off the glassed-in walkway of the house. "All I can figure is something's plugging the drain."

"I'm sorry?"

"Aren't you the plumber?"

"No."

"Oh. I knew she was a woman, and I thought . . . Who are you, then?"

I took out my identification and showed it to her. Told her why I was there.

Steff Rivers seemed to shrink inside her loose slicker. She drew her knees up and hugged them with her arms.

"He needs to see you," I concluded. "He wants to make amends."

She shook her head. "It's too late for that."

"Maybe. But he *is* sincere."

"Too bad." She was silent for a moment, turning her gaze back toward the sea. "How did you find me? Atlas and my agent know better than to give out my address."

"Once I knew Stephanie Weiss was Steff Rivers, it was easy."

"And how did you find *that* out?"

"The first clue I had was 'It Never Stops Hurting.' You adapted the melody of 'My Little Girl' for it."

"I what?" She turned her head toward me, features frozen in surprise. Then she was very still, seeming to listen to the song inside her head. "I guess I did. My God . . . I *did*!"

"You didn't do it consciously?"

"No. I haven't thought of that song in years. I . . . I broke the only copy of the record that I had the day my mother died." After a moment she added, "I suppose the son of a bitch will want to sue me."

"You know that's not so." I sat down beside her on the wet bench, turned my collar up against the mist. "The lyrics of that song say a lot about you, you know."

"Yeah—that everybody's left me or fucked me over as long as I've lived."

"Your grandfather wants to change that pattern. He wants to come back to you."

"Well, he can't. I don't want him."

A good deal of her toughness was probably real—would have to be, in order for her to survive in her business—but I sensed some of it was armor that she could don quickly whenever anything threatened the vulnerable core of her persona. I remained silent for a few minutes, wondering how to get through to her, watching the waves ebb and flow on the beach at the foot of the cliff. Eroding the land, giving some of it back again. Take and give, take and give . . .

Finally I asked, "Why were you sitting out here in the rain?"

"They said it would clear around three. I was just waiting. Waiting for something good to happen."

"A lot of good things must happen to you. Your career's going well. This is a lovely house, a great place to escape to."

"Yeah, I've done all right. 'It Never Stops Hurting' wasn't my first hit, you know."

"Do you remember a neighbor of yours in Petaluma—a Mrs. Caubet?"

"God! I haven't thought of her in years either. How is she?"

"She's fine. I talked with her yesterday. She mentioned your talent."

"Mrs. Caubet. Petaluma. That all seems so long ago."

"Where did you go after you left there?"

"To my Aunt Sandra, in L.A. She was married to a record-company flack. It made breaking in a little easier."

"And then?"

"Sandra died of a drug overdose. She found out that the bastard she was married to had someone else."

"What did you do then?"

"What do you think? Kept on singing and writing songs. Got married."

"And?"

"What the hell is this and-and-and? Why am I even talking to you?"

I didn't reply.

"All right. Maybe I need to talk to somebody. That didn't work out—the marriage, I mean—and neither did the next one. Or about a dozen other relationships. But things just kept clicking along with my career. The money kept coming in. One weekend a few years ago I was up here visiting friends at Sea Ranch. I saw this place while we were just driving around, and . . . now I live here when I don't have to be in L.A. Alone. Secure. Happy."

"Happy, Steff?"

"Enough." She paused, arms tightening around her drawn-up knees. "Actually, I don't think much about being happy anymore."

"You're a lot like your grandfather."

She rolled her eyes. "Here we go again!"

"I mean it. You know how he lives? Alone in the back of his store. He doesn't think much about being happy either."

"He still has that store?"

"Yes." I described it, concluding, "It's a place that's just been forgotten by time. *He's* been forgotten. When he dies, there won't be anybody to care—unless you do something to change that."

"Well, it's too bad about him, but in a way he had it coming."

"You're pretty bitter toward someone you don't even know."

"Oh, I know enough about him. Mama saw to that. You think *I'm* bitter? You should have known her. She'd been thrown out by her own father, had two rotten marriages, and then she got cancer. Mama was a very bitter, angry woman."

I didn't say anything, just looked out at the faint sheen of sunlight that had appeared on the gray water.

Steff seemed to be listening to what she'd just said. "I'm turning out exactly like my mother, aren't I?"

"It's a danger."

"I don't seem to be able to help it. I mean, it's all there in that song. It never *does* stop hurting."

"No, but some things can ease the pain."

"The store—it's in the Glen Park district, isn't it?"

"Yes. Why?"

"I get down to the city occasionally."

"How soon can you be packed?"

She looked over her shoulder at the house, where she had been secure in her loneliness. "I'm not ready for that yet."

"You'll never be ready. I'll drive you, go to the store with you. If it doesn't work out, I'll bring you right back here."

"Why are you doing this? I'm a total stranger. Why didn't you just turn my address over to my grandfather, let him take it from there?"

"Because you have the right to refuse comfort and happiness. We all have that."

Steff Rivers tried to glare at me but couldn't quite manage it. Finally—as a patch of blue sky appeared offshore and the sea began to glimmer in the sun's rays—she unwrapped her arms from her knees and stood.

"I'll go get my stuff," she said.

Somewhere in the City

1990

At 5:04 p.m. on October 17, 1989, the city of San Francisco was jolted by an earthquake that measured a frightening 7.1 on the Richter scale. The violent tremors left the Bay Bridge impassable, collapsed a double-decker freeway in nearby Oakland, and toppled or severely damaged countless homes and other buildings. From the Bay Area to the seaside town of Santa Cruz some 100 miles south, 65 people were killed and thousands left homeless. And when the aftershocks subsided, San Francisco entered a new era—one in which things would never be quite the same. As with all cataclysmic events, the question "Where were you when?" will forever provoke deeply emotional responses in those of us who lived through it.

WHERE I WAS WHEN: the headquarters of the Golden Gate Crisis Hotline in the Noe Valley district. I'd been working a case there—off and on, and mostly in the late afternoon and evening hours, for over two weeks—with very few results and with a good deal of frustration.

The hotline occupied one big windowless room behind a rundown coffeehouse on Twenty-fourth Street. The location, I'd been told, was not so much one of choice as of convenience (meaning the rent was affordable), but had I not known that, I would have considered it a stroke of genius. There was something instantly soothing about entering through the coffeehouse, where the aromas of various blends permeated the air and steam rose from huge stainless steel urns. The patrons were unthreatening—mostly shabby and relaxed, reading or conversing with their feet propped up on chairs. The pastries displayed in the glass case were comfort food at its purest—reminders of the days when calories and cholesterol didn't count. And the round face of the proprietor, Lloyd Warner, was welcoming and kind as he waved troubled visitors through to the crisis center.

On that Tuesday afternoon I arrived at about twenty to five, answering Lloyd's cheerful greeting and trying to ignore the chocolate-covered doughnuts in the case. I had a dinner date at seven thirty, had been promised some of the best French cuisine on Russian Hill, and was unwilling to spoil my appetite. The doughnuts called out to me, but I turned a deaf ear and hurried past.

The room beyond the coffeehouse contained an assortment of mismatched furniture: several desks and chairs of all vintages and materials; phones in colors and styles ranging from standard black Touchtone to a shocking turquoise Princess; three tattered easy chairs dating back to the fifties; and a card table covered with literature on health and psychological services. Two people manned the desks nearest the door. I went to the desk with the turquoise phone, plunked my briefcase and bag down on it, and turned to face them.

"He call today?" I asked.

Pete Lowry, a slender man with a bandit's mustache who was director of the center, took his booted feet off the desk and swiveled to face me. "Nope. It's been quiet all afternoon."

"Too quiet." This came from Ann Potter, a woman with dark frizzed hair who affected the aging-hippie look in jeans and flamboyant overblouses. "And this weather—I don't like it one bit."

"Ann's having one of her premonitions of gloom and doom," Pete said. "Evil portents and omens lurk all around us—although most of them went up front for coffee a while ago."

Ann's eyes narrowed to a glare. She possessed very little sense of humor, whereas Pete perhaps possessed too much. To forestall the inevitable spat, I interrupted. "Well, I don't like the weather much myself. It's muggy and too warm for October. It makes me nervous."

"Why?" Pete asked.

I shrugged. "I don't know, but I've felt edgy all day."

The phone on his desk rang. He reached for the receiver. "Golden Gate Crisis Hotline, Pete speaking."

Ann cast one final glare at his back as she crossed to the desk that had been assigned to me. "It has been too quiet," she said defensively. "Hardly anyone's called, not even to inquire about how to deal with a friend or a family member. That's not normal, even for a Tuesday."

"Maybe all the crazies are out enjoying the warm weather."

Ann half smiled, cocking her head. She wasn't sure if what I'd said was funny or not, and didn't know how to react. After a few seconds her attention was drawn to the file I was removing from my briefcase. "Is that about our problem caller?"

"Uh-huh." I sat down and began rereading my notes silently, hoping she'd go away. I'd meant it when I'd said I felt on edge, and was in no mood for conversation.

The file concerned a series of calls that the hotline had received over the past month—all from the same individual, a man with a distinctive raspy voice. Their content had been more or less the same: an initial plaint of being all alone in the world with no one to care if he lived or died; then a gradual escalating from despair to anger, in spite of the trained counselors' skillful responses; and finally the declaration that he had an assault rifle and was going to kill others and himself. He always ended with some variant on the statement, "I'm going to take a whole lot of people with me."

After three of the calls, Pete had decided to notify the police. A trace was placed on the center's lines, but the results were unsatisfactory; most of the time the caller didn't stay on the phone long enough, and in the instances that the calls could be traced, they turned out to have originated from booths in the Marina district. Finally, the trace was taken off, the official conclusion being that the calls were the work of a crank—and possibly one with a grudge against someone connected with the hotline.

The official conclusion did not satisfy Pete, however. By the next morning he was in the office of the hotline's attorney at All Souls Legal Cooperative, where I am chief investigator. And half an hour after that, I was assigned to work the phones at the hotline as often as my other duties permitted, until I'd identified the caller. Following a crash course from Pete in techniques for dealing with callers in crisis—augmented by some reading of my own—they turned me loose on the turquoise phone.

After the first couple of rocky, sweaty-palmed sessions, I'd gotten into it:

become able to distinguish the truly disturbed from the fakers or the merely curious; learned to gauge the responses that would work best with a given individual; succeeded at eliciting information that would permit a crisis team to go out and assess the seriousness of the situation in person. In most cases, the team would merely talk the caller into getting counseling. However, if they felt immediate action was warranted, they would contact the SFPD, who had the authority to have the individual held for evaluation at S. F. General Hospital for up to seventy-two hours.

During the past two weeks the problem caller had been routed to me several times, and with each conversation I became more concerned about him. While his threats were melodramatic, I sensed genuine disturbance and desperation in his voice; the swift escalation of panic and anger seemed much out of proportion to whatever verbal stimuli I offered. And, as Pete had stressed in my orientation, no matter how theatrical or frequently made, any threat of suicide or violence toward others was to be taken with the utmost seriousness by the hotline volunteers.

Unfortunately, I was able to glean very little information from the man. Whenever I tried to get him to reveal concrete facts about himself, he became sly and would dodge my questions. Still, I could make several assumptions about him: he was youngish, reasonably well-educated, and Caucasian. The traces to the Marina indicated he probably lived in that bayside district— which meant he had to have a good income. He listened to classical music (three times I'd heard it playing in the background) from a transistor radio, by the tinny tonal quality. Once I'd caught the call letters of the FM station—one with a wide-range signal in the Central Valley town of Fresno. Why Fresno? I'd wondered. Perhaps he was from there? But that wasn't much to go on; there were probably several Fresno transplants in his part of the city.

When I looked up from my folder, Ann had gone back to her desk. Pete was still talking in low, reassuring tones with his caller. Ann's phone rang, and she picked up the receiver. I tensed, knowing the next call would cycle automatically to my phone.

When it rang some minutes later, I glanced at my watch and jotted down the time while reaching over for the receiver. Four fifty-eight. "Golden Gate Crisis Hotline, Sharon speaking."

The caller hung up—either a wrong number or, more likely, someone who lost his nerve. The phone rang again about twenty seconds later and I answered it in the same manner.

"Sharon. It's me." The greeting was the same as the previous times, the raspy voice unmistakable.

"Hey, how's it going?"

A long pause, labored breathing. In the background I could make out the strains of music—Brahms, I thought. "Not so good. I'm really down today."

"You want to talk about it?"

"There isn't much to say. Just more of the same. I took a walk a while ago, thought it might help. But the people, out there flying their kites, I can't take it."

"Why is that?"

"I used to . . . ah, forget it."

"No, I'm interested."

"Well, they're always in couples, you know."

When he didn't go on, I made an interrogatory sound.

"The whole damn world is in couples. Or families. Even here inside my little cottage I can feel it. There are these apartment buildings on either side, land I can feel them pressing in on me, and I'm here all alone."

He was speaking rapidly now, his voice rising. But as his agitation increased, he'd unwittingly revealed something about his living situation. I made a note about the little cottage between the two apartment buildings.

"This place where the people were flying kites," I said, "do you go there often?"

"Sure—it's only two blocks away." A sudden note of sullenness now entered his voice—a part of the pattern he'd previously exhibited. "Why do you want to know about that?"

"Because . . . I'm sorry, I forgot your name."

No response.

"It would help if I knew what to call you."

"Look, bitch, I know what you're trying to do."

"Oh?"

"Yeah. You want to get a name, an address. Send the cops out. Next thing I'm chained to the wall at S. F. General. I've been that route before. But I know my rights now; I went down the street to the Legal Switchboard, and they told me . . ."

I was distracted from what he was saying by a tapping sound—the stack trays on the desk next to me bumped against the wall. I looked over there, frowning. What was causing that . . . ?

". . . gonna take the people next door with me . . ."

I looked back at the desk in front of me. The lamp was jiggling.

"What the hell?" the man on the phone exclaimed.

My swivel chair shifted. A coffee mug tipped and rolled across the desk and into my lap.

Pete said, "Jesus Christ, we're having an earthquake!"

". . . The ceiling's coming down!" The man's voice was panicked now.

"Get under a door frame!" I clutched the edge of the desk, ignoring my own advice.

I heard a crash from the other end of the line. The man screamed in pain. "Help me! Please help—" And then the line went dead.

For a second or so I merely sat there—longtime San Franciscan, frozen by my own disbelief. All around me formerly inanimate objects were in motion. Pete and Ann were scrambling for the archway that led to the door of the coffeehouse.

"Sharon, get under the desk!" she yelled at me.

And then the electricity cut out, leaving the windowless room in blackness. I dropped the dead receiver, slid off the chair, crawled into the kneehole of the desk. There was a cracking, a violent shifting, as if a giant hand had seized the building and twisted it. Tremors buckled the floor beneath me.

This is a bad one. Maybe the big one that they're always talking about.

The sound of something wrenching apart. Pellets of plaster rained down on the desk above me. Time had telescoped; it seemed as if the quake had been going on for many minutes, when in reality it could not have been more than ten or fifteen seconds.

Make it stop! Please make it stop!

And then, as if whatever powers-that-be had heard my unspoken plea, the shock waves diminished to shivers, and finally ebbed.

Blackness. Silence. Only bits of plaster bouncing off the desks and the floor.

"Ann?" I said. "Pete?" My voice sounded weak, tentative.

"Sharon?" It was Pete. "You okay?"

"Yes. You?"

"We're fine."

Slowly I began to back out of the kneehole. Something blocked it— the chair. I shoved it aside, and emerged. I couldn't see a thing, but I could feel fragments of plaster and other unidentified debris on the floor. Something cut into my palm; I winced.

"God, it's dark," Ann said. "I've got some matches in my purse. Can you—"

"No matches," I told her. "Who knows what shape the gas mains are in."

"Oh, right."

Pete said, "Wait, I'll open the door to the coffeehouse."

On hands and knees I began feeling my way toward the sound of their voices. I banged into one of the desks, overturned a wastebasket, then finally reached the opposite wall. As I stood there, Ann's cold hand reached out to guide me. Behind her I could hear Pete fumbling at the door.

I leaned against the wall. Ann was close beside me, her breathing erratic. Pete said, "Goddamned door's jammed." From behind it came voices of the people in the coffeehouse.

Now that the danger was over—at least until the first of the after-shocks—my body sagged against the wall, giving way to tremors of its own manufacture. My thoughts turned to the lover with whom I'd planned to have dinner: where had he been when the quake hit? And what about my cats, my house? My friends and my coworkers at All Souls? Other friends scattered throughout the Bay Area?

And what about a nameless, faceless man somewhere in the city who had screamed for help before the phone went dead?

The door to the coffeehouse burst open, spilling weak light into the room. Lloyd Warner and several of his customers peered anxiously through it. I prodded Ann—who seemed to have lapsed into lethargy— toward them.

The coffeehouse was fairly dark, but late afternoon light showed beyond the plate glass windows fronting on the street. It revealed a floor that was awash in spilled liquid and littered with broken crockery. Chairs were tipped over—whether by the quake or the patrons' haste to get to shelter I couldn't tell. About ten people milled about, talking noisily.

Ann and Pete joined them, but I moved forward to the window. Outside, Twenty-fourth Street looked much as usual, except for the lack of traffic and pedestrians. The buildings still stood, the sun still shone, the air drifting through the open door of the coffeehouse was still warm and muggy. In this part of the city, at least, life went on.

Lloyd's transistor radio had been playing the whole time—tuned to the station that was carrying the coverage of the third game of the Bay Area World Series, due to start at five-thirty. I moved closer, listening.

The sportscaster was saying, "Nobody here knows *what's* going on. The Giants have wandered over to the A's dugout. It looks like a softball game where somebody forgot to bring the ball."

Then the broadcast shifted abruptly to the station's studios. A newswoman was relaying telephone reports from the neighborhoods. I was relieved to hear that Bernal Heights, where All Souls is located, and my own small district near Glen Park were shaken up but for the most part undamaged. The broadcaster concluded by warning listeners not to use their phones except in cases of emergency. Ann snorted and said, "Do as I say but not . . ."

Again the broadcast made an abrupt switch—to the station's traffic helicopter. "From where we are," the reporter said, "it looks as if part of the upper deck on the Oakland side of the Bay Bridge has collapsed onto the bottom deck. Cars are pointing every which way, there may be some in the water. And on the approaches—" The transmission broke, then resumed after a number of static-filled seconds. "It looks as if the Cypress structure on the Oakland approach to the bridge has also collapsed. Oh my God, there are cars and people—" This time the transmission broke for good.

It was very quiet in the coffeehouse. We all exchanged looks—fearful, horrified. This was an extremely bad one, if not the catastrophic one they'd been predicting for so long.

Lloyd was the first to speak. He said, "I'd better see if I can insulate the urns in some way, keep the coffee hot as long as possible. People'll need it tonight." He went behind the counter, and in a few seconds a couple of the customers followed.

The studio newscast resumed. ". . . fires burning out of control in the Marina district. We're receiving reports of collapsed buildings there, with people trapped inside . . ."

The Marina district. People trapped.

I thought again of the man who had cried out for help over the phone. Of my suspicion, more or less confirmed by today's conversation, that he lived in the Marina.

Behind the counter Lloyd and the customers were wrapping the urns in dishtowels. Here—and in other parts of the city, I was sure—people were already overcoming their shock, gearing up to assist in the relief effort. There was nothing I could do in my present surroundings, but I hurried to the back room and groped until I found my purse on the floor beside the desk. As I picked it up, an aftershock hit—nothing like the original trembler, but strong enough to make me grab the chair for support. When it stopped, I went shakily out to my car.

Twenty-fourth Street was slowly coming to life. People bunched on the sidewalks, talking and gesturing. A man emerged from one of the shops, walked to the center of the street and surveyed the facade of his building. In the parking lot of nearby Bell Market, employees and customers gathered by the grocery cans. A man in a butcher's apron looked around, shrugged, and headed for a corner tavern. I got into my MG and took a city map from the side pocket.

The Marina area consists mainly of early twentieth-century stucco homes and apartment buildings built on fill on the shore of the bay—which meant the quake damage there would naturally be bad. The district extends roughly from the Fisherman's Wharf area to the Presidio—not large, but large enough, considering I had few clues as to where within its boundary my man lived. I spread out the map against the steering wheel and examined it.

The man had said he'd taken a walk that afternoon, to a place two blocks from his home where people were flying kites. That would be the Marina Green near the Yacht Harbor, famous for the elaborate and often fantastical kites flown there in fine weather. Two blocks placed the man's home somewhere on the far side of Northpoint Street.

I had one more clue: in his anger at me he'd let it slip that the Legal Switchboard was "down the street." The switchboard, a federally funded assistance group, was headquartered in one of the piers at Fort Mason, at the east end of the Marina. While several streets in that vicinity ended at Fort Mason, I saw that only two—Beach and Northpoint—were within two blocks of the Green as well.

Of course, I reminded myself, "down the street" and "two blocks" could have been generalizations or exaggerations. But it was somewhere to start. I set the map aside and turned the key in the ignition.

The trip across the city was hampered by near-gridlock traffic on some streets. All the stoplights were out; there were no police to direct the panicked motorists. Citizens helped out: I saw men in three-piece suits, women in heels and business attire, even a ragged man who looked to be straight out of one of the homeless shelters, all playing traffic cop. Sirens keened, emergency vehicles snaked from lane to lane. The car radio kept reporting further destruction; there was another aftershock, and then another, but I scarcely felt them because I was in motion.

As I inched along a major crosstown arterial, I asked myself why I was doing this foolhardy thing. The man was nothing to me, really—merely a voice on the phone, always self-pitying, and often antagonistic and potentially violent. I ought to be checking on my house and the folks at All Souls; if I wanted to help people, my efforts would have been better spent in my own neighborhood or Bernal Heights. But instead I was traveling to the most congested and dangerous part of the city in search of a man I'd never laid eyes on.

As I asked the question, I knew the answer. Over the past two weeks the man had told me about his deepest problems. I'd come to know him in spite of his self-protective secretiveness. And he'd become more to me than just the subject of an investigation; I'd begun to care whether he lived or died. Now we had shared a peculiarly intimate moment—that of being together, if only in voice, when the catastrophe that San Franciscans feared the most had struck. He had called for help; I had heard his terror and pain. A connection had been established that could not be broken.

After twenty minutes and little progress, I cut west and took a less-traveled residential street through Japantown and over the crest of Pacific Heights. From the top of the hill I could see and smell the smoke over the Marina; as I crossed the traffic-snarled intersection with Lombard, I could see the flames. I drove another block, then decided to leave the MG and continue on foot.

All around I could see signs of destruction now: a house was twisted at a tortuous angle, its front porch collapsed and crushing a car parked at the curb; on Beach Street an apartment building's upper story had slid into the street, clogging it with rubble; three bottom floors of another building were flattened, leaving only the top intact.

I stopped at a corner, breathing hard, nearly choking on the thickening smoke. The smell of gas from broken lines was vaguely nauseating—frightening, too, because of the potential for explosions. To my left the street was cordoned off; fire department hoses played on the blazes—weakly, because of damaged water mains. People congregated everywhere, staring about with horror-struck eyes; they huddled together, clinging to one another; many were crying. Firefighters and police were telling people to go home before dark fell. "You should be looking after your property," I heard one say. "You can count on going seventy-two hours without water or power."

"Longer than that," someone said.

"It's not safe here," the policeman added. "Please go home."

Between sobs, a woman said, "What if you've got no home to go to anymore?"

The cop had no answer for her.

Emotions were flying out of control among the onlookers. It would have been easy to feed into it—to weep, even panic. Instead, I turned my back to the flaming buildings, began walking the other way, toward Fort Mason. If the man's home was beyond the barricades, there was nothing I could do for him. But if it lay in the other direction, where there was a lighter concentration of rescue workers, then my assistance might save his life.

I forced myself to walk slower, to study the buildings on either side of the street. I had one last clue that could lead me to the man: he'd said he lived in a little cottage between two apartment buildings. The homes in this district were mostly of substantial size; there couldn't be too many cottages situated in just that way.

Across the street a house slumped over to one side, its roof canted at a forty-five-degree angle, windows from an apartment house had popped out of their frames, and its iron fire escapes were tangled and twisted like a cat's cradle of yarn. Another home was unrecognizable, merely a heap of rubble. And over there, two four-story apartment buildings leaned together, forming an arch over a much smaller structure.

I rushed across the street, pushed through a knot of bystanders. The smaller building was a tumble-down mass of white stucco with a smashed red tile roof and a partially flattened iron fence. It had been a Mediterranean-style cottage with grillwork over high windows; now the grills were bent and pushed outward; the collapsed windows resembled swollen-shut eyes.

The woman standing next to me was cradling a terrified cat under her loose cardigan sweater. I asked, "Did the man who lives in the cottage get out okay?"

She frowned, tightened her grip on the cat as it burrowed deeper. "I don't know who lives there. It's always kind of deserted-looking."

A man in front of her said, "I've seen lights, but never anybody coming or going."

I moved closer. The cottage was deep in the shadows of the leaning buildings, eerily silent. From above came a groaning sound, and then a piece of wood sheared off the apartment house to the right, crashing onto what remained of the cottage's roof. I looked up, wondering how long

before one or the other of the buildings toppled. Wondering if the man
was still alive inside the compacted mass of stucco.

A man in jeans and a sweatshirt came up and stood beside me. His face
was smudged and abraded; his clothing was smeared with dirt and what
looked to be blood; he held his left elbow gingerly in the palm of his
hand. "You were asking about Dan?" he said.

So that was the anonymous caller's name. "Yes. Did he get out okay?"

"I don't think he was at home. At least, I saw him over at the Green
around quarter to five.

"He was at home. I was talking with him on the phone when the
quake hit."

"Oh, Jesus." The man's face paled under the smudges. "My name's Mel;
I live . . . lived next door. Are you a friend of Dan's?"

"Yes," I said, realizing it was true.

"That's a surprise." He stared worriedly at the place where the two
buildings leaned together.

"Why?"

"I thought Dan didn't have any friends left. He's pushed us away ever
since the accident."

"Accident?"

"You must be a new friend, or else you'd know. Dan's woman was killed
on the freeway last spring. A truck crushed her car."

The word "crushed" seemed to hang in the air between us. I said, "I've
got to try to get him out of there," and stepped over the flattened portion
of the fence.

Mel said, "I'll go with you."

I looked skeptically at his injured arm.

"It's nothing, really," he told me. "I was helping an old lady out of my
building, and a beam grazed me."

"Well—" I broke off as a hail of debris came from the building to the left.

Without further conversation, Mel and I crossed the small front yard,
skirting fallen bricks, broken glass, and jagged chunks of wallboard. Dusk
was coming on fast now; here in the shadows of the leaning buildings it
was darker than on the street. I moved toward where the cottage's front

door should have been, but couldn't locate it. The windows, with their protruding grillwork, were impassable.

I said, "Is there another entrance?"

"In the back, off a little service porch."

I glanced to either side. The narrow passages between the cottage and the adjacent buildings were jammed with debris. I could possibly scale the mound at the right, but I was leery of setting up vibrations that might cause more debris to come tumbling down.

Mel said, "You'd better give it up. The way the cottage looks, I doubt he survived."

But I wasn't willing to give it up—not yet. There must be a way to at least locate Dan, see if he was alive. But how?

And then I remembered something else from our phone conversations.

I said, "I'm going back there."

"Let me."

"No, stay here. That mound will support my weight, but not yours." I moved toward the side of the cottage before Mel could remind me of the risk I was taking.

The mound was over five feet high. I began to climb cautiously, testing every hand- and foothold. Twice, jagged chunks of stucco cut my fingers; a piece of wood left a line of splinters on the back of my hand. When I neared the top, I heard the roar of a helicopter, its rotors flapping overhead. I froze, afraid that the air currents would precipitate more debris, then scrambled down the other side of the mound into a weed-choked backyard.

As I straightened, automatically brushing dirt from my jeans, my foot slipped on the soft, spongy ground, then sank into a puddle, probably a water main was broken nearby. The helicopter still hovered overhead; I couldn't hear a thing above its racket. Nor could I see much: it was even darker back here. I stood still until my eyes adjusted.

The cottage was not so badly damaged at its rear. The steps to the porch had collapsed and the rear wall leaned inward, but I could make out a door frame opening into blackness inside. I glanced up in irritation at the helicopter, saw it was going away. Waited, and then listened . . .

And heard what I had been hoping to. The music was now Beethoven—his third symphony, the *Eroica*. Its strains were muted, tinny. Music played by an out-of-area FM station, coming from a transistor radio. A transistor whose batteries were functioning long after the electricity had cut out. Whose batteries might have outlived its owner.

I moved quickly to the porch, grasped the iron rail beside the collapsed steps, and pulled myself up. I still could see nothing inside the cottage. The strains of the *Eroica* continued to pour forth, close by now.

Reflexively I reached into my purse for the small flashlight I usually kept there, then remembered it was at home on the kitchen counter—a reminder for me to replace its weak batteries. I swore softly, then started through the doorway, calling out to Dan.

No answer.

"Dan!"

This time I heard a groan.

I rushed forward into the blackness, following the sound of the music. After a few feet I came up against something solid, banging my shins. I lowered a hand, felt around. It was a wooden beam, wedged crosswise.

"Dan?"

Another groan. From the floor—perhaps under the beam. I squatted and made a wide sweep with my hands. They encountered a wool-clad arm; I slid my fingers down it until I touched the wrist, felt for the pulse. It was strong, although slightly irregular.

"Dan," I said, leaning closer, "it's Sharon, from the hotline. We've got to get you out of here."

"Unh, Sharon?" His voice was groggy, confused. He'd probably been drifting in and out of consciousness since the beam fell on him.

"Can you move?" I asked.

"Something on my legs."

"Do they feel broken?"

"No, just pinned."

"I can't see much, but I'm going to try to move this beam off you. When I do, roll out from under."

"Okay."

From the position at which the beam was wedged, I could tell it would have to be raised. Balancing on the balls of my feet, I got a good grip on it and shoved upward with all my strength. It moved about six inches and then slipped from my grasp. Dan grunted.

"Are you all right?"

"Yeah. Try it again."

I stood, grasped it, and pulled this time. It yielded a little more, and I heard Dan slide across the floor. "I'm clear," he said—and just in time, because I once more lost my grip. The beam crashed down, setting up a vibration that made plaster fall from the ceiling.

"We've got to get out of here fast," I said. "Give me your hand."

He slipped it into mine—long-fingered, work-roughened. Quickly we went through the door, crossed the porch, jumped to the ground. The radio continued to play forlornly behind us. I glanced briefly at Dan, couldn't make out much more than a tall, slender build and a thatch of pale hair. His face turned from me, toward the cottage.

"Jesus," he said in an awed voice.

I tugged urgently at his hand. "There's no telling how long those apartment buildings are going to stand."

He turned, looked up at them, said "Jesus" again. I urged him toward the mound of debris.

This time I opted for speed rather than caution—a mistake, because as we neared the top, a cracking noise came from high above. I gave Dan a push, slid after him. A dark, jagged object hurtled down, missing us only by inches. More plaster board—deadly at that velocity.

For a moment I sat straddle-legged on the ground, sucking in my breath, releasing it tremulously, gasping for more air. Then hands pulled me to my feet and dragged me across the yard toward the sidewalk—Mel and Dan.

Night had fallen by now. A fire had broken out in the house across the street. Its red-orange flickering showed the man I'd just rescued: ordinary-looking, with regular features that were now marred by dirt and a long cut on the forehead, from which blood had trickled and dried. His pale eyes were studying me; suddenly he looked abashed and shoved both hands into his jeans pocket.

After a moment he asked, "How did you find me?"

"I put together some of the things you'd said on the phone. Doesn't matter now."

"Why did you even bother?"

"Because I care."

He looked at the ground.

I added, "There never was any assault rifle, was there?"

He shook his head.

"You made it up, so someone would pay attention."

"Yeah."

I felt anger welling up—irrational, considering the present circumstances, but nonetheless justified. "You didn't have to frighten the people at the hotline. All you had to do was ask them for help. Or ask friends like Mel. He cares. People do, you know."

"Nobody does."

"Enough of that! All you have to do is look around to see how much people care about each other. Look at your friend here." I gestured at Mel, who was standing a couple of feet away, staring at us. "He hurt his arm rescuing an old lady from his apartment house. Look at those people over by the burning house—they're doing everything they can to help the firefighters. All over this city people are doing things for one another. Goddamn it, I'd never laid eyes on you, but I risked my life anyway!"

Dan was silent for a long moment. Finally he looked up at me. "I know you did. What can I do in return?"

"For me? Nothing. Just pass it on to someone else."

Dan stared across the street at the flaming building, looked back into the shadows where his cottage lay in ruins. Then he nodded and squared his shoulders. To Mel he said, "Let's go over there, see if there's anything we can do."

He put his arm around my shoulders and hugged me briefly, then he and Mel set off at a trot.

The city is recovering now, as it did in 1906, and as it doubtless will when the next big quake hits. Resiliency is what disaster teaches us, I guess—

along with the preciousness of life, no matter how disappointing or bur-
densome it may often seem.

Dan's recovering, too: he's only called the hotline twice, once for a
referral to a therapist, and once to ask for my home number so he could
invite me to dinner. I turned the invitation down, because neither of us
needs to dwell on the trauma of October seventeenth, and I was fairly sure
I heard a measure of relief in his voice when I did so.

I'll never forget Dan, though—or where I was when. And the strains
of Beethoven's Third Symphony will forever remind me of the day after
which things would never be the same again.

Final Resting Place

1990

T he voices of the well-dressed lunch crowd reverberated off the chromium and Formica of Max's Diner. Busy waiters made their way through the room, trays laden with meatloaf, mashed potatoes with gravy, and hot turkey sandwiches. The booths and tables and counter seats of the trendy restaurant—one of the forerunners of San Francisco's fifties revival—were all taken, and a sizable crowd awaited their turn in the bar. What I waited for was Max's famous onion rings, along with the basket of sliders—little burgers—I'd just ordered.

I was seated in one of the window booths overlooking Third Street with Diana Richards, an old friend from college. Back in the seventies, Diana and I had shared a dilapidated old house a few blocks from the U.C. Berkeley campus with a fluctuating group of anywhere from five to ten other semi-indigent students, but nowadays we didn't see much of each other. We had followed very different paths since graduation: she'd become a media buyer for the city's top ad agency, drove a new Mercedes, and lived graciously in one of the new condominium complexes near the financial district; I'd become a private investigator with a law cooperative, drove a beat-up MG, and lived chaotically in an old cottage that was constantly in the throes of renovation. I still liked Diana, though—enough that when she'd called that morning and asked to meet with me to discuss a problem, I'd dropped everything and driven downtown to Max's.

Milkshakes—the genuine article—arrived. I poured a generous dollop into my glass from the metal shaker. Diana just sat there, staring out at the passersby on the sidewalk. We'd exchanged the usual small talk while waiting for a table and scanning the menu ("Have you heard from any of the old gang?" "Do you still like your job?" "Any interesting men in your life?"), but then she'd grown uncharacteristically silent. Now I sipped and waited for her to speak.

After a moment she sighed and turned her yellow eyes toward me. I've never known anyone with eyes so much like a cat's; their color always startles me when we meet to renew our friendship. And they are her best feature, lending her heart-shaped face an exotic aura and perfectly complementing her wavy light brown hair.

She said, "As I told you on the phone, Sharon, I have a problem."

"A serious one?"

"Not serious so much as . . . nagging."

"I see. Are you consulting me on a personal or a professional basis?"

"Professional, if you can take on something for someone who's not an All Souls client." All Souls is the legal cooperative where I work; our clients purchase memberships, much as they would in a health plan, and pay fees that are scaled to their incomes.

"Then you actually want to hire me?"

"I'd pay whatever the going rate is."

I considered. At the moment my regular caseload was exceptionally light. And I could certainly use some extra money; I was in the middle of a home-repair crisis that threatened to drain my checking account long before payday. "I think I can fit it in. Why don't you tell me about the problem."

Diana waited while our food was delivered, then began: "Did you know that my mother died two months ago?"

"No, I didn't. I'm sorry."

"Thanks. Mom died in Cabo San Lucas, at a second home she and my father have down there. Dad had the cause of death hushed up; she'd been drinking a lot and passed out and drowned in the hot tub."

"God."

"Yes." Diana's mouth pulled down grimly. "It was a horrible way to go. And so unlike my mother. Dad naturally wanted to keep it from getting into the papers, so it wouldn't damage his precious reputation."

The bitterness and thinly veiled anger in her voice brought me a vivid memory of Carl Richards: a severe, controlling man, chief executive with a major insurance company. When we'd been in college, he and his wife, Teresa, had crossed the Bay Bridge from San Francisco once a month to take Diana and a few of her friends to dinner. The evenings were not great successes; the restaurants the Richardses chose were too elegant for our preferred jeans and T-shirts, the conversations stilted to the point of strangulation. Carl Richards made no pretense of liking any of us; he used the dinners as a forum for airing his disapproval of the liberal political climate at Berkeley, and boasted that he had refused to pay more than Diana's basic expenses because she'd insisted on enrolling there. Teresa Richards tried hard, but her ineffectual social flutterings reminded me of a bird trapped in a confined space. Her husband often mocked what she said, and it was obvious she was completely dominated by him. Even with the nonwisdom of nineteen, I sensed they were a couple who had grown apart, as the man made his way in the world and the woman tended the home fires.

Diana plucked a piece of fried chicken from the basket in front of her, eyed it with distaste, then put it back. I reached for an onion ring.

"Do you know what the San Francisco Memorial Columbarium is?" she asked.

I nodded. The Columbarium was the old Odd Fellows mausoleum for cremated remains, in the Inner Richmond district. Several years ago it had been bought and restored by the Neptune Society—a sort of All Souls of the funeral industry, specializing in low-cost cremations and interments, as well as burials at sea.

"Well, Mom's ashes are interred there, in a niche on the second floor. Once a week, on Tuesday, I have to consult with a major client in South San Francisco, and on the way back I stop in over the noon hour and . . .

visit. I always take flowers—carnations, they were her favorite. There's a little vaselike thing attached to the wall next to the niche where you can put them. There were never any other flowers in it until three weeks ago. But then carnations, always white ones with a dusting of red, started to appear."

I finished the onion ring and started in on the little hamburgers. When she didn't go on, I said, "Maybe your father left them."

"That's what I thought. It pleased me, because it meant he missed her and had belatedly come to appreciate her. But I had my monthly dinner with him last weekend." She paused, her mouth twisting ruefully. "Old habits die hard. I suppose I do it to keep up the illusion we're a family. Anyway, at dinner I mentioned how glad I was he'd taken to visiting the Columbarium, and he said he hadn't been back there since the interment."

The man certainly didn't trouble with sentiment, I thought. "Well, what about another relative? Or a friend?"

"None of our relatives live in the area, and I don't know of any close friend Mom might have had. Social friends, yes. The wives of other executives at Dad's company, the neighbors on Russian Hill, the ladies she played bridge with at her club. But no one who would have cared enough to leave flowers."

"So you want me to find out who is leaving them."

"Yes."

"Why?"

"Because since they've started appearing it's occurred to me that I never really knew my mother. I loved her, but in my own way I dismissed her almost as much as my father did. If Mom had that good a friend, I want to talk with her. I want to see my mother through the eyes of someone who *did* know her. Can you understand that?"

"Yes, I can," I said, thinking of my own mother. I would never dismiss Ma—wouldn't *dare* dismiss the hundred-and-five-pound dynamo who warms and energizes the McCone homestead in San Diego—but at the same time I didn't really know much about her life, except as it related to Pa and us kids.

"What about the staff at the Columbarium?" I asked. "Could they tell you anything?"

"The staff occupy a separate building. There's hardly ever anyone in the mausoleum, except for occasional visitors, or when they hold a memorial service."

"And you've always gone on Tuesday at noon?"

"Yes."

"Are the flowers you find there fresh?"

"Yes. And that means they'd have to be left that morning, since the Columbarium's not open to visitors on Monday."

"Then it means this friend goes there before noon on Tuesdays."

"Yes. Sometime after nine, when it opens."

"Why don't you spend a Tuesday morning there and wait for her?"

"As I said, I have regular meetings with a major client then. Besides, I'd feel strange, just approaching her and asking to talk about Mom. It would be better if I knew something about her first. That's why I thought of you. You could follow her, find out where she lives and something about her. Knowing a few details would make it easier for me."

I thought for a moment. It was an odd request, something she really didn't need a professional investigator for, and not at all the kind of job I'd normally take on. But Diana was a friend, so for old times' sake . . .

"Okay," I finally said. "Today's Monday. I'll go to the Columbarium at nine tomorrow morning and check it out."

Tuesday dawned gray, with a slowly drifting fog that provided a perfect backdrop for a visit to the dead. Foghorns moaned a lament as I walked along Loraine Court, a single block of pleasant stucco homes that dead-ended at the gates of the park surrounding the Columbarium. The massive neoclassical building loomed ahead of me, a poignant reminder of the days when the Richmond district was mostly sand dunes stretching toward the sea, when San Franciscans were still laid to rest in the city's soil. That was before greed gripped the real estate market in the early decades of the century, and developers decided the limited acreage was too valuable to be wasted on cemeteries. First cremation was outlawed within the city, then burials, and by the late 1930s the last bodies were moved south to the necropolis of Colma. Only the Columbarium remained, protected from destruction by the Homestead Act.

When I'd first moved to the city I'd often wondered about the verdi-grised copper dome that could be glimpsed when driving along Geary Boulevard, and once I'd detoured to investigate the structure it topped. What I'd found was a decaying rotunda with four small wings jutting off. Cracks and water stains marred its facade; weeds grew high around it; one stained-glass window had buckled with age. The neglect it had suffered since the Odd Fellows had sold it to an absentee owner some forty years before had taken its full toll.

But now I saw the building sported a fresh coat of paint: a medley of lavender, beige, and subdued green highlighted its ornate architectural details. The lawn was clipped, the surrounding fir trees pruned, the names and dates on the exterior niches newly lettered and easily readable. The dome still had a green patina, but somehow it seemed more appropriate than shiny copper.

As I followed the graveled path toward the entrance, I began to feel as if I were suspended in a shadow world between the past and the present. A block away Geary was clogged with cars and trucks and buses, but here their sounds were muted. When I looked to my left I could see the side wall of the Coronet Theater, splattered with garish, chaotic graffiti; but when I turned to the right, my gaze was drawn to the rich colors and harmonious composition of a stained-glass window. The modern-day city seemed to recede, leaving me not unhappily marooned on this small island in time.

The great iron doors to the building stood open, inviting visitors. I crossed a small entry and stepped into the rotunda itself. Tapestry-cushioned straight chairs were arranged in rows there, and large floral offerings stood next to a lectern, probably for a memorial service. I glanced briefly at them and then allowed my attention to be drawn upward, toward the magnificent round stained-glass window at the top of the dome. All around me soft, prismatic light fell from it and the other windows.

The second and third floors of the building were galleries—circular mezzanines below the dome. The interior was fully as ornate as the exterior and also freshly painted, in restful blues and white and tans and gilt that highlighted the bas-relief flowers and birds and medallions. As I turned and walked toward an enclosed staircase to my left, my heels clicked on the mosaic marble floor; the sound echoed all around me. Otherwise the rotunda was hushed and chill; as near as I could tell, I was the only person there.

Diana had told me I would find her mother's niche on the second floor, in the wing called Kepheus—named, as the others were, after one of the four Greek winds. I climbed the curving staircase and began moving along the gallery. The view of the rotunda floor, through railed archways that were banked with philodendrons, was dizzying from their height; the wall opposite the arches was honeycombed with niches. Some of them were covered with plaques engraved with people's names and dates of birth and death; others were glass-fronted and afforded a view of the funerary urns. Still others were vacant, a number marked with red tags—meaning, I assumed, that the niche had been sold.

I found the name Kepheus in sculpted relief above an archway several yards from the entrance to the staircase. Inside was a smallish room—no more than twelve by sixteen feet—containing perhaps a hundred niches. At its front were two marble pillars and steps leading up to a large niche containing a coffin-shaped box; the ones on the walls to either side of it were backed with stained-glass windows. Most of the other niches were smaller and contained urns of all types—gold, silver, brass, ceramics. Quickly I located Teresa Richards's: at eye level near the entry, containing a simple jar of hand-thrown blue pottery. There were no flowers in the metal holder attached to it.

Now what? I thought, shivering from the sharp chill and glancing around the room. The reason for the cold was evident: part of the leaded-glass skylight was missing. Water stains were prominent on the vaulted ceiling and walls; the pillars were chipped and cracked. Diana had mentioned that the restoration work was being done piecemeal, because the Neptune Society—a profit-making organization—was not eligible for funding usually available to those undertaking projects of historical significance. While I could appreciate the necessity of starting on the ground floor and working upward, I wasn't sure I would want my final resting place to be in a structure that—up here, at least—reminded me of Dracula's castle.

And then I thought, just listen to yourself. It isn't as if you'd be peering through the glass of your niche at your surroundings! And just think of being here with all the great San Franciscans—Adolph Sutro, A. P. Hotaling, the Stanfords and Folgers and Magnins. Of course, it isn't as if you'd be creeping out of your niche at night to hold long, fascinating conversations with them, either.

I laughed aloud. The sound seemed to be sucked from the room and whirled in an inverted vortex toward the dome. Quickly I sobered and considered how to proceed. I couldn't just be standing here when Teresa Richards's friend paid her call—*if* she paid her call. Better to move about on the gallery, pretending to be a history buff studying the niches out there.

I left the Kepheus room and walked around the gallery, glancing at the names, admiring the more ornate or interesting urns, peering through archways. Other than the tapping of my own heels on the marble, I heard nothing. When I leaned out and looked down at the rotunda floor, then up at the gallery above me, I saw no one. I passed a second staircase, wandered along, glanced to my left, and saw familiar marble pillars.

What is this? I wondered. How far have I walked? Surely I'm not already back where I started.

But I was. I stopped, puzzled, studying what I could discern of the Columbarium's layout.

It was a large building, but by virtue of its imposing architecture it seemed even larger. I'd had the impression I'd only traveled partway around the gallery, when in reality I'd made the full circle.

I ducked into the Kepheus room to make sure no flowers had been placed in the holder at Teresa Richards's niche during my absence. Disoriented as I'd been, it wouldn't have surprised me to find that someone had come and gone. But the little vase was still empty.

Moving about, I decided, was a bad idea in this place of illusion and filtered light. Better to wait in the Kepheus room, appearing to pay my respects to one of the other persons whose ashes were interred there.

I went inside, chose a niche belonging to someone who had died the previous year, and stood in front of it. The remains were those of an Asian man—one of the things I'd noticed was the ethnic diversity of the people who had chosen the Columbarium as their resting place—and his urn was of white porcelain, painted with one perfect, windblown tree. I stared at it, trying to imagine what the man's life had been, its happiness and sorrows. And all the time I listened for a footfall.

After a while I heard voices, down on the rotunda floor. They boomed for a moment, then there were sounds as if the tapestried chairs were being rearranged. Finally all fell as silent as before. Fifteen minutes passed. Footsteps came up the staircase, slow and halting. They moved along the gallery and went by. Shortly after that there were more voices, women's that came close and then faded.

Was it always this deserted? I wondered. Didn't anyone visit the dead who rested all alone?

More sounds again, down below. I glanced at my watch, was surprised to see it was ten thirty.

Footsteps came along the gallery—muted and squeaky this time, as if the feet were shod in rubber soles. Light, so light I hadn't heard them on the staircase. And close, coming through the archway now.

I stared at the windbent tree on the urn, trying to appear reverent, oblivious to my surroundings.

The footsteps stopped. According to my calculations, the person who had made them was now in front of Teresa Richards's niche.

For a moment there was no sound at all. Then a sigh. Then noises as if someone was fitting flowers into the little holder. Another sigh. And more silence.

After a moment I shifted my body ever so slightly. Turned my head. Strained my peripheral vision.

A figure stood before the niche, head bowed as if in prayer. A bunch of carnations blossomed in the holder—white, with a dusting as red as blood. The figure was clad in a dark blue windbreaker, faded jeans, and worn athletic shoes. Its hands were clasped behind its back.

It wasn't the woman Diana had expected I would find. It was a man,

slender and tall, with thinning gray hair. And he looked very much like a
grieving lover.

At first I was astonished, but I had to control the urge to laugh at Diana's
and my joint naïveté. A friend of mine has coined a phrase for that kind
of childlike thinking: "teddy bears on the brain." Even the most cynical of
us occasionally falls prey to it, especially when it comes to relinquishing
the illusion that our parents—while they may be flawed—are basically
infallible. Almost everyone seems to have difficulty setting that idea aside,
probably because we fear that acknowledging their human frailty will
bring with it a terrible and final disappointment. And that, I supposed,
was what my discovery would do to Diana.

But maybe not. After all, didn't this mean that someone had not only
failed to dismiss Teresa Richards, but actually loved her? Shouldn't Diana
be able to take comfort from that?

Either way, now was not the time to speculate. My job was to find out
something about this man. Had it been the woman I'd expected, I might
have felt free to strike up a conversation with her, mention that Mrs.
Richards had been an acquaintance. But with this man, the situation was
different: he might be reluctant to talk with a stranger, might not want his
association with the dead woman known. I would have to follow him, use
indirect means to glean my information.

I looked to the side again; he stood in the same place, staring silently
at the blue pottery urn. His posture gave me no clue as to how long he
would remain there. As near as I could tell, he'd given me no more than
a cursory glance upon entering, but if I departed at the same time he did,
he might become curious. Finally I decided to leave the room and wait on
the opposite side of the gallery. When he left, I'd take the other staircase
and tail him at a safe distance.

I went out and walked halfway around the rotunda, smiling politely at
two old ladies who had just arrived laden with flowers. They stopped at
one of the niches in the wall near the Kepheus room and began arguing
about how to arrange the blooms in the vase, in voices loud enough to
raise the niche's occupant. Relieved that they were paying no attention to

me, I slipped behind a philodendron on the railing and trained my eyes on the opposite archway. It was ten minutes or more before the man came through it and walked toward the staircase.

I straightened and looked for the staircase on this side. I didn't see one.

That can't be! I thought, then realized I was still a victim of my earlier delusion. While I'd gotten it straight as to the distance around the rotunda and the number of small wings jutting off it, I hadn't corrected my false assumption that there were two staircases instead of one.

I hurried around the gallery as fast as I could without making a racket. By the time I reached the other side and peered over the railing, the man was crossing toward the door. I ran down the stairs after him.

Another pair of elderly women were entering. The man was nowhere in sight. I rushed toward the entry, and one of the old ladies glared at me. As I went out, I made mental apologies to her for offending her sense of decorum.

There was no one near the door, except a gardener digging in a bed of odd, white-leafed plants. I turned left toward the gates to Loraine Court. The man was just passing through them. He walked unhurriedly, his head bent, hands shoved in the pockets of his windbreaker.

I adapted my pace to his, went through the gates, and started along the opposite sidewalk. He passed the place where I'd left my MG and turned right on Anza Street. He might have parked his car there, or he could be planning to catch a bus or continue on foot. I hurried to the corner, slowed, and went around it.

The man was unlocking the door of a yellow VW bug three spaces down. When I passed, he looked at me with that blank, I'm-not-really-seeing-you expression that we city dwellers adopt as protective coloration. His face was thin and pale, as if he didn't spend a great deal of time out-doors; he wore a small beard and mustache, both liberally shot with gray. I returned the blank look, then glanced at his license plate and consigned its number to memory.

"It's a man who's been leaving the flowers," I said to Diana. "Gordon DeRosier, associate professor of art at S. F. State. Fifty-three years old.

He owns a home on Ninth Avenue, up the hill from the park in the area near Golden Gate Heights. Lives alone; one marriage, ending in divorce eight years ago, no children. Drives a 1979 VW bug, has a good driving record. His credit's also good—he pays his bills in full, on time. A friend of mine who teaches photography at State says he's a likable enough guy, but hard to get to know. Shy, doesn't socialize. My friend hasn't heard of any romantic attachments."

Diana slumped in her chair, biting her lower lip, her yellow eyes troubled. We were in my office at All Souls—a big room at the front of the second floor, with a bay window that overlooks the flat Outer Mission district. It had taken me all afternoon and used up quite a few favors to run the check on Gordon DeRosier; at five Diana had called wanting to know if I'd found anything, and I'd asked her to come there so I could report my findings in person.

Finally she said, "You, of course, are thinking what I am. Otherwise you wouldn't have asked your friend about this DeRosier's romantic attachments."

I nodded, keeping my expression noncommittal.

"It's pretty obvious, isn't it?" she added. "A man wouldn't bring a woman's favorite flowers to her grave three weeks running if he hadn't felt strongly about her."

"That's true."

She frowned. "But why did he start doing it now? Why not right after her death?"

"I think I know the reason for that: he's probably done it all along, but on a different day. State's summer class schedule just began; DeRosier is probably free at different times than he was in the spring."

"Of course." She was silent a moment, then muttered, "So that's what it came to."

"What do you mean?"

"My father's neglect. It forced her to turn to another man." Her eyes clouded even more, and a flush began to stain her cheeks. When she continued, her voice shook with anger. "He left her alone most of the time, and when he was there he ignored or ridiculed her. She'd try so hard—at

being a good conversationalist, a good hostess, an interesting person—
and then he'd just laugh at her efforts. The bastard!"

"Are you planning to talk with Gordon DeRosier?" I asked, hoping to
quell the rage I sensed building inside her.

"God, Sharon, I can't. You know how uncomfortable I felt about
approaching a woman friend of Mom's. This . . . the *implications* of this
make it impossible for me."

"Forget it, then. Content yourself with the fact that someone loved her."

"I can't do that, either. This DeRosier could tell me so much about her."

"Then call him up and ask to talk."

"I don't think . . . Sharon, would you—"

"Absolutely not."

"But you know how to approach him tactfully, so he won't resent the
intrusion. You're so good at things like that. Besides I'd pay a bonus."

Her voice had taken on a wheedling, pleading tone that I remembered
from the old days. I recalled one time she'd convinced me that I really
wanted to get out of bed and drive her to Baskin-Robbins at midnight for
a gallon of pistachio ice cream. And I don't even like ice cream much,
especially pistachio.

"Diana—"

"It would mean so much to me."

"Dammit—"

"Please."

I sighed. "All right. But if he's willing to talk with you, you'd better
follow up on it."

"I will, I promise."

Promises, I thought. I knew all about promises . . .

"We met when she took at art class from me at State," Gordon DeRosier
said. "An oil painting class. She wasn't very good. Afterward we laughed
about that. She said that she was always taking classes in things she wasn't
good at, trying to measure up to her husband's expectations."

"When was that?"

"Two years ago last April."

Then it hadn't been a casual affair, I thought.

We were seated in the living room of DeRosier's small stucco house on Ninth Avenue. The house was situated at the bottom of a dip in the road, and the evening fog gathered there; the branches of an overgrown plane tree shifted in a strong wind and tapped at the front window. Inside, however, all was warm and cozy. A fire burned on the hearth, and DeRosier's paintings—abstracts done in reds and blues and golds—enhanced the comfortable feeling. He'd been quite pleasant when I'd shown up on his doorstep, although a little puzzled because he remembered seeing me at the Columbarium that morning. When I'd explained my mission, he'd agreed to talk with me and graciously offered me a glass of an excellent zinfandel.

I asked, "You saw her often after that?"

"Several times a week. Her husband seldom paid any attention to her comings and goings, and when he did she merely said she was pursuing her art studies.

"You must have cared a great deal about her."

"I loved her," he said simply.

"Then you won't mind talking with her daughter."

"Of course not. Teresa spoke of Diana often. Knowing her will be a link to Teresa—something more tangible than the urn I visit every week."

I found myself liking Gordon DeRosier. In spite of his ordinary appearance, there was an impressive dignity about the man, as well as a warmth and genuineness. Perhaps he could be a friend to Diana, someone who would make up in part for losing her mother before she really knew her.

He seemed to be thinking along the same lines, because he said, "It'll be good to finally meet Diana. All the time Teresa and I were together I'd wanted to, but she was afraid Diana wouldn't accept the situation. And then at the end, when she'd decided to divorce Carl, we both felt it was better to wait until everything was settled."

"She was planning to leave Carl?"

He nodded. "She was going to tell him that weekend, in Cabo San Lucas, and move in here the first of the week. I expected her to call on Sunday night, but she didn't. And she didn't come over as she'd promised she would on Monday. On Tuesday I opened the paper and found her obituary."

"How awful for you!"

"It was pretty bad. And I felt so . . . shut out. I couldn't even go to her memorial service—it was private. I didn't even know how she had died— the obituary merely said 'suddenly.' "

"Why didn't you ask someone? A mutual friend? Or Diana?"

"We didn't have any mutual friends. Perhaps that was the bond between us; neither of us made friends easily. And Diana . . . I didn't see any reason for her ever to know about her mother and me. It might have caused her pain, colored her memories of Teresa."

"That was extremely caring of you."

He dismissed the compliment with a shrug and asked, "Do you know how she died? Will you tell me, please?"

I related the circumstances. As I spoke DeRosier shook his head as if in stunned denial.

When I finished, he said, "That's impossible."

"Diana said something similar—how unlike her mother it was. I gather Teresa didn't drink much—"

"No, that's not what I mean." He rose and began to pace, extremely agitated now. "Teresa did drink too much. It started during all those years when Carl alternately abused her and left her alone. She was learning to control it, but sometimes it would still control her."

"Then I imagine that's what happened during that weekend down in Cabo. It would have been a particularly stressful time, what with having to tell Carl she was getting a divorce, and it's understandable that she might—"

"That much is understandable, yes. But Teresa would *not* have gotten into that hot tub—not willingly."

I felt a prickly sense of foreboding. "Why not?"

"Teresa had eczema, a severe case, lesions on her wrists and knees and elbows. She'd suffered from it for years, but shortly before her death it had spread and become seriously aggravated. Water treated with chemicals, as it is in hot tubs and swimming pools, makes eczema worse and causes extreme pain."

"I wonder why Diana didn't mention that."

"I doubt she knew about it. Teresa was peculiar about illness—it stemmed from having been raised a Christian Scientist. Although she wasn't religious anymore, she felt physical imperfection was shameful and wouldn't talk about it."

"I see. Well, about her getting into the hot tub—don't you think if she was drunk, she might have anyway?"

"No. We had a discussion about hot tubs once, because I was thinking of installing one here. She told me not to expect her to use it, that she had tried the one in Cabo just once. Not only had it aggravated her skin condition, it had given her heart palpitations, made her feel she was suffocating. She hated that tub. If she really did drown in it, she was put in against her will. Or after she passed out from too much alcohol."

"If that was the case, I'd think the police would have caught on and investigated."

DeRosier laughed bitterly. "In Mexico? When the victim is the wife of a wealthy foreigner with plenty of money to spread around, and plenty of influence?" He sat back down, pressed his hands over his face, as if to force back tears. "When I think of her there, all alone with him, at his mercy . . . I never should have let her go. But she said the weekend was planned, that after all the years she owed it to Carl to break the news gently." His fist hit the arm of the chair. "*Why* didn't I stop her?"

"You couldn't know." I hesitated trying to find a flaw in his logic. "Mr. DeRosier, why would Carl Richards kill his wife? I know he's a proud man, and conscious of his position in the business and social communities, but divorce really doesn't carry any stigma these days."

"But a divorce would have denied him the use of Teresa's money. Carl had done well in business, and they lived comfortably. But the month before she died, Teresa inherited a substantial fortune from an uncle. The inheritance was what made her finally decide to leave Carl; she didn't want him to get his hands on it. And, as she told me in legalese, she hadn't commingled it with what she and Carl held jointly. If she divorced him immediately, it wouldn't fall under the community property laws."

I was silent, reviewing what I knew about community property and inheritances. What Teresa had told him was valid—and it gave Carl Richards a motive for murder.

DeRosier was watching me. "We could go to the police. Have them investigate."

I shook my head. "It happened on foreign soil; the police down there aren't going to admit they were bribed, or screwed up, or whatever happened. Besides, there's not hard evidence."

"What about Teresa's doctor? He could substantiate that she had eczema and wouldn't have gotten into that tub voluntarily."

"That's not enough. She was drunk; drunks do irrational things."

"Teresa wasn't an irrational woman, drunk or sober. Anyone who knew her would agree with me."

"I'm sure they would. But that's the point: you knew her; the police didn't."

DeRosier leaned back, deflated and frustrated. "There's got to be some way to get the bastard."

"Perhaps there is," I said, "through some avenue other than the law."

"How do you mean?"

"Well, consider Carl Richards: he's very conscious of his social position, his business connections. He's big on control. What if all that fell apart—either because he came under suspicion of murder or if he began losing control because of psychological pressure?"

DeRosier nodded slowly. "He *is* big on control. He dominated Teresa for years, until she met me."

"And he tried to dominate Diana. With her it didn't work so well."

"Diana . . ." De Rosier half rose from his chair.

"What about her?"

"Shouldn't we tell her what we suspect? Surely she'd want to avenge her mother somehow. And she knows her father and his weak points better than you or I."

I hesitated, thinking of the rage Diana often displayed toward Carl Richards. And wondering if we wouldn't be playing a dangerous game by telling her. Would her reaction to our suspicions be a rational one? Or would she strike out at her father, do something crazy? Did she really need to know any of this? Or did she have a right to the knowledge? I was ambivalent: on the one hand, I wanted to see Carl Richards punished in some way; on the other, I wanted to protect my friend from possible ruinous consequences.

DeRosier's feelings were anything but ambivalent, however; he waited, staring at me with hard, glittering eyes. I knew he would embark on some campaign of vengeance, and there was nothing to stop him from contacting Diana if I refused to help. Together their rage at Richards might flare out of control, but if I exerted some sort of leavening influence . . .

After a moment I said, "All right, I'll call Diana and ask her to come over here. But let me handle how we tell her."

It was midnight when I shut the door of my little brown-shingled cottage and leaned against it, sighing deeply. When I'd left Gordon DeRosier's house, Diana and he still hadn't decided what course of action to pursue in regard to Carl Richards, but I felt certain it would be a sane and rational one.

A big chance, I thought. That's what you took tonight. Did you really have a right to gamble with your friend's life that way? What if it had turned out the other way?

But then I pictured Diana and Gordon standing in the doorway of his house when I'd left. Already I sensed a bond between them, knew they'd forged a united front against a probable killer. Old Carl would get his, one way or the other.

Maybe their avenging Teresa's death wouldn't help her rest more easily in her niche at the Columbarium, but it would certainly salve the pain of the two people who remembered and loved her.

Silent Night

1990

Larry, I hardly know what to say!"

What I *wanted* to say was, "What am I supposed to do with this?" The object I'd just liberated from its gay red-and-gold Christmas wrappings was a plastic bag, about eight by twelve inches, packed firm with what looked suspiciously like sawdust. I turned it over in my hands, as if admiring it, and searched for some clue to its identity.

When I looked up, I saw Larry Koslowski's brown eyes shining expectantly; even the ends of his little handlebar mustache seemed to bristle as he awaited my reaction. "It's perfect," I said lamely.

He let his bated breath out in a long sigh. "I thought it would be. You remember how you were talking about not having much energy lately? I told you to try whipping up my protein drink for breakfast, but you said you didn't have that kind of time in the morning."

The conversation came back to me—vaguely. I nodded.

"Well," he went on, "put two tablespoons of that mixture in a tall glass, add water, stir, and you're in business."

Of course—it was an instant version of his infamous protein drink. Larry was the health nut on the All Souls Legal Cooperative staff; his fervent exhortations for the rest of us to adopt better nutritional standards often fell upon deaf ears—mine included.

"Thank you," I said. "I'll try it first thing tomorrow."

Larry ducked his head, his lips turning up in shy pleasure beneath his straggly little mustache.

It was late in the afternoon of Christmas Eve, and the staff of All Souls was engaged in the traditional gift exchange between members who had drawn each other's names earlier in the month. The yearly ritual extends back to the days of the co-op's founding, when most people were too poor to give more than one present; the only rule is Keep It Simple.

The big front parlor of the co-op's San Francisco Victorian was crowded. People perched on the furniture or, like Larry and me, sat cross-legged on the floor, oohing and aahing over their gifts. Next to the Christmas tree in the bay window, my boss, Hank Zahn, sported a new cap and muffler, knitted for him—after great deliberation and consultation as to colors—by my assistant, Rae Kelleher. Rae, in turn, wore the scarf and cap I'd purchased (because I can't knit to save my life) for her in the hope she would consign relics from her days at U. C. Berkeley to the trash can. Other people had homemade cookies and sinful fudge, special bottles of wine, next year's calendars, assorted games, plants, and paperback books.

And I had a bag of instant health drink that looked like sawdust.

The voices in the room created such a babble that I barely heard the phone ring in the hall behind me. Our secretary, Ted Smalley, who is a compulsive answerer, stepped over me and went out to where the instrument sat on his desk. A moment later he called, "McCone, it's for you."

My stomach did a little flip-flop, because I was expecting news of a personal nature that could either be very good or very bad. I thanked Larry again for my gift, scrambled to my feet, and went to take the receiver from Ted. He remained next to the desk; I'd confided my family's problem to him earlier that week, and now, I knew, he would wait to see if he could provide air or comfort.

"Shari?" My youngest sister Charlene's voice was composed, but her use of the diminutive of Sharon, which no one but my father calls me unless it's a time of crisis, made my stomach flip.

"I'm here," I said.

"Shari, somebody's seen him. A friend of Ricky's saw Mike!"

"Where? When?"

"Today around noon. Up there—in San Francisco."

I let out my breath in a sigh of relief. My fourteen-year-old nephew, oldest of Charlene and Ricky's six kids, had run away from their home in Pacific Palisades five days ago. Now, it appeared, he was alive, if not exactly safe.

The investigator in me counseled caution, however. "Was this friend sure it was Mike he saw?"

"Yes. He spoke to him. Mike said he was visiting you. But afterward our friend got to thinking that he looked kind of grubby and tired, and that you probably wouldn't have let him wander around that part of town, so he called us to check it out."

A chill touched my shoulder blades. "What part of town?"

"Somewhere near City Hall, a sleazy area, our friend said."

A very sleazy area, I thought. Dangerous territory to which run-aways are often drawn, where boys and girls alike fall prey to pimps and pushers . . .

Charlene said, "Shari?"

"I'm still here, just thinking."

"You don't suppose he'll come to you?"

"I doubt it, if he hasn't already. But in case he does, there's somebody staying at my house—an old friend who's here for Christmas—and she knows to keep him there and call me immediately. Is there anybody else he knows here in the city?"

"I can't think of anybody."

"What about that friend you spent a couple of Christmases with—the one with the two little girls who lived on Sixteenth Street across from Mission Dolores?"

"Ginny Shriber? She moved away about four years ago." There was a noise as if Charlene was choking back a sob. "He's really just a little boy yet. So little, and so stubborn."

But stubborn little boys grow up fast on the rough city streets. I didn't want that kind of coming-of-age for my nephew.

"Look at the up side of this, Charlene," I said, more heartily than I felt. "Mike's come to the one city where you have your own private investigator. I'll start looking for him right away."

It had begun with, of all things, a moped that Mike wanted for Christmas. Or maybe it had started a year earlier, when Ricky Savage finally hit it big.

During the first fourteen years of his marriage to my sister, Ricky had been merely another faceless country-and-western musician, playing and singing backup with itinerant bands, dreaming seemingly improbable dreams of stardom. He and Charlene had developed a reproductive pattern (and rate) that never failed to astound me, in spite of its regularity: he'd get her pregnant, go out on tour, return after the baby was born; then he'd go out again when the two o'clock feedings got to him, return when the kid was weaned, and start the whole cycle all over. Finally, after the sixth child, Charlene had wised up and gotten her tubes tied. But Ricky still stayed on the road more than at home, and still dreamed his dreams.

But then, with money borrowed from my father on the promise that if he didn't make it within one more year he'd give up music and go into my brother John's housepainting business, Ricky had cut a demo of a song he'd written called "Cobwebs in the Attic of My Mind." It was about a lovelorn fellow who, besides said cobwebs, had a "sewer that's backed up in the cellar of his soul" and "a short in the wiring of his heart." When I first heard it, I was certain that Pa's money had washed down that same pipe before it clogged, but fate—perverse creature that it is—would have it otherwise. The song was a runaway hit, and more Ricky Savage hits were to follow.

In true *nouveau* style, Ricky and Charlene quickly moved uptown—or in this case up the coast, from West Los Angeles to affluent Pacific Palisades. There were new cars, new furniture and clothes, a house with a swimming pool, and toys and goodies for the children. *Lots* of goodies, anything they wanted—until this Christmas when, for reasons of safety, Charlene had balked at letting Mike have the moped. And Mike, headstrong little bastard that he was, had taken his life's savings of some fifty-five dollars and hitched away from home on the Pacific Coast Highway.

It was because of a goddamned moped that I was canceling my Christmas Eve plans and setting forth to comb the sleazy streets and alleys of the area known as Polk Gulch for a runaway.

The city was strangely subdued on this Christmas Eve, the dark streets hushed, although not deserted. Most people had been drawn inside to the warmth of family and friends; others, I suspected, had retreated to nurse the loneliness that is endemic to this season. The pedestrians I passed moved silently, as if reluctant to call attention to their presence; occasionally I heard laughter from the bars as I went by, but even that was muted. The lost, drifting souls of the city seemed to collectively hold their breath as they waited for life to resume its everyday pattern.

I had started at Market Street and worked my way northwest, through the Tenderloin to Polk Gulch. Before I'd started out, I'd had a photographer friend who likes to make a big fee more than he likes to celebrate holidays run off a hundred copies of my most recent photo of Mike. Those I passed out, along with my card, to clerks in what liquor stores, corner groceries, cheap hotels, and greasy spoon restaurants I found open. The pictures drew no response other than indifference or sympathetic shakes of the head and promises to keep an eye out for him. By the time I reached Polk Street, where I had an appointment in a gay bar at ten, I was cold, footsore, and badly discouraged.

Polk Gulch, so called because it is in a valley that has an underground river running through it, long ago was the hub of gay life in San Francisco. In the seventies, however, most of the action shifted up Market Street to the Castro district, and the vitality seemed to drain out of the Gulch. Now parts of it, particularly those bordering the Tenderloin, are depressingly sleazy. As I walked along, examining the face of each young man I saw, I became aware of the hopelessness and resignation in the eyes of the street hustlers and junkies and winos and homeless people.

A few blocks from my destination was a vacant lot surrounded by a chain-link fence. Inside gaped a huge excavation, the cellar of the building that had formerly stood there, now open to the elements. People had scaled the fence and taken up residence down in it; campfires blazed, in defiance of the NO TRESPASSING signs. The homeless could rest easy—at least for this one night. No one was going to roust them on Christmas Eve.

I went to the fence and grasped its cold mesh with my fingers, staring down into the shifting light and shadows, wondering if Mike was among the ragged and hungry ranks. Many of the people were middle-aged to elderly, but there were also families with children and a scattering of young people. There was no way to tell, though, without scaling the fence and climbing down there. Eventually I turned away, realizing I had only enough time to get to the gay bar by ten.

The transvestite's name was Norma and she—he? I never know what to call them—was coldly beautiful. The two of us sat at a corner table in the bar, sipping champagne because Norma had insisted on it. ("After all, it's Christmas Eve, darling!") The bar, in spite of winking colored lights on its tree and flickering bayberry candles on each table, was gloomy and semideserted; Norma's brave velvet finery and costume jewelry had about it more than a touch of the pathetic. She'd been sitting alone when I'd entered and had greeted me eagerly.

I'd been put in touch with Norma by Ted Smalley, who is gay and has a wide-ranging acquaintance among all the segments of the city's homosexual community. Norma, he'd said, knew everything there was to know about what went on in Polk Gulch; if anyone could help me, it was she.

The photo of Mike didn't look familiar to Norma. "There are so many runaways on the street at this time of year," she told me. "Kids get their hopes built up at Christmas time. When they find out Santa isn't the great guy he's cracked up to be, they take off. Like your nephew."

"So what would happen to a kid like him? Where would he go?"

"Lots of places. There's a hotel—the Vinton. A lot of runaways end up there at first, until their money runs out. If he's into drugs, try any flophouse, doorway, or alley. If he's connected with a pimp, look for him hustling."

My fingers tightened involuntarily on the stem of my champagne glass. Norma noticed and shook her elaborately coiffed head in sympathy. "Not a pretty thought, is it? But what do you see around here that's pretty—

except for me?" As she spoke the last words, her smile became self-mocking.

"He's been missing five days now," I said, "and he only had fifty-some dollars on him. That'll be gone by now, so he probably won't be at the hotel, or any other. He's never been into drugs. His father's a musician, and a lot of his cronies are druggies; the kid actually disapproves of them. The other I don't even want to think about—though I probably will have to, eventually."

"So what are you going to do?"

"Try the hotel. Go back and talk to the people at that vacant lot. Keep looking at each kid who walks by."

Norma stared at the photo of Mike that lay face up on the table between us. "It's a damned shame, a nice-looking kid like that. He ought to be home with his family, trimming the tree, roasting chestnuts on the fire, or whatever other things families do."

"The American Christmas dream, huh?"

"Yeah." She smiled bleakly, raised her glass. "Here's to the American Christmas dream—and to all the people it's eluded."

I touched my glass to hers. "Including you and me."

"Including you and me. Let's just hope it doesn't elude young Mike forever."

The Vinton Hotel was a few blocks away, around the corner on Eddy Street. Its lobby was a flight up, over a closed sandwich shop, and I had to wait to be buzzed in before I could climb carpetless stairs that stank strongly of disinfectant and faintly of urine. Lobby was a misnomer, actually: it was more a narrow hall with a desk to one side, behind which sat a young black man with a tall afro. The air up there was thick with the odor of marijuana; I guess he'd been spending his Christmas Eve with a joint. His eyes flashed panic when I reached in my bag for my identification. Then he realized it wasn't a bust and relaxed somewhat.

I took out another photo of Mike and laid it on the counter. "You seen this kid?"

He barely glanced at it. "Nope, can't help you."

I shoved it closer. "Take another look."

He did, pushed it back toward me. "I said no."

There was something about his tone that told me he was lying—would lie out of sheer perversity. I could get tough with him, make noises about talking to the hotel's owners, mentioning how the place reeked of grass. The city's fleabags had come under a good bit of media scrutiny recently; the owners wouldn't want me to cause any trouble that would jeopardize this little goldmine that raked in outrageously high rents from transients, as well as government subsidized payments for welfare recipients. Still, there had to be a better way.

"You work here every night?" I asked.

"Yeah."

"Rough, on Christmas Eve."

He shrugged.

"Christmas night, too?"

"Why do you care?"

"I understand what a rotten deal that is. You don't think I'm running around here in the cold because I like it, do you?"

His eyes flickered to me, faintly interested. "You got no choice, either?"

"Hell, no. The client says find a kid, I go looking. Not that it matters. I don't have anything better to do."

"Know what you mean. Nothing for me at home, either."

"Where's home?"

"My real home, or where I live?"

"Both, I guess."

"Where I live's up there." He gestured at the ceiling. "Room goes with the job. Home's not there no more. Was in Motown, back before my ma died and things got so bad in the auto industry. I came out here thinking I'd find work." He smiled ironically. "Well, I found it, didn't I?"

"At least it's not as cold here as in Detroit."

"No, but it's not home either." He paused, then reached for Mike's picture. "Let me see that again." Another pause. "Okay. He stayed here. Him and this blonde chick got to be friends. She's gone, too."

"Do you know the blonde girl's name?"

"Yeah. Jane Smith. Original, huh?"

"Can you describe her?"

"Just a little blonde, maybe five-two. Long hair. Nothing special about her."

"When did they leave?"

"They were gone when I came on last night. The owner don't put up with the ones that can't pay, and the day man, he likes tossing their asses out on the street."

"How did the kid seem to you? Was he okay?"

The man's eyes met mine, held them for a moment. "Thought this was just a job to you."

"He's my nephew."

"Yeah, I guessed it might be something like that. Well, if you mean was he doing drugs or hustling, I'd say no. Maybe a little booze, that's all. The girl was the same. Pretty straight kids. Nobody's gotten to them yet."

"Let me ask you this: what would kids like that do after they'd been thrown out of here? Where would they hang out?"

He considered. "There's a greasy spoon on Polk, near O'Farrell. Owner's an old guy, Iranian. He feels sorry for the kids, feeds them when they're about to starve, tries to get them to go home. He might of seen those two."

"Would he be open tonight?"

"Sure. Like I said, he's Iranian. It's not his holiday. Come to think of it, it's not mine anymore, either."

"Why not?"

Again the ironic smile. "Can't celebrate peace-on-earth-good-will-to-men when you don't believe in it anymore, now can you?"

I reached into my bag and took out a twenty-dollar bill, slid it across the counter to him. "Peace on earth, and thanks."

He took it eagerly, then looked at it and shook his head. "You don't have to."

"I *want* to. That makes a difference."

The "greasy spoon" was called The Coffee Break. It was small—just five tables and a lunch counter, old green linoleum floors, Formica and molded plastic furniture. A slender man with thinning gray hair sat behind the counter smoking a cigarette. A couple of old women were hunched over coffee at a corner table. Next to the window was a dirty-haired blonde girl; she was staring through the glass with blank eyes—another of the city's casualties.

I showed Mike's picture to the man behind the counter. He told me Mike looked familiar, thought a minute, then snapped his fingers and said, "Hey, Angie."

The girl by the window turned. Full-face, I could see she was red-eyed and tear-streaked. The blankness of her face was due to misery, not drugs.

"Take a look at the picture this lady has. Didn't I see you with this kid yesterday?"

She got up and came to the counter, self-consciously smoothing her wrinkled jacket and jeans. "Yeah," she said after glancing at it, "that's Michael."

"Where's he now? The lady's his aunt, wants to help him."

She shook her head. "I don't know. He was at the Vinton, but he got kicked out the same time I did. We stayed down at the cellar in the vacant lot last night, but it was cold and scary. These drunks kept bothering us. Mr. Ahmeni, how long do you think it's going to take my dad to get here?"

"Take it easy. It's a long drive from Oroville. I only called him an hour ago." To me, Mr. Ahmeni added, "Angie's going home for Christmas."

I studied her. Under all that grime, a pretty, conventional girl hid. I said, "Would you like a cup of coffee? Something to eat?"

"I wouldn't mind a Coke. I've been sponging off Mr. Ahmeni for hours." She smiled faintly. "I guess he'd appreciate it if I sponged off somebody else for a change."

I bought us both Cokes and sat down with her. "When did you meet Mike?"

"Three days ago, I guess. He was at the hotel when I got into town. He kind of looked out for me. I was glad; that place is pretty awful. A lot of addicts stay there. One OD'd in the stairwell the first night. But it's cheap and they don't ask questions. A guy I met on the bus coming down here told me about it."

"What did Mike do here in the city, do you know?"

"Wandered around, mostly. One afternoon we went out to Ocean Beach and walked on the dunes."

"What about drugs or—"

"Michael's not into drugs. We drank some wine, is all. He's . . . I don't know how to describe it, but he's not like a lot of the kids on the streets."

"How so?"

"Well, he's kind of . . . sensitive, deep."

"This sensitive soul ran away from home because his parents wouldn't buy him a moped for Christmas."

Angle sighed. "You really don't know anything about him, do you? You don't even know he wants to be called Michael, not Mike."

That silenced me for a moment. It was true: I really didn't know my nephew, not as a person. "Tell me about him."

"What do you want to know?"

"Well, this business with the moped—what was that all about?"

"It didn't really have anything to do with the moped. At least not much. It had to do with the kids at school."

"In what way?"

"Well, the way Michael told it, his family used to be kind of poor. At least there were some months when they worried about being able to pay the rent."

"That's right."

"And then his father became a singing star and they moved to this awesome house in Pacific Palisades, and all of a sudden Michael was in school with all these rich kids. But he didn't fit in. The kids, he said, were really into having things and doing drugs and partying. He couldn't relate to it. He says it's really hard to get into that kind of stuff when you've spent your life worrying about real things."

"Like if your parents are going to be able to pay the rent."

Angie nodded, her fringe of limp blonde hair falling over her eyes. She brushed it back and went on. "I know about that; my folks don't have

much money, and my mom's sick a lot. The kids, they sense you're different and they don't want to have anything to do with you. Michael was
lonely at the new school, so he tried to fit in—tried too hard, I guess, by
having the latest stuff, the most expensive clothes. You know."

"And the moped was part of that."

"Uh-huh. But when his mom said he couldn't have it, he realized what
he'd been doing. And he also realized that the moped wouldn't have done
the trick anyway. Michael's smart enough to know that people don't fall
all over you just because you've got another new toy. So he decided he'd
never fit in, and he split. He says he feels more comfortable on the streets,
because life here is real." She paused, eyes filling, and looked away at the
window. "God, is it *real*."

I followed the direction of her gaze: beyond the plate glass a girl of perhaps thirteen stumbled by. Her body was emaciated, her face blank, her
eyes dull—the look of a far-gone junkie.

I said to Angie, "When did you last see Mike . . . Michael?"

"Around four this afternoon. Like I said, we spent the night in that
cellar in the vacant lot. After that I knew I couldn't hack it anymore, and
I told him I'd decided to go home. He got pissed at me and took off."

"Why?"

"Why do you think? I was abandoning him. I could go home, and he
couldn't."

"Why not?"

"Because Michael's . . . God, you don't know a thing about him! He's
proud. He couldn't admit to his parents that he couldn't make it on his
own. Any more than he could admit to them about not fitting in at
school."

What she said surprised me and made me ashamed. Ashamed for
Charlene, who had always referred to Mike as stubborn or bullheaded,
but never as proud. And ashamed for myself, because I'd never really seen
him, except as the leader of a pack jokingly referred to in family circles as
"the little savages."

"Angie," I said, "do you have any idea where he might have gone after
he left you?"

She shook her head. "I wish I did. It would be nice if Michael could have a Christmas. He talked about how much he was going to miss it. He spent the whole time we were walking around on the dunes telling me about the Christmases they used to have, even though they didn't have much money: the tree trimming, the homemade presents, the candlelit masses on Christmas Eve, the cookie decorating and the turkey dinners. Michael absolutely loves Christmas."

I hadn't known that either. For years I'd been too busy with my own life to do more than send each of the Savage kids a small check. Properly humbled, I thanked Angie for talking with me, wished her good luck with her parents, and went back out to continue combing the dark, silent streets.

On the way back down Polk Street toward the Tenderloin, I stopped again at the chain-link fence surrounding the vacant lot. I was fairly sure Mike was not among the people down there—not after his and Angie's experience of the night before—but I was curious to see the place where they had spent that frightening time.

The campfires still burned deep in the shelter of the cellar. Here and there drunks and addicts lay passed out on the ground; others who had not yet reached that state passed bottles and shared joints and needles; one group raised inebriated voices in a chorus of "Rudolph, the Red-Nosed Reindeer." In a far corner I saw another group—two women, three children, and a man—gathered around a scrawny Christmas tree.

The tree had no ornaments, wasn't really a tree at all, but just a top that someone had probably cut off and tossed away after finding that the one he'd bought was too tall for the height of his ceiling. There was no star atop it, no presents under it, no candy canes or popcorn chains, and there was certain to be no turkey dinner tomorrow. The people had nonetheless gathered around it and stood silently, their heads bowed in prayer.

My throat tightened and I clutched at the fence, fighting back tears. Even though I spent a disproportionate amount of my professional life probing into events and behavior that would make the average person gag, every now and then the indestructible courage of the human spirit absolutely stuns me.

I watched the scene for a moment longer, then turned away, glancing at my watch. Its hands told me why the people were praying: Christmas Day was upon us. This was their midnight service.

And then I realized that those people, who had nothing in the world with which to celebrate Christmas except somebody's cast-off treetop, may have given me a priceless gift. I thought I knew now where I would find my nephew.

When I arrived at Mission Dolores, the neoclassical facade of the basilica was bathed in floodlights, the dome and towers gleaming against the post-midnight sky. The street was choked with double-parked vehicles, and from within I heard voices raised in a joyous chorus. Beside the newer early twentieth-century structure, the small adobe church built in the late 1700s seemed dwarfed and enveloped in deep silence. I hurried up the wide steps to the arching wooden doors of the basilica, then took a moment to compose myself before entering.

Like many of my generation, it had been years since I'd been even nominally a Catholic, but the old habit of reverence had never left me. I couldn't just blunder in there and creep about, peering into every worshipper's face, no matter how great my urgency. I waited until I felt relatively calm before pulling open the heavy door and stepping over the threshold.

The mass was candlelit; the robed figures of the priest and altar boys moved slowly in the flickering, shifting light. The stained-glass window behind the altar and those on the side walls gleamed richly. In contrast, the massive pillars reached upward to vaulted arches that were deeply shadowed. As I moved slowly along one of the side aisles, the voices of the choir swelled to a majestic finale.

The congregants began to go forward to receive Communion. As they did, I was able to move less obtrusively, scanning the faces of the young people in the pews. Each time I spotted a teenaged boy, my heart quickened. Each time I felt a sharp stab of disappointment.

I passed behind the waiting communicants, then moved unhurriedly up the nave and crossed to the far aisle. The church was darker and sparsely populated toward the rear; momentarily a pillar blocked my view of the altar. I moved around it.

He was there in the pew next to the pillar, leaning wearily against it. Even in the shadowy light, I could see that his face was dirty and tired, his jacket and jeans rumpled and stained. His eyes were half-closed, his mouth slack; his hands were shoved between his thighs, as if for warmth.

Mike—no, Michael—had come to the only safe place he knew in the city, the church where on two Christmas Eves he'd attended mass with his family and their friends, the Shribers, who had lived across the street.

I slipped into the pew and sat down next to him. He jerked his head toward me, stared in open-mouthed surprise. What little color he had drained from his face; his eyes grew wide and alarmed.

"Hi, Michael." I put my hand on his arm.

He looked at me as if he wanted to shake it off. "How did you . . . ?"

"Doesn't matter. Not now. Let's just sit quietly till mass is over."

He continued to stare at me. After a few seconds he said, "I bet Mom and Dad are really mad at me."

"More worried than anything else."

"Did they hire you to find me?"

"No, I volunteered."

"Huh." He looked away at the line of communicants.

"You still go to church?" I asked.

"Not much. None of us do anymore. I kind of miss it."

"Do you want to take Communion?"

He was silent. Then, "No. I don't think that's something I can do right now. Maybe never."

"Well, that's okay. Everybody expresses his feelings for . . . God, or whatever, in different ways." I thought of the group of homeless worshippers in the vacant lot. "What's important is that you believe in something."

He nodded, and then we sat silently, watching people file up and down the aisle. After a while he said, "I guess I do believe in something. Otherwise I couldn't have gotten through this week. I learned a lot, you know."

"I'm sure you did."

"About me, I mean."

"I know."

"What're you going to do now? Send me home?"

"Do you want to go home?"

"Maybe. Yes. But I don't want to be sent there. I want to go on my own."

"Well, nobody should spend Christmas Day on a plane or a bus anyway. Besides, I'm having ten people to dinner at four this afternoon. I'm counting on you to help me stuff the turkey."

Michael hesitated, then smiled shyly. He took one hand from between his thighs and slipped it into mine. After a moment he leaned his tired head on my shoulder, and we celebrated the dawn of Christmas together.

Benny's Space

1992

Amorfina Angeles was terrified, and I could fully empathize with her.
Merely living in the neighborhood would have terrified me—all the
more so had I been harassed by members of one of its many street gangs.

Hers was a rundown side street in the extreme southeast of San Francisco,
only blocks from the crime- and drug-infested Sunnydale public housing
projects. There were bars over the windows and grilles on the doors of the
small stucco houses; dead and vandalized cars stood at the broken curbs; in
the weed-choked yard next door, a mangy guard dog of indeterminate breed
paced and snarled. Fear was written on this street as plainly as the graffiti on
the walls and fences. Fear and hopelessness and a dull resignation to a life
that none of its residents would willingly have opted to lead.

I watched Mrs. Angeles as she crossed her tiny living room to the front
window, pulled the edge of the curtain aside a fraction, and peered out at
the street. She was no more than five feet tall, with rounded shoulders,
sallow skin, and graying black hair that curled in short, unruly ringlets.
Her shapeless flower-printed dress did little to conceal a body made soft
and fleshy by bad food and too much childbearing. Although she was only
forty, she moved like a much older woman.

Her attorney and my colleague, Jack Stuart of All Souls Legal Cooperative, had given me a brief history of his client when he'd asked me
to undertake an investigation on her behalf. She was a Filipina who had
emigrated to the states with her husband in search of their own piece
of the good life that was reputed to be had here. But as with many of
their countrymen and -women, things hadn't worked out as the Angeleses had envisioned: first Amorfina's husband had gone into the
import-export business with a friend from Manila; the friend
absconded two years later with Joe Angeles's life savings. Then, a year
after that, Joe was killed in a freak accident at a construction site where
he was working. Amorfina and their six children were left with no
means of support, and in the years since Joe's death their circumstances
had gradually been reduced to this two-bedroom rental cottage in one
of the worst areas of the city.

Mrs. Angeles, Jack told me, had done the best she could for her family,
keeping them off the welfare rolls with a daytime job at the Mission district sewing factory and nighttime work doing alterations. As they grew
older, the children helped with part-time jobs. Now there were only two
left at home: sixteen-year-old Alex and fourteen-year-old Isabel. It was
typical of their mother, Jack said, that in the current crisis she was more
concerned for them than for herself.

She turned from the window now, her face taut with fear, deep lines
bracketing her full lips. I asked, "Is someone out there?"

She shook her head and walked wearily to the worn recliner opposite
me. I occupied the place of honor on a red brocade sofa encased in the
same plastic that had doubtless protected it long ago upon delivery from
the store. "I never see anybody," she said. "Not till it's too late."

"Mrs. Angeles, Jack Stuart told me about your problem, but I'd like to
hear it in your own words—from the beginning, if you would."

She nodded, smoothing her bright dress over her plump thighs. "It
goes back a long time, to when Benny Crespo was . . . they called him the
Prince of Omega Street, you know."

Hearing the name of her street spoken made me aware of its ironic
appropriateness: the last letter of the Greek alphabet is symbolic of endings,

and for most of the people living here, Omega Street was the end of a steady decline into poverty.

Mrs. Angeles went on, "Benny Crespo was Filipino. His gang controlled the drugs here. A lot of people looked up to him; he had power, and that don't happen much with our people. Once I caught Alex and one of my older boys calling him a hero. I let them have it pretty good, you bet, and there wasn't any more of *that* kind of talk around this house. I got no use for the gangs—Filipino or otherwise."

"What was the name of Benny Crespo's gang?"

"The *Kabalyeros*. That's Tagalog for Knights."

"Okay—what happened to Benny?"

"The house next door, the one with the dog—that was where Benny lived. He always parked his fancy Corvette out front, and people knew better than to mess with it. Late one night he was getting out of the car and somebody shot him. A drug burn, they say. After that the *Kabalyeros* decided to make the parking space a shrine to Benny. They roped it off, put flowers there every week. On All Saints Day and the other fiestas, it was something to see."

"And that brings us to last March thirteenth," I said.

Mrs. Angeles bit her lower lip and smoothed her dress again.

When she didn't speak, I prompted her. "You'd just come home from work."

"Yeah. It was late, dark. Isabel wasn't here, and I got worried. I kept looking out the window, like a mother does."

"And you saw . . . ?"

"The guy who moved into the house next door after Benny got shot, Reg Dawson. He was black, one of a gang called the Victors. They say he moved into that house to show the *Kabalyeros* that the Victors were taking over their turf. Anyway, he drives up and stops a little way down the block. Waits there, revving his engine. People start showing up; the word's been put out that something's gonna go down. And when there's a big crowd, Reg Dawson guns his car and drives right into Benny's space, over the rope and the flowers.

"Well, that started one hell of a fight—Victors and *Kabalyeros* and folks from the neighborhood. And while it's going on, Reg Dawson just stands there in Benny's space acting macho. That's when it happened, what I saw."

"And what was that?"

She hesitated, wet her lips. "The leader of the *Kabalyeros*, Tommy Dragón—the Dragon, they call him—was over by the fence in front of Reg Dawson's house, where you couldn't see him unless you were really looking. I was, 'cause I was trying to see if Isabel was anyplace out there. And I saw Tommy Dragón point this gun at Reg Dawson and shoot him dead."

"What did you do then?"

"Ran and hid in the bathroom. That's where I was when the cops came to the door. Somebody'd told them I was in the window when it all went down and then ran away when Reg got shot. Well, what was I supposed to do? I got no use for the *Kabalyeros* or the Victors, so I told the truth. And now here I am in this mess."

Mrs. Angeles had been slated to be the chief prosecution witness at Tommy Dragón's trial this week. But a month ago the threats had started: anonymous letters and phone calls warning her against testifying. As the trial date approached this had escalated into blatant intimidation: a fire was set in her trash can; someone shot out her kitchen window; a dead dog turned up on her doorstep. The previous Friday, Isabel had been accosted on her way home from the bus stop by two masked men with guns. And that had finally made Mrs. Angeles capitulate; in court yesterday, she'd refused to take the stand against Dragón.

The state needed her testimony; there were no other witnesses, Dragón insisted on his innocence, and the murder gun had not been found. The judge had tried to reason with Mrs. Angeles, then cited her for contempt—reluctantly, he said. "The court is aware that there have been threats made against you and your family," he told her, "but it is unable to guarantee your protection." Then he gave her forty-eight hours to reconsider her decision.

As it turned out, Mrs. Angeles had a champion in her employer. The owner of the sewing factory was unwilling to allow one of his long-term workers to go to jail or to risk her own and her family's safety. He brought her to All Souls, where he held a membership in our legal-services plan, and this morning Jack Stuart asked me to do something for her.

What? I'd asked. What could I do that the SFPD couldn't to stop vicious harassment by a street gang?

Well, he said, get proof against whoever was threatening her so that they could be arrested and she'd feel free to testify.

Sure, Jack, I said. And exactly why *hadn't* the police been able to do anything about the situation?

His answer was not surprising: lack of funds. Intimidation of prosecution witnesses in cases relating to gang violence was becoming more and more prevalent and open in San Francisco, but the city did not have the resources to protect them. An old story nowadays—not enough money to go around.

Mrs. Angeles was watching my face, her eyes tentative. As I looked back at her, her gaze began to waver. She'd experienced too much disappointment in her life to expect much in the way of help from me.

I said, "Yes, you certainly are in a mess. Let's see if we can get you out of it."

We talked for a while longer, and I soon realized that Amor—as she asked me to call her—held the misconception that there was some way I could get the contempt citation dropped. I asked her if she'd known beforehand that a balky witness could be sent to jail. She shook her head. A person had a right to change her mind, hadn't she? When I set her straight on that, she seemed to lose interest in the conversation; it was difficult to get her to focus long enough to compile a list of people I should talk with. I settled for enough names to keep me occupied for the rest of the afternoon.

I was ready to leave when angry voices came from the front steps. A young man and woman entered. They stopped speaking when they saw the room was occupied, but their faces remained set in lines of contention. Amor hastened to introduce them as her son and daughter, Alex and Isabel. To them she explained that I was a detective "helping with the trouble with the judge."

Alex, a stocky youth with a tracery of mustache on his upper lip, seemed

disinterested. He shrugged out of his high school letter jacket and vanished through a door to the rear of the house. Isabel studied me with frank
curiosity. She was a slender beauty, with black hair that fell in soft curls to
her shoulders; her features had a delicacy lacking in those of her mother
and brother. Unfortunately, bright blue eyeshadow and garish orange lipstick detracted from her natural good looks, and she wore an imitation
leather outfit in a particularly gaudy shade of purple. However, she was
polite and well-spoken as she questioned me about what I could do to help
her mother. Then, after a comment to Amor about an assignment that was
due the next day, she left through the door her brother had used.

I turned to Amor, who was fingering the leaves of a philodendron plant
that stood in a stand near the front window. Her posture was stiff, and
when I spoke to her she didn't meet my eyes. Now I was aware of a tension in her that hadn't been there before her children returned home.
Anxiety, because of the danger her witnessing the shooting had placed
them in? Or something else? It might have had to do with the quarrel
they'd been having, but weren't arguments between siblings fairly
common? They certainly had been in my childhood home in San Diego.

I told Amor I'd be back to check on her in a couple of hours. Then,
after a few precautionary and probably unnecessary reminders about
locking doors and staying clear of windows, I went out into the chill
November afternoon.

The first name on my list was Madeline Dawson, the slain gang
leader's widow. I glanced at the house next door and saw with some relief
that the guard dog no longer paced in its yard. When I pushed through
the gate in the chain link fence, the creature's whereabouts became
apparent: a bellowing emanated from the small, shabby cottage. I went up
a broken walk bordered by weeds, climbed the sagging front steps, and
pressed the bell. A woman's voice yelled for the dog to shut up, then a
door slammed somewhere within, muffling the barking. Footsteps
approached, and the woman called, "Yes, who is it?"

"My name's Sharon McCone, from All Souls Legal Cooperative. I'm
investigating the threats your neighbor, Mrs. Angeles, has been
receiving."

A couple of locks turned and the door opened on its chain. The face that peered out at me was very thin and pale, with wisps of red hair straggling over the high forehead; the Dawson marriage had been an interracial one, then. The woman stared at me for a moment before she asked, "What threats?"

"You don't know that Mrs. Angeles and her children have been threatened because she's to testify against the man who shot your husband?"

She shook her head and stepped back, shivering slightly—whether from the cold outside or the memory of the murder, I couldn't tell. "I . . . don't get out much these days."

"May I come in, talk with you about the shooting?"

She shrugged, unhooked the chain, and opened the door. "I don't know what good it will do. Amor's a damned fool for saying she'd testify in the first place."

"Aren't you glad she did? The man killed your husband."

She shrugged again and motioned me into a living room the same size as that in the Angeles house. All resemblance stopped there, however. Dirty glasses and dishes, full ashtrays, piles of newspapers and magazines covered every surface; dust balls the size of rats lurked under the shabby Danish furniture. Madeline Dawson picked up a heap of tabloids from the couch and dumped it on the floor, then indicated I should sit there and took a hassock for herself.

I said, "You *are* glad that Mrs. Angeles was willing to testify, aren't you?"

"Not particularly."

"You don't care if your husband's killer is convicted or not?"

"Reg was asking to be killed. Not that I wouldn't mind seeing the Dragon get the gas chamber—he may not have killed Reg, but he killed plenty of other people—"

"What did you say?" I spoke sharply, and Madeline Dawson blinked in surprise. It made me pay closer attention to her eyes; they were glassy, their pupils dilated. The woman, I realized, was high.

"I said the Dragon killed plenty of other people."

"No, about him not killing Reg."

"Did I say that?"

"Yes."

"I can't imagine why. I mean, Amor must know. She was up there in the window watching for sweet Isabel like always."

"You don't sound as if you like Isabel Angeles."

"I'm not fond of flips in general. Look at the way they're taking over this area. Daly City's turning into another Manila. All they do is buy, buy, buy—houses, cars, stuff by the truckload. You know, there's a joke that the first three words their babies learn are 'Mama, Papa, and Serramonte.' " Serramonte was a large shopping mall south of San Francisco.

The roots of the resentment she voiced were clear to me. One of our largest immigrant groups today, the Filipinos are highly westernized and by and large better educated and more affluent than other recently arrived Asians—or many of their neighbors, black or white. Isabel Angeles, for all her bright, cheap clothing and excessive makeup, had behind her a tradition of industriousness and upward mobility that might help her to secure a better place in the world than Madeline Dawson could aspire to.

I wasn't going to allow Madeline's biases to interfere with my line of questioning. I said, "About Dragón not having shot your husband—"

"Hey, who knows? Or cares? The bastard's dead, and good riddance."

"Why good riddance?"

"The man was a pig. A pusher who cheated and gouged people—people like me who need the stuff to get through. You think I was always like this, lady? No way. I was a nice Irish Catholic girl from the Avenues when Reg got his hands on me. Turned me on to coke and a lot of other things when I was only thirteen. Likes his pussy young, Reg did. But then I got old—I'm all of nineteen now—and I needed more and more stuff just to keep going, and all of a sudden Reg didn't even *see* me anymore. Yeah, the man was a pig, and I'm glad he's dead."

"But you don't think Dragón killed him."

She sighed in exasperation. "I don't know what I think. It's just that I always supposed that when Reg got it it would be for something more personal than driving his car into a stupid shrine in a parking space. You know what I mean? But what does it matter who killed him, anyway?"

"It matters to Tommy Dragón, for one."

She dismissed the accused man's life with a flick of her hand. "Like I said, the Dragon's a killer. He might as well die for Reg's murder as for any of the others. In a way, it'd be the one good thing Reg did for the world."

Perhaps in a certain primitive sense she was right, but her off-handedness made me uncomfortable. I changed the subject. "About the threat to Mrs. Angeles—which of the *Kabalyeros* would be behind them?"

"All of them. These guys in the gangs, they work together."

But I knew about the structure of street gangs—my degree in sociology from U. C. Berkeley hadn't been totally worthless—to be reasonably sure that wasn't so. There is usually one dominant personality, supported by two or three lieutenants; take away these leaders, and the followers become ineffectual, purposeless. If I could turn up enough evidence against the leaders of the *Kabalyeros* to have them arrested, the harassment would stop.

I asked, "Who took over the *Kabalyeros* after Dragón went to jail?"

"Hector Bulis."

It was a name that didn't appear on my list; Amor had claimed not to know who was the current head of the Filipino gang. "Where can I find him?"

"There's a fast-food joint over on Geneva, near the Cow Palace. Fat Robbie's. That's where the *Kabalyeros* hang out."

The second person I'd intended to talk with was the young man who had reportedly taken over the leadership of the Victors after Dawson's death, Jimmy Willis. Willis could generally be found at a bowling alley, also on Geneva Avenue near the Cow Palace. I thanked Madeline for taking the time to talk with me and headed for the Daly City line.

The first of the two establishments that I spotted was Fat Robbie's, a cinderblock-and-glass relic of the early sixties whose specialties appeared to be burgers and chicken-in-a-basket. I turned into a parking lot that was half full of mostly shabby cars and left my MG beside one of the defunct drive-in speaker poles.

The interior of the restaurant took me back to my high school days:

orange leatherette booths beside the plate glass windows, a long Formica
counter with stools, laminated color pictures of disgusting-looking food
on the wall above the pass-through counter from the kitchen. Instead of
a jukebox there was a bank of video games along one wall. Three Filipino
youths in jeans and denim jackets gathered around one called "Invader!"
The *Kabalyeros*, I assumed.

I crossed to the counter with only a cursory glance at the trio, sat, and
ordered coffee from a young woman who looked to be Eurasian. The
Kabalyeros didn't conceal their interest in me; they stared openly, and after
a moment one of them said something that sounded like "tick-tick," and
they all laughed nastily. Some sort of Tagalog obscenity, I supposed. I
ignored them, sipping the dishwater-weak coffee, and after a bit they
went back to their game.

I took out the paperback that I keep in my bag for protective coloration
and pretended to read, listening to the few snatches of conversation that
drifted over from the three. I caught the names of two: Sal and Hector—
the latter presumably Bulis, the gang's leader. When I glanced covertly at
him, I saw he was tallish and thin, with long hair caught back in a ponytail; his features were razor-sharp and slightly skewed, creating the
impression of a perpetual sneer. The trio kept their voices low, and
although I strained to hear, I could make out nothing of what they were
saying. After about five minutes Hector turned away from the video
machine. With a final glance at me he motioned to his companions, and
they all left the restaurant.

I waited until they'd driven away in an old green Pontiac before I called
the waitress over and showed her my identification. "The three men who
just left," I said. "Is the tall one Hector Bulis?"

Her lips formed a little "O" as she stared at the ID. Finally she nodded.

"May I talk with you about them?"

She glanced toward the pass-through to the kitchen. "My boss, he
don't like me talking with the customers when I'm supposed to be
working."

"Take a break. Just five minutes."

Now she looked nervously around the restaurant. "I shouldn't—"

I slipped a twenty-dollar bill from my wallet and showed it to her. "Just five minutes."

She still seemed edgy, but fear lost out to greed. "Okay, but I don't want anybody to see me talking to you. Go back to the restroom—it's through that door by the video games. I'll meet you there as soon as I can."

I got up and found the ladies' room. It was tiny, dimly lit, with a badly cracked mirror. The walls were covered with a mass of graffiti; some of it looked as if it had been painted over and had later worked its way back into view through the fading layers of enamel. The air in there was redolent of grease, cheap perfume, and stale cigarette and marijuana smoke. I leaned against the sink as I waited.

The young Eurasian woman appeared a few minutes later. "Bastard gave me a hard time," she said. "Tried to tell me I'd already taken my break."

"What's your name?"

"Anna Smith."

"Anna, the three men who just left—do they come in here often?"

"Uh-huh."

"Keep pretty much to themselves, do they?"

"It's more like other people stay away from them." She hesitated. "They're from one of the gangs; you don't mess with them. That's why I wanted to talk with you back here."

"Have you ever heard them say anything about Tommy Dragón?"

"The Dragon? Sure. He's in jail; they say he was framed."

Of course they would claim that. "What about a Mrs. Angeles—Amorfina Angeles?"

"Not that one, no."

"What about trying to intimidate someone? Setting fires, going after someone with a gun?"

"Uh-uh. That's gang business; they keep it pretty close. But it wouldn't surprise me. Filipinos—I'm part Filipina myself, my mom met my dad when he was stationed at Subic Bay—they've got this saying, *kumukuló ang dugó*. It means, 'the blood is boiling.' They can get pretty damn mad 'specially the men. So stuff like what you said—sure they do it."

"Do you work on Fridays?"

"Yeah, two to ten."

"Did you see any of the *Kabalyeros* in here last Friday around six?" That was the time when Isabel had been accosted.

Anna Smith scrunched up her face in concentration. "Last Friday . . . oh, yeah, sure. That was when they had the big meeting, all of them."

"*All* of them?"

"Uh-huh. Started around five-thirty, went on a couple of hours. My boss, he was worried something heavy was gonna go down, but the way it turned out, all he did was sell a lot of food."

"What was the meeting about?"

"Had to do with the Dragon, who was gonna be character witnesses at the trial, what they'd say."

The image of the three I'd seen earlier—or any of their ilk—as character witnesses was somewhat ludicrous, but I supposed in Tommy Dragón's position you took what you could get. "Are you sure they were all there?"

"Uh-huh."

"And no one at the meeting said anything about trying to keep Mrs. Angeles from testifying?"

"No. That lawyer the Dragon's got, he was there too."

Now that was odd. Why had Dragon's public defender chosen to meet with his witnesses in a public place? I could think of one good reason: he was afraid of them, didn't want them in his office. But what if the *Kabalyeros* had set the time and place—as an alibi for when Isabel was to be assaulted?

"I better get back to work," Anna Smith said. "Before the boss comes looking for me."

I gave her the twenty dollars. "Thanks for your time."

"Sure." Halfway out the door she paused, frowning. "I hope I didn't get any of the *Kabalyeros* in trouble."

"You didn't."

"Good. I kind of like them. I mean, they push dope and all, but these days, who doesn't?"

These days, who doesn't? I thought. *Good Lord . . .*

—˄—

The Starlight Lanes was an old-fashioned bowling alley girded by a rough cliff face and an auto dismantler's yard. The parking lot was crowded, so I left the MG around back by the garbage cans. Inside, the lanes were brightly lit and noisy with the sound of crashing pins, rumbling balls, shouts, and groans. I paused by the front counter and asked where I might find Jimmy Willis. The woman behind it directed me to a lane at the far end.

Bowling alleys—or lanes, as the new upscale bowler prefers to call them—are familiar territory to me. Up until a few years ago my favorite uncle Jim was a top player on the pro tour. The Starlight Lanes reminded me of the ones where Jim used to practice in San Diego—from the racks full of tired-looking rental shoes to the greasy-spoon coffeeshop smells to the molded plastic chairs and cigarette-burned scorekeeping consoles. I walked along it, soaking up the ambience—some people would say lack of it—until I came to lane 32 and spotted an agile young black man bowling alone. Jimmy Willis was a left-hander, and his ball hooked out until it hung on the edge of the channel, then hooked back with deadly accuracy and graceful form. His concentration was so great that he didn't notice me until he'd finished the last frame and retrieved his ball.

"You're quite a bowler," I said. "What's your average?"

He gave me a long look before he replied, "Two hundred."

"Almost good enough to turn pro."

"That's what I'm looking to do."

Odd, for the head of a street gang that dealt in drugs and death. "You ever heard of Jim McCone?" I asked.

"Sure. Damned good in his day."

"He's my uncle."

"No kidding." Willis studied me again, now as if looking for a resemblance.

Rapport established, I showed him my ID and explained that I wanted to talk about Reg Dawson's murder. He frowned, hesitated, then nodded. "Okay, since you're Jim McCone's niece, but you'll have to buy me a beer."

"Deal."

Willis toweled off his ball, stowed it and his shoes in their bag, and led me to a typical smoke-filled, murkily lighted bowling alley bar. He took one of the booths while I fetched us a pair of Buds.

As I slid into the booth I said, "What can you tell me about the murder?"

"The way I see it, Dawson was asking for it."

So he and Dawson's wife were of a mind about that. "I can understand what you mean, but it seems strange, coming from you. I hear you were his friend, that you took over the Victors after his death."

"You heard wrong on both counts. Yeah, I was in the Victors, and when Dawson bought it, they tried to get me to take over. But by then I'd figured out—never mind how, doesn't matter—that I wanted out of that life. Ain't nothing in it but what happened to Benny Crespo and Dawson—or what's going to happen to the Dragon. So I decided to put my hand to something with a future." He patted the bowling bag that sat on the banquette beside him. "Got a job here now—not much, but my bowling's free and I'm on my way."

"Good for you. What about Dragón—do you think he's guilty?"

Willis hesitated, looking thoughtful. "Why do you ask?"

"Just wondering."

"Well, to tell you the truth, I never did believe the Dragon shot Reg."

"Who did, then?"

He shrugged.

I asked him if he'd heard about the *Kabalyeros* trying to intimidate the chief prosecution witness. When he nodded, I said, "They also threatened the life of her daughter last Friday."

He laughed mirthlessly. "Wish I could of seen that. Kind of surprises me, though. That lawyer of Dragón's, he found out what the *Kabalyeros* were up to, read them the riot act. Said they'd put Dragón in the gas chamber for sure. So they called it off."

"When was this?"

"Week, ten days ago."

Long before Isabel had been accosted. Before the dead dog and the shooting incidents, too. "Are you sure?"

"It's what I hear. You know, in a way I'm surprised that they'd go after Mrs. Angeles at all."

"Why?"

"The Filipinos have this macho tradition. 'Specially when it comes to their women. They don't like them messed with, 'specially by non-Filipinos. So how come they'd turn around and mess with one of their own?"

"Well, her testimony *would* jeopardize the life of one of their fellow gang members. It's an extreme situation."

"Can't argue with that."

Jimmy Willis and I talked a bit more, but he couldn't—or wouldn't—offer any further information. I bought him a second beer, then went out to where I'd left my car.

And came face-to-face with Hector Bulis and the man called Sal.

Sal grabbed me by the arm, twisted it behind me, and forced me up against the latticework fence surrounding the garbage cans. The stench from them filled my nostrils; Sal's breath rivaled it in foulness. I struggled, but he got hold of my other arm and pinned me tighter. I looked around, saw no one, nothing but the cliff face and the high board fence of the auto dismantler's yard. Bulis approached, flicking open a switchblade, his twisty face intense. I stiffened, went very still, eyes on the knife.

Bullis placed the tip of the knife against my jawbone, then traced a line across my cheek. "Don't want to hurt you, bitch," he said. "You do what I say, I won't have to mess you up."

The Tagalog phrase that Anna Smith had translated for me—*kumukuló ang dugó*—flashed through my mind. *The blood is boiling.* I sensed Bullis's was—and dangerously so.

I wet my dry lips, tried to keep my voice from shaking as I said, "What do you want me to do?"

"We hear you're asking around about Dawson's murder, trying to prove the Dragon did it."

"That's not—"

"We want you to quit. Go back to your own part of town and leave our business alone."

"Whoever told you that is lying. I'm only trying to help the Angeles family."

"They wouldn't lie." He moved the knife's tip to the hollow at the base of my throat. I felt it pierce my skin—a mere pinprick, but frightening enough.

When I could speak, I did so slowly, phrasing my words carefully. "What I hear is that Dragón is innocent. And that the *Kabalyeros* aren't behind the harassment of the Angeleses—at least not for a week or ten days."

Bullis exchanged a look with his companion—quick, unreadable.

"Someone's trying to frame you," I added. "Just like they did Dragón."

Bullis continued to hold the knife to my throat, his hand firm. His gaze wavered, however, as if he was considering what I'd said. After a moment he asked, "All right—who?"

"I'm not sure, but I think I can find out."

He thought a bit longer, then let his arm drop and snapped the knife shut. "I'll give you till this time tomorrow," he said. Then he stuffed the knife into his pocket, motioned for Sal to let go of me, and the two quickly walked away.

I sagged against the latticework fence, feeling my throat where the knife had pricked it. It had bled a little, but the flow already was clotting. My knees were weak and my breath came fast, but I was too caught up in the possibilities to panic. There were plenty of them—and the most likely was the most unpleasant.

Kumukuló ang dugó. The blood is boiling . . .

Two hours later I was back at the Angeles house on Omega Street. When Amor admitted me, the tension I'd felt in her earlier had drained. Her body sagged, as if the extra weight she carried had finally proved to be too much for her frail bones; the skin of her face looked flaccid, like melting putty; her eyes were sunken and vague. After she shut the door and motioned for me to sit, she sank into the recliner, expelling a sigh. The house was quiet—too quiet.

"I have a question for you," I said. "What does 'tick-tick' mean in Tagalog?"

Her eyes flickered with dull interest. *"Tiktík."* She corrected my pro-
nunciation. "It's a word for detective."

Ever since Hector Bulis and Sal had accosted me I'd suspected as
much.

"Where did you hear that?" Amor asked.

"One of the *Kabalyeros* said it when I went to Fat Robbie's earlier.
Someone had told them I was a detective, probably described me. Who-
ever it was said I was trying to prove Tommy Dragón killed Reg
Dawson."

"Why would—"

"More to the point, *who* would? At the time, only four people knew
that I'm a detective."

She wet her lips, but remained silent.

"Amor, the night of the shooting, you were standing in your front
window, watching for Isabel."

"Yes."

"Do you do that often?"

"Yes."

"Because Isabel is often late coming home. Because you're afraid she
may have gotten into trouble."

"A mother worries—"

"Especially when she's given good cause. Isabel is running out of control, isn't she?"

"No, she—"

"Amor, when I spoke with Madeline Dawson, she said you were
standing in the window watching for 'sweet Isabel, like always.' She didn't
say 'sweet' in a pleasant way. Later, Jimmy Willis implied that your
daughter is not . . . exactly a vulnerable young girl."

Amor's eyes sparked. "The Dawson woman is jealous."

"Of course she is. There's something else: when I asked the waitress at
Fat Robbie's if she'd ever overheard the *Kabalyeros* discussing you, she
said, 'No, not that one.' It didn't register at the time, but when I talked to
her again a little while ago, she told me Isabel is the member of your
family they discuss. They say she's wild, runs around with the men in the

gangs. You know that, so does Alex. And so does Madeline Dawson. She just told me the first man Isabel became involved with was her husband."

Amor seemed to shrivel. She gripped the arms of the chair, white-knuckled.

"It's true, isn't it?" I asked more gently.

She lowered her eyes, nodding. When she spoke her voice was ragged. "I don't know what to do with her anymore. Ever since that Reg Dawson got to her, she's been different, not my girl at all."

"Is she on drugs?"

"Alex says no, but I'm not so sure."

I let it go; it really didn't matter. "When she came home earlier," I said, "Isabel seemed very interested in me. She asked questions, looked me over carefully enough to be able to describe to the *Kabalyeros*. She was afraid of what I might find out. For instance, that she wasn't accosted by any men with guns last Friday."

"She was!"

"No, Amor. That was just a story, to make it look as if your life—and your children's—were in danger if you testified. In spite of what you said early on, you haven't wanted to testify against Tommy Dragón from the very beginning.

"When the *Kabalyeros* began harassing you a month ago, you saw that as the perfect excuse not to take the stand. But you didn't foresee that Dragón's lawyer would convince the gang to stop the harassment. When that happened, you and Isabel, and probably Alex, too, manufactured incidents—the shot-out window, the dead dog on the doorstep, the men with the guns—to make it look as if the harassment was still going on."

"Why would I? They're going to put me in jail."

"But at the time you didn't know they could do that—or that your employer would hire me. My investigating poses yet another danger to you and your family."

"This is . . . why would I do all that?"

"Because basically you're an honest woman, a good woman. You didn't want to testify because you knew Dragón didn't shoot Dawson. It's my

guess you gave the police his name because it was the first one that came
to mind."

"I had no reason to—"

"You had the best reason in the world: a mother's desire to protect her
child."

She was silent, sunken eyes registering despair and defeat.

I kept on, even though I hated to inflict further pain on her. "The day
he died, Dawson had let the word out that he was going to desecrate
Benny's space. The person who shot him knew there would be fighting
and confusion, counted on that as a cover. The killer hated Dawson—"

"Lots of people did."

"But only one person you'd want to protect so badly that you'd accuse
an innocent man."

"Leave my mother alone. She's suffered enough on account of what I did."

I turned. Alex had come into the room so quietly I hadn't noticed. Now
he moved midway between Amor and me, a Saturday night special
clutched in his right hand.

The missing murder weapon.

I tensed, but one look at his face told me he didn't intend to use it.
Instead he raised his arm and extended the gun, grip first.

"Take this," he said. "I never should of bought it. Never should of used
it. I hated Dawson on account of what he did to my sister. But killing him
wasn't worth what we've all gone through since."

I glanced at Amor; tears were trickling down her face.

Alex said, "Mama, don't cry. I'm not worth it."

When she spoke, it was to me. "What will happen to him?"

"Nothing like what might have happened to Dragón; Alex is a juvenile.
You, however—"

"I don't care about myself, only my children."

Maybe that was the trouble. She was the archetypal selfless mother:
living only for her children, sheltering them from the consequences of
their actions—and in the end doing them irreparable harm.

There were times when I felt thankful that I had no children. And
there were times when I was thankful that Jack Stuart was a very good

criminal lawyer. This was a time I was thankful on both counts. I went to the phone, called Jack, and asked him to come over here. At least I could leave the Angeles family in good legal hands.

After he arrived, I went out into the gathering dusk. An old yellow VW was pulling out of Benny's space. I walked down there and stood on the curb. Nothing remained of the shrine to Benny Crespo. Nothing remained to show that blood had boiled and been shed here. It was merely a stretch of cracked asphalt, splotched with oil drippings, littered with the detritus of urban life. I stared at it for close to a minute, then turned away from the bleak landscape of Omega Street.